# NIGHT IN TEHRAN

# PHILIP KAPLAN
# *NIGHT IN TEHRAN*

MELVILLE HOUSE

Brooklyn
London

Night in Tehran
Copyright © Philip Kaplan, 2020
All rights reserved
First Melville House Printing: November 2020

Melville House Publishing
46 John Street
Brooklyn, NY 11201
and
Melville House UK
Suite 2000
16/18 Woodford Road
London E7 0HA

Book design by Richard Oriolo

mhpbooks.com
@melvillehouse

ISBN: 978-1-61219-850-7
ISBN: 978-1-61219-851-4 (eBook)

Library of Congress Control Number: 2020932927

Printed in the United States of America

10 9 8 7 6 5 4 3 2 1

A catalog record for this book is available from the Library of Congress

For Barbara

# NIGHT IN TEHRAN

# 1

## PARIS

**A** FOGGY MORNING IN the Place de la Concorde.

Poking above the rooftops of the left bank of the Seine, a blinking red light was all that could be seen of the Eiffel Tower. David Weiseman shook the drizzle from his overcoat, and then dodged through the cars streaming into the great square. He hustled past the Hotel de Crillon and across to Avenue Gabriel. Get on with it, he told himself.

He strode past the US embassy, casting only a quick glance at the tough-looking French flics twirling police batons, staring down nosy American tourists. A clap of thunder hastened his step. Ten minutes later he crossed the ornate Pont Alexander III, homage to the Russian Tsar who supported the Holy Alliance that endured for a hundred years, until the guns of the First World War shattered a century of post-Napoleonic peace in Europe.

Diplomacy rarely if ever succeeded like that.

Across the Seine, he took in the Quai d'Orsay, said to be the home of the French mandarins who considered themselves masters of the stylized international ballet known as diplomacy. This fine art meant staying on one's toes, sustaining the process, never letting it break down. But it did break down, Weiseman knew, remembering Berlin . . . the Grue-newald . . . every twenty years or so in Europe, leading to the two world wars of the twentieth century.

And so he saw things differently, reminding himself diplomacy wasn't just about process, or compromise. It was about persuading the other country that it was in *their* interest to do what *you* wanted them to do. Trevor said Gramont, the man Weiseman was on his way to meet, could be trusted. Well, he didn't quite say that. Trevor—Weisman's boss, the director of the Central Intelligence Agency—didn't trust anyone. He said Laurent Gramont was important, the door into the French elites.

At the Foreign Ministry, a young woman in outsized amber glasses led him to the secretary general's office. Gramont was with an aide, giving instructions. He held himself tall and straight in a perfectly tailored, double-breasted gray suit with a subtle dark stripe, a silver tie with a pearl tie tack, matching cufflinks on his white shirt. His hair was a richly toned silver gray. He was a French Trevor, knowing and discreet, no doubt ready to be ruthless.

*"Monsieur Weiseman, quel plaisir."*

Gramont's inner office was a gorgeous Empire spectacle, separated from the outer world by mauve, silk drapes. The gilt inlaid desk was devoid of any papers. A revolving globe stood to the right. Europe on top, France in the middle.

Weiseman gestured toward it. "Still the center of civilization, I see."

Gramont allowed the kind of half smile that also reminded Weiseman of Trevor. "It's our mission," he said. "But please, have a seat." He lifted the phone, whispered, *"Deux cafés."*

"Justin Trevor suggested I see you first. I'll be—"

"Yes, of course. I know your role. Justin called me from Washington."

*I need you to find me someone to replace the Shah, to run the country for us. A general, a cutthroat, a cleric. But our man. Our entire position in the Middle East depends on it.*

Gramont sat perfectly still, a modern day Renaissance prince, a Machiavelli waiting to grant a trivial favor. Like Trevor. What exactly is their relationship? Weiseman wondered.

"You and Justin go back a long way."

"Oh yes, one could say that. We were in Moscow together, as ambassadors, before he went to Prague. He told me about his promising young protégé during the Prague Spring, an idealist who stood his ground, made him reconsider his own positions. Not easy to do with Justin. So it seems you're *un homme serieux*, someone we can work with."

"Well then, has there been any progress on the New Year's Eve incident?"

"Ah, yes, the ritual executions. Quite grisly—in bed, nude, their throats were slit. The man was an anti-Shah exile, a bazaari, a businessman who came to Paris when things got hot."

Weiseman took that in without comment. Gramont had been calm in relating the barbaric acts, but it was obvious that the French were concerned Iranian infighting in France might spread.

He asked, "Who did it? What do your services think?"

"*Tiens, tiens*, it's a bit of a puzzle. The woman was a relative of Empress Farah. Fabulously wealthy. The word was that she liked to play."

"A puzzle indeed," Weiseman said, wanting him to get to the point.

Gramont turned his head ever so slightly, his Adam's apple bobbing a bit, a trait Weiseman had noticed before among high French dignitaries. "Perhaps a political assassination by SAVAK," Gramont suggested.

Weiseman shook his head, recalling what Trevor told him. "The Shah's security service? In Paris? Well, the French *would* say that, wouldn't they. The Shah's our man. The French are betting he'll be gone soon, so they pin it on SAVAK and wait to displace our influence in Iran."

"I see. Of course it's not just a police matter," he said. "Something political."

"Oh, yes. With the Middle East it's always political. In France we have bitter memories of the Algerian war, of blasts in our Metro stations. That was just twenty years ago. Our Muslim community has been quiet since then, but I have no illusions. New Year's Eve and then the Sorbonne killing of that young woman. Suicide bombings are quite possible."

"And?"

"We monitor the Iranian factions. They could wage a jihad against each other in Paris."

Ah.

The door opened and a man in a white starched jacket with gold epaulettes came in bearing two white china cups and saucers and two tiny glasses of water on a silver tray. Gramont's little finger rose ever so slightly as he drank down the espresso. "It won't be easy," he said morosely, "what Justin is asking you to do. You'll rather stand out on the streets of Tehran. Of course, you'll be monitored from the day you arrive. By SAVAK, and by the others."

No doubt your people, too, and mine, thought Weiseman.

The phone rang and Gramont spoke softly into it, switching to an indecipherable Breton dialect. Weiseman looked around the office. There was a watercolor that looked like a Monet. He got up to examine a gold plaque on a nearby walnut table. The dedication was to Le Comte Laurent Gramont from former President Charles de Gaulle. Royalty then. And next to it was a facsimile of the ribbons in Gramont's suit lapel: *Le Croix de Guerre*.

Gramont hung up the phone. He was sure, he said, that there was much he could offer a colleague of Justin Trevor's as it affected matters in Iran. He would be honored to put his new American friend in touch with the right people. And then, smooth as silk, "Please, call me Laurent. You'll come to dinner at my home on Saturday. We have to do our work quietly, under the radar, as Justin would say."

**SAINT-GERMAIN-DES-PRÉS WAS A** short walk away, through the tangle of narrow streets and alleys that flowed up from the Seine, between seventeenth-century buildings once occupied by French royals, by the noble facade of the École des Beaux Arts, on to the medieval church.

On the boulevard, a man with a salt-and-pepper beard, slightly stooped, was walking his dachshund, urging him on whenever he fell into a stubborn crouch, refusing to take another step. A young couple went by, holding hands, fingers linked, engrossed in each other. A beggar in baggy pants limped toward Weiseman, his cane tapping on the cobblestones, holding out his beret. Weiseman dropped in a franc and watched the withered old man hold it up, bite on it, then bow theatrically, sweeping the cap before him like some character in Molière.

Weiseman glanced across to the Café de Flore, where Sartre still held forth. During the war, many of the French intellectuals had taken care not to confront the Nazis, Weiseman knew. He himself had been a small child in Hitler's Berlin, but he hadn't forgotten what Johann had taught him about what it was like to live under a dictator. It's why he became a diplomat, to engage and make sure the horror didn't come again, didn't swallow up other innocents.

He paused and thought of Trevor, how the new CIA director had surprised him the day after Jimmy Carter's inauguration by plucking him out of the State Department and assigning him on detail as his personal agent to deal with the looming crisis in Iran, supposedly a reward for his work during the Prague Spring on his first Foreign Service assignment. There were others Trevor could have chosen—Mideast experts fluent in Farsi—but he had insisted on Weiseman, "because I trust you."

Weiseman had no illusions about the game of espionage, or who would take the fall should things go wrong . . . as well they might.

He started up again, crossing the street, heading down Saint-Germain, turning left on Rue du Dragon, by the fast-food joints and oriental restaurants, He reflected on how Gramont could help him on Iran, on what Trevor had told him about Gramont's game, on whether the French count could be trusted. In a doorway of a *hôtel particulier*, a woman in white platform shoes, a short red skirt, and a red beret tapped ashes of a cigarette against the building. She raised her eyebrows.

*"Non, merci,"* Weiseman said.

He picked up the pace and rounded the corner to Rue Grenelle, over to Boulevard Raspail. In less than five minutes he turned onto the Rue de Varenne, pushed on double doors, and entered an enclave, Rue Cité de Varenne, an upper-class oasis insulating its residents from the hurly-burly of the city—the sounds and smells, the stream of pedestrians, the blaring Klaxons of speeding taxis. He started down a dark path, past enclosed tennis courts. Overhead lights came on, illuminating four white town houses. Number 8 was at the end of the road. He stepped up to the door and pressed the bell. A barely audible chime sounded. A maid in a black dress and white apron opened the door. *"Bonsoir, Monsieur Weiseman."*


**A BRONZE EQUESTRIAN** statue with a stern Roman gladiator guarded the stairwell. At the top of the stairs, Laurent Gramont, in a three-piece, black-tie ensemble, stood on a finely woven Persian carpet—a Tabriz, Weiseman thought, based on the cream-and-red ornamental patterns. The town house was a mélange of East and West. The walls were a beige silk decorated with a motif that looked like Louis XV, before the revolution, when aristos still ruled the roost in well-guarded enclaves. Behind Gramont, guests whispered under the chandelier he had seen from outside. It was a formal affair—black ties for men, women in long silk dresses.

Like Trevor, Weisman thought again, Gramont was tough, even ruthless when need be, but now the bon vivant. He followed his host into the salon, tasting his champagne. "This is David Weiseman," Gramont announced, "en route to Tehran." Heads nodded ever so slightly. A muscular man with a shock of gray hair approached, followed by an elegant woman, offered his hand and introduced his wife. He was the minister of defense. Next, a shipping magnate and a younger woman, not his wife. A professor at ENA, the elite French École National d'Administration, his wife a couturier. Across the room, Weiseman saw a tall man with a white Van Dyck beard and sunken cheekbones, yet deeply tanned for all that, with a tiny white mustache beneath a prominent nose. "Someone you will want to meet," Gramont said, and he led Weismeman over there.

"Alain de Rose," the man said. He looked a bit like James Angleton, the old paranoid CIA counterintelligence chief—chain-smoking, brushing ashes off his tux onto the superb Tabriz carpet. Sûreté was written all over him.

"Alain monitors the *Proche Orient* for our services," Gramont confirmed. "The Near East from Egypt to Iran, the Saudis and Gulf emirates. And of course, Israel."

"Then you're involved in the investigation," Weiseman said casually. He knew the Paris social scene, the little tricks and moral pieties that enabled one to inquire without breaching the code of the French upper crust.

"Yes, of course." De Rose's voice was gruff, almost as if his larynx had been removed. "The Iranian girl at the Sorbonne. But it's more than one assassination. We've got a sticky web of Iranians in Paris, fighting it out by proxy over what will happen when the Shah goes."

Well, this is someone worth talking to, Weiseman thought.

"You expect the Shah to be deposed?"

De Rose shrugged. "Everyone goes at some point. Your president was forced to resign, to avoid impeachment."

Weiseman nodded, recalling past encounters as a young diplomat with Nixon, that working dinner at San Clemente when the president was drunk, Nixon's diplomatic mastery in dealing with Kremlin leaders.

"Yes, we're all on short-term leases," he conceded

Heels tapped. *"Et enfin,"* Gramont said. "Our hostess has appeared, finally."

Weiseman turned to see a five-foot-ten woman in black silk; dark hair cut short, almost boyish; a rakishly tied belt that highlighted her narrow waist. This was Margot Gramont. She thanked him for the flowers he had sent along that afternoon, then introduced a lovely young woman in an emerald-green silk dress, with long, glossy, black hair. Yasmine de Rose was a student at the Sorbonne, and the daughter of Alain de Rose.

A tuxedoed waiter came up and whispered into Margo Gramont's ear. "Dinner is served," she said. "There is one more couple expected, but we may begin."

Weiseman offered his arm to Yasmine de Rose and led her to her place, held her chair. She smiled shyly and gestured to the place marker with his name. *"Asseyez vous, monsieur."*

He sat at the place next to her and took in her porcelain-like facial features, her two luminous dark eyes, the way she lowered them modestly. Is she Iranian? he wondered.

A fork tapped on a glass. Laurent Gramont welcomed his guests with words that flowed like the Seine.

The maid entered and announced, *"Monsieur Schreiber et Madame d'Antou."*

The chunky man wore a tuxedo with a red bow tie and pocket square, red braces and cummerbund—gray-black hair was combed straight back and brilliantined flat against his skull. The woman was altogether different: in her early thirties, slim, a gold gown highlighting lustrous blond hair in a chignon with a jeweled clasp.

The host and hostess embraced the woman, then shook hands formally with the man. Laurent Gramont said, "We're pleased to welcome dear Françoise once again to our home. And Jacques Schreiber. Just in time for dinner."


**A BLACK-TIE WAITER** swept away the coquillage, a formidable array of prawns and scallops, clams and moules, oysters from Normandy. Seated between Yasmine de Rose and Françoise d'Antou, Weiseman chatted easily in French with each, aware of those across the table inspecting him. He asked Françoise what Jacques did, wondering, What is their relationship?

The waiter began to serve the grilled *turbotin* and to offer a sterling silver pitcher of hollandaise sauce. "Jacques is in the armaments business," Françoise said.

"In the Middle East?"

"*Oui*. In Iran and Saudi, also in Libya."

"And when he travels there . . ."

"He goes alone."

"And you?"

"I'm a diplomatic correspondent for *Le Figaro*, specializing in Iran. I speak Farsi and go there often, and to Iraq." She sipped the wine, the napkin caressed her lips. She caught his eye. "We're not a couple. *Vous comprenez?*"

Her glass was empty and Weiseman signaled to the waiter, who came over and filled it with more white wine. He gestured toward Yasmine and the waiter filled her glass, too.

"You were in Tehran recently, Jacques," Alain de Rose said from the center of the table. "How goes the Shah?"

"Mohammad Reza Pahlavi," he said, "is America's puppet." Jacques Schreiber sliced into the *turbotin*. "All Tehran is waiting for him to fall. The factions are arming to the teeth."

"Well, you would know, Jacques," the ENA professor said. "You sell to all of them."

"And why not?" Schreiber said. "Jobs for our people. But regrettably, the Anglo-Saxons keep the Shah well equipped. Perhaps it was American weapons that SAVAK used here in Paris on New Year's Eve."

Weiseman noticed Schreiber staring hard at him, daring him to respond. Françoise whispered, "Let it pass. Jacques is trying to bait you."

"Do you know that, monsieur?" Weiseman asked. "That SAVAK carried out the murder?"

Schreiber rolled his eyes, as if only the village idiot would doubt it. Weiseman looked first at Gramont, then Alain de Rose.

"Of course, you're right to ask," Gramont said softly. "The matter is unsettled."

De Rose shot Weiseman a glance. His lips seemed to synch, *Later . . .*

Margot Gramont smiled sweetly, "Who would like more of the turbot?"

"But you know Jacques may be right," the professor's wife said. "The Shah is a tyrant. The Americans have been propping him up for years, averting their eyes from the torture." A pause for effect. "Look, I don't have any use for French arms dealers"—here, a nasty glance at Jacques Schreiber—"but why not give the Shah's political opponents a chance?"

Weiseman wondered, Why not indeed?

"And who are these opponents?" he asked. "Would we want to see them in power? Religious fundamentalists are operating right here in Paris. Isn't that true, Laurent?"

"Well, we've seen those reports," Gramont said. "It's very complicated, rather opaque."

"Not so opaque," Yasmine suddenly said aloud. "Iranian exiles at the Sorbonne are organizing into cells, pro and anti-Shah. There are SAVAK agents in training, religious fanatics spreading the word of the Ayatollah. Students are being beaten up—one was even killed. And that Iranian couple murdered here on New Year's Eve—"

Weiseman thought she seemed extremely agitated. It was more than the usual fevered debate at a diplomatic dinner party.

Françoise d'Antou said, "I interviewed Ayatollah Khomeini in Iraq recently. He was expelled by the Shah years ago; he's the Shah's *bête noir*." She stared directly at Schreiber who seemed about to burst a blood vessel. "One of your customers, Jacques, I believe."

Weiseman looked down the table at Gramont and de Rose, studying their fingers.


**AFTER DINNER, THE** men and women separated into two groups—the ladies in the salon, the men in a den where drinks and cigars were distributed. As Jacques went off to use the phone in the next room, Gramont led Weiseman into a huddle with de Rose. Gramont told him that Françoise's father had been close to him. De Rose said Jacques Schreiber was a man of the far right, fiercely Catholic, a *collaborateur* who did the bidding of the gestapo in the war, a schemer who advanced himself on the backs of others.

"It's a sordid story," Gramont added. "He's here because we find him useful."

*Useful?*

"The violence at the Sorbonne," Weiseman said to de Rose. "It's not just old wounds."

"Of course not," de Rose said, "What my daughter spoke about is correct. Those things are happening now, and it brings back memories of our past. We haven't forgotten the bombings. It's still a scar on our politics. Now we see it coming again."

Gramont led them to a corner set of three fauteuils. "You leave tomorrow for Tehran, David. You'll want to meet everyone in the government, civil society, even the mullahs. But discreetly. There's a man called Hanif; he heads SAVAK. Justin knows Hanif. So do I."

Gramont paused, as if deciding whether to say more. "We know the opposition, even some ayatollahs."

I'll bet you do, thought Weiseman.

"And intermediaries?" he asked.

"Yasmine will introduce you to student leaders," de Rose said softly. "She was born there. She's very attuned to the *reseau*. The network."

"And there are others," Gramont said. "Françoise—"

Jacques Schreiber reentered the room. "It's time to go," he said abruptly.

Weiseman looked up, startled by the peremptory tone. What was this about?

Gramont led them back into the salon.

Françoise d'Antou appeared a moment later, stunning in a shimmering black fur cloak. She gave Weiseman a subtle but meaningful look, as if anxious to tell him something.

"Monsieur," Jacques said crisply, then turned on his heel and headed toward the door.

Françoise stepped forward, slipped a note into Weiseman's hand, then kissed him on both cheeks, and pulled her cloak tightly about her as she followed Jacques Schreiber out into the cold Paris night.

**YASMINE. WEISEMAN HAD** a feeling she would be able to tell him more about the murder at the Sorbonne. He excused himself and went to look for her.

He found her sitting alone in a small book-lined den. She appeared to have been crying. She looked up, but didn't say anything.

"When you spoke in there about the Sorbonne student being killed," he said, "it didn't seem like something you'd only heard about. If you can tell me, I'd like to know. Perhaps it would help."

Yasmine shook her head, was silent for a moment. "She was a friend of mine," Yasmine finally said. "A gentle girl named Shirin Majid. From a good family. Her father is a banker in Tehran. She was completely apolitical."

For an instant it looked as if Yasmine would resume crying, but she stifled it and continued. "It was the headscarf," she said. "Shirin wore it every day. It didn't cover the hair in the front of her head—that was her tiny statement, her freedom. They warned her to cover up, but she wouldn't wear the chador. She was a modern Iranian woman, like me. She told me she wouldn't abandon her identity. And now . . ."

Weiseman felt a gathering force in what she was saying, the way a small wave can crest into something terrifying. "Shirin was walking on the Boul'Mich," Yasmine said softly. "I was about a hundred meters behind her when I recognized her headscarf. I was about to call out to her when I saw three Muslim guys wearing skullcaps cross the street toward her. They grabbed her by the arms and pushed her against a wall. One of them pulled the scarf down over her hair so that all of it was covered. Then he tied it very tightly around her throat. Shirin started screaming. She pulled the knot open and fixed it again, her way. They started up again, and she screamed at them, saying she was a woman, not their property."

Yasmine's voice had risen, so that it seemed she was the one who was crying out against the attackers. Suddenly, she seemed to shrink down into her body, as if retelling the words had intensified Shirin's terror—and her own.

Weiseman saw before his eyes the two slain nudes from New Year's Eve; he felt the wave swelling, ready to crash. "And then?" he said, urgently.

Yasmine took a deep breath. "A Mercedes was parked there. A man got out. He was huge, a big man in a jellaba."

Yasmine was sobbing now. He reached out to steady her, but she had to get it out, to tell everything. "The man drew a long sword out of his jellaba."

She sobbed hysterically as she relived what she had seen. "He raised the sword over his shoulder, and then he swung it at Shirin. She was standing there, and then—"

But the words wouldn't come.

## 2

# *PASSAGE TO IRAN*

**T**HE NEXT DAY, before departing for Tehran, Weiseman waited for Françoise d'Antou in a café, wondering why she wanted to see him. She professed to be a journalist, to travel around the Middle East, and to meet Arab and Iranian leaders. She was beautiful and sophisticated and worldly. And she was with Jacques Schreiber, a collaborator during the Nazi occupation.

Why?

He wondered, was she placed in his path by Gramont as bait? Did that explain the departure kiss at the dinner party and the note she had secretly passed to him?

He sipped his espresso and suddenly she was there, standing before him. They exchanged air-kisses and she slipped gracefully into the booth, smoothing her skirt and crossing her legs. He signaled to the waiter and a cappuccino was placed before her. She got right to her message, speaking to him of Iran, about the conflicting forces he was about to confront there. She told him that fear was the Shah's only remaining weapon, but now hatred was overcoming that fear. When the SAVAK secret police rolled out their dragnet to sweep up the middle-class opposition and student rebels, they only stirred the cauldron of regime hatred.

"And the mullahs?" he asked.

"When the mullahs take over," Françoise said, "the people will dance in the streets. They'll celebrate the Shah's departure and cheer on the new regime. They'll chant the prayers. Then they'll realize what they've allowed to happen. Black robes will replace military epaulettes. Everyone will conceal his true feelings. People will report their neighbors, as they do now. It will remain Iran . . . all the blundering and deceit, the suffering and self-preservation, the conspiracies and secret police."

He was struck by the comprehensiveness and realism of her perspective, conveyed in just a few moments, and how it corresponded with his own reflections about Iran—except she had been there frequently as a journalist, knew the languge, and had anecdotal detail to bolster her views. And he was struck that her depiction of life under a future regime run by ayatollahs hardly supported Trevor's belief that the French were out to replace the Shah.

Was there more that grounded her insights? He'd have to find out.

The penetrating mind almost made him forget her beauty, the tendrils of blond hair that caressed a long graceful neck; but her passionate commitment forced his attention back to the fissures in Iranian society. She told him everyone in Iran was a hostage: the Shah, the soldiers and bazaari, the students and peasants. The ayatollahs. Even the SAVAK. "As soon as you get off the plane," she warned, "you'll be a hostage, too."

"And you," he said. "Are you a hostage as well?"

He had not meant to pry; it was incompatible with his character, his insistence on guarding his privacy and respecting that of others—qualities inherited from Johann, his father—values he considered well suited to his life as a diplomat.

But she seemed to brush it aside, leaning forward and speaking softly, even intimately. "I met Jacques when I was in the university and he was a man of the world. He flattered me, took me to fine restaurants, to concerts. At that time, there were so few eligible young men who had come back from World War II and the German occupation."

She paused, as if awaiting his reaction, then said, "We never know what is inside the gold wrapping paper. It ended before it started."

Clever, he thought, and encouraging. But be discreet; how was she still linked to that beast?

"You need to understand the Iranians, David. They have their own rituals of decorum, politeness, and social etiquette. When they flatter, or say something they don't necessarily mean you to take literally, they expect you to understand. And they expect the same in return. They have a word for it. *Taarof.* In Tehran, you must practice *taarof* like the Iranians."

And did she practice *taarof* as well? Weiseman wondered. Was she doing so now?

She stood to leave and led him out of the café, up the Faubourg Saint-Honoré, past the upscale boutiques and the Élysée. The sun had warmed the day, and Françoise removed her gloves. A long black Citroën flashed by and entered into the courtyard of a massive gray building just up a narrow street. "It's the minister of the interior," she said.

Two blocks more and she stopped at Saint-Philippe du Roule, a church with a single spire that he had often passed but never entered. *"Vous permettez?"* she asked.

He watched her enter Saint-Philippe, kneel, and cross herself, then rise to light a candle. Eyes tightly shut, she said a silent prayer, crossed herself again, and walked out of the church, the sun casting its glow on her blond hair.

She led him to a bistro across the street, and they sat at a table with a red and black tablecloth. Over their quiches lorraine and salads and glasses of pinot gris, he asked her about her work. How often did she go to the Middle East . . . to Iran?

She spoke knowingly, describing visits for *Le Figaro* to Iraq and Iran, to Lebanon and Egypt—even to Saudi Arabia, not the easiest place for a woman to cover. She had learned Arabic and become rather proficient in Farsi. The paper's editor was a crusty old man who doubted a woman's ability to operate in such countries. It was a point of pride that now, it seemed, the editor came to her to take on the tough assignments . . . as Trevor did with him.

He respected that, her intellect, and the way she had put Jacques down at Gramont's dinner party. But he wanted to know more. How could she be with Jacques? What was their relationship? Who was her mentor at the quai . . . her patron?

"You've risen . . . quickly," he said.

"I've met a number of the mullahs," she said. "Businessmen, even some military officers. I can help you contact them, once you get there."

She was cool and calm. He wondered, his mind going back to Gramont, to "useful" Jacques, was journalism her cover? He asked, "How long have you worked for *Le Figaro*?"

"Since I graduated from the Sciences Po. I read Oriental Political Studies. Laurent arranged my first job, as a *stagaire*, an intern, at the quai."

Ah. Gramont. Of course.

"And then?"

"Then a call to *Le Figaro* and they took me on." She paused, as if seeking to gauge his reaction, and added, "I was very grateful to him."

"Of course," he said, wondering how grateful, and why she was telling him all this, and whether she had really met with Saddam and Khomeini.

"They're close," she said knowingly. "Laurent and your Justin Trevor. Really two of a kind."

He watched her dab at her lips, refresh her lipstick. She was sophisticated, practiced in the arts of intrigue, a journalist who could open doors to mullahs ostracized by Washington, a way to make contact.

And beautiful.

"You told me that you and Jacques were not a couple. And yet . . ."

"Yes," she said. "We arrived together last night and departed together. *N'importe*. He's old enough to be my father. But he could never be my father."

A man came into the café carrying yellow roses and walked up to their table. *"Pour l'amour,"* he murmured.

Weiseman selected a rose and handed it to her. "It matches your hair."

The man drew a pin from his green apron, and Weiseman helped affix it to her dress. His hands fumbled with the pin; it took three tries, and finally it was done.

"So, a collaboration," he said, breaking the pregnant silence.

"Yes, we could call it that, if you wish."

He watched her rise to go and stood as she glided away, turned at the door, and gently waved, the fingers in the white glove dancing seductively, performed as only a Frenchwoman can. He looked again at the note she had slipped to him at the dinner party: *Café Castiglione: 8 A.M., and Tehran.*

She was charming, while at the same time possessing the cool demeanor and intellect of the European professional woman. She had denied any relationship with the depraved Jacques Schreiber. He had to assume she was close to Laurent Gramont, perhaps the asset Trevor had mentioned. What was she not telling him? Could it be more than that?

Yet he sensed in her a kindred spirit, someone using the cover of *Le Figaro*, perhaps to carve out a measure of autonomy from Gramont just as he sought to do from Trevor. And there was their common past, how each had lost a father very close to them, her reaction to that.

And what else? Suddenly this woman had appeared in his path, an expert on Iran. Could that be a coincidence? Unlikely. Had he revealed too much?

He had lost Eva and remained unattached. There had been other women as he moved about Europe on missions for Trevor, most of them Europeans who shared his interest in the theater and music. And, of course, there was Regina Trevor, but the thought of marrying into Justin

Trevor's family . . . well, his father, Johann, had schooled him on Goethe's *Faust*, had cautioned him never to sell his soul to anyone, for any price.

Growing up on a farm in Illinois after their harrowing escape from Germany, Weiseman often heard Johann say, *"Never again."* Now, years later as a diplomat tested by hard experience, he knew that terror and genocide had not ended in the ruins of Hitler's bunker. It continued to reside in the lower depths of the human condition and could not be wished away. Those who have power can and often do abuse it beyond the limits of human decency.

He relied on the counsel of two fathers: the good and gentle Johann and the coldly realistic Justin. Johann had saved his life and sensitized him to the importance of self-reliance, of helping others, to redeem a life that was nearly forfeited. Justin had enrolled him in the service of the American empire, promoting him in Prague, turning to him to wage the good fight in Europe for America's interests and ideals in the Cold War. But Iran—that was different, a blank slate for him. As director of central intelligence, Trevor had told him America's entire position in the Middle East depended on the Shah's secret alliance with Israel and Turkey, and of course with the United States.

They were so different in personal manner and in social station, Johann and Justin, yet Weiseman's own mind and methods were touched symbiotically by both. He still heard his father's words echo in his ears. "Our new country was carved out by individuals ready to dare, not by sheep who do what they are told. Remember what Bonaparte said, *'Audace, toujours audace.'"* And with his remarkable intuition, Trevor seemed to know just how to draw the best out of his protégés, touching their innermost drives to stir them to surmount what they themselves thought they could achieve.

Yet he still felt a missing personal dimension. Maybe it was because he lost his mother at such a young age, in Hitler's war. A bomb had exploded in her path. A psychiatrist he saw once in Vienna—only once—told him the death of a mother was like being torn a second time from the womb. He didn't have much time for psychobabble; he accepted the uncertainty of life, and so was pragmatic, ready to take events as they were served up, to use his skills and internal discipline to confront any challenge. But he suspected he would have been a better man if his mother had been there to give him the love he missed amid the stress of growing up in an adopted country.

He remained in the café and ordered another espresso, his thoughts returning to Françoise, what she had said, and—"*Salaud!*" the waiter suddenly cried out, turning up the television over the bar. The TV screen was replaying that terrible night at the Sorbonne. Shirin Majid was on a stretcher, covered up before the gates. The camera panned in farther, and he felt a chill, reliving Yasmine's horror. Everyone at the bar stared at the TV, their faces flush with rage. A TV reporter explained what happened. Shirin was an Iranian student who spoke fluent French. She had a brilliant career before her. She was murdered because she didn't observe the precepts of some radical prelate of a foreign country far away. It was time to send them home if they dared to ignore French laws and customs.

At the bar, the patrons were all cursing the foreigners. The old fellow with a white mustache and fisherman's cap was telling how he had fought at the battle of Algiers and shown them a thing or two. Next to Weiseman, a rail-thin woman with a gravelly voice said, "These people, they live in my quartier, they stay up late, play loud music, and keep me awake. Their place stinks from their strange cooking. It's like a souk; a person can't get any sleep. I don't have any peace."

Coins hit the counter, and a thin, dark-skinned man slipped out of the café, apprehension on his face. The innocent would get caught up in all this, Weiseman thought. They always did.

**WEISEMAN SAT ON** the Air France flight east, peering down at the Balkans, the mountains drenched in blood from centuries of conflict. The stark contrast reminded him graphically that he had a job to do, and his mind flashed back to the exodus from Germany across the Baltic Sea, onward to America, across the Atlantic on a barely seaworthy freighter. A lifetime ago.

There had been a man in a black turtleneck with big thick eyeglasses and wavy brown hair huddled alongside them just outside the boiler room. The man entertained young David with card tricks and tall tales of adventure, telling him of life's possibilities, granting a frightened child the precious gift of hope.

Johann had asked the stranger what he had done before ending up on a ship of refugees. The man said he was a member of the honored profession of survivors. A small town doctor from the French Auvergne, he had married a German woman who cursed the Nazis, swore to him that she hated Hitler. When she learned that he had joined the Resistance, she turned him in to the gestapo. They clapped him in Drancy, just outside Paris, the way station to Auschwitz. But he decided to survive. You couldn't fight back in Drancy, the doctor told them. You had to outsmart them. "I made myself into a whole camp of different characters: a magician, a gypsy violinist. I did card tricks for the camp commandant's children, and even seduced his wife. You see, you have to get into the head of your enemy, to think like him. You have to comprehend what he believes in, to imagine the rules *he* lives by. Then you can know what he will do."

"And so I stayed alive."

As did I, Weiseman thought, snapping back to the task at hand. He was on his way to Iran, a country he knew only from briefing books. Trevor had given him a mission: Replace the Shah; find a successor we can bend to our will. Be discreet, but get the job done. Stay out of the newspapers. That was the way Trevor operated. Trevor always gave him plenty of latitude, leaving him to sink or swim on his own.

He picked up a magazine and saw the Shah's photo, thought, this is the *Zeitgeist*. We depend on dictators till one day our leaders find them distasteful. And when they falter, we want them out. But replacing a tyrant with something decent . . . that's another matter. And sheltering the people from the ugly aftermath, the inevitable violence? Well, that's much harder.

He took out the Farsi language cards he had received from the Foreign Service Institute before departure and began methodically working his way through them. He was good at languages and began to feel the rhythm of Farsi. Once he arrived in Tehran he would practice on the tapes he also had with him.

An Air France stewardess came by, offering him a drink. He shook his head; *non, merci.* She shrugged in the Gallic way: your loss, she seemed to say.

Ah, yes, Trevor's bottom line: do it any way you must. Find me a successor to run the country for us. Our guy: a general, a cleric, a cut-throat. We can't be too fastidious.


**AT ANKARA THEY** stopped to refuel. Arab and Iranian families joined the flight. Veiled Arab women incongruously nursed their babies in plain sight.

Over the Caucasus Mountains the plane soared. Out the window, Weiseman saw mountains give way to water. They headed southwest across Azerbaijan, and he could see the oil rigs, offshore from the port city of Baku. The Caspian Sea and Iran beckoned.

He opened the briefing book and read, seeking to steep himself in the psychology and culture of the Iranians, in the split between Sunni and Shia Islam, and especially in what existed in Iran *before* Islam. The Zoro-astrian faith, closer to Christianity or Judaism, emphasized the responsi-bility of every person to work for social justice. Citizens had the inalienable right to enlightened leadership. Iranian kings were seen as the represen-tatives of God on earth as long as they enjoyed *farr*, a divine blessing they had to earn through consistently moral behavior. Subjects had the duty to obey just kings and to rise up against wicked ones.

Like Confucian China, he thought. Shahs and emperors ruled by the mandate of heaven. Any ruler who violated that principle invited rebel-lion and his own ouster.

He pulled out a yellow pad and jotted down his priorities. Establish Iranian agents in place. Court the vulnerable. See the Iranians, and Turks, and Israelis, the British agent Trevor had mentioned. Co-opt

Hanif, the SAVAK chief. He paused and thought of his own harrowing escape with Johann from Germany. *Check the borders to arrange egress for exiles*, he wrote. *And reach out to the ayatollahs, just in case.*

He had to put a face to all these people, fill in the blanks. There were only bad options: Stick with the Shah, cancer or not, or one of his men. Accommodate the ayatollahs and hope they'd mellow over time. Find a white knight to save the day, what Graham Greene—whose reckoning with the moral compromises of espionage Weiseman admired—once called a third force. Stage a coup. Invade. Mind our own business.

But even his brief list was too complicated. The Shah would go, so it came down to this: find a credible leader we could work with or tie the ayatollahs in knots. That was the bottom line. That and finding a way to stay out of Evin Prison.

Meddling with another nation's future was a dicey business. We had done it before in Iran, in 1953, a quarter century before. Operation Ajax—overthrowing a regime, then bringing the Shah back. Iranians hadn't forgotten that; they probably never would. But taking on the ayatollahs? The very thought brought nightmares.

He locked the briefing book inside his attaché case, knowing that a briefing book was like a strategic war plan, to be abandoned at the first engagement with the enemy. He'd get to Tehran in a couple of hours and do his walk-arounds, imbibing the sights and smells, taking the measure of the city. He'd burrow in with the students, the mullahs, the troublemakers, as well as the military and business class. Find out what they're up to, before Iran goes up in flames. Then would come the hard part: deciding who to trust and who to avoid.

He thought back to what Françoise had said. *They were all hostages.* Iran was poised on the edge of an earthquake, exactly two hundred years after the French and American revolutions.

He was a hostage, too. And if it all went down, there'd be no one to claim him and bring him home.

**A STEWARDESS STROLLED** up the central aisle. *"Un quart d'heure pour l'atrerrissage,"* she said. "Fifteen minutes to landing." She drew a lavender silk scarf from her bag and covered her head, tucking her auburn hair under the scarf.

Mehrabad International Airport came into view, as if slowly revealing itself from behind cloud cover, hiding Persia's secrets from Western intruders. From the air he could see miles of squat buildings mottled with centuries of pollution, while in the distance high-rise structures beckoned visitors to the new Iran the Shah was constructing as part of his White Revolution.

The wheels touched down and the aircraft bounced once, then again, before heading toward the bleak, gray terminal.

In Mehrabad, security guards with wraparound sunglasses surrounded the arriving passengers, demanding that one or another display his or her papers. At immigration, the customs official glanced at his black US diplomatic passport and quickly waved him on. America was still in good standing in the Shah's Iran, Weiseman thought.

He passed a tweny-four–hour prayer room where a half dozen heads were bent toward Mecca. Women in chadors rushed by, their faces covered except for slits for their eyes. Younger women in miniskirts, holding hands, floated along like butterflies, displaying coiffed hair, tottering in high heels.

Outside the airport, throngs of Iranians waited for relatives. Cops and soldiers were everywhere. Horns blared, impatient taxis revved their motors. Security blanketed the airport.

A taxi pulled up. The black-bearded driver wore a white robe and white knit kofi cap. As a woman with glossy dark hair got out, her expensive knit dress rode up her legs to reveal a glimpse of lilac bikini panties. The driver took her Italian lire, tucked them in his billfold, placed his hand over his heart, then leaned forward and kissed the photo of Khomeini on his dashboard.

A cop with a swagger stick, a remnant of British colonial rule, thumped on the taxi's trunk to hasten him along. The rickety cab pulled up a few feet, scouting for another fare.

Weiseman surveyed the scene, searching for his new "escorts"—SAVAK agents, mullahs, US or French embassy spooks. He saw a short, wiry American in a brown suit and tie, head as bald as an eagle, studying an Iranian newspaper. Weiseman hustled over to the still lingering cab, got in, and slammed the door. He glanced back toward the bald American, who was no longer there.

"Let's go," he said.


**THE RIDE INTO** Tehran was a journey into the past. Men led mules that pulled carts laden with farm produce. Women balanced baskets on their heads. Small children kicked a rubber ball near a polluted pond. Soldiers along the highway gripped automatic weapons.

They were in the suburbs now. The gray concrete buildings that lined both sides of the road resembled the featureless Stalinist architecture Weismann knew from Moscow. Pedestrians were bundled in padded coats to protect them from the frigid February weather. A billboard showed a smiling Shah and Empress Farah escorting two children into a model school.

A few miles farther on, there was another billboard. This one was a shot of the Ayatollah Khomeini's eyes burning with righteous wrath. "The Shah allows that?" Weiseman asked.

"No, sir," the driver said. "They tear them down but they're back up the next day. In the bazaar, priests pass out leaflets cursing the American devil. They say the Shah must go."

The taxi entered the city. Soldiers were everywhere, patrolling the streets, riding in armored personnel carriers. Through the window, Weiseman could hear the din of the crowds in the streets, where merchants were plying their wares from modest storefronts, and women were boiling chickens in sizzling clay pots. He rolled down the window to sniff the aromas of the street. The driver ordered him to snap it right back up. "Security," he said sharply.

Weiseman spotted the marquee of the Intercontinental Hotel, and then the car was heading up the front drive. A doorman in a green uniform and red turban opened the door.

In the lobby, the Shah's picture was everywhere.

## 3

## *TWO TEHRANS*

**W**EISEMAN FELT AS though he had plunged into a Third World, amorphous city that sprawled under a heavy cloud of smog, across a vast plain surrounded by breathtaking mountains. Los Angeles without the glitz. Except, he knew Tehran was a city where spies and cops lurked in every doorway.

After checking into his room at the Intercontinental, he set out to explore Tehran. He took a taxi along Pahlavi Avenue, toward the Shah's Niavaran Palace in North Tehran, past skyscrapers and luxury apartments, parks with trimmed hedges and immaculate gardens, climbing to the summit of a steep hill where rich Persians enjoyed the pleasures that money afforded. Those who ruled resided here. High walls sequestered the affluent in handsome villas. On a nearby rooftop he spotted surveillance cameras and uniformed men with automatic rifles.

Alighting from the cab at Mellat Park, he took a seat on a bench—a tourist observing the passing parade. Across the street a black limo pulled up. The chauffeur opened the right rear door for a stocky pockmarked man in a colonel's dress uniform; a moment later a younger woman in a blue dress and fur stole took his arm, and they moved up the steps to a private club. Across the road, a man in the white robes of a Muslim high priest entered a mosque, a cigarette drooping from his lower lip. Women passed by, their faces covered in black with tiny openings for their eyes. Yet Weiseman knew they could discern more of this panorama of paradox than he.

He rose from the bench and walked into the mosque. He found himself amidst pillars stretching to a vaulted stone ceiling where an enormous white banner with the red crescent of Islam called the faithful to prayer. Persian carpets covered the concrete floor space. Up front, an ulema was chanting at an altar. Perhaps two dozen men on their knees murmured their devotions, bending their bodies forward until their heads, covered by simple caps of knitted white wool, touched the ground. Behind a railing, women were segregated from the men. Most of the women were in long garments; one or two wore the veil, several were in chadors. Some younger women and girls wore Western clothes, heels, skirts at the knee, but each was wearing a scarf that covered every strand of hair—all bent toward Mecca, like the men a hundred feet away.

Weiseman moved toward the side wall of the mosque and felt he was entering a caravan. Grizzled old men in prayer caps sat hunched over water pipes, imbibing whatever narcotic the pipes might offer. An aroma of apple tobacco, rose water, and a distinctly stronger opiate wafted toward the high ceilings. The men fingered worry beads and gossiped in a guttural Persian dialect. He saw one of the old men staring at him. The man removed a pipe from between rows of stained yellow teeth. "You would like the tea, sir?" the man asked in English.

Weiseman said, "No, thank you," and slipped away.

The mosque was filling up with young people in Western clothes, schoolgirls in green sweater and skirt combinations, matching green ribbons in their hair. Students in pairs of two held hands and followed their teachers, chattering like teenagers everywhere. More paradox, he thought—the old and modern, religious and secular, East and West—a country seeking its identity.

Exiting the mosque, he walked back across the park to where it ended at the edge of a cliff. He peered down the mountain, south, toward the poorer part of the immense city, to the anonymous alleys and dull gray facades of South Tehran, hiding its secrets. He knew the mullahs would have their strength, and it was there.

Suddenly he was aware of a man behind him. He turned and saw the wiry, bald man in the brown suit he had first noticed at Mehrabad Airport. Dark eyes flitted back and forth under severely trimmed eyebrows. "I'm Serge Klein," the man said.

Klein was the embassy station chief whom Trevor had told him to avoid. They were bound to meet, though, so better to get it over with.

Klein eyed him. "I know you're close to Trevor, but you're on my turf. We have to reach an understanding."

"Go ahead."

"You and I share, or we'll be crossing wires, sending false signals. That's dangerous."

Klein's dark eyes drilled in. "Agreed?"

"Agreed," Weiseman said. He extended his hand and gripped Klein's. Sharing was an ambiguous concept; his relationship with Trevor, not to mention his mission, would stay private. And, thought Weiseman, Klein would only share what he wanted me to know; that much was certain.

Apparently assuming a compact had been closed, Klein became the consummate professional intelligence officer, concisely charting the lay of the land. Multiple conflicting forces existed here. The palace was a nest of vipers, and in addition to anti-Shah dissidents and students, there were the bazaari, businessmen who sucked up to the palace and left Tehran when things got hot. Klein himself was the point man with SAVAK.

"And the Islamists?" Weiseman asked.

Klein squinted, although there was no sun. "We don't deal with them," he said. "It's policy, from Washington."

"I see."

"Do you? If you plan to see them, you'd better have Trevor give you authority to do so, in writing."

**WEISEMAN PASSED UP** the new Mercedes taxis parked in front of the club for a tumbledown job with a smoking tailpipe he found down the street. As he climbed in, he noticed a lime-green Peugeot pull away from the curb. They drove down the mountain, and modernity dissolved. Skyscrapers were replaced by shacks. Posh glass-enclosed restaurants with tuxedo-clad waiters became roadside *kebabi*, and then pushcarts. A man on a mule started across the road, and his driver slammed on the brakes.

Behind them, there was the screech of skidding tires, and a car pulled up alongside them. The lime-green Peugeot. Inside were two rough-looking men wearing bottle-green police jackets and caps. Each had what seemed to be a two-day-old beard; each wore aviator sunglasses. They both stared straight ahead while their radio blared Persian popular songs.

SAVAK, Weiseman thought. Klein's friends?

Along the side of the road, two women walked arm in arm, one in a long flowing skirt, the other in a chador. They could have been mother and daughter, but it was impossible to judge their ages. A man sat on a log nearby, smoking the stub of a cigarette, staring blankly at the mule. Other cars arrived. Drivers shouted at the delay, and leaned on their horns.

The man with the mule patted his beast and grinned. The people from North Tehran would just have to wait.

Finally, the mule was across the road. The taxi edged forward. The Peugeot waited, then slid back behind them, trailing at about thirty feet. Why so obvious? Weiseman wondered. Clumsy, or just letting him know that they were on to him, a warning not to get out of line?

The cab arrived at a covered bazaar. Surely a place to see, and to lose his police escort—if they were indeed cops.

The driver said, "You get out here, mister."

Weiseman got out and watched the Peugeot roll by. He paid the taxi driver and walked into the warren of alleys and stands. Merchants hawked their carpets, bracelets, religious icons, and street food. A young man held a silk scarf. "Lovely . . . lovely," he crooned, his dark eyes sparkling. "Made in Paris," he said, sure it was the deal clincher.

"No, thank you," Weiseman said.

"Please, sir. It is woven in Tabriz, worth thousands of rials. For you, one hundred dollars!"

He shook his head at the merchant. "I bought one at the other stand."

The man was wringing his hands; he knew there would be no other Westerner passing by his stand today. "Please, mister, you will take the scarf, free, for the honor of my house."

"No thanks," he said, and moved on, before remembering. *Taarof.* The elaborate behavioral system, a culture comprised of cues and traps, courtesy and deceit, as their protective cloak. You'll run into it everywhere, he'd been told, in the bazaar and in the palace, and in the mosque.

If the scarf was really any good, he thought, the hawker wouldn't offer to give it away. But that's not quite it. What had Françoise said? He offers it to you free, but doesn't mean it. He expects you to be sufficiently civilized to pay him his price. *Taarof.* That's the way it works here.

He wandered out of the bazaar, across the road and onto a dirt soccer field with shredded nets on either end. Young boys and men in mixed jerseys and short pants were racing back and forth, kicking the ball ferociously, intercepting each other, butting heads, battering shins. A shirtless kid made a neat tackle on a man wearing a Barcelona shirt, then grasped the ball with both hands as though doing so was essential to prove his manhood, even if it meant violating the rules of the game. The kid then kicked the ball sharply, peered toward the goal, then shrieked and laughed as it curved into the upper right corner of the net, over the outstretched arms of the tall older man who was the goalkeeper.

A green Peugeot pulled up. Startled, Weiseman wondered if it was the same one that had been following him?

Two cops in bottle-green uniforms strode onto the dirt field, grabbed the goalkeeper by his arms and began to beat him with their batons. The other men and boys all stood with their heads down, saying nothing. One of the boys, no more than eight, edged slowly toward Weiseman and meekly extended his hand. Weiseman stared at him. The boy wore a tattered, sleeveless yellow sweater, like the one Weiseman himself wore to school a lifetime ago in Berlin. He didn't know why the cops were beating the goalkeeper but grasped the boy's outstretched hand tightly, as if the boy were his son, knowing he had at least to give this frightened boy some protection.

SAVAK, Weiseman thought, snapping out of his momentary reverie. He hated knowing he couldn't interfere, could do nothing to help them. Why do they do it? he asked himself. But he knew: to show they can.

And the others, why don't they do anything? But he knew that, too: the first imperative is to survive to fight another day. The savage beating brought back memories of his childhood in Berlin, of other innocents he had seen beaten for no good reason, other than so Hitler's hoodlums could show that they could.

One day, he thought, those other boys will be foot soldiers of the revolution. They'll join whatever SAVAK the mullahs establish. They won't forget what happened here today.

He walked slowly off the field, careful not to attract attention, grasping the boy's hand. At the end of the street, he saw a cop watching them, then look off at the beating on the playing field. He gave the boy a push. "Go now," he said. "Run!" Then watched, breathless, as the youngster raced away down a dirt road.


THE ELEVATOR IN the British embassy was creaky. Weiseman rode down to the basement offices and rang a bell beside a metal door. A thin man in a faded blue shirt, tartan necktie, with a monk's tonsure of gray hair and round eyeglasses stood before him.

"Justin Trevor sends greetings," Weiseman said, and Ronald Sims smiled as if it took some effort.

"Right. Shall we?" Sims stepped back to slip on a Harris Tweed jacket and a gray peaked cap hanging behind the door, then snatched a long black umbrella and led Weiseman up a flight of stairs and out the back way, into a car park. A moment later they were driving slowly up the road in an antique Jaguar that had already clocked 200,000 miles. "They don't make them this way anymore," Sims said.

He gave off the air of a small-town English Midlands constable, accountant, or door-to-door insurance salesman, hardly the type you'd expect to be MI6. Back in Washington, Trevor had cautioned Weiseman not to underestimate Sims, which would have been easy to do. He had cultivated an air of inconsequence since entering MI6 but he had a first class mind, Trevor confided, and a bag of tricks he'd accumulated over a lifetime. There was a wife, Millicent, who, Trevor implied, added something extra to Ronald's repertoire.

"You've been monitored since you arrived," Sims said. "By SAVAK, by the French, and of course by your own people. The American ambassador doesn't much care for our types."

That didn't surprise Weiseman; that's the way it was going to be.

The smog made for reduced visibility. Sims swerved the Jag across a lane of traffic, then pulled up to a white mansion. A white sign said BRITISH CLUB IN TEHRAN. The place was an oasis of Britain's former empire and might have been transplanted from the British Raj in India. Doric columns supported the roof that overhung a wooden porch packed with white cane chairs and tartan cushions. The dining room décor was faded Victorian plush—red velour banquettes, chandeliers from the subcontinent, and portraits of Disraeli, Gladstone, and Chamberlain.

"Here's someone you need to know," Sims said, the lines at his mouth crinkling again.

"Foster," said a six-foot-four man in a gray striped suit, standing by the banquette.

"Your deputy chief of mission here," Sims said.

They all slipped into a booth. Sims filled out a luncheon chit, and a waiter came by and picked it up. "Well, that's done then."

It was 1:00 p.m., and only three tables were occupied. Foster folded his hands in front of himself on the table. "Serge Klein told me you were a troublemaker," he said. "He told me to keep an eye on you." Foster stared hard at him, then said, "Klein is a rat. I take my orders from Justin Trevor."

"And the ambassador?" Weiseman asked.

"Lyman Palmer? He's a disaster."

Neither Foster nor Sims seemed to find it odd that the American was airing his embassy's dirty linen in front of a British operative. Apparently the special relationship that fostered the Ajax operation in 1953 was still functioning in Iran.

The waiter arrived with Dover sole—flown in fresh every day, Sims assured him.

"Trevor's going to dump the Shah, isn't he," Foster said.

Weiseman dipped a slice of the sole in the dill, ate it, then sipped the Frascati Sims had ordered. "What would you do?" he asked.

"Not much choice," Foster said. "The bazaari, the army—no guts, nothing there."

"And it won't buy us much time," Sims added, then suddenly stood to greet a tall woman in a floral dress who appeared at their table. "Millicent," Sims said, "our friend David works for Justin Trevor."

She slid into the booth, and her husband squeezed in after her. "Yes, Farah told me."

So he'd already been announced to the Empress. And therefore the Shah.

He studied Millicent more closely. The curly red hair and the sensuous mouth and the flowery Dior outfit all were offset by a protruding nose with rounded nostrils that evoked, in his mind, the image of a bloodhound.

"You want to know what to do," she said. "What have Ronald and Thomas told you?"

"Nothing yet," Weiseman said, and raised his glass to her.

"Of course, nothing," she said. "But you're here to advise Justin. You need to know." She picked up Foster's glass proprietarily and sipped his wine.

Ronald Sims never stopped cutting and eating his Dover sole in neat, tiny bites.

"Here's what I think," Millicent said. "We can do it again." Her whole aspect brightened and she seemed to grow larger. "Another Ajax would keep Mohammad Reza and our dear Farah on their thrones. Mrs. Thatcher would know what to do . . ." She shrugged stoically. "I suppose your people wouldn't have the stomach for *that*."

"It won't happen, my dear," Sims said. He seemed to turn reflective, as if about to say something of significance, but he kept whatever it was to himself. Weiseman decided he'd need to devote more time to Ronald Sims.

"Then you simply must wait for the Imam," Millicent said. "Will Justin like *that*?"

Foster nodded conspiratorially. "Millicent has it spot-on."

Ronald Sims looked up from his sole. Weiseman sensed that there were other options careening through his brain, but he kept them to himself. The little man was a pro.

"That's about it, Dave," Foster said. "What are you going to tell Trevor?"

"There's nothing to tell." Millicent focused on him, as if taking his measure, then raised her glass. "Welcome to Iran," the bloodhound said.


**BACK AT THE** hotel, Weiseman slipped by the people sipping tea in an oak-paneled lounge that could have been taken from the club he'd just left. He rode the tiny elevator up to his room, unlocked the door, and there was the Shah's face staring through the window into the room—from a huge billboard on the facing building: the high forehead; the outsized ears and prominent nose; the coal black eyes staring at him as if peeling away the layers of guilt he should, by rights, feel for coming to Iran to take away his Peacock Throne.

He sat on the bed, emotionally exhausted from jet lag and his first day in Tehran, then eased his head back on the pillow. Françoise had sent him a message; she would arrive in the morning—there were Iranians she wanted him to meet.

Only half-awake now, he tried to sort out signals flashing from a lighthouse in the center of an alien world. He was back at the soccer field, at that moment with the little boy he helped escape, repeating, "Hurry!" And then the nightmare reappeared: he saw a small child hidden behind the high hedge in Berlin's Grünewald park, gestapo dogs sniffing ever closer . . .

# 4

# PRIEST & PROFESSOR

"**COME, I'LL SHOW** you Tehran," Françoise said the next morning, waiting for him in the breakfast room, sipping an espresso. She stood and put on her black wool coat.

A taxi took them to another upscale part of the vast city, where stone villas cloistered behind high walls and guard booths heedlessly called attention to the lucrative targets inside. They stopped at a two-story house with a tile roof and multiple TV antennas.

"Ready?" she asked, and adjusted her green, silk headscarf. He nodded, and she led him into the house, to the living room where they were greeted by a mullah with well-tailored clerical robes, a leathery face, and carefully trimmed white beard under a circular turban. "*Sobh bakheir*, Mr.

Weiseman," the mullah said. "Madame d'Antou said you wished to visit us."

"Good morning."

At a side table, a framed photograph showed the mullah as a young man, with a young Ruhollah Khomeini.

"David, this is Ayatollah Seyyed," Françoise said. "His name means 'Descendant of the Prophet.'" She took a seat and inclined her head. Seyyed's bony hand emerged from beneath the sleeve of his black robe and gestured to a window. He was in his fifties—a serious, self-assured man with a taste for luxury, if the gold embroidery on his robe was any indicator. At the window, they looked south, toward the decay below, poverty not erased by the Shah's reforms—the so-called White Revolution.

"We will find our recruits to overthrow the Shah there," Seyyed said, "*Alam dollah*. Thank God, it will be done without violence."

Weiseman, recalling the mayhem on the soccer field, asked how that might happen.

"We have a secret weapon," Seyyed replied. "Pahlavi himself. The people despise him. They will sweep him aside, and we will return this land to Allah."

So it wasn't just the cancer, Weiseman thought; already there was plotting to oust the Shah. And the first contact arranged by Françoise was with a lieutenant of Khomeini. Perhaps Trevor was right—that the French thought Islamist rule was inevitable.

Seyyed picked up a pack of Gauloises and put it in his pocket. On the table, Weiseman spotted a book, *Anatomy of a Revolution*. This ayatollah was no Gandhi, he thought.

"You know, the Shah will resist," Weiseman said.

Seyyed held up a finger for silence. He pointed to a door. Weiseman and Françoise followed Seyyed down a flight of stairs, into a dark cellar with one bare light bulb. The strong scent of wine was incongruous in an orthodox Muslim house.

The priest spoke in a low voice. "I agreed to see you," he told Weiseman, "because we trust Madame Françoise. Soon we may be in charge of this country. We don't want the CIA to try to install another strongman; it would tear this country apart." He lit up a Gauloise, took a deep drag on it, and vented the smoke into the fetid air of the dark cellar. "We will not accept the son of a shah, as we had to do when the Shah's father was deposed by the British in 1941. We will not receive an exiled shah dumped on us by the Americans, like 1953."

Seyyed referred, of course, to Operation Ajax, which had stashed the Shah in Rome just long enough to remove Mossadeq, the opposition prime minister, before returning Mohammad Reza Pahlavi to power. Did Seyyed take him down to this cellar, out of reach of the listening devices undoubtedly located upstairs, to pledge allegiance to the cause of the Islamic Revolution? That hardly seemed necessary. And why was he saying all this in front of Françoise?

Trevor said that Paris had another agenda. Maybe Seyyed was keeping all options open.

"The photograph upstairs of you with Ayatollah Khomeini," Weiseman said. "When was it taken?"

Seyyed took a final drag on the cigarette and dropped it to the concrete floor, lifting his robe to grind the butt with his black leather wing tip. He inched closer to Weiseman: they were almost forehead to forehead. "I have known the Imam for many years. There are those around him who hate America, who speak of *gharbzadegi*, of 'Westoxication.'"

"And this concerns you?" Weiseman spoke in a whisper. It seemed as if some secret was about to be imparted.

"Sheikh Khalaji and Montana are dangerous," Seyyed said. These were new names to Weiseman. He hadn't seen them in the briefing material Trevor had given him.

Seyyed kept talking. "Those two fanatics mean to use the Imam. He is old and frail."

"But there are others," Weiseman said, "who would tread the true path of Islam."

Seyyed said nothing, but Weiseman could tell there was *something* he meant to say.

The idea crystallized at once. An ayatollah, Weiseman thought. An old friend of the ailing Ayatollah, fearful of fundamentalists around Khomeini.

Could he be thinking of opposing the radical ayatollahs? Would he?

"Please go on," Weiseman said quietly.

The sound of a car pulling up startled them. Seyyed moved the shade at a small window near the low ceiling and peered warily outside. He seemed taken aback at whatever he saw.

A sharp rap on the door. A head with a long white beard poked in and spoke in Farsi.

"And now it seems I am summoned," Seyyed said. "I'm told we are honored by a visit from General Hanif. Perhaps you two will be so good as to depart through the rear door."


**"DANESHGAH," FRANÇOISE TOLD** the taxi driver—the university—as Weiseman turned over the possibility that Seyyed could be an avenue into Khomeini's inner circle. Yet it seemed too easy, and Françoise seemed to read his thoughts. "In a revolution," she said, "everyone keeps one eye open while sleeping."

A half mile before the gates of the university she told the driver to let them out. She led him across a rough terrain and into a grove of cedar trees. She pointed to a house through the trees and led him forward.

Leaves rustled, a tree branch snapped. An Iranian man emerged from the woods, very close to them, with a lean foxhound bounding free. The man wore a trilby hat and had a rifle tucked under his arm. The dog barked and bared his teeth.

Weiseman stepped in front of Françoise. The dog surged toward them, stopping only a few feet away. Spittle dribbled from his yellow teeth. The man in the trilby hat stood impassively.

"Call him off," Weiseman said quietly, not wanting to provoke the dog.

The man did nothing. The dog moved closer, snarling at Weiseman.

*"Please,"* Weiseman said. *"The lady . . ."*

"Reza!" the man commanded. The dog backed off, following his master back across the glen and into the trees.

Weiseman was shaken, wondering if the man with the dog was just off on a walk through the woods or was one of Hanif's lieutenants. He took a deep breath and tried to decipher the sphinx-like calm of Françoise.

He saw a trace of smoke floating out of the chimney of the house they'd been headed toward. "This way," Françoise said. He offered his hand as they climbed over hard ground, up the hill. Reaching the house, the door sprang open without their knocking. Inside, a man in a tweed sport jacket with leather elbow patches stood smoking a pipe.

"Karim Nasir," he said, extending a hand, and then leading them into a den. The walls were covered by bookcases.

They sat at a card table before a redbrick fireplace, and Weiseman studied the man whom Françoise had referred to as the professor. His hair was black and wet, as if he had just taken a shower. Horn-rimmed glasses perched on his eagle-beak nose. His chin slimmed to a point and was covered by a neat salt-and-pepper goatee.

"Did you see Seyyed?" he asked Françoise, but didn't wait for her to answer. Nasir told them that he and Seyyed had gone to school together, had played soccer, had chased girls together. But Seyyed had then discovered he had a religious calling, a destiny to serve people. He was no revolutionary, though; you could reason with him.

Weiseman recalled the photo with Khomeini and asked about the mullahs, about their factions. Were there others like Seyyed? Could any of them be trusted?

"Let me explain," Nasir said, stopping to fill a briar pipe and take several puffs. "The ulema hated Reza Shah," he said, "the present shah's father. But not because he was an autocrat. He ruled in the thirties, the age of dictators. He was convinced that a poor country needed reforms— made with a firm hand. And he had a perfect model nearby."

"Of course," Weiseman said. "Kemal Atatürk."

"Exactly," Nasir said. He explained how Reza Shah applied the Turkish model to Iran—army rule, imposing Western ways and dress, banning the veil, a secular public sphere—all of which had enraged the mullahs.

A door opened and a young man appeared, perhaps eighteen. *"Baba,"* he said, and kissed Nasir on both cheeks, then turned toward Françoise and pressed his hand to his heart. He sat beside her at the table.

"This is Selim Nasir," Françoise said. "He is my assistant. He works here for *Le Figaro*."

"And he is my son," Nasir said. He continued with his briefing as if there had been no interruption. "Mohammad Reza Pahlavi is unlike his father in many ways," he said, "but in the most important ways he is the same. He is secular. He rules by force and fear." Nasir stopped to gauge Weiseman's reaction. "You see, these autocrats are everything until they go, when all at once they become nothing. That is the important fact the others miss."

"It won't happen," Selim blurted out. "The Americans won't permit it."

Over Selim's shoulder, Weiseman spotted another framed photograph, of two teenagers on a soccer field—Karim Nasir and Seyyed. Well, then. Françoise was leading him to influential Iranians, but there were ties among them that he didn't begin to understand. He turned to Nasir. "You said, 'Until they go.' Do you think the Shah will go now?"

"Very soon," Nasir said. "The hatred and despair grows and grows. Soon the people will march up the mountain and surround the palace. They will risk everything. They'll hound him till he flees, and—"

"The Imam will be our shield," Selim interrupted, his face flushed with pride. "What will America do then? Will you be on the side of the people, Mister David?"

Weiseman knew that when that day came, SAVAK would be at the palace to meet the marchers, tanks against sticks and rocks. He realized the tanks would be made in the United States. He said nothing.

"My dear," Nasir said softly to his son, "we'll wait to see what our American friends do. Then we will decide."

Selim's chair scraped as he abruptly pushed it back and rushed out of the room. Apparently the Nasir family was as divided as the Iranian nation, Weiseman thought.

He glanced at Françoise, wondering why she had taken on young Selim as her local stringer. Françoise rose from her chair and followed the young man out the door.

"I was like that once," Nasir said with a faraway look. "Reza Shah killed my father. And yet, a man must go on with his life . . . We can afford idealism only when we are young."

Weiseman flinched at the mention of the death of Nasir's father. It made him think of Johann and their near death in Berlin.

"And if the Shah goes?" he asked. "Professors never flourish in theocratic states. Not in Calvin's Geneva or Savonarola's Florence.

"Ah, yes," Nasir said. "It's true. We are skeptical and we challenge the self-righteous. Mullahs offer certainty and demand submission to doctrine."

"Then, it will be worse for you than it has been under the Shah."

Nasir shrugged and extended his hands in the eternal gesture of doubt.

"Worse?" Françoise said to Weiseman. She had returned with Selim at her side. "No, it's the same. Shahs and mullahs have doctrines, but they're never much more than rationalizations for keeping or gaining power. I told you that before you left Paris."

Weiseman nodded. Yes, all autocrats shared a lust for power, for control, but he knew instinctively that there were differences among them that mattered hugely. So why was she here? To help him? Perhaps. But no doubt also to steer him toward Gramont's goals.

Selim's taut facial muscles went slack. "It drives us crazy," he said. His hands coiled into two tight fists. "What kind of life will there ever be for us?"

Nasir said, "It will be the way it always is. The strong will do what they can, the weak will do what they must. Will America have any more time for Iran?"

"Of course," Weiseman assured them and realized that he was pursing his lips, a nervous habit he had developed long ago.

But it was true. It was why he was here, after all, seeking to forge a network to keep Iran in America's camp, knowing that Karim Nasir and many others would soon rely on him to save them from the storms brewing around them.

BACK AT THE hotel, he walked her down the corridor to her room. She inclined her head toward the room, gave him a taut smile, and then stepped inside.

His first two days already had revealed how tough it would be to get the job done. Yes, she was alluring . . . but better not to get distracted.

He went to his own room, took off his jacket and tie, sat at the desk to clear his mind and reduce his thoughts to paper, to inform Trevor as to what he had learned. It was his habit to do so promptly, in order not to lose important insights. He would add his assessments of Ayatollah Seyyed and Karim Nasir to those of Ronald Sims, taking his first steps toward building a network for a post-Shah Iran.

But the memory of Françoise d'Antou's scent remained with him. She was a puzzle: seductive one moment, businesslike the next; a beautiful Western journalist, nevertheless, able to call on ayatollahs in a country where women were cloaked from head to toe; and linked to a man who served the Nazis in World War II, and yet was welcomed with her into the parlor of a French count.

He shook his head and focused on Iran. On Seyyed.

In all his missions for Trevor, there had been an unexpected driving figure, one who brought what the philosopher Henri Bergson termed an élan vital to his cause, as well as high risk. Weiseman asked himself, was Seyyed such a man? If so, he wondered why Françoise—especially if she was working for Gramont—had led him to Seyyed? Was this part of a double game she was playing?

He took up his pen. It was time to expand his network. He'd contact the Israeli agent Trevor had recommended to him as well as the opposition figures who could lead him to plausible alternative leaders. His thoughts returned to the meeting with Seyyed, interrupted by the arrival of Hanif. Why was the Shah's single most important man, the head of SAVAK, calling on an ayatollah? Especially this ayatollah?

Well then, Hanif should be his next port of call. The man must know everyone and everything that was going on here. At the very least, David Weiseman would need to know what to look out for, to gauge Hanif's purposes, and if possible neutralize him as a threat to his mission.

The phone rang. It was Trevor, telling him that the president would be celebrating New Year's Eve with the Shah and that he should be available.

"Of course, Justin." Then, "Justin, we need to talk."

"Of course, David. When I get to Tehran with the president. Oh, by the way, I'm hearing things. Best be wary with the lady."

Trevor rang off, the click of the phone accentuating the warning.

# 5

## HANIF

**F**RANÇOISE WAS GONE the next morning—on a business trip she had said, location undisclosed. The meetings she had arranged with Seyyed and Karim Nasir were valuable, but Weiseman knew now it was time for him to assemble his own assets to carry out his mission.

He had been in Tehran less than a week, but he could already discern the trapdoors that threatened to swallow his operation. The society was split between the regime supporters who received special favors and the silent majority cowed by SAVAK torture and intimidation. Here was the perennial danger faced by autocratic rule: once the aura of invincibility surrounding the regime was punctured, the country would fall into chaos. There would be a power vacuum at the top, leaving the perfect seedbed for the radical Islamists. A reign of terror would follow the revolution the way it had in France, two hundred years before. It was always the same. He'd lived through it himself as a child, when bakers and butchers donned armbands and paraded the streets with their chests puffed out.

He stared at a decoded cable he'd received from Trevor. The National Security Council in Washington was debating options—national security cabinet officials looking for political cover. Weiseman knew the NSC debate was diplomatic Kabuki; their options had everything to do with Washington politics and nothing to do with the realities he was encountering in Iran. The cable was classic Trevor: a prompt to cut through the morass and solve the problem before Washington politicians or bureaucrats made it worse.

His father had taught him to resist the temptation of perfection. Survival required compromise, Johann said. Even a partial and imperfect victory was worth having. He had imbibed this philosophy on the small farm in Springfield, Illinois, where they had emigrated from Germany. The good Lutherans who lived nearby believed that redemption was gained through faith. David and his father had seen too much to rely on faith alone. Sometimes you had to make hard choices.

HOSEIN HANIF RECEIVED him in a private residence secluded in a grove of linden trees in North Tehran, not far from the Niavaran Palace. Weiseman found him examining an illuminated globe in a walnut frame. He was tall, muscular, erect as an oak, with a high forehead, white hair cut close to his scalp, and a tight white moustache. He wore a well-tailored, double-breasted white suit and monochromatic blue tie. He evoked the understated power expected of the director general of the Iranian National Security and Information Organization—known by its Persian acronym, SAVAK.

Hanif's readiness to welcome him to what appeared to be his private residence was a favorable omen. The SAVAK chief showed him to an easy chair and offered chilled papaya juice. He said the Shah was looking forward to the president's visit. He took a cigarette from a silver case, a

Chesterfield, inserted it into an ivory cigarette holder, drew deeply, and exhaled.

"I have known Reza Shah since he, himself, was a lad," Hanif said. "Now, that was a man. He ruled this country with an iron hand. And when he was deposed by Britain," Hanif confided, "Reza Shah directed me to look after his son and to guide him in his work."

Hanif expelled the smoke from his cigarette in a circle that rose as if on command toward the high ceiling. "I was there, you know, concealed in the stone tower of the palace that day in 1941 when Sir Reader Bullard came and took away His Majesty, dismissing him as if he were a servant of a minor English manor house rather than the ruler of a great civilization."

Hanif recounted the story with palpable anger, the event constituting a trauma he was unlikely ever to forget or forgive. Weiseman felt he was beginning to understand something of Hanif's power and purpose: his life was not just about commanding the forces of SAVAK. His was a sacred call to preserve the Pahlavi dynasty founded by Reza Shah, to keep the young shah out of trouble, and to guide him as a ruler—to be the indispensable right-hand man.

It had taken some time, Hanif conceded, flicking his ashes neatly into a lacquer ashtray. The young shah was shy, unsure of his mission, always looking over his shoulder at the past, wondering what his father would have done. Hanif remained by his side, gently leading, teaching him how to keep foreigners from intruding, how to control the mullahs and the radical nationalists who would destroy the monarchy and Iranian state if allowed to do so. When the crisis came in 1953, he was the one who advised the young shah to take a Roman holiday while Hanif sorted things out with friends and counterparts in the CIA and MI6. "Operation Ajax," he said with relish. "Mossadeq was placed under house arrest for years; he never bothered us again."

*Yes*, Weiseman thought, *but Mossadeq now was a dead martyr who haunted the regime.*

Hanif stubbed out the cigarette, cleaned his ivory cigarette holder and carefully restored it to a small mahogany box. When the Shah returned from Rome, he told Weiseman, order was restored. "Young Mohammad Reza suddenly found his vocation. Before my eyes stood a shah, almost as if Reza Shah had returned. Ruthless as a king must be to control our Iranian state."

"And you were there with him," Weiseman said, encouraging him.

"Indeed," Hanif said. "Iran, you see, had become endangered, and it takes a strong hand to save us from those who would seize our ancient culture. America would not want to see its Iranian ally ruled from the mosque." His eyebrows raised, soliciting confirmation. "Would it?"

"Certainly not."

Weiseman recalled what Trevor had once told him: *There's no limit to the flattery men will accept. The more you give them, the more perceptive they think you are.*

"I hope you won't consider it presumptuous, General, but you bear a strong resemblance to Reza Shah himself. I believe he, too, was a general, before he ascended to the throne."

Hanif sat silently taking that in. Weiseman waited, allowing the SAVAK chief to think that perhaps, one day, he could, with US support, succeed Mohammad Reza as the current Shah once succeeded his father.

*A general, a cutthroat. Plant the seed, but make sure it never poisons the garden.*

Hanif stiffened his martial posture. His face remained a mask, until the lines softened about his mouth. "Reza Shah was my mentor," he said. "Do you know who his model was?" He paused. "Kemal Atatürk. I accompanied the Shah when he met the great man who dragged the polluted remains of the Ottoman Empire into the twentieth century. Reza Shah told me we were in the presence of a modernizer, a reformer who had cast out the ulema, and a leader who knew what had to be done to rouse a sleeping nation." Hanif looked directly at Weiseman. "Atatürk and Reza Shah were gods."

He led Weiseman to the window. "Later," he said, "His Majesty sent me to Ankara, as defense attaché, to learn from Ataturk, his *effendi*." He pointed across the lawns toward the Niavaran Palace. "Now, Mohammad Reza is never out of my sight."

*No doubt*, Weiseman thought. It was said the father had intimidated Mohammad Reza with his stern discipline. Now Hanif was there, still the regent, keeping track of his charge.

"He's lucky to have you so dedicated to him," Weiseman said, and immediately felt the cold eyes searching him as intently as a thief cleaning out a safe.

Hanif seemed to draw himself up even straighter. "We exiled Khomeini, the way Kemal Atatürk removed the caliph. I guide Mohammad Reza, but, well, there still is much to be done. Our Mohammad Reza is running out of time."

Hanif flexed his fingers, then cracked his knuckles. Weiseman braced himself for the message Hanif had summoned him to convey,

"Mr. Weiseman, you must try to understand. We're used to deception and betrayal, especially from the West. When a country is as dependent on another as we are on America, we study the tea leaves very closely. Your people give us assurances, but we sense hesitation, second thoughts . . . You say more than you mean."

Hanif stared at the palace, deep in thought, then turned back to Weiseman. "My country is in crisis, Mr. Weiseman. The bazaari are withdrawing support. Our universities are riddled with troublemakers. There's discontent in the barracks. The radical clergy is a lethal threat to His Majesty. His Majesty needs your president's support. We need the arms we requested from the United States. We need public gestures of support. We need our ally to support us in all ways. Do you understand?"

Weiseman understood completely, feeling the blast of the rage and frustration expressed by every Mideast Muslim leader who had to deal with the inconstancy of an America pulled hither and yon by its global interests. Ally and protector one day, but the next—who knew? Leaving them dependent, fearful of reaping the whirlwind.

Hanif continued to speak in a confidential tone, taking the role of trusted ally sharing ideas about their mutual interests. "We know, of course, about the president's commitment to human rights. And certainly, we agree with it."

He poured Weiseman another glass of papaya juice. "You know the

Shah is the great reformer of the entire Middle East. He and his father introduced female suffrage, land reform; they ended rural illiteracy. Those are genuine human rights, not just words. They are the results of the Shah's great White Revolution, which will be completed in two years, in October 1979."

"Of course," Weiseman said. "And we support the Shah. But sometimes, openness and inclusion can bring even greater order. Trusting your own people can generate security."

Hanif cracked his knuckles again, a clear sign of displeasure. "Yes," he finally said. "Sometimes. In some countries. But if you compel the ruler of Iran to behave in the American way, to break with centuries of tradition, to violate the customs and expectations of his nation and its culture, and yes, the will of his people, you will destroy your ally and lose your influence. You will find yourself talking to ayatollahs. And they will not hear you."

Hanif lit another cigarette and blew the smoke from the Turkish tobacco so that it formed a circle between them. "I've learned one thing in my life," he said. "One has to choose between democracy and security, between order and false idols—such as 'human rights for all.' A decent society cannot allow its enemies to rule. It cannot afford to hand the nation to the worst elements. Strong leaders must protect their people."

Weiseman spoke very carefully. Managing the SAVAK chief was central to his plan, and he did not want to send a wrong signal. "General, I understand what you're saying," he said. "But the United States is also concerned about the risks of repression. You mentioned university students, for example. You mustn't lose their support—"

"Mr. Weiseman," Hanif interrupted. "Justin Trevor told me I could trust you. I hope so. I have known other American agents in Iran, and some came to grief."

Hanif stared at him meaningfully, and Weiseman stared back, knowing the SAVAK chief was laying the cards on the table. Hanif said, "If we are to work together, I must be sure about why Justin sent you to my country."

"I'm here, General, to safeguard our alliance, our mutual interest in a strong Iran led by the Shah. Our talk this morning has deepened my understanding of your key role and my confidence in our working together to make this happen."

Hanif rose from his gilded chair, extended his hand and shared a stiff smile. But Weiseman knew he had been put on notice, that Hanif would be monitoring his every move, and he recalled once again Françoise's cautionary words that he would be a hostage the moment he landed in Tehran.

# 6

# NEW YEAR'S EVE

**J**USTIN TREVOR SAT at a large desk in the presidential suite of the Intercon hotel in Tehran, immaculately dressed in a striped suit and gray suede vest with pearl buttons that marked him as a statesman of the American century. Weiseman studied his patron, the high forehead and ruddy cheeks, the intense blue eyes, the gold cuff links. He was still in his prime after serving as ambassador to Moscow and Prague. But he wasn't a Carter man. Not at all. He was a rock-ribbed Republican, kept on to give the new White House political cover.

Before Trevor was a stack of briefing papers with marginal notations made in pencil by a clear, firm hand. Portraits of the Shah in full military regalia and Empress Farah in crown and gown hung behind the desk. An illustrated presentation book on Persepolis rested between ivory Persian miniatures on an oriental table inlaid with precious stones. "Our people have swept the room," he told Weisman. "So. Are we walking into a trap?"

Weiseman had been waiting for the question for the last half hour as his boss had asked him about his reports. Trevor had only arrived in the country that morning, but, as ever, his focus was on the unknown contingencies he and the president might encounter on their visit to Tehran.

Weiseman said, "There were protests at Tehran University after the Shah's visit to the White House last winter. SAVAK cracked down. There was systematic intimidation . . ."

Trevor looked up. "Because of the tear gas incident on the White House lawn?"

Weiseman remembered the day of the Shah's visit to the Carter White House only a few months before. Tear gas fired by DC police against protestors in Lafayette Park floated across to the White House south lawn and caused the two leaders to choke on their exchange of greetings, ruining the arrival ceremony. "The students figured it had to be on our orders," he told Trevor. "They thought it was a signal we were abandoning the Shah."

"That's ridiculous," Trevor snapped. "We rolled out the red carpet for the Shah, gave him all the reassurances in the world."

Weiseman thought Trevor looked tight as a drum. His eyes seemed red from lack of sleep; his temper was short.

"Yes, yes, of course we did," he told Trevor. "But the Iranians assume statements of support are camouflage. That's the way it's done in their culture, so they assume we do it, too."

Trevor tugged at his cuff links. "By the way," Weiseman said, "I saw Hanif. He's very suspicious about my mission, and why you sent me here."

Trevor rolled his eyes. "He should be," he exclaimed. "They want us to get out of the way *and* they want us to get rid of the Shah. Both things. Of course, they blame their troubles on us wanting to control their oil. They blame the US for backing the Shah. They blame the CIA for overthrowing Mossadeq and restoring the Shah to the throne. They blame us for everything."

Trevor got up and stood at the window. Weiseman stared out, too, at the panorama of modern office buildings, at roads jammed with cars, and at crowded sidewalks—all under a layer of smog and soot that obscured the summit of Mount Damavand. But both men could see the parade of demonstrators beneath them waving signs at the hotel: CARTER GO HOME! DOWN WITH PAHLAVI!

"You know Carter would like to do just that," Trevor said. "Get out of this stinking pit. Cut our losses. He hates being caught in the middle between a tyrant and religious fanatics. He's convinced we lose either way. There's a White House political advisor, Beauford, who is egging him on to dump the Shah."

"He's wrong," Weiseman said, and recalled Johann preaching to him on their Illinois farm—after their last minute, miraculous escape from Berlin—about the costs of America abandoning its global responsibilities. It would be like an orchestra horribly out of tune, dissonant, Johann the German violinist had explained—like a medical organism dying from the failure of bodily functions. If America the liberator of Hitler's Europe and the postwar international stabilizer retreated, who would step forward to prevent a similar seizure of world peace? No one, Johann had insisted, and Weiseman knew that his father was right.

Johann had given him a book by Santayana with a bookmark on the page of the Spanish-American philosopher's famous quote: "He who forgets the past is condemned to repeat it." It was a lesson he hoped America would never forget.

"Yes, Iran is messy, worse than that," Weiseman conceded. "But you told me Iran was vital to keeping the peace in the Mideast, and you sent me here to get it right, or to try to. Give me time to do the job, Justin. You know I'm right. Keep Carter on track, or he'll regret the consequences as much as we do."

Trevor took it all in, his eyes drilling into Weiseman's, calculating the policy he knew was right and the politics of managing his president. "This is the hardest job I've given you. Gramont means to undermine our position, to ease out the Shah, America's ally, and to play footsie instead with the ayatollahs, so when the Shah goes, France can step in to displace us in Iran. Are you up to this, David? Tell me now. I need to know you won't be distracted."

He's talking about Françoise.

"I get it," Weiseman replied, deflecting the warning and asking, "Does Carter?"

Trevor's eyes looked toward the ceiling. "The president can't abide SAVAK's methods. He thinks the ayatollahs, as religious men, may respect religious diversity and human rights."

"Justin, is that you speaking? You're my mentor; you know what we're dealing with—the collapse of this society and its takeover by medieval mullahs determined to take this country back to an autocratic, premodern epoch. When that happens human rights will not belong in their vocabulary."

Sirens sounded. Both men returned their attention to the street below to see policemen leaping out of black vehicles and charging at the orderly demonstrators. Trevor flinched as cops with batons pummeled the protestors. Weiseman saw the paradox clearly: the regime the United States couldn't afford to abandon was holding on to power by beating up peaceful demonstrators—students and kids. But the question remained: Could the United States afford to hand power over to the Ayatollah Khomeini?

It was a Hobson's choice.

The sound of the muezzin's call over tinny loudspeakers pierced the late afternoon silence, startling them both. Weiseman checked his watch. "It's 5:00 p.m.," he said. "The call to prayers."

"Yes, of course," Trevor said.

"It comes down to this, Justin. It's better not to deal with dictators, but we needn't commit suicide by exchanging the Shah for the Islamists. Centrist democrats would be better than the Shah or Ayatollah, but Iran is no democracy. They can't win. Unless . . ."

"Yes?" Trevor said. He was fully attentive now.

"Unless we can find a way to help them do so. A businessman, perhaps another general."

"Exactly," Trevor said. "That's what we should do. That's why I sent you here."

Trevor poured himself a glass of the champagne cooling in an ice bucket provided for the Shah's honored guests. "Of course, if the Islamists take over . . ."

"Then we deal with the mullahs," Weiseman said. "I'm going to contact them."

He knew he was moving on to entirely new ground and that Trevor wouldn't respond. He'd be entirely on his own.

He pointed at the savage scene below. "Tell the Shah it's unacceptable."

"Of course it is," Trevor said, "but he won't be there forever."

Weiseman had almost forgotten his illness. "How long?"

Trevor shrugged. "His doctors are hedging."

*So are you, Justin,* Weiseman thought.

But he'd have to go carefully. He hadn't forgotten Hanif's warning. Without Trevor's support, he'd be on a high wire without a net.

"You were right, Justin. The Shah is going to go, so we should be talking to everyone. But we shouldn't be the ones to push him out—until we're ready."


**TREVOR WAS TRANSFORMED** by the sweatshirt, blue jeans, and rough worker's cap that Weiseman had gotten for him. Weiseman had urged him to come out onto the streets of Tehran and see for himself what they were confronting. To his surprise, Trevor had immediately agreed to do so even though it was completely out of character.

On the street the remaining protestors came into focus. They were middle-class professionals in coats and ties and dresses, kids in blue jeans, even the odd major or colonel or noncommissioned officer, probably caught up in the protest and sympathetic to the cause.

They stopped in a café and ordered lemonades. No wines or champagne here.

A young man approached. Selim Nasir.

"Françoise is back, sir. To cover the dinner for *Le Figaro*. She'll see you there."

"Your father, Selim. Is he all right?"

"All right?" he said curiously. "He was out here, during the demo. He wanted to understand me, and now he's coming around. It's going to happen."

Selim turned to go, but Trevor called him back. "I'm John. Tell me—what is it you wanted your father to understand?"

Selim stared at Weiseman, who nodded, *Yes, tell him*.

"We're going to take over, Mister John. We'll force Pahlavi out, then the mullahs will lead us. We'll clean out the stables, all the corruption. We'll hang Hanif in Azadi Square."

Trevor got up, abruptly said, "Thank you, Selim," then turned to Weiseman. "What else did you want me to see," he asked, as an apparently earlier-scheduled car drove up.

Weiseman had the driver take them through the two Tehrans, rich and poor. Down in the valley, cops carrying billy clubs watched by the roadside as a dozen men dragged a mock coffin under a white cloth banner, mourning the absence of freedom. Back up the mountain, near the palace, Weiseman saw men and women dressed for a formal affair. "They're getting ready for the dinner," Trevor said quietly.

First his curt dismissal of Selim, now his reflectiveness—as they drove on in silence. Weiseman, unable to read his chief, thought of the first time he met Trevor, when he was the ambassador in Weiseman's first posting as a diplomat. He had been wandering in the garden behind the Prague embassy when he came upon a man in a straw hat with an ascot around his neck, reading *Macbeth*. There's a lot to learn from this play about human nature, Trevor had explained, and when Weiseman had offered his own thoughts about how human beings could go wrong, Trevor had taken an instant liking for him, as if he might be the son he and Clarissa never had. He had made Weiseman his personal aide, assigned him to duties well above his grade. They had clashed repeatedly, the cynical veteran diplomat and the young idealist. But the bond between them had never torn. And Clarissa was always there for him, too, as his champion, to ensure Justin's backing when things got hot.

The car swerved to avoid a pothole, breaking into Weiseman's reverie. "This place is going to blow," he told Trevor, "and it will take only a single spark. We're hostage to the Shah; he's hostage to us. This whole country is a powder keg."

"I know," Trevor said. "Now take me back. There's someone who's asked to see you."


THE RECEPTION WAS in the apartment of an American oil company executive, no doubt a contributor to the last presidential campaign. It was in one of those scarred buildings Weiseman had spotted from Trevor's hotel suite. The reception appeared to be little more than a happy hour with US businessmen and their wives preparing to attend the palace dinner hosted by the Shah.

Weiseman arrived alone. A young woman, Caitlin, who worked in the White House, led him to a private room. There a slim, athletic looking man with corn-yellow hair was regaling a half dozen guests with his war stories from Washington.

Caitlin announced him. "Mr. Beauford, David's here."

Beauford kept up his patter, radiating the confident air of a White House aide. Two embassy wives came in, Peggy and Allison. After air-kisses, Bobby Beauford got an *embrazo* from one of the husbands, accepted a glass of whiskey from the bar. There were plenty of smiles, chatter between Beauford and the man about their Oxford days. Keats and cats.

Weiseman stood back, listening as they shared memories. In a lull, he extended his hand. Beauford took it, fixed his deep blue pupils on Weiseman and said, "So, Trevor's prodigal son."

Weiseman had met these White House types before: inflated; self-aggrandizing; completely dedicated to the president as their channel to power, no matter their private views. Trevor's earlier message about him was, *The guy's a knife: out to get me, out to get you.*

"Actually, I work for Mr. Carter," Weiseman said. "Like you, I work for the president."

"Do tell us about Jimmy, Bobby," Peggy slipped in diplomatically, knowing that White House staffers don't need to be asked twice to expound on their own importance. Weiseman winked his thanks and smoothed a bit of salmon pâté on a baguette, accepted a glass of port. Let Beauford showboat, he thought, he'll get around to me in due course. And indeed, after explaining how Carter was altering the world by insisting on respect for human rights and after voicing his dedication to Carter's political visions, Bobby Beauford did exactly as Weiseman predicted.

"Case in point, Weiseman, you're backing the Shah of Iran!"

"Never met him, Mr. Beauford," he said, finishing off the port.

Beauford frowned. "Best not do so. My job is to protect the chief. This Pahlavi is a dictator. Our base would tar and feather us if we backed him, say we're hypocrites."

Weiseman smiled at the sanctimony, the situational ethics adopted by pols like Beauford. "I simply take soundings of the Iranians," he said. "It's undramatic. You folks set policy."

Beauford wasn't buying it. "You're Trevor's man," he said with finality. "Trevor backs the Shah."

"Actually, I don't know what Trevor thinks about Iran. As for the Shah—"

"But don't you see?" one of the embassy wives—Allison—interjected. "We're so lucky to have Jimmy after those horrid Nixon years." She extended her glass and a waiter did the honors, then she was telling them where things stood. "America can't back the Shah and Mrs. Shah with all her diamonds. Everyone knows SAVAK staged the New Year's Eve murders, and the Sorbonne killing, that nice young woman . . ." She sipped. "It would be a mockery!"

"You've got that right," Beauford said. He swallowed his whiskey, then stepped away. From the pantry, he could be heard asking the international operator to dial the White House, barking out orders to whomever was on the other side of the Atlantic. Then he was back.

"So," he said, an index finger tapping onto Weiseman's chest. "Take that as your guidance. The Shah is on his own."

So am I, Weiseman thought, realizing that Trevor had brought him together with Bobby Beauford so he'd see what even Trevor was up against.

The oil company executive suddenly materialized. "Got it?" Beauford demanded.

"Got it," Weiseman said. "Now have the State Department send me that instruction in writing."


**THE PALACE WAS** resplendent, like a Persian Versailles. Weiseman, wearing white tie and tails, spotted Françoise, whose blond hair fell off bare shoulders onto a lilac evening gown, a vision of loveliness. He had no doubt what the mullahs would think about the outfits they were wearing, nor about what they would regard a decadent scene.

Françoise joined him, and together they walked up the marble steps, just behind Justin and Clarissa Trevor and a tall man with iron-gray hair and a frozen face: Lyman Palmer, the American ambassador.

At the top of the steps, Trevor gestured to Weiseman and Françoise to join him next to a marble balustrade. And then he was Justin the cavalier, embracing Françoise, telling her how Laurent Gramont had told him she was his most valued colleague. A kiss on the cheek, a wink to his wife, and Clarissa escorted Françoise a few meters ahead of the men, telling her how her own daughter, Regina, had had her eye on David . . .

"The president met with the Shah alone for ninety minutes," Trevor was confiding to Weiseman. "We gave him what he asked for: a five year military aid list, nuclear power plants."

What did a major oil producer need with nuclear power plants? Weiseman wondered, but the question answered itself: the Shah was hoping to build his own nuclear deterrent rather than rely exclusively on what might turn out to be an unreliable American protector.

Trevor pursed his lips tightly. He waved at someone below and flashed a bright smile. When he turned back to Weiseman, the smile had vanished. "Carter told him he'd have to rein in SAVAK, let the students blow off some steam, and keep the lid on. The Shah stared into space as if he were on drugs, then he let POTUS have it. He said we didn't understand Iran, that America would never comprehend Iran. If he followed our advice, reforms would end and there'd be chaos. We'd end up dealing with the mullahs."

"He might be right, you know," Weiseman remarked.

"I know," he said. "That's why you're here."

Suddenly, a chamberlain was before them in a white silk uniform, red shoulder sashes and puffy pants, a shiny, long sword snaking down his leg. "Mr. Director, His Majesty and Empress Farah await you and Mrs. Trevor."

Trevor nodded. Clarissa took his arm. The procession was underway again. They moved under royal blue silk canopies that evoked a harlot's bed. Amber lanterns sparkled, casting an ambiance from Scheherazade.

At the head of the receiving line, the Shah, in full military dress, greeted the Carters. The tight smiles and formal handshakes said it all. The two despised each other but were tied together out of necessity.

Justin Trevor stepped right up and praised the Shah for transforming the palace into a magnificent bridge to the New Year. He remarked at how beautiful the Empress looked, that the Shah was surely a fortunate man. Weiseman watched the old fox perform, the effortless finesse, and admired the way Clarissa brushed an invisible nothing from the monarch's lapel, then exchanged air-kisses with the Empress and dangled shameless flattery that brought a sad smile to the Shah's lips. Clarissa was ten years younger than Justin, a lustrous brunette with green eyes and turned-up nose, stylish in a long, black sheath silk dress.

Waiting his turn, Weiseman gazed around the room. The luxury smacked of *fin de siecle* France, of kings and queens soon to be led to the guillotine, of the French Revolution and the generations of blood and war it spawned. They must know, he told himself, Justin and Clarissa, that the New Year could bring Iran despair and tragedy.

Françoise tugged on his arm, and they were greeting the Shah. He was struck by the prominent nose and the lean face framed by outsized ears—a near carbon copy of Reza Shah, though without his father's bushy mustache. The monarch seemed self-assured. Perhaps the gifts that Carter had bestowed that afternoon—along with having put Carter in his place—had restored his confidence.

When Weiseman and Françoise came to the Empress, he noted that beneath the practiced smile and the compliment to Weiseman for his beautiful lady was a tremor in the hand she extended to greet them, as if she knew she was playing a tragic part.

As the Empress turned to her next guest in the receiving line, Weiseman and Françoise found themselves facing a beaming General Hanif, like his boss also in full-dress military uniform. No doubt the Shah had told him over a non-Muslim drink how he had rebuffed the American president's demand that he muzzle SAVAK. Hanif gripped his arm, a manly gesture between friends that also served to reinforce the message.

Clarissa Trevor called to them, and when Weiseman and Françoise caught up, she leaned in to whisper in Weiseman's ear so Françoise couldn't hear. "You two are perfect together," she said.

She then elbowed him to offer Françoise his arm, which Weisemann did rather awkwardly, and together they all followed the chamberlain into the Grand Ballroom, decorated in festive red and green, the colors of Christmas and of Islam. Brilliant candelabra illuminated the starched, white tablecloth and glistening silver, the gold trimmed, white bone china from Germany, party favors in yellow wrappers.

The Shah and the Empress led the Carters and Trevors to the head table, situated on an elevated dais overlooking the sea of tables at which the elites of the Shah's kingdom were seated. Trevor had told Weiseman that it was best to keep him and Carter apart. "Deniability," he said tersely.

Waiters in white jackets with gold sashes served Caspian caviar, sturgeon and lamb shashlik, and partridge, with Baked Alaska and other flaming desserts.

At 11:00 p.m., an American dance band appeared. The president was on his feet. "Empress Farah has informed me that Earl 'Fatha' Hines and Dizzy Gillespie are the Shah's favorite jazz instrumentalists. We have brought them here as a gesture of friendship to our friend, the Shah."

A moment later the pianist and trumpeter were on stage, riffing away in a spirited jam while the Shah sat stiffly in his place. When it was over, Empress Farah, in her green brocade and emeralds, urged her husband to go onto the stage. Finally, she grasped his arm and virtually propelled him to the stage, where, in evident discomfort, he shook hands all around.

Looking on, Weiseman wondered if this man, so practiced in the orchestrated ritual of formal statecraft, could cope when confronted with the unexpected and the need for improvisation. Was this just a trivial event or did it reveal a character flaw, a fatally missing ingredient in the Shah's capacity to lead his nation?

At 11:45 p.m., the Shah rose, donned black horn-rimmed reading glasses, and read his toast. "Honored guests and dear friends . . . President and Mrs. Carter . . . enduring friendship . . . common interests . . ." It was diplomatic boilerplate served up by the Foreign Ministry, a script he must have read to many prior American presidents.

Finally, the Shah removed his glasses, dispensed a half smile, and raised his glass. Carter stood. Weiseman and Françoise rose along with the whole room, as a single wave heading for the shore. The Shah and Carter clinked glasses lightly. At the microphone, the Shah said, "God bless America."

Across the ballroom, Weiseman picked out Ronald and Millicent Sims. Françoise touched his arm and nodded to a nearby table where Ayatollah Seyyed rearranged his robes.

"Teamwork," she said softly, reaching to straighten out Weiseman's bow tie.

It was now Carter's turn. The buzz in the ballroom suddenly ceased. Weiseman watched the kingdom's elites and bejeweled ladies slide up in their seats. There was a tangible sigh of anticipation. The Shah, *comme il faut*, maintained his composure, as monarchs did.

Carter was smiling now, the politician currying favor, though Weiseman knew how much he must hate this particular burden of office. "Rosalyn and I are delighted to welcome in the New Year with the Shah and

Empress Farah. It's a special pleasure to do so in Tehran. We have noted the special respect and the love Iranians feel for their leader. There is no leader for whom I have a deeper sense of personal gratitude and personal friendship." And then the coda: "Iran is an island of stability in a turbulent corner of the world."

*Wait till that hits the streets!*

As Carter continued, Weiseman glanced at Trevor, sitting there with a straight face. Trevor had seen it all before. Tonight was about shoring up the Shah . . . for now. After the tour of the city, he had said to Weiseman, "We need the Shah until we don't need him anymore."

Weiseman heard Carter speak the name of Saadi, then begin a verse.

*Human beings are like parts of a body,*
*created from the same essence,*
*when one part is hurt and in pain, others*
*cannot remain in peace and be quiet*
*If the misery of others leaves you indifferent*
*and with no feelings of sorrow, then you*
*can not be called a human being*

Carter paused. Weiseman saw heads nodding around the hall, heard a smattering of applause at the quotation from the great Persian national poet.

At the center of the table, the Empress shifted in her chair. The Shah stared straight ahead, a frown now on his face. Jimmy Carter had presented his human rights calling card in an excruciatingly public way, in the Shah's own royal palace.

"So it was written," Carter said, "in beautiful, elegiac verse. This I also believe."

Then taking his glass, he raised it toward the royal couple. "To the Shah and Empress Farah, to the enduring friendship between the Iranian and American people."

Once again the wave of guests rose for the toast. The Shah shook his head, then stood up slowly, as if exhausted. He stepped toward Carter and lifted his own glass, but this time, Weiseman noticed, the two glasses did not quite touch.

The chamberlain began the countdown. Justin Trevor kissed his wife.

Weiseman turned toward Françoise and she came closer; their lips touched.

Over her shoulder across the ballroom, as the crowd shouted, "Happy New Year!" he glimpsed a red bow tie and cummerbund: Jacques Schreiber.

# 7

# MOHARRAM

**T**EHRAN AT 10:00 A.M. The city was still awakening to 1978. Electronically amplified cries emanated from minarets—the muezzin calling out the *adhan*, the traditional summons to prayer.

A rickety bus went by, empty. There were few cars on the usually clogged roads. Most of the stores were zipped up tight with padlocks securing lowered steel shutters. Curbside, vendors roasted chestnuts on coal, lamb on iron spits, and chicken on wooden sticks. Weiseman found the vendors more to his liking than the palace with its white-gloved waiters offering caviar on silver trays.

The winter chill was sharp enough to cut through his fleece jacket, wool sweater, and corduroy pants. Françoise in a chic, fur-lined tan coat and Hermès headscarf, held his arm tightly, stirring in him memories of their lovemaking in the early dawn hours of the New Year. He hadn't mentioned seeing Jacques in the palace ballroom, but he knew Jacques must have seen them together.

Yet Jacques hadn't intervened. Why not? Too public a place?

They strolled into a coffee bar where their appointment was to take place and took a table covered in red and white plastic. She ordered a pot of the chamomile tea and he a double espresso. Next to them he saw an elderly woman dolloping orange marmalade on buttered toast, her lined face a map of the Shah's long reign. A young couple in matching designer jeans held hands; they could have been in Berlin or Paris or New York. A television set beamed a soccer match from Madrid, or was it Milan? In the corner, a simple man in a white knit cap bent over on his prayer mat, facing Mecca.

Still observing the room, he asked her, as if offhandedly, "Did you know Jacques saw us, last night, at midnight?" Turning back, he saw in her eyes how she snapped to attention, the seductive side of her personality quickly supplanted by the elite professional.

She looked at him pensively for a moment, then said simply, "Yes." Then, "I didn't care." She lifted her eyebrows, as if to say, Did you? "He is not so important."

Now it was Weisman's turn for a pensive stare, followed by a slowly widening smile. He reached across the table for her hand, but before he could quiz her further about Jacques, or indeed their growing attraction and the situation it put them in, the door to the café creaked open and a young woman entered, followed quickly by a man of a similar age. She paused a moment, made eye contact with Weisman, then headed their way.

"Excuse me, Mr. Weiseman," she said. Her short car coat was open over a cashmere sweater and tartan skirt. Black hair peeked out of the scarf casually draped around her head. "I'm Alana Khoury. Yasmine de Rose and I were friends of Shirin Majid, the girl at the Sorbonne." Alana nodded toward the man hovering at her side. "This is Mahmoud."

Weiseman rose and held a chair for her. "This is Madame d'Antou."

"Yes," Alana said. "We know about you."

Weiseman wondered what that meant, but Françoise ignored it and said, "Thank you for joining us."

Alana and Mahmoud took their seats. "Tell me, please," Alana said to Weiseman, "what was it like last night? First your president embraces the Shah, then quotes Saadi at him on human rights."

Weiseman poured her some of the chamomile tea. He said, "Maybe the president doesn't think it's a matter of black and white. And you, Alana? Do you think the mullahs would be better than the Shah?"

"It couldn't be worse," she said, then paused. "The Shah put my father in Evin Prison. I can't see him or speak to him. They torture him there. Could the Ayatollah do worse?"

Weiseman felt caught short. For Alana, nothing else mattered. How could it?

It was America's global predicament: You backed a dictator to ensure stability, paying the price with the people he ruled. So when the dictator crashes, what do you do?

"Your president did a lot of harm here, sir," Alana said. She put her hand over her mouth, as if surprised by her own boldness, then realized she had lipstick on her hand, blushed, and blotted it off with a napkin. "I'm sorry."

"It's all right," Weiseman said, admiring her candor. He asked what would happen next.

"It's already started," she said. "My phone started ringing at seven this morning; our network is arranging meetings all around the city. Posters will go up today of Carter and the Shah clinking glasses."

Alana continued talking, noting Carter's "island of stability" remark, but Weiseman fixed on the word *network*. He was a realist. He didn't believe Iranian students could overthrow a king or counter the power of the mosque, but he wanted to give them a chance, and to back them. He needed every lever he could find to bring about change. He asked Alana whether her friends could do more than make phone calls. What, he wondered, could her network actually do?

Françoise said, "David can help you, Alana. And your friends."

Alana replied cautiously, perhaps knowing she had few options and that this American official might actually support them. She slowly told him about the network, without mentioning names. She and her friends were more than a small cell, they were connected to students throughout the city who were organizing a people-power movement. And there were others, not only students. When he asked whether she believed they had a chance against the power of the state, she said, "Kings only rule until they're challenged."

*Right . . . but he's our man in Tehran, at least for now.*

Weiseman shifted his attention to Mahmoud. He had a neatly trimmed beard, a prominent nose and dark eyes, an open white shirt and Nike white sneakers, and the air of a student.

"Introduce us to Mahmoud, Alana."

"Mahmoud is with us." she said. "He was in Paris. He was engaged to Shirin."

Weiseman recalled what Johann once told him: nothing radicalizes a man as much as the death of an intimate friend.

"The Shah and SAVAK are on one side," Mahmoud said, "the Islamists are on the other. The people are squeezed in between. There's nothing for us either way."

"Exactly," Weiseman said. "Neither the Shah nor the Ayatollah."

But it was the Shah that Mahmoud went on about. SAVAK was everywhere, suborning students, coercing them to act as informants. Life was oppressive. The Shah had to go.

Weiseman asked about the Islamists, and Alana said it reminded her of an American novel she had read: *The Scarlet Letter*. "The night before I flew to Paris, I was at a disco in Tehran, lots of nice young men and women. One of my girlfriends was dancing, her body swaying, her kerchief had come undone and her hair was flowing back and forth . . . The next day, her date reported her. She was arrested, and they cut off her beautiful hair, shaved her head, said she was a wanton woman. They could easily have killed her, and she had done nothing."

She looked around nervously to see if she was overheard, and Weiseman thought again of the soccer field, and how SAVAK could act with impunity. He wondered if Alana and Mahmoud were also on Hanif's watch list. Of course they were; maybe their entire network as well.

"And if the Ayatollah were to take over?" Weiseman asked. When they didn't respond he said, "General Hanif told me the Shah was the most enlightened ruler in the Middle East. I told him he was seen in America as an autocrat."

"*You said that to Hosein Hanif?*" Alana said, her eyes wide in wonderment. "Well, in a way, what he said is true. The Shah did set up free clinics. And if the Islamists take over, we'll all be wrapped in chadors, like portable black coffins."

"But still, you would prefer to see the Shah overthrown?"

"I could never support Pahlavi. Never!"

Her rage almost set her aglow. Whatever might happen under the rule of a fundamentalist Islam, life under the Shah's boot aroused Alana's visceral hatred. She didn't want freedom if it were a gift from a king.

Alana picked up her glass and drank down the white wine she'd ordered. She smiled tightly.

Weiseman was impressed. In his book, to persist in the face of danger marked a person as trustworthy, a person of character.

"Yes, the reforms," she said thoughtfully. "That's the irony."

Of course, thought Weiseman. Each time the Shah does what we tell him to do, the Islamists are more determined to take him down. We order him to liberate women, they end up in chadors.

"Alana wants America to make it all work," Mahmoud interjected, "to keep the Islamists in their mosques, to convince the Shah to rein in Hosein Hanif—but not to intrude. Right?"

Exactly, Weiseman thought. We're in a box, paying the price for supporting the Shah *and* for pressing him to reform.

The young man began to tap his finger on the side of his chair. His eyes darted back and forth toward Alana, hesitantly, as if asking her if this American could be trusted.

Alana said, "Tell Mr. Weiseman."

"I work in the central mosque here, for Sheikh Khalaji. He provides harbor for Khomeini's people. One of them killed Shirin."

"David." Now it was Françoise's turn to reveal the New Year's second secret. "Mahmoud has infiltrated the mosque for Alain de Rose. To pass on their plans to Sûreté."

"I see." So the mosque is a safe house, thought Weiseman. Yasmine must be the vital link between her spymaster father and Mahmoud, who had agreed to spy on the mullahs that had murdered Shirin. He could only imagine the danger in which Mahmoud had placed himself. And where did Françoise fit into this cabal, with her frequent visits to Iran, and to Iraq, on behalf of Gramont? Of course, the journalism and the work for Gramont went together. No doubt her collaboration with me as well, Weiseman understood.

"Who is he?" Weiseman asked. "The killer. What's his name?"

The finger tap-tapped. Mahmoud gave Alana another searching glance. "He goes by Guido Montana. He was, for a while, an exile in Italy. He's a contract assassin. He hates the Shah."

"His Iranian name is Hamid Fazli," Alana said. "There's something else. In a week, the holy month of Moharram ends. Then the mullahs will exploit Carter's embrace of the Shah. They'll say Pahlavi is America's puppet. If SAVAK does anything foolish, the end of Moharram will lead to an explosion in this country."

**WEISEMAN WALKED WITH** Françoise along a street of grimy apartment towers. Beggars patrolled the street. A feral, black cat with yellow eyes darted in front of them, then stopped and stared up at him, giving him the evil eye, its tail curling up as if ready to strike. From here, the White Revolution looked more like empty propaganda than promises fulfilled.

They approached a kiosk, and there on page one were Carter and the Shah toasting each other. Next to the photo, in a black box, the island of stability remark was quoted in bold text.

"You know, David, she may be right."

"I know." The talk with Alana and Mahmoud had affected him deeply. Johann had often reminded him never to ignore the human dimension. It was the aspect, he thought, that Trevor, with all of his political cunning, sometimes missed.

Françoise said, "The Shah is over, David, *finished*."

He studied her profile—lips drawn together, hair slightly askew as she made her points.

"Khomeini is no threat. France and America can contain him. Do you want your good name linked to SAVAK?"

He sought to comprehend her role, whether she was a disciplined operative who simply sought to use him. The question was becoming ever more important to him as he found himself drawn increasingly to her.

But he thought she was dead wrong about Khomeini. He was sure that if the Islamists took over, they would do to Iran what Robespierre did to France. *Couldn't she see that?*

He contained it. "You said you could connect me to the Islamists."

"Yes, *chérie*. There's a lawyer, an expat Lebanese. He has an office here. He's a bit of a radical himself, marching for the Palestinians and so forth. He's close to the people you need to see."

Why was she so close to this Lebanese lawyer and his Islamist friends? he asked himself. What did she really believe at her core? Then Weiseman realized that was a question he often asked about himself.

"Do you want me to call him for you?" she asked.

"Yes, please."

He thought about Alana's network, and wondered when Hanif would round them up. He dreaded the thought of what would happen to Mahmoud if the Sheikh in the mosque found him out . . .

More and more, he was finding himself being drawn into the lives of Iranians, and feeling responsibility for their safety in ways that he knew Justin Trevor would not approve of . . .

THAT EVENING, WEISEMAN typed up a cable to Trevor. Iran was catapulting into crisis, he warned, emphasizing that the holy month of Moharram would end in a week and that demonstrations were already planned. He urged Trevor to call Hanif and caution him not to use excessive force against the demonstrators. He told him that the French had planted an agent in Tehran's central mosque which was giving harbor to the assassin who decapitated the Iranian student in Paris. He did not disclose any names. He wasn't about to risk a White House leak that could place Mahmoud in even greater danger.

And then he thought, no, even disclosing that much could risk Mahmoud's life, and he deleted the reference to the mosque. He reread the cable, then went down and flagged a hotel taxi. The old car rattled through grungy slums and fifteen minutes later pulled up outside high brick walls.

"American embassy," the driver said. "I wait for you?"

"Yes, please."

He hopped out of the cab, hustled up to the art deco entrance of the huge brick structure, and pressed the night bell. The stars and stripes fluttered in the wind, and its hoisting rope clanked loudly against the pole. A marine guard buzzed him in.

At the guard booth in the lobby, Weiseman slid his black, diplomatic passport under the opening in the bulletproof glass window. Cleared by the marine to the third floor, he took the elevator up and walked across linoleum tiles to the Comm-Center. He rang the buzzer and a window opened. A face appeared—from the lips up—pallid and pimply, hair uncombed.

Weiseman handed over the cable. "Director Trevor's channel. You have that code?"

"We have it," the young man said. The window closed before Weiseman could say anything else.

Weiseman rushed back down the steps, anxious to get out, thinking what a desolate building it was, how he'd hate to work here. Back at the guard booth, he retrieved his passport. The marine eyed him crookedly but said nothing. Well, no one liked presidential visits, he thought: the constant demands from prima donnas wanting everything immediately.

He exited the building and trotted down the steps to where he left the taxi.

But the car was gone, the driver apparently deciding it was better to get out of here rather than take an American's money.

Standing on the curb, he signaled for another cab. Five minutes went by while he waved his hand in the wind. A rickety bus passed.

It was getting colder. A lot colder. Snow, light flakes, fell among gusts of wind.

He started to walk. It had taken a quarter hour to get to the embassy by cab, so it would be a long walk back in the dark, and he didn't know his way. There were no streetlights, but ahead he saw a white sign, splattered with mud. He made out the words HOTEL DISTRICT and trudged off in the direction of the sign. Then he remembered: in his wallet he had a card Trevor had given him with information about a safe house near the embassy if things got hot. He glanced at the card and confirmed the address.

He walked steadily, alert to the ice beneath his feet. The snow came down now in heavy flurries. Behind him he heard faint footfalls kicking the slush; it sounded like more than one person. He turned and saw behind him three men wearing black leather bomber jackets.

He crossed the street and felt their eyes follow him. A block away he saw a flickering light and headed that way. He picked up his pace; they followed.

He accelerated again, and they crossed the street after him. Glancing back, he noticed werewolf insignias on their jackets.

Were they SAVAK? A warning from Hanif? Radical Islamists? Or just street thugs, preying on foreigners? Didn't much matter; the priority now was to get to the safe house.

They were closing in on him now. A guttural voice called out in English. *"Weiseman!"*

At the flickering light he knocked at the front door of a café. It was the right address.

The men were running toward him. He banged on the door. The voice cried out, again calling his name. He remembered the instruction on the card: the rear entrance. He slipped around to the back under cover of darkness.

He gave the rear door three loud raps and it suddenly creaked ajar. He shoved it open and rushed in, slamming it shut behind him and quickly throwing the lock bolt back into place. Then he fell back against the door in a cold sweat.

He heard confused, muffled shouts on the street, feet shuffling in the snow.

Inside, the light was dim. He coughed against the dust and smell of camphor. After the cold outside, the room felt very warm. Behind the zinc bar, he caught the blurred image of a man. Across the room, a woman sat at a table, dealing cards.

He heard the confusion and anger growing in the voices outside. They'd lost him.

"You are the American." The woman spoke softly, in English, but he couldn't make out the accent that inflected her gravely voice.

"Yes, I'm American." He fingered the card Trevor had given him, but decided to wait before showing it.

She continued to deal what appeared to be playing cards, although laying them out in front of her in a pattern that suggested tarot. His eyes darted again at the door.

"Nouri will bring you some warm tea now," she said.

"I need a taxi to get back to my hotel," he said. "The Intercontinental." She dealt another card. She clapped her hands once.

"You're with Mr. Carter."

"Well, he's gone now, and I'm still here."

The figure from the bar brought steaming tea in a glass with a rusty, silver handle.

"Drink," she said. "Then I'll have Nouri drive you to your hotel."

He lifted the glass; the handle was so hot he had to set it down. The woman dealt another card. He tried the glass again, with a napkin, and sipped the tea. It tasted of mint. He reached into his pocket and took out the card with her name on it. It said Madame Zed, the name Trevor had given him for one of his agents.

"You are Madame Zed?" he asked.

"Take a card," she told him.

Weiseman focused on her. She was heavyset, with thick rimless glasses above a prominent nose and double chin. Stark white hair peeked out from beneath a black headscarf.

He took a card. It was the Queen of Hearts. He placed it facedown.

"The Queen of Hearts, Mister David. There is a woman . . .?"

It seemed a classic start to him—wasn't there always "a woman"? He was more struck by the question of whether it was disconcerting or reassuring that she knew who he was.

He said, simply, "Yes?"

"Take another card."

It was the Jack of Clubs.

"There is a man in town. Jack?"

This did give him pause. "Jacques," he said.

She dealt another card.

It was the Ace of Spades.

Even Weiseman knew that one. Death

She said, "You should go now."

Fortune tellers were fakes, he reminded himself. And besides, it was just a cover. She was no more Madame Zed than he.

She said, "I will be here if you need me again."


**IN THE CAR,** Nouri told Weiseman there were djinn lurking in the city. Evil spirits. Weiseman had read that some Iranians believed such things, but it was his first encounter with such belief.

At the front door of the Intercon, Nouri handed him a three-by-five card with a name and a South Tehran address. Weiseman put it into his pocket without looking at it, thanked Nouri for coming out to get him, and hurried into the hotel. The whole evening had unnerved him—especially learning he was on SAVAK's radar—and he wanted to find Françoise.

Stopping at his room, he found his key wouldn't turn. Spotting a chambermaid, a teenage girl, he said "Room 1012. It's my room. The key doesn't work."

"The bellboy took your luggage downstairs for you, mister," she said. "A lady and a gentleman asked me to give you this."

He took the sheet of hotel stationery. Gentleman? He wondered. Jacques? The note said: *Be safe. I'll call you when I can.*

He rushed back down to the lobby. It was late at night, but several people were waiting at the reception desk. He stepped in front of them. "It's very urgent."

"A moment, mister," the female clerk said, and tugged her headscarf as tight as a plaster gauze around her scalp. "You must wait your turn."

Beside the desk was a door with a sign on it that said MANAGER. As he headed for it he heard the clerk mutter in English, "Americans. They think they own us."

He opened the office door to find a fat, bald man in a black cutaway jacket and striped pants at a desk, squinting through thick, rimless eyeglasses at a newspaper. Weiseman told him there'd been some mistake, about his room, about the luggage.

The bald man listened quietly, nodding and inspecting his fingernails. Then he said, "You are finished, Mr. Weiseman? I am Daud." The bald man hoisted his flabby frame out of his chair and handed Weiseman an outsized business card. "You will come with me, please."

He led Weiseman across the lobby to the concierge's desk.

"And do you know if Madame d'Antou checked out?" Weiseman asked.

Before answering, Daud called to a bellman. He turned to Weiseman. "Madame d'Antou left with Monsieur Jacques. Osman took her luggage to the taxi. Correct?" he asked the bellman.

"Yes," Osman said, eyes averted.

"We have packed your luggage for you, Mr. Weiseman. Osman will get it."

"Did madame leave a forwarding address?"

"None," Daud said. "Just this," and he handed over a hotel card with a name on the back. *Pierre Jubril, avocat,* and an address. It was the Lebanese lawyer Françoise said could connect him to Khomeini's people.

"I see. Please ask Osman to return my luggage to my room."

"I'm afraid that will not be possible. You vacated the room. Someone else has it."

Weiseman took a deep breath, striving to hold his anger in check. "Then, another room."

"I regret to inform you," Daud said, "that the hotel is fully booked." He walked toward the reception desk, then turned, held his hand with a ruby ring across his heart. "Bye, bye, mister."

At the reception desk, the female clerk glared at Weiseman.

## 8

# DOING THE 40-40

O N JANUARY 9, a week after Carter's departure from Tehran, Weiseman was slouched against the plaster wall of a room in a dormitory at the University of Tehran, where he had been staying since being evicted from the Intercon. Mahmoud hovered nearby, plucking the seeds from a pomegranate and popping them one by one into his mouth. Alana sat next to Yasmine de Rose on a wooly khaki army blanket tossed over a cot. Yasmine's Paris party dress was replaced by blue jeans, the worldwide uniform of university students.

And, as it turned out, Yasmine knew where Françoise was.

"She's in Paris," she told him. "With my father. She'll contact you."

So. She was with de Rose at the Sûreté now, not Gramont? And not *Le Figaro*.

Was she part of a French security tag team? Françoise and Yasmine, working for Alain de Rose? He trusted Alain de Rose and, judging by Yasmine's private comments to him at the Paris dinner party, he tended to trust her as well.

He led Yasmine into the next room and closed the door. "Tell me about your father and Gramont," he said.

"You know that already," she replied. "Laurent is the one calling the shots in Paris; he has the access in the Élysée, but my father speaks for Sûreté. Laurent needs him for the intelligence and for support of the national security team."

"I see."

"Of course you do, but that's not what you're asking, David. Is it?"

"Françoise," he said cautiously. ". . . Is she working with your father, or Gramont?

"Trust her, David," Yasmine said.

Before them a tiny black-and-white TV showed images of protestors in religious regalia: black robes and circular turbans. There were flowing white beards on the men, peach fuzz on the cheeks of novices, and, in the hands of nearly everyone, placards depicting Ayatollah Khomeini. A news reader out of Dubai intoned: *Qom, the religious capital of Iran. This protest comes two days after the mysterious death of the Ayatollah's son. Many Iranians attribute that death to SAVAK.*

The news report cut back to Carter's "island of stability" remark. It had been played over and over on Iranian television, held up by the Shah's PR flacks as proof of White House support, and mocked by Iran's opposition as a colossal insult. The irony was that Carter despised the Shah. He hadn't meant a word he'd said.

Weiseman led Yasmine off to the side and called to Mahmoud and Alana to join them. "What's going on," he asked.

"Moharram is over," Mahmoud explained. "It's starting—the 40-40."

"The 40-40?" Weisman asked.

"In Iran, politics and religion are intertwined. We hold a religious ceremony forty days after a death like that of the Ayatollah's son. After each ceremony there's a rolling wave of demonstrations for forty more days."

For some reason Weiseman remembered the night during his first posting when Soviet tanks rolled in and turned the Prague Spring into a brutal Soviet winter, how Trevor concluded nothing could be done, that the outcome was inevitable, that the mission was to safeguard American interests. That's all.

Trevor had warned him not to become involved with the Czechs. Involved!

Weiseman hadn't accepted such fatalism then, and he didn't accept it now. Just getting out of the way while a cloud of misery and oppression engulfed the Iranians wasn't good enough. He was determined to keep the Islamist mullahs out, and if that wasn't possible, to throw obstacles in their path. He would extend his outreach to disaffected young people, military officers and business executives; to the poor foot soldiers in South Tehran; to honest politicians and their corrupt counterparts; to Seyyed and others in the clergy; even to those in the Shah's entourage who sought to advance themselves once Mohammad Reza Pahlavi was gone.

Among these disparate forces, he would seek out someone who might become America's new man in Iran, someone who could be relied on. That was Trevor's mandate. But Weiseman also wanted someone capable of running the country effectively, and if possible, honestly.

Let them all think he was their friend, but in the end, if it worked, he would need to be the one to pull it together, to integrate the strategy. Weiseman pondered these thoughts. Of course, it might not work. He recalled once asking his college philosophy professor: How can you know anything for sure? The professor told him, "If you want certainty in life, there's a church on every street corner."

"David," Yasmine said, breaking into his trance. "They want to know what you're going to do."

"What *we* are going to do?" he repeated. Pulling his thoughts together, he told them what he'd need from their network, whom they could recruit, how they could spread their influence. He would help arrange safe houses, teach them codes to maintain contact, provide simple communication equipment—walkie-talkies to start. Trevor could get some to him through Foster. These young people knew the country and brought to their cause passion and readiness to sacrifice. With the material assistance he could provide, and the network of Alana's and Mahmoud's followers, they could keep the Shah's men and the mullahs off balance while he sought to keep everyone from Hanif to Seyyed in the tent, and to identify potential successors and the foreign support necessary to back a new regime.

Above all, he needed to ensure that he had Trevor's support. Trevor had warned him once, "Your principal enemies will be those of your own household," meaning Washington. Weiseman hadn't forgotten that. It would be Trevor's task to make sure that the White House didn't pull the plug on him for domestic political reasons that would then forever remain opaque.

Sirens screamed from the TV, interrupting their planning. Cameras panned to SAVAK units leaping out of their vehicles and rushing toward an orderly line of mullahs. Warnings blared from megaphones. The police brandished their batons. The marchers moved slowly but relentlessly toward the police units.

Shots cracked, like hammers hitting a block of wood. As Weiseman and the others stared, horrified at the TV, mullahs and novices, older men and young students, fell, wounded or killed. Blood channeled through the holy streets of Qom.


IT WAS TIME to leave the dormitory, establish a safe base, and set things in motion. He asked Foster, the American embassy minister, to call the Intercon on his behalf, thinking it was best to hide in plain view. "Good idea," Foster replied, "I'll take care of it."

When he returned to the hotel, Daud greeted him at the front door, bowing and scraping as if the earlier incident had never happened. Apparently, the little opportunist had been impressed by the call from the embassy. And through him, no doubt, Hanif would now learn about his return to the hotel. Good. It was time to follow up with the SAVAK chief.

"Our best room," Daud said, and a team of bellmen carried his one bag and escorted him, anxious to see to his every comfort. When he reached into his wallet to tip them, they backed out the door, bowing, hands to heart. "Oh, no, Your Honor, we couldn't accept, please, do not insist . . ."

He remembered what Johann had taught him: beware of false flattery, even while doling it out to others.

ON THE HIGHLY polished walnut table of his hotel suite was a crystal vase with white orchids next to Beluga caviar with all the accompaniments and a bottle of Chablis. The red light was blinking on the phone. Weiseman dialed for the operator, and Daud picked up.

"A call for you, Excellency. General Hanif."

Before Weiseman could say anything, he was holding for Hosein Hanif. He wondered whether the call would be followed by a team of SAVAK agents escorting him to Mehrabad and out of the country, or worse, to Evin. But no, Hanif was cordial. Hard men compartmentalize their duties; it was as if he had nothing to do with the repression in the square.

"I'm glad we had that chat at my residence, Weiseman. There is someone you need to meet. Colonel Mustafa Yilmaz. He's the Turkish military attaché."

"I would like to meet Colonel Yilmaz," Weiseman said, "and to stay in touch with you."

"Oh, yes, we'll be in touch," said Hanif. Weiseman heard the hacking cough of a longtime smoker. Then Hanif said, "Good that you're back in the Intercon. It makes it easier for us to look out for you."

A slight rephrasing, Weiseman knew, would have been more accurate: *It makes it easier for us to keep an eye on you.*

**THE BATTERED PONTIAC** clattered past a truck on the highway that ran through the city. Alana's scarf slipped back and her hair spilled onto her forehead. From the front passenger seat, Mahmoud cursed a passing car, then touched his forehead. "I'm sorry, Mister David, sometimes my head gets hot. With the 40-40, there is so much death." Mahmoud slapped the dashboard. "The US is giving SAVAK tear gas to disable demonstrators. There are signs at Tehran University warning students to behave. *BEHAVE!* OR YOU'LL CHOKE ON AMERICAN GAS."

The driver swiveled in his seat and extended his hand in greeting. "Shapour is my brother," Alana said.

Weiseman briefly gripped Shapour's outstretched hand. "Better watch the road," he added.

Lumbering along the highway, the Pontiac suddenly swerved to the center of the road, barely avoiding a pothole big enough to swallow it up, just missing an oil tanker truck carrying the lifeblood of the Iranian economy coming the other way. It started to rain, and the downpour beat so hard on the Pontiac that he imagined they might be swept away. Horns blared in the wet night.

Another sound joined in: the *adhan*, rising everywhere in the city. "We're near the central mosque now," Alana said.

They passed by the modernistic Azadi Tower, the Freedom Tower. After twenty minutes, they reached South Tehran. The Pontiac thundered up an alley.

"We're here," Shapour said. "And please, call me Sammy. I prefer it."

**SAMMY GOT OUT** of the car and approached a soldier patrolling nearby. Sammy gave him the high sign, then handed him an envelope. The soldier opened it, pocketed the bills inside, and then handed the envelope back to Sammy. The soldier tossed his cigarette butt onto the ground, and a small boy dashed over, snatched it up, and fled the alley. Sammy handed the soldier another cigarette from his own pack. They shook hands and

Sammy swaggered toward the car, strutting like the mayor of the shabby slum, letting Weiseman know he had set things up.

"Let's go," Alana said. She led the way into the dull gray-brick school, down a dark corridor and across a modern well-lit basketball court, into an auditorium. A student assembly was listening to a speaker dressed in a Western suit and tie. The sight of the students brought to mind the boy Weiseman had helped escape from the soccer field; he decided he needed to see how the youngster was doing; that was important, something he must do. Maybe Sammy could help him find the boy.

They walked across the back of the auditorium and out, into another unlit corridor, then entered a classroom where one dim light bulb barely illuminated the faces around a scratchy pine table. "You asked whether we could do more than make phone calls," Alana said. "We're going to tell you."

He peered across the table and saw a half dozen young people, barely twenty years old, burning with passion and commitment. They wanted the Shah out of Iran but didn't know how to make it happen. They wanted Weiseman to show them.

"Fires are burning a mile from here," Mahmoud said. "Khomeini's priests got some thugs to torch one of the Shah's palaces." He stepped out of the room.

Had Mahmoud already infiltrated the mullah command center? Weiseman wondered.

Instead, he asked, "And SAVAK?"

"They're rounding up suspects," Alana said. "But the wrong people—students who are no threat to the regime."

"The mullahs are the threat now," someone down the table called out. Good, thought Weiseman. Perhaps there's hope for this network.

"Hanif wants to go after them," the voice added, "but the Shah is holding him back. Pahlavi is afraid to confront the ayatollahs."

"He'd better be," a young woman's voice replied from behind a niqab.

Weiseman was mesmerized by the eyes peering out at him from the two slits in her black niqab. He knew this was a different culture, but he couldn't comprehend how a woman, or any human being, would consent to being imprisoned that way.

The young woman sat up and adjusted her niqab; she seemed uncomfortable. Weiseman thought he detected red lipstick from the slight opening for her mouth. She took a cigarette from her purse and he reached across the table to light it. "Thank you," she said in an accented English, and then told Weiseman of her life. Her mother married a German banker close to young Mohammad Reza during Hitler's war. He bought oil at bargain basement prices and traded it at a huge profit. "He played the young shah for a fool." She puffed two times, tiny drags on the cigarette, and exhaled the smoke, then shrugged. When the war ended, Mohammad Reza summoned her father. "He said, 'You don't swindle a king.'"

The woman adjusted her niqab again. "The Shah ordered my father's execution. General Hanif personally shot him. My mother died in an asylum a year later."

"Your father?" Weiseman said. "He was?"

"German intelligence. He served Hitler the way most Iranians serve the Shah—"

"No," Weiseman interrupted. "I know about Hitler. They're not comparable. Hitler and the Shah. Not remotely."

"Of course not. Not for Americans." Her eyes were blazing through the eyelets. "And my father was a Nazi spy? Right? That's what you're thinking. But—"

"I didn't say that—"

Silence swallowed the space between them. Then she said, "It's all right, mister. Perhaps he was—of course he was—serving his country. But for me, it doesn't matter. The Pahlavis have been pillaging this country for fifty years." She paused. "Hanif and his men raped my mother before sending her to the asylum."

Weiseman took it all in and felt frozen. "I'm sorry," was all he could muster.

"Of course you are, but I know what you're thinking. Will it be any better when we have the Ayatollah? The answer is no. Of course not. But it will be different."

Weiseman stared at all the young faces. "And that's enough?" he asked her.

"Do you have a better idea?"

Well, he thought, that's what we're here for. "And what do you want of me?" he asked.

The young woman glanced meaningfully at Alana, and Weiseman saw Alana nod. Two young women whose parents were victims of the ghastly treatment by the regime.

"I want to help you destroy Pahlavi and Hanif."

Revenge, he thought, the most elemental of human emotions.

"And how could you do that?"

Alana said, "Hannah is the personal secretary of Hosein Hanif."

Jolted, Weiseman let it sink in, then realized with satisfaction: agents were already in place. Hannah was with Hanif; Mahmoud with the Sheikh and his hired killer, Montana; and, perhaps, Ayatollah Seyyed with Khomeini. Beyond that, Yasmine was acting for her father, and Françoise, Gramont's agent in place, was reporting back channel to Alain de Rose.

Mahmoud came back into the room. "There's been another death. A mullah set himself on fire. The crowd stood around and watched him burn. The cycle has started again."

# 9

# THE GREAT GAME

FORTY DAYS. WEISEMAN knew it was time to expand his assets. The network of young Iranians could lead him to local centrists who wanted an alternative to the Shah or the Ayatollah, but he knew the center was weak. Moderates were . . . moderate. They folded when faced with violence. And if they didn't, they were crushed.

But even the brave could be crushed: he was preoccupied with Hannah. The cultivated Hanif had already shot her German father and raped her Iranian mother; if she were found out, Hanif wouldn't hesitate to kill her.

To succeed, Weiseman knew that he needed more powerful forces who shared his strategic aim. That meant foreigners, countries who shared

America's interest in keeping the Mideast from blowing up. If it meant reviving the Great Game at the end of the twentieth century—with the United States taking over the role of Great Britain in the contest with Russia for control of the Mideast—well, that was better than an Islamist Iran that would threaten the entire region.

Meanwhile, there was Hanif himself, stealthily plotting to succeed the Shah. Weiseman knew he had taken a risk in flattering Hanif and egging him on. He thought of Kipling's warning: Don't hustle the East!

For the time being, though, he would have to keep the SAVAK chief on his side. The confrontation with him would come soon enough.

The phone rang and he heard what he now knew was Hannah's voice. "General Hanif is calling," she said, and he pursed his lips.

Hanif came on with that same faux cordial voice. "Mustafa Yilmaz, the Turkish military attaché, has agreed to see you. Tomorrow morning." He paused, as if considering his next question. "Do you ride?"


**WEISEMAN FOUND YILMAZ** sipping tea on the verandah of the Tehran Polo Club, clad in a houndstooth sport jacket and fedora, sporting a slick, black mustache: the complete Turkish gentleman. The only horses in sight were cantering lazily around a dirt track.

The Turk recognized him at once. "We're expected," he said, not adding by whom, and moments later they were traveling in an olive green sedan. At Mehrabad, Yilmaz led Weiseman up the stairs of a fixed-wing, executive airplane with no identifying markings. The plane rose into the smoggy Persian sky. Yilmaz said, "There are briefing papers by your seat. You'll excuse me, I have some things to attend to," and he disappeared into the plane's cockpit.

Weiseman opened the loose-leaf, three-ring binder and began to flip through a briefing on Turkey's secular politics. First came a narrative of Kemal Atatürk's ban on sultans and priests after World War I, which led to the end of Ottoman traditions; then an account of his successful propulsion of Turkey into the modern world following the First World War; finally a review of the dominant (and beneficent, of course) role of the army. Unsurprisingly, there was nothing on the military coups that had been precipitated by civilian governments that dared to innovate, nor was there any mention of recent reports that another coup could be imminent. The brief might well have been prepared by Hanif.

It was easy to see how the Turks and Iranians got along. They were two moderate Muslim states run from the top, born of civilizations encrusted in longstanding legends. The Turks were mostly Sunni Muslims, the Iranians Shiite by way of a Zoroastrian past. But neither were Arab; and neither trusted their Arab neighbors.

Weisman stared down at the uncultivated, sun-dried Iranian earth, where the essential crop was the magic black liquid that fueled Western manufacturing plants. Yilmaz reappeared, his jacket buttoned snuggly around his athletic frame. "We'll be passing over Tabriz soon, before we enter Turkish airspace. There were riots in Tabriz on January 9. They will doubtless start again soon."

The small plane leveled off when it entered Turkey. Down below, Weiseman spotted men bent over with rudimentary plows and dray horses, working the land as their ancestors had done for centuries. They passed over small villages with dirt roads and a marked absence of commerce or the refinements of city life. The plane began a sharp turn and circled over Ankara's international airport, then flew on for several minutes before diving rapidly and touching down at an air force base on the edge of the city.

The door of the plane was drawn open and Weiseman followed Yilmaz past a flank of saluting airmen. A staff car awaited them, and a motorcycle escort whisked them through the sprawling capital, around the stalled parade of vintage autos spewing exhaust fumes into the leaden air of Anatolia. At midday, the pollution could be cut with a knife. The city seemed to Weiseman utterly without charm. Maybe that's why Atatürk located the capital here in Ankara, far from the decadent distractions of Istanbul.

A quarter hour later, the car pulled up under a large red Turkish flag with a white half crescent. They entered a redbrick block building where the floors were buffed to a brilliant sheen, matching the shoes of the four-star general who awaited them at the head of a highly polished conference table. The steel-gray hair of the commander of the Turkish general staff was combed straight back, as if plastered to his skull. There were razor sharp creases in his gray uniform slacks. Next to him slouched a man in a wrinkled blue suit, squinting through sunglasses. "I'm Moshe Regev," he said.

Weiseman shook the firm hand of the Turkish general and the calloused one of the Mossad man, then took his seat at the table. Two slender, dark-haired young women in miniskirts appeared with Turkish coffee and biscuits, then vanished.

There were no Englishmen present, no one from France.

He certainly could not tell Françoise about Ankara.

So, thought Weiseman, this was the Iranian-Turkish-Israeli alliance that Trevor had described as America's security regime for the Arab Middle East.

Now he'd see how he could put it to use.


**THERE WAS NO** palaver. These were hard men with no time for diplomatic niceties. The Turkish general—the name tag on his blouse said Irmak—crisply set out the agenda. "We're here to rearrange things in Iran," he said. And then General Irmak made clear what he had in mind. "Our brother, Mohammad Reza, is mortally ill. We need to fill the vacuum before the ayatollahs take over. If that happens, our own Islamists may get ideas. You understand?"

Weiseman nodded.

"We need our own man," Irmak said, as though he was taking his script from Justin Trevor. And perhaps he was. Had Hanif really arranged for this trip to Ankara to depose his shah, opening the place on the Peacock Throne for him to claim? Was Trevor in on the plot?

But Irmak wasn't finished. "This time, the powers around this table have to solve the problem. Hanif is too ambitious; he can't be trusted."

And what was that supposed to mean? Weiseman inclined his head toward Moshe Regev.

The Israeli took off his sunglasses, one stem at a time, as if they might crack. He began to clean them, carefully. "Our American friend," he said, as if coaching the Turk.

Yilmaz leaned forward. "We invited you, Mr. Weiseman, because the United States is our partner. We need your help to make this come out right."

So the table was set. He felt their eyes upon him as he succinctly presented his program. He spoke softly and had their complete attention. It was time for Ajax Two, he told them, but with a central Asian twist. This time the Shah would not return. That was the endgame, and it would be his task to win the Shah's confidence, and eventually lead him to the plane carrying him away. A bit of a white lie, perhaps, he said, but surely it was in the Shah's interest and that of all of those around this table. It was, after all, only a matter of time before illness or political circumstance would force the Shah out. Surely a decent exit would be preferable, more dignified for a king than what the ayatollahs had in mind for him.

But arranging the Shah's exit, Weiseman added, would depend on keeping his trust while simultaneously and, secretly, finding a reliable successor.

He detected slight smiles as he spoke.

Then he sat back and took in the fabled cynicism of the East. The allies of the Shah were ready to sell him out and replace him with a figurehead who would serve them. That was how London and Moscow had deposed his father in 1941. Except now the regional powers, deciding that Britain was out of the game and France was too cozy with the mullahs, were stepping into the vacuum, apparently eager to work with America.

Good. It fit into his plans to replace the Shah and preempt the ayatollahs. He would gain assets necessary to get the job done—political support from Iran's neighbors, and military assets should they become necessary—capabilities the student network could not muster. Perhaps a Turkish plane could take the Shah out on the fateful day. Perhaps the neighbors would provide military forces if it came to that. Yes, there would be many tactical details to be sorted out—but he felt a sense of relief that the strategic concept was finally on the table.

Of course, he knew he shouldn't trust what they say. If the price was right, Yilmaz would report everything to Hanif. Turkey and Israel would cut each others' throats for an imagined tactical advantage with the next shah. Whoever he might be.

When they concluded their discussions, Moshe Regev handed him a card with his name and the simple title, *Representative*. "Yes, Israel has an embassy to the Shah's court," he added. "I see the Shah rather often, when I need to."

General Irmak told him that Colonel Yilmaz would be at his disposal, then invited them all for a stroll in his private gardens. Outside, Weiseman spotted a man with owlish glasses in a charcoal-gray suit and green tam-o'-shanter strolling in a grove of trees. Irmak exchanged a brisk handshake with the man, then moved off to sniff the roses.

Regev kept his distance. He shrugged, as if saying, a necessary evil.

Mustafa Yilmaz introduced Weiseman to Tariq Aziz, Saddam Hussein's foreign minister. Aziz steered him away from the others, toward the hedges.

Weiseman had never been to Baghdad, but he knew about Aziz, Saddam's odious right-hand man, ready to pronounce whatever messages Saddam put in his mouth. This man was someone who served the Iraqi dictator the way those around Hitler once served the führer.

Weiseman felt himself tighten up. He knew of the need, sometimes, to deal with abominable people. But Saddam's man?

Who set this up? The Turks? Perhaps. The Israelis? Regev the professed chum of the Shah? Unlikely, but who knew? Most likely Trevor, fond of quoting nineteenth-century British statesman Palmerson's adage that power politics were guided by permanent national interests. Trevor, always keeping his options open, probably saw an Iraqi connection as a gift to David Weiseman.

Aziz gripped his arm. "I think one day we may be working together."

Weiseman nodded and extracted his arm from the Iraqi's grasp. "Good evening," he said, and made his way back to the car where Colonel Yilmaz was awaiting him, ready for the flight back to Tehran.

## 10

# MOSSAD'S MAN

**W**EISEMAN WAS BACK in Tehran by nightfall, mapping out the plan, asking himself hard questions. The hardest one, always, was, Where could it go wrong?

He had made good progress. He now had allies among the regional powers who knew the territory and their own interests. They shared his distrust of Hanif and had been intrigued by the plan he called Ajax Two. He hadn't gone into the inner layers of the plan, of course; details were still to be worked out. He let them read into his words what they wanted, doubtless more and less than his true intentions. He hadn't worked for Trevor for nothing.

But this was no game. These were sovereign governments that would focus relentlessly on their own individual interests. It was a rough neighborhood, where diplomacy was like brokering a truce among rival street gangs in order to fight the police together. Bizarrely, Weiseman had been introduced to them all by Hanif, the very person they were all ready to betray. Nevertheless, each would—for his own nation's interest—do all he could to avoid an Iran ruled by Ayatollah Khomeini. They wanted, they *needed*, America's help to do so.

Still, Hanif was dangerous, Weiseman thought. He could find himself in Evin Prison if Hanif got wind of his plans. What could Trevor do about *that*?

And then there was the business with Tariq Aziz, hinting at future cooperation but leaving it undefined, deniable for the moment—the diplomatic practice of constructive ambiguity with an Iraqi spin. Weiseman had faced distasteful choices before, but this one bordered, perhaps transgressed, the line of moral turpitude. Did the end justify the means? Wasn't Saddam worse than the Shah? Wasn't Aziz worse than Hanif?

Weiseman knew he was treading close to the edge of the envelope—near the boundary line between Johann's values and Trevor's methods. He wondered, how did one make such calculations?

He knew there was no barometer of morality in this game, but one thing was sure: if this transpired, Saddam's agent would one day present America with an invoice for payment in kind, perhaps a slice of Iran or an assurance of silence while Saddam liquidated his own dissenters. Or worse.

**THE NEXT EVENING,** Weiseman made a phone call from a booth outside his hotel and quickly found the cab with the right number. Sammy grinned to see him again and shot off into the night. It took twenty minutes to reach the brick building tucked away in an alley in North Tehran. He rang the doorbell once. A peephole opened; a blue eye examined his own. Moshe Regev drew him inside.

Weiseman stared up at the light fixture above their heads, a tired old chandelier, rusty gold trimming utterly lacking in charm. Regev said, "Don't worry. We swept the room before you arrived. It's clean."

Of course it was, Weiseman thought. The only bugs here would have been those placed by Mossad.

The Israeli went to a wet bar, returning with a vodka for each of them. Weiseman didn't ordinarily drink vodka, but he felt he needed to do so in the circumstances. He swallowed it in one shot and felt the liquid burn his throat and stomach. Regev offered him a refill. "No, enough," Weiseman said.

Regev led him to a small table and came right to the point. "America put all its chips on the Shah," he said, "and now he's called your bet—the way he did in '53. That's why your idea—Ajax Two—intrigued me. I shared it with Jerusalem. The prime minister wants to know more."

Regev pointed to a map on the wall. "Iran is in our neighborhood. The Shah is our ally. We don't make a big display of it, but everybody knows. We work together to check the wild beasts in our neighborhood, like Aziz and his master. If Mohammad Reza goes, it won't be decent moderates who take his place. We remember what happened to Saul."

"Saul?"

"Our king who died at the hands of the Philistines. The name we used for Reza Shah."

Weiseman understood at once. For Israelis, this was an existential matter. It impacted their essential security. Islamists were their new Philistines.

"Agreed," he said. "We can't let that happen here."

"Yes, yes, I know," Regev said, and gave Weiseman the weary smile he half-expected. It was like talking to Trevor.

"Listen to me, David. There'll be madmen like Qadhafi among these ayatollahs, and who knows, one of them may build a nuclear bomb. Can Washington live with that? What will you do when some mullah threatens to destroy Israel? Would you wait until Menachem decides to obliterate Iran first?"

"He would do that?"

"You have to ask?"

Weiseman glanced at the empty glass before him and Regev refilled it. They both swallowed their vodkas simultaneously. Weiseman said, "Then you're on board."

Regev gave him an incredulous look. "David, on board what? We're a small country. We find the Shah a reliable partner. Hanif, too."

"And you know the Shah is mortally ill."

Weiseman waited for Regev to respond but got only slightly arched eyebrows, as if the Mossad man wondered how he could imagine the Israelis knew less than the Americans.

The silence was suffocating.

He was there to enlist Israeli intelligence and perhaps military assets to beat back an enemy they both found beyond the pale. They were good at this sort of thing, but Regev was guarding his options, wanting to know how the Americans intended to solve the problem.

Weiseman finally asked, "Okay. What do you suggest we do?"

"Do? Well, David, you kick this king's ass, tell *him* what to do. Or, you replace him— and then, you'd better get it right."

CARRYING OUT TREVOR'S orders had suddenly become far more complex. Everyone was playing double games. It was no accident that diplomacy was called the second oldest profession. And there was his double game with Françoise.

From his hotel room, Weiseman peered out at the city. Despite the huge oil resources there were few lights outside; Tehran was covered by a blanket of darkness. Sitting in the dark room, his mind turned over the horrid choices he now faced. His plan was full of trapdoors, vulnerable to all sorts of imponderables, deceptions, and other unknowns. He thought of Trevor and Gramont, of Hanif and the hard men at Ankara, of Moshe Regev who had left no doubt that Israel would act in its own unilateral interest, and of Tariq Aziz, Saddam's man from Baghdad.

Who do you trust, he wondered, in a community of spymasters? His father had once warned him you should always keep an eye on your enemies, but above all beware of those who pretend to be your friends. He knew that, when it came down to it, Jimmy Carter wouldn't want to save the Shah. Surely this was something the Turks and the Israelis, not to mention the Iraqis, also understood.

And then there was Regev: there was no happy talk with him. No sentiment. Regev was a man scarred by the battles of a lifetime. When Weiseman referred to the alliance of Iranians, Turks, and Israelis that was supposed to guarantee peace and security in the Middle East, Regev had reminded him that there were no Arabs in the arrangement. "Turks are Turks and Iranians are Iranians," he had said. "Arabs are Arabs."

And Israelis?"

"Ah, Israel." There was a sad smile. "You see, David, we look after ourselves." And that's when Regev had given him that deep brace of reality, the nuclear scenario he'd outlined.

So, Weiseman understood. There were to be no heroes in this mission, only survivors.

He got up, switched on a light and walked into the bathroom to wash his face with cold water. He stared in the mirror. Whenever he grappled with a problem beyond his control, Johann would say, *"Erfrisch, David!"* Freshen up. Focus.

Returning to the suite, he saw the red light on the phone and called the operator.

Daud again. "A call for you, Excellency, the American ambassador." Before Weiseman could say anything, he was holding for Lyman Palmer.

Trevor had warned him that Palmer was known for guarding his turf. He didn't like outsiders interfering with his mandate.

Palmer spoke in a deep, Irish-tinted baritone. "Justin Trevor told me you'd be in my country," he said. "Did you plan to call on the American ambassador, Weiseman?"

"It would be my honor, sir."

Silence, for maybe ten seconds. "Then I'll see you the day after tomorrow at six-thirty, at my residence." Palmer wheezed. "Do you need a car?"

"No, sir. I'll get there myself."

"Very well, Weiseman. I've been told you may have your own agenda."

"Sir?"

"And the room? Trevor asked me to look after you. You are at the Intercon, aren't you?"

"Of course, Ambassador. The room . . . it's splendid, more than I need."

Palmer cleared his throat. "Six-thirty, Sunday evening, then. Good-bye."

**WEISEMAN TURNED ON** the television news station and switched the channel to Dubai. A peaceful demonstration coursed through Tehran's dark streets—young people in casual Western wear, older ones in coats and ties and dresses, or sober traditional Iranian dress. Their signs called on the Shah to open up Evin and let the prisoners out.

The camera panned through the marchers. He couldn't spot any signs demanding the end of the monarchy. But it was eerie, a silent procession of those who would be repressed if the Islamists took over.

Suddenly, the camera stuck on a tall erect man with a thin mustache at the edge of the crowd. Hanif raised his right hand, as if giving a command. The TV screen seemed to crackle in light, flares lit up the parade. Some people froze, most scattered, but every corner was filled with steel-helmeted riot police carrying metal shields and upright batons.

Rifle shots burst across the screen. Demonstrators fell. The new-model German color TV caught the bodies sagging to the asphalt road, the sticky red flow of blood.

Hanif, the enforcer, believed he was protecting his shah, but he was doing so from the wrong enemies. His victims today were the good people the Shah would need in order to survive. Hanif's men mowed them down the way the czar's police did on that Bloody Sunday in 1905 in St.

Petersburg, opening the way to the Russian Revolution. The way those bakers and butchers marching with puffed up chests had seized Berlin Jews and sent them east.

Weiseman stared in rage at the TV, knowing that Khomeini's mullahs were watching it as well, all with grim pleasure.

## 11

# PALMER & THE SHAH

**A**FTER THE GRUELING visit to Turkey and the follow up with Regev, Weiseman spent the next day recovering in the hotel, doing laps in the indoor pool and lifting weights in the gym, studying his Farsi language cards, going over and over his language tapes. He treated himself to an American-style hamburger and prepared himself for Lyman Palmer.

On Sunday night, down the street from the hotel, he saw the beat-up Pontiac with the long tail fins. Alana's brother, Shapour, was in the driver's seat. Weiseman climbed in and gave him an address. The Pontiac stuttered slowly in the maddening Tehran traffic, past countless dull high-rises, and the ever-present piles of uncollected curbside refuse. The late afternoon air had turned frigid. Sleet drew icy designs on the windshield. Peering through the obstructed view, Shapour shook his head. "The defroster, it's broken. Like this country."

They stopped at the stone wall that encircled the ambassador's residence like a moat around a Persian palace. A security guard, in an outlandish red uniform, a blue cape, leather gloves, and spurred boots, opened the iron gate and frowned at the dirty Pontiac. Weiseman rolled down the window and said his name. The guard snapped a salute, froze for a moment in the cold air of protocol, and accepted Weiseman's passport. After checking a visitors list in his guard booth, he handed back the passport and said, "I'm afraid you'll have to alight here, sir. We have no record of this . . . automobile."

Weiseman, bundled up in his overcoat, walked between sculptured hedges coated with evening frost toward a splendid redbrick mansion that was said to be one of the finest American ambassadorial residences in the world. Lyman Palmer was waiting for him in a small parlor with dark green walls and dark wood wainscoting. The ambassador was tall and lean, ascetic in appearance; he stood slightly slouched, hands on hips, and peered at Weiseman from under thick eyebrows as if suspecting his visitor was an intruder.

"Sir."

"Yes, yes, Weiseman. You'd better come in, then. Take a seat, over there on the sofa."

Weiseman sank into the cushions, and felt immediately uncomfortable, at a disadvantage. Palmer stood on the plush mauve carpet, examining him, seeking to decipher his purpose. Finally, he picked up a tumbler from the piano and polished off the contents.

On the piano, Weiseman spotted a gold framed photo of the Shah. He pushed himself out of the cushion and went over. "May I?" he asked and saw Palmer nod. The inscription read: *To our trusted friend and brother Lyman, in peace. Mohammad Reza Pahlavi.*

"As a matter of fact," Palmer said, "the Shah has no friends, only

Farah. He sits on a throne of thorns. He's hated as an autocrat for giving the whip to Hanif and SAVAK, and despised by those of us who know him for his vacillation."

Weiseman thought back to when he had first seen the Shah on New Year's Eve, a mere two months before. Now the man was surrounded by enemies on all sides, the product of many years of tyranny. Yet the American ambassador was saying the Shah was incapable of decisive action.

Palmer gestured back to the sofa and took a seat in a huge leather chair—a throne of his own. There was a chair on the other side of a coffee table, facing Palmer. "May I?" Weiseman said, and sat. Better, he thought, and pushed himself back into the chair.

Palmer rang a little silver bell on the table, and the butler brought two tumblers filled nearly to the brim. They each took one, and Palmer said, "*Santé*," then downed the whiskey. Weiseman sipped his. The butler returned with a silver dish with Beluga caviar on ice. Weiseman picked up the little mother of pearl spoon and enjoyed the tiny black eggs that burst in his mouth with the essence of the Caspian Sea.

Go easy, he cautioned himself. This ambassador does not wish you well.

"I've read your cables, sir," he began cautiously. "They didn't convey such a dark sense of the Shah's dilemma."

Palmer was tapping his fingers on the side of his chair, still eying him. Weiseman decided he'd have to ask Trevor whether the two of them had had some kind of confrontation.

"Why would I tell them that?" Palmer finally said, enunciating his words distinctly. "Washington does not know how to digest bad news. What would they do with it?"

What indeed, Weiseman thought. Probably file away the report in a circular file.

"Are you saying the Shah is finished?" he asked.

Palmer picked up his glass and found it empty. He eyed the caviar and shrugged. The butler, hovering, edged forward with refills, but Palmer waggled an index finger of dismissal.

"I didn't say that, nor would I say that even if I believed it."

"I'm lost," Weiseman said.

"Are you, Weiseman? No, I think not."

Palmer got up from his chair and walked back to the piano. He lifted the framed photo of the Shah. "My pathetic friend," he said derisively, then put the photo back down and started out of the room. "Come along. If you're truly lost, I'll help you find your way."

Weiseman rose and followed him through the archway and past the butler still standing there with two more filled glasses, into a study lined with books and illuminated by recessed amber lighting that cast an eerie glow around the room. The ambassador led him to one section after another of his collection: Vietnam, Guatemala, Congo. "That's where I served our Republic," he said, pointing to a raft of books in Spanish and English on Cuba. "This was my first posting, where I lost my illusions. Fidel and Che sent Batista packing, in the name of liberty, then they snuffed out the last spark of it."

Well, thought Weiseman, at least we have something in common, though it was Prague where I lost my innocence. Under Trevor.

"So here we are with a dying autocrat," Palmer said, pointing at a biography of the Shah. "These absolute rulers lose all sense of why they're there. They have nowhere else to go, so they stay and stay, clinging to power till they're brought down."

"And what do we do in the meantime?" Weiseman asked. "What do you do?"

"We tell the Shah we support him, all the way, until we support his successor. I did that in Saigon, with Diem, until Washington arranged to have him . . . removed from office."

*Removed from office*—what a quaint way to describe Diem's assassination, Weiseman thought. He said, "You would let the mullahs take over this country?"

Palmer elevated his eyebrows as if to express his disappointment. "Weiseman, it's their country," he said. "It doesn't do to get emotional. We Americans think we must solve all the world's problems. We can't. Washington won't admit that, of course. We're the superpower; we're America."

"Mr. Ambassador, you meet the bazaari, the middle class, the professionals. There must be a capable business executive among all those Iranians who hate the Shah. There must be men with the ability to run a modernizing society efficiently. Isn't that what we need here?"

Palmer nodded to the butler and accepted another tumbler, which he dispatched. He shook his head vehemently. "I'm afraid it's their problem. We'll live with the outcome."

Weiseman felt a wave of disgust at Palmer. He'd been in the East too long, had drunk in the spirit of resignation that pervaded this place. He'd given up. Trevor should pull him out.

"It will be the mullahs," Palmer suddenly said. "We'll say we support them. We'll say we'll work with them."

"And if they tell us to go to the devil?"

"Then we'll go, and let them sink with their stinking nostrums until they call for us to return and bail them out. And they will. And we'll return . . . on our own terms, I hope."


**IN THE END,** Lyman Palmer surprised Weiseman by inviting him to accompany him the next day for his weekly Wednesday morning audience with the Shah. This would be his first time with the man Trevor had sent him here to displace. He hadn't planned to meet the Shah; now he'd be dealing with a human being, not just the image conjured up by his friends and enemies.

At the palace, Weiseman was surprised to meet a mere shadow of the regal figure who had gotten his way with Jimmy Carter on New Year's Eve. His face was gaunt with worry; he had lost weight. His martial posture had given way to a slight stoop, like the slouch that afflicted Lyman Palmer.

The Shah granted Weiseman a sad smile. "So," he said, "Director Trevor has sent you here to see if we will overcome the present difficulties, Lyman Palmer and I."

Weiseman turned toward Palmer, but the ambassador stared straight ahead, as if he were merely a silent observer. The fierce turf warrior now seemed all too content to let Weiseman occupy his space.

"Your Majesty," Weiseman said, "I bring you greetings from Director Trevor. America wants you to act, to—"

"To do what, Mr. Weiseman? Our friend Lyman assures me of American support every Wednesday at this hour, but he offers no advice. He tells me I am the Shah, so I must decide."

"And so you are, and you must do, Your Majesty," Palmer said, suddenly stirring to life.

"Yes, Lyman, thank you for that. And you, Mr. Weiseman, what message do you bring from Washington? Do you have something more specific to offer?"

"This is my first trip to Iran, Your Majesty, but I hear many things around the city. The mullahs are stoking religious fervor since Moharram, since—"

"Since your president's unfortunate remark on New Year's Eve. Yes, statesmen should not flatter each other in such an inept manner."

"Frankly, sir, Washington believes your security services are making things worse. We hear in the bazaars and universities that many who fear the mullahs are nevertheless turning against the Shah."

The Shah listened calmly as Weiseman urged him to reach out to his people.

"Of course, Your Majesty," Palmer interjected, "these are merely anecdotal impressions of one who speaks no Farsi, who has been in this country only a short time, who is not well acquainted with all the forces that are influential here."

The Shah shook his head. "Is that true, Lyman? Or is Mr. Weiseman speaking as a keen observer with a fresh eye on our present situation? Perhaps he has been investigating our city in some old, dirty car with Iranian friends who speak our language. Or perhaps he is simply offering us today the views of the CIA."

Weiseman felt a chill at the reference to Shapour's Pontiac. The Shah fixed him with a stare that said he knew more than he revealed, that SA-VAK kept him well briefed.

Weiseman hesitated for an instant, then said, "Your Majesty, the best I can do is refer to a book that you may wish to consider. It's called *The*

*Leopard*, and it's the story of how change came to Sicily late in the last century. A young man dares to say to the prince something we all might do well to consider now: 'If we want things to stay as they are, things will have to change.'"

The Shah permitted himself a bittersweet smile. "I have read this book," he said. "So tell me, my friend, what would you have us change?"

"Trust your people, Your Majesty. There are too many of them simply to be rounded up. And there are educated people who share the aspirations of your White Revolution and who fear the mullahs. You need to give them an alternative. Reach out to them. Appeal for their support."

*"Appeal?"* The Shah spoke the word as if it were an epithet. "Mr. Weiseman, a Persian monarch does not beg his people. The Shah of Iran is the embodiment of his people. We are one. My people will follow me." The Shah stood to signal that the audience was over. "You tell that to Director Trevor."

**"EXACTLY WHAT DID** *you think you were doing in there?"* Palmer exploded as the Cadillac steered out of the palace gates.

"He seemed lifeless, as though he's lost his will to survive. All right, I shouldn't have said appeal—but maybe they would give him a chance rather than surrendering to the mullahs."

Palmer was only inches away in the back seat. "You really are rather naïve, aren't you, Weiseman. He *is* almost lifeless. His doctors give him two years to live. At most! He knows it's too late, that after all these years there are no more chances. And you really need to accept that."

"So we walk away?" Weiseman asked. "We let them turn Iran into a repressive theocracy? Khomeini will attack our interests across the Middle East. He'll carry the sword of revolution against his neighbors, lead the battle against Israel. And you're content to sit and let it happen?"

Palmer was silent. Weiseman knew he had said too much to a powerful ambassador who wouldn't forget or forgive. A diplomat shouldn't indulge himself this way. But the man's indifference was infuriating. And he felt a tremor of satisfaction that he had told it as it was.

The Cadillac sped up and darted through an open gate, past redbrick walls, into the embassy complex, into the cold basement. Palmer climbed out of the car and pointed to an embassy Ford. "I've done my duty to Trevor," he said. "That car will drive you to your hotel. Don't give Hanif an excuse to pick you up. I won't be there to help if they toss you in Evin."

Weiseman absorbed the warning as Lyman Palmer disappeared behind the doors of the parking garage elevator, then watched it bear him to the office at the top of America's diplomatic fortress.

## 12

# A VISIT

**THE NEXT MORNING,** the ringing of Weiseman's phone awoke him from a deep sleep.

"It's Françoise," she said, her voice as clear as if she were down in the lobby. "We need to talk, but not here. There's a private club. A Citroën will wait for you at noon, at the hotel entrance. The driver's name is Luic."

He hadn't seen Françoise since she disappeared from the hotel with Jacques Schreiber, the night after the New Year's Eve celebration at the palace. He realized he was relieved to hear from her.

The French driver arrived at the front door of the hotel at twelve noon, sharp. Weiseman eased into the back seat of the dark blue Citroën and they sped away. The driver said nothing as they went across town to a district Weiseman didn't know. Twenty-five minutes later, the car pulled up in front of an ordinary, gray, two-story brick building, and Luic turned off the key. Weiseman stepped out and looked around, but there was no one to be seen on the street.

He climbed the three steps to the front door and, unbidden, the door opened and Françoise was there, looking pale and uncharacteristically uncertain. He stepped forward and greeted her with air-kisses.

"Come, David," she said. "There's a small park where we can talk."

She slipped her arm in his and led him silently a couple of blocks away, into a secluded park where they sat side by side on a green wooden park bench.

He began to say how pleased he was to see her again, but she spoke quickly. "There is something I need to clarify with you. Laurent summoned me to meet with him. He had received a report that made him angry, that made him suspect your intentions. I listened to what he said and told him I would take care of it. *Chérie*, Laurent wants to know what you were doing in Ankara."

He had dreaded this moment. He knew he couldn't tell her the entire truth. She would then be obliged to tell Gramont about Ajax Two, the plan to keep the ayatollahs out of power.

"There was intel from Trevor," he said. "Elements of the Turkish military considering options that could upset the delicate diplomacy in Iran. I was asked to visit Ankara, to get things under control. Of course, they denied it all."

"Of course," she said. He could tell she didn't believe him. "*C'est tout?* That's all?"

It was true as far as he told her, and the least he could say. He was determined not to lie to her, and he had cleared it with Trevor in case Gramont called to check up.

"Of course," he said, "you can never exclude some majors and colonels embroidering the story to make themselves look important."

"David, you expect me to rely on this?"

He thought for a moment, then said, "We can't always share everything, but we can each accomplish our mission if we work together when we can."

Françoise stared at him, mulling it over, conceding nothing.

"How about this," he said. "We each go about our separate duties, me reporting to Trevor and you to Gramont. But privately, we'll be a committee of two. Trevor once told me no effective intel operation could be run without at least two confidential agents, protecting each other's backs."

"I've got to go," she said, rising off the bench. "Laurent wants me back in Paris tonight. I need to speak with Alain de Rose."

He knew she hadn't agreed to anything, but neither had he.

But there weren't even air-kisses goodbye this time.

## 13

# REACHING THE
# RADICALS

**A**FTER THE DEPRESSING encounters with Palmer and the Shah, Weiseman decided it was time to explore whether an accommodation with the mullahs was possible, before it was too late. He had no illusions on that score, and he knew that Hanif's men would be watching him even more closely once Hanif reviewed the taped transcript of his conversation with the Shah. And he recalled Serge Klein warning him about reaching out to the mullahs. But there was no choice; he had to play all the cards in the deck and keep all his options open.

Meanwhile: Françoise. He knew she was deciding how much she could trust him. She was a thorough intelligence professional, weighing the options, capable of compartmentalizing the personal and the professional, like him. Perhaps he should call her, he thought.

Instead, Weiseman called the Lebanese lawyer she'd recommended, the one she had said could get him a meeting with Khomeini's people. Pierre Jubril told him he had already spoken to Françoise, and he was finalizing the arrangements. Leave it all to him, Jubril said. He'd call Weiseman back with the time and place.

**IT WAS ALREADY DARK,** the dirty skies cold and windy, by the time Weiseman approached the square in Tehran's Jewish quarter where Jubril told him they'd meet. Weiseman strode past soot-stained windows, through a stench of home-fire cooking, and into the desolate square, wondering why the mullahs Jubril was supposed to introduce him to would choose this place to meet. Weiseman was flying blind, and hating it.

A man in a sidewalk stall pointed him to a bookstore, and Weiseman crossed the street. Once in the bookstore he asked again, then walked through the back door and found himself in an inner courtyard. He spotted a bench on the left side, under a big leafy tree, and sat down. It was seven fifteen. He was a quarter hour late. He hoped Jubril hadn't left without him.

After a while, the back door of the bookshop opened. The proprietor came out clutching a paperback and walked right by without a word. No one else was in the square. It was cold. Weiseman, in a light topcoat, checked his watch. It was 7:25.

The wind started blowing through the trees and a branch fell from above, landing in his lap. He picked it up and tossed it on the ground, brushed off his trousers. Thinking again, he stood and picked up the branch, wondering if perhaps a message were on it? But there was nothing.

He stared into the darkening night, wondering if he had been set up. A streetcar could be faintly heard beyond the courtyard, clanging once, twice, a third time.

He checked his watch again: 7:40. It began to rain, a cold drizzle. A door closed, so slowly he could hear it squeak. Then the square was dead silent. He cursed, blamed himself for not taking an umbrella, and stood up from the bench, heading for the bookstore. He trotted up the stairs and turned the handle.

Locked.

He knocked on the door, calling out for someone to open up. Down the steps, he peered through the windows, but no one was there, so he jogged to the other side of the square, staring through the dark, but saw no doors. Who was this Jubril, he wondered, this champion of leftist causes? Why had Françoise entrusted his security to this Lebanese lawyer? And where was she?

Worried, ready to cut his losses, he edged his way under the dark arcades, searching for a way out.

He heard footsteps.

A hand gripped his shoulder.

Through his peripheral vision he glimpsed a black leather glove and a pair of thick, dark glasses before a hood slipped over his head.

He turned, putting his strength into it, before it was too late.

A second set of ungloved hands forced his hands behind his back, and a rough rope tightened around his wrists, cutting into his skin.

A guttural voice said, "Come with us."


ONE OF THE men smelled of onions; the other smoked a cigarette. The windows of the car were closed. Weiseman was squeezed between the two men in the back seat as the car moved slowly in the city traffic. The driver grunted in an odd dialect. He knew a bit of Farsi but didn't recognize what they were saying, thought it might be a dialect.

The car broke out of traffic and accelerated, apparently leaving the city. "Where is Pierre?" he demanded. The smoker said something in Farsi, then, "Shut up."

The car swung around a curve, and he felt a blast of cold wind and rain as the driver apparently lowered his window, then the sound of coins hitting an automatic coin trough. A gate creaked. The window squeaked back up, cutting off the fresh air. The hood was oppressive; he was claustrophobic and found it really hard to take. Slouching down in his seat, he tried to surrender to the monotonous rhythm of the road.

It didn't compute. Françoise had led him to Jubril, who set up the contact and the Islamists agreed to it. Jubril was a radical, but surely not this radical. Why would they kidnap an American diplomat?

Surely Françoise hadn't set him up?

He started drilling Iranian names. It was an old trick: when under duress, discipline yourself by exercising your mind. He hated being tied up. He moved, trying to get comfortable. One of the thugs slapped him, hard. He felt his adrenaline, rising. Cool down, he warned himself.

The motion of the car finally lulled him to sleep. After an hour, it might have been two, the car swerved off the highway, bounded down a dirt path, and slowed to a stop. He smelled manure; someone must have finally opened a window.

The doors opened. He felt very much on his own.


**INSIDE WHAT HE** assumed was a farmhouse, they led him to a chair at a table. He seemed to be in a kitchen, and the aroma of coffee and fresh bread revived him. He thought he smelled farm butter.

A man quietly entered the room. "Untie him, take off that hood," he said in a gentle voice. "We're not barbarians."

The rope was removed from his wrists, then the hood, and his captors were gone. Weiseman rubbed his eyes. The quiet man was short and thin, with a trimmed, gray beard. He wore a black suit, white shirt buttoned at the neck, no tie, and black slippers with a satiny finish.

"There was no need to bind you," the man said. "I apologize. Everyone is high-strung."

"Where is Pierre?"

"He is not here. Perhaps I'm the one you wanted to speak to. Pierre made the connection, that's all."

The man spoke American English, almost without accent.

"Where in the United States were you born?"

"I was born in Tehran, but I've lived in America for many years. In Austin."

"Do you have a name?"

"Yes, Mr. Weiseman. Iranians have names, like Americans."

The Iranian got up and poured him coffee, then gestured to the bread and butter on the wooden table. He took a tin of sardines from a shelf, opened it, and placed it on the table, took a seat facing Weiseman. "My name is Ali Amin," he said. "I'm a professor of history at the University of Texas. Now, please, you're my guest, have something to eat."

Weiseman was hungry; it had been a long time since he'd eaten. He watched Ali Amin cover a slice of brown bread with the sardines, and did the same.

"Of course you're free to go whenever you wish," Amin said." We'll drive you back to Tehran. This time you'll be treated correctly."

Weiseman took a bite of the bread. "We're here now. I appreciate your hospitality. Was there something you wanted to tell me?"

Amin gave him a quizzical look. "Are you sure your government will allow you to talk to us? We've tried before, you know. We've always been rebuffed."

"When you say 'we,' Mr. Amin, who do you mean?"

Amin got up to refill the coffee. His posture was a bit bent over—perhaps, Weiseman thought, from seeking to serve both Iranian and American masters. Despite his outwardly calm demeanor, Amin appeared tense to Weiseman, high-strung.

His ruminations were abruptly interrupted by a thought. *Could he be one of ours?*

*Trevor would certainly love to plant one of ours among the mullahs.*

"Our group opposes the Shah," Amin spoke again. "We're banned by the Shah, so your embassy shuns us."

*Yes,* Weiseman recalled. *So Klein told me.*

"But, of course, you do more than express your opinions," he said.

Amin waved a hand at that. "You asked to see us, didn't you?"

Weiseman changed his tack. "The murder of the Iranian student. Shirin—"

"Please, Mr. Weiseman, the Ayatollah is a holy man. We never—"

"Mr. Amin, we've read the Ayatollah's statements. His words are inflammatory, violent, viciously anti-American, the kind of things that turn a man or woman into a suicide bomber."

Weiseman had regained his confidence; the food helped, and being free of the bonds. Amin wanted this meeting, too, he thought, or at least someone wanted contact with the United States.

Amin started to reply, then seemed to think better of it.

"Yes?" Weiseman prompted.

"We're going to win. You must know that. Americans wait too long, they dangle their puppets until they can no longer dance for them." Amin paused, apparently searching for a word. "Steam. Americans run out of steam; they don't feel the rhythm of history. In China, Cuba, Vietnam— you wait till it's too late."

Weiseman got up and walked to the window. It was storming outside; the cold drizzle had become a heavy spring rain pounding on the isolated farmhouse. There were no other buildings to be seen, only fields of wheat that bent over in the wind. The ride back in this weather would be treacherous.

"Well, this American has waited too long this time," he said to Amin's reflection in the window.

Amin chuckled. "Yes, the roads will be muddy," he said. "If you wish, you can stay here. There's a spare bedroom; you'll have your privacy. You are my guest."

Weiseman stared out at the storm. He recoiled at the thought of the thugs driving him. Besides, he'd come this far.

"I suppose there's not much choice. And we can talk."

Ali Amin smiled shyly. "Yes, we can talk . . . if you wish . . ."

**HE'D BEEN ASLEEP** for two hours when the thunder woke him. It was pitch-black outside, except when lightening crackled in the sky. Too tense to sleep, he threw off the blankets. The door handle turned easily and he walked down a dark corridor to the front room.

Amin was sitting in a plump chair under a dim light fixture. "What are you reading?" Weiseman asked.

"Did you sleep well?"

"Yes, thank you, until the storm woke me."

"This book, it's our holy scriptures, the Koran. You know it?"

"I've heard that your ayatollah wants to revive the caliphate."

Amin carefully placed the book down on a side table, removed a prayer shawl from his neck, kissed it, and laid it by the Koran. He looked curiously at Weiseman.

"Iran is a small country, Mr. Weiseman," he said, spreading his arms as if referring to the walls that surrounded him. "We've been ruled by the British, and the Shah is your puppet. Your CIA takes our oil and tells him what to do. The United States of America is the most powerful country on earth. How could we set ourselves against America?"

How indeed? Weiseman wondered. If the Shah fell, was an accommodation with the mullahs possible? And what would *that* lead to?

Amin sat there stolidly, then got up and gazed out the window. "The storm is letting up," he said. "You'll want to go soon."

"That's all you have to say? That the storm is letting up?"

Amin came back and sat across from him. "All right. Muslims have been divided for centuries. Shia and Sunnis, Arabs and Persians."

"And factions among your own people?"

"Of course. Americans will never understand us. My Texas neighbors go to church on Sunday, then leave their religion in the pews and go about their lives all week long. For us, the Prophet is always with us. Misery as well. You resolve your differences through open debate and elections, both of which the Shah bans. You have your first amendment, we have SAVAK. I've been a guest in the Shah's Evin Prison, the first circle of hell. I know what torture and terror mean."

There was a twitching in Ali Amin's right cheek. He seemed not to realize it.

"If the Shah were to go," Weiseman asked, "what would be the Ayatollah's role?"

"The Ayatollah, God protect him, is seventy-five years old. He was in Evin; now he's in exile among the infidels, in Iraq. He's a mystic. He could not govern."

*Could* not? Weiseman wondered at the word.

"He would go to our holy city of Qom," Amin went on, "to pray. He'd be revered as a saint."

"Then who *would* govern?" Weiseman asked, wondering again why they had put him with this particular representative. "What would be your policies?"

Amin leaned across the table, a little man suddenly come to life. "We would dismantle the Shah's dictatorship. We would dissolve the SAVAK and release all political prisoners. We'd establish a new constitutional democracy. We'd be America's good friend in the Middle East."

"And we'd embrace you," Weiseman said, equally ridiculously, watching the little man's eyebrows rise in disbelief. He wondered if Amin actually believed what he was saying. Was he a true believer who never lets facts get in the way of his ideology? More likely, he was naïve, or being used. Or, was it all *taarof*? That he expected Weiseman to grasp a message the direct opposite of the words he uttered.

Yes, perhaps that was it.

And yet, how else was he to reach the radicals, Weiseman wondered. At least Amin knew something of America. This was a first step.

"Will there be more murders in Paris? Will your assassins be unleashed in Tehran?"

Amin shrugged. "I detest violence, but I don't decide such things."

Weiseman understood that dodge well enough. *Take my word for it, but my word doesn't count.*

So what did this meeting amount to? Maybe an opening bid out in a remote place, unseen and unheard by others, deniable by both sides.

As a diplomat, Weiseman had been taught to play it safe. Don't make waves. But having escaped Germany long ago, he had learned that sometimes you had to act, to put yourself at risk. Nothing ever got done through timidity.

"You asked me if I was able to meet with your people," Weiseman said carefully, knowing he was embarking on a voyage that might come back to haunt him. "I can do that, discreetly. But I'd need to speak with someone with authority."

"I'll inquire," Amin said. "Then we shall wait and see."

"Not for long," Weiseman said.

It was a phrase that lingered in his mind on the slow journey back to Tehran.

## 14

# RACE AGAINST TIME

**W**EISEMAN DIDN'T SLEEP that night. Arriving in Tehran at midnight, he got up at 5:00 a.m., determined to set things in motion, to manipulate his assets and move Ajax Two ahead.

He knew all too well from his childhood that often it was what you didn't do that came back to haunt you, sometimes in blood. He'd have to work with the full array of knaves and naïfs, regional and European powers, and possible Iranian successors—pulling the strings, making sure they didn't entangle him. He had no illusion of the difficulty of that. Or the danger. Or the compromises he'd need to make with his values.

At 9:00 a.m., he received a call from Hanif saying that Jacques Schreiber was in town. His first thought was whether Françoise was with him. He still couldn't reconcile it, the lovely woman and the predator. As well, he needed to know why she had led him to Jubril. Why the thugs?

Hanif told him that Jacques had been meeting with Khomeini's people and was now seeking an audience with the Shah. Hanif said he would tell Jacques the Shah was unavailable and would warn him to stay away from the mullahs.

Weiseman wondered why Hanif was calling him at all? Was it some sort of warning? Did Hanif know about the meeting with Ali Amin? Had the Shah told Hanif what Weiseman had said about SAVAK?

That evening, Alana came to the hotel with a parcel from Hannah— Xerox copies of order forms on Jacques's letterhead: tear gas, stun guns, small arms. The customer was Hosein Hanif.

Weiseman began to fear that the trip to Ankara had been a big con, arranged by Hanif to put him off the track while the Turks and Israelis lined up behind the Shah, and Hanif used Jacques Schreiber as a supplier of arms for the coming showdown. Yilmaz and Regev doubtless were playing their own games, pitting Hanif against the Shah, cooing pledges of loyalty to the Islamists, while hoping that Weiseman would find a way to avoid an Islamist Iran.

Which was precisely what he was trying to do.

Weiseman quickly scanned the parcel of arms orders—artillery, armored personnel carriers, lots of guns and ammunition—then secured them in in a safe.

He went out into a piercing winter sun. There was no one he could fully trust, but he did need someone savvy, someone who knew Iran well and who shared his interests. He needed to call again on MI6's man in Tehran.

**"WELL, YOU'RE QUITE RIGHT,"** Ronald Sims said. "We're in a race against time."

Sims had worked the Ajax project as an apprentice spy twenty-five years before. He had to know the details of how MI6 and CIA did their business after a rattled Mohammad Reza Pahlavi flew to Rome. The idea of sending the Shah off again brought a smile to Sims's lips.

Puffing on a Havana cigar, Sims seemed perfectly at home in the big Queen Anne chair in the safe house near the university. "Of course," he said, "we don't need to decide now whether he'll return this time, or who else might get the throne. That comes later."

"Exactly," Weiseman said, though they both knew this would be a one-way ticket.

"Not too much later, though," he added. "The Shah looks shaky. The French are ready to move. Hanif and the others are all laying plans. We could wait too long, and then—"

Sims broke into a coughing spell; his pink cheeks now were all red. Weiseman rose to assist him, but a deep breath brought the British agent out of it. He went to a double-door cabinet where he stored his spirits, and poured them each a snifter of dry sherry. Sims tossed his down straight away, in a single swallow, and breathed deeply again.

"Better," he said.

"Ajax," Weiseman reminded him, and heard Sims cough again.

"You know," he said, "I convinced London to select another name for the operation. In Greek drama—Sophocles, I recall—Ajax was a buffoon who slaughtered a flock of sheep imagining them to be enemy warriors, then committed suicide."

"And you called it . . ."

Sims stepped to a desk and unlocked it with a gold key attached to a chain affixed to his belt. He smiled and said, "Boot. We called it Boot, for what we were about to do to Mossadeq. So we could keep our man in place."

*Our man.* The Brits ousted the father, and now the son Mohammad Reza—"our man"—was about to get the boot as well.

Sims pulled a two-page telephone/address list out of a yellow plastic folder. "These are the key people—military and intelligence circles, businessmen and intellectuals, politicians." He picked up a felt pen and checked off several names. "Here are the ones you should see first. Yourself or your friends." Right index finger raised. "Best not be too trusting."

The Brit stood and removed his jacket. He pushed back a few remaining strands of hair. Something about him with those spotted eyeglasses invited trust.

"I'd start with a certain general; he's called Mehdi. He's getting on now. You'll learn more about what happened in '53. And he's still well connected with the present generals."

"Will you be coming with me?"

"Oh, no, David. I don't think so." He refilled his glass of sherry and swallowed it down in a gulp again. "Too much history, too little power."

Weiseman cast his eye over the list. It was a gold mine of contacts. Apparently the special relationship remained in good working order, at least in Tehran.

"You'll have to get on with it," Sims told him. "You'll be the one up-front. We'll work out the execution together, though. The plan."

"Of course," Weiseman said, knowing he'd do no such thing.

"Oh yes," Sims said. An impish smile lit up his gray face. "Mustn't tell Millicent; she's devoted to the Shah and Farah."


WEISEMAN MADE THE ROUNDS, contacting the key names on Sims's list. He zeroed in on key business executives, army colonels and majors, and university activists to recruit the foot soldiers for his own network. The bottom-line message to all was the same: Give us an alternative to the Shah and Ayatollah. We'll wait for your lead. And if you act, we'll be there.

He was cautious in exploiting their fears, restrained in validating their hatred of the Shah, careful not to press too hard. They were all at risk of ending up in Evin—as was he. Especially him, left as he was by Trevor to operate without a lifeline; he would get no more help from the American embassy than they would. So he offered hope and financial support, saying the time for action was coming soon. More often than not, it worked, and he recruited new assets.

Throughout, he kept in touch with Hanif, telling him he was assessing the mood and scouting the political environment, while being careful to never report on individuals, and always being flattering—thus maintaining the SAVAK chief's hope that Washington might back him after the Shah departed. It seemed to be enough, though Weiseman never failed to see the edge of suspicion in Hanif's eyes.

Meanwhile, Seyyed arranged for him to see a novice priest whom Mahmoud told him was alarmed by Khomeini's fire-and-brimstone fundamentalism. Trita, not more than twenty-three years old, met him in the recesses of a seminary—his young hawklike face tense with fear, his lips pressed tightly together. He said SAVAK was on a rampage, filling the cells of Evin Prison with dissidents of all kinds. He said Hanif was after his brother, a SAVAK officer who was in hiding, gone to ground. Could Weiseman possibly help get his brother out of Iran?

Weiseman thought Sims and MI6 could arrange it. But if Hanif found out? He thought then of his own escape from Germany . . . and he told the young priest he would try.

It was time to reconnect with Trevor; he knew he mustn't let that line of communication to his home base go cold. He phoned Trevor on the secure line, keeping his briefing on Ali Amin vague.

"Yes, I know," Trevor said. "Gramont phoned."

*Had Françoise told him? How had she known?*

"Anything new?" Weiseman asked.

He heard the slight cough Trevor retreated to when covering up with him.

"Nothing you wouldn't know, David."


**AS SIMS SUGGESTED,** Weiseman met General Mehdi in a safe house on a side street not far from army headquarters. Sims had been right. The man was as old as Methuselah, with a full head of stark white hair, cheeks dry as parchment, hooded eyes that harbored countless secrets. He walked curved over a steel cane, but when he stood still he forced his body to unbend, to the straight posture of a commanding general. Now he sat with his hands in his lap. "I was there," he said to Weiseman. "Did Sims tell you?"

"He said you would tell me, General. He said no one knew the details as well as you."

The general drew a long cigar from a humidor, lit it carefully, and watched the smoke rise in circles that obscured his face. "It's true," he said. "No one except Hanif."

Weiseman waited for the general to summon his recollections and continue at his own pace.

"Of course," he seemed to assure himself. "We did it."

"Of course," Weiseman said. "Together," willing to share the credit or blame.

"No, no, young man," pointing at his chest. "*We!* We Iranians. All those folktales about Ajax. About Kim Roosevelt and the British." The hooded eyes opened wide a moment; he slapped his thigh and chortled, as if seeing Americans and Brits bollocksing it up. "Absurd."

"Tell me about it, sir."

The general puffed on his cigar as if to stir his memory, then smiled.

"Your Mr. Roosevelt was everywhere, shoring up our shah, paying thugs, even bringing in the communists to demonstrate against Mossadeq." A snort. "But it was, you say, a sideway?"

"Sideshow?"

"Yes. That's it. Sideshow. We were in a serious economic mess. After Mossadeq nationalized Anglo-Iranian Oil, there was an embargo against us. Our middle classes were all worried. The businessmen. Even the professors disliked Mossadeq—he was so arrogant."

The old man leaned forward and shook his head. "We had to step in." He cupped his gnarled fingers around his mouth, then whispered, "There will be another coup in Ankara. Soon." He nodded emphatically. "Colonel Yilmaz told me, in strict confidence."

A maid came in and poured them cups of tea with hot milk, then vanished.

"So, General. 1953. You stepped in."

The general puffed on his cigar, ignoring the white tea. He nodded. "Of course, Kim kept busy. CIA wanted to get Mossadeq out and replace him with General Zahedi." Mehdi let loose a belly laugh. "Kim got the

Shah to sign a decree dismissing Mossadeq, the old dreamer. It was to be served on him August 15. Yes, I'll never forget that date."

And then, another outburst of laughter. "The commander who was to deliver the message got arrested. Kim's plan was"—the eyes popped open—"kaput!"

Weiseman joined the general's laughter, and soon the two of them were roaring with glee at the way self-important officials invariably fouled up. And then, the general's memory kindled, on he went, unprompted by Weiseman. The Shah decided to take a little holiday in Rome. The Americans didn't have a backup plan. The Iranian military stepped in. "But it was the clergy that sold out Mossadeq. The ayatollahs preferred a conservative and vacillating shah to Mossadeq with all his radical plans. The clerics saved the Shah in order to remove him."

"Then, it wasn't America that pulled off Ajax? That's just a myth?"

Amazing, Weiseman thought. But if true, why not once more?

Get the military to do it again, and this time a competent general could be raised up.

Mehdi seemed to read his mind. He fingered his cigar. "Kim tried," he said. "Ajax was his child, but we adopted it. We did it ourselves, and everybody gave Kim the credit."

He paused. "You have to work with our local people, David." Weiseman hadn't even needed to ask. Mehdi gave him the names of two generals. "They'll expect your call."


**BACK AT THE HOTEL,** Weiseman tried to put it together, to find the kernel of truth in the old general's ramblings.

*They didn't have a backup plan.* Was that just an old man concocting tales of Iranian derring-do, or was it the inside story of how the CIA failed? What did it say about pulling off *his* mission, about keeping the mullahs out of power, about whether the ayatollahs might rule more pragmatically than they preached? What did it say about the Shah's generals and middle-class Iranians who should find Khomeini more repugnant than Mossadeq? He thought of Seyyed and wondered, What did it say about a worldly mullah who had his doubts about Ruhollah Khomeini?

Or was Mehdi's entertaining tale woven of whole cloth? It had been Ronald Sims who sent him to meet Mehdi, to learn the real details. Had it simply been to whitewash the British role? He had asked General Mehdi what role the British played in Ajax. After another laugh, the old man said, "They held your coat. It's the way they operate. Drop a few clues, step back, and let the other fellow supply the boot."

The boot! It was almost funny. The phone interrupted his thoughts.

It was Françoise, from Baghdad. Finally. There were things he needed to know. She would stop in Beirut the following Wednesday. Could he possibly meet her there?

## 15

# BEIRUT

THE TAXI SWERVED around the Mediterranean cornice, and Weiseman gripped the strap above his head. At the waterfront Long Beach Club, bikini-clad European women reclined on chaise lounges while, across the road, pastel pink buildings pockmarked by bullet holes hovered over Muslim women walking along hot sidewalks clad in black from head to toe.

The taxi windows were open and Beirut was stifling. The AC was out, the driver explained. Soon it would be Ramadan, the ninth month of the Muslim year, the "hot month," when the faithful fasted from sunrise to sunset.

A traffic light seemed to leap up before them. The taxi driver slammed on his brakes and muttered a mélange of French and Arabic words. *"Où allons nous?"* he asked for the third time.

*"La Cathédrale,"* Weiseman repeated, wondering why Françoise had chosen to meet him there.

The glaze of the morning sun slanted around the high-rise hotels, bearing down on the city, producing a flimsy veil of gossamer. Weiseman felt the bath of humidity on his brow and under his shirt. On his way to a meeting whose purpose was unclear, he recalled Trevor's maxim: *Diplomacy is chess played by gentlemen who understand the rules.* And if the other fellow isn't a gent? Weiseman had asked. If he smashes his fist on the board and throws over all the pieces?

"Then you deal with it," Trevor had replied.

Weiseman knew that the sectarian civil war which began in Lebanon in 1975 was a warning. It was tearing apart Lebanese cities—the same thing might happen in Iran if Khomeini were permitted to take over, or if the Shah were allowed to stay on and rob Iranians of hope.

Weiseman continued to be struck by the ironies of his situation. Jimmy Carter was the world's most powerful man, and he loathed the Shah. Carter would never forgive himself for his false tribute to the Shah that New Year's Eve in Tehran, yet he could no more abandon Mohammad Reza Pahlavi than bring Richard Nixon back from his post-Watergate exile in New Jersey. So he handed off Iran to Trevor, who passed it on to Weiseman. But when the Shah called for help, Carter would probably bite his tongue and save the Shah again.

Out the window, Weiseman saw an attractive European woman walk by and thought of Françoise. Memory was a tyrant, giving him only fragments, air bubbles that left him searching for more.

Happiness. How did it compare with playing a role in the great events of your time? Once he would have been sure that being at the center of things was what it was all about. Now, thinking of all the compromises, the cynical sellouts, the ways he might be betrayed, he wasn't so sure. Could it all be a great con? He still wondered. Was Françoise only Gramont's bait?

Enough, he told himself. There was a job to do. If she was playing him like a pawn for Gramont, he knew how to pretend, to use her as Trevor would wish him to do. He had learned from the master.

The cab stopped. He looked up at the spires of Beirut's main cathedral, paid the driver in Lebanese lire, and walked into the cathedral, to the middle pew where Laurent Gramont was kneeling in prayer.


**GRAMONT WORE AN** open sky-blue shirt with a bright polka-dot green ascot, a boulevardier able to enter any door in Paris. The outfit lent him the look of Charles Boyer, the French heartthrob of the forties. Gramont had the charm of an actor all right, but also the cunning of a snake. A French Trevor.

All right, Weiseman thought, bracing himself. Play the game.

*"David, mon vieux."* Gramont stood and led him along the nave of the church toward golden double doors, into a large office suitable for a cardinal, or an ambassador. Then came the bantering about nothing, the easy dropping of names, references to headlines about crises hither and yon, sly jokes, each man lightly putting down his own leader, laughing, reassuring his friend. Well, the banter implied, we diplomats are here now, ready to clean up after the politicians.

Finally, they got to it.

"You know about Khomeini," Gramont said. "We'll stuff him in a suburb for now, just outside Paris, where he can't do any mischief, keep an eye on him. A kind of house arrest."

Weiseman said, "Why not leave him in Iraq with Saddam Hussein as his jailer? Saddam's done a good job of that for sixteen years now."

Gramont folded his arms as if there was nothing more to say. "Iran is coming apart," he finally added. "We told you that when you first arrived. Ask Moshe Regev. Jews know their enemies."

Sly . . . sly, just above the line. But the point was made. So, Trevor was right: the French intended to stage-manage replacement of the Shah with the ayatollahs and supplant American influence in Iran.

And if Gramont was the chess master, did that mean Françoise was nothing more than his pawn? The thought dampened his spirit.

"We don't surrender to fundamentalists," Weiseman said, sure that Gramont would register the reference to the French knuckling under to the Nazis in World War II.

*"Mon vieux,"* Gramont drew out the two words sarcastically. "Wasn't that below the belt? I'd rather say *sauve qui peut*. We're diplomats; we do what we can, what we must. We deal with whatever, whomever is there. France will fight no Pyrrhic battles."

Gramont rose and led Weiseman back out of the opulent office, back along the pews toward the back of the church, pointing to the stained glass windows as they passed. He'd always loved them, he said, the abstraction of the design, mirroring the mysteries of life. No reliable patterns, haphazard events that defied understanding. It was why he relied on the church and—just to be safe, he acknowledged with a chuckle—on his intuition about people.

"And Khomeini," Weiseman said. "You really think you can work with him?"

Gramont strolled on, pointing to a likeness of the Virgin. "Few of us are pure," he said. "But we have those in our beloved country who would do anything for a price. *Tu comprends?*"

Oh, yes, he got the reference to Jacques, another piece of the puzzle he couldn't decrypt.

They were at the front door of the cathedral. A priest strolled in, a yellow cord at the waist of his brown tunic. A blast of heat blew in from the street.

"Ramadan is coming," Gramont said. "It's a bit like our Catholic Lent—long days followed by a burst of pent-up energy."

"You're playing with fire, Laurent. The mullahs will use you and then toss you away."

*"Qui sait? Peut-être le dèluge.* When it rains, flowers bloom. Sometimes there are floods."

**WEISEMAN WATCHED GRAMONT** leave and turned back into the cathedral to find Françoise. She was wearing a white dress, arms bare, covered by an exquisite lattice shawl, inspecting the portrait of a saint being slaughtered by the devil, a testament to the civil war that was demolishing the harmony of the many faiths that once prevailed in pre–civil war Lebanon. Now it was a cauldron of religious and ethnic conflict that was about to claim Iran as its next victim.

She turned and saw him. Her cheeks colored in an instant. Was it out of excitement at the sight of him or embarrassment at being caught in tawdry service for Laurent Gramont?

She gave him chaste kisses on both cheeks and silently led him out of the cathedral to a black sports car, and they sped off into Beirut's hot afternoon. The Phoenician Hotel came into view, but she parked the car along the seaside and said, "Let's walk . . . fewer ears."

They strolled silently along the Mediterranean, past waves colliding with the shore. She seemed somewhere else. The furrow on her brow bespoke preoccupation, and his own concerns deepened. She had come here with Gramont to do his bidding, Weiseman thought; to convince Weiseman to accede to France's will.

She nodded toward an outdoor café near a dock where European women took the rays of the sweltering Lebanese sun. He heard a quiet buzz of Latin languages—French and Italian, some Spanish, tourists out for a good time amidst the travails of the civil war. But this was Beirut, with its daily paradoxes and dangers. The proprietor of the café, a tall, bald, hawk-nosed man in a black T-shirt with a parrot decal, arrived unbidden with two cappuccinos, then left them alone.

"You saw Khomeini," he prompted.

"Yes, in Iraq, and Saddam Hussein in Baghdad. One is a fanatic, the other an assassin."

She took off her big round designer sunglasses and put them on the table, then put them back on, but not before he detected the dark circles under her eyes. She was putting something off, as if delaying the moment of truth.

"The Ayatollah is in Najaf, Iraq's holy city, proselytizing the Iraqi Shia," she said. "Saddam has had enough of him. Laurent intends to bring him to Paris."

"I know," he told her.

She took that in silently, as if unsurprised. So she was clued into Gramont's game.

He held his silence, too, willing her to tell him the truth.

"It's only a stopover," she finally said, "before he returns to Iran."

Well then, at least she had told him that.

"You know, Trevor will be incensed with Gramont. They both agree the Shah has to go, but to replace him with Khomeini . . . that's obscene."

He waited, asking himself, yet again where she fit into this game, whether Gramont had used her to pass messages to Khomeini and Saddam, to arrange it all, before Jacques would arrive with payment for the Iraqis and armaments for the Ayatollah.

She shook her head and her lovely blond hair fell across her eyes.

"They don't know who they're dealing with, what they're getting into," she said. "When I was in Baghdad, Saddam told me he had called the Shah and said it was time to dispose of Khomeini. He asked for the Shah's agreement. The Shah told him no."

Astounding, Weiseman thought. And then, he had to ask.

"Françoise, did Gramont prompt Saddam to make that call?"

"I just don't know," she said. "It's possible, of course, but Saddam didn't say so."

Now her eyes were fixed on his. "Our people come up with these schemes because of their Cartesian intellectual training. We're taught in our *grandes écoles* to devise theories and put them into action. We are absolutely certain about our conclusions but we lack grounding in experience, what Anglo-Saxons call the scientific method. Our arrogance is our shield."

She sipped thoughtfully on her cappuccino. "It goes deeper than you realize," she finally said. "And I'm stuck, bound to Laurent Gramont and Jacques Schreiber."

She shuddered. Was it the sea air, or was it due to her personal prison? He took off his jacket and draped it over her shoulders.

But as he did so, out of the corner of his eye, he saw a rocket streak overhead. He whirled and saw it strike the Phoenician Hotel, sparking a fire in the heart of the city, shooting flames into the burnished orange sky. They were close enough to hear the screams of the victims, and they watched, aghast, as a man leapt out of the building to his death. On the beach below, bathers scattered.

Weiseman grabbed her hand and they ran across the dock and down to the now empty beach, a safe distance away. From there they watched the column of smoke rising above the hotel. "The Paris of the Middle East is now a war zone," she said. "It's like the religious wars in Europe three hundred years ago. The Middle East is going to repeat Europe's bloody history."

As they stared at the hotel, engulfed in flames, she told him her sister used to live here. Iréne was married to an engineer, a Lebanese Druze who was dedicated to bringing people together. One day a bomb landed on their house, a random event in which Iréne was killed, as were Abdul and their two small children. Françoise came for the funeral, her first time in the Middle East.

There were no tears as she recounted this story. At first he thought it was because she was so self-controlled, but she told him no, all her tears had been shed long ago.

Perhaps, he thought, that's what made her so elusive, so hard to comprehend.

A long moment passed as the flames leapt from the hotel like the Phoenix toward the fading sun and the waves of the Mediterranean Sea rushed against the nearby shore.

"It will happen in Iran as well," she finally said. "And in Iraq, when Saddam goes. All the rest. Once the rules of civilization fail, it's a fast descent into hell."

He said, "Laurent—"

"*Le Comte Gramont*," she said snidely. "Alain de Rose opposed him. He doesn't want France to capitulate to terror. He wants to stay close to America. *Mais, comme tu vois . . .*"

They walked away from the scene of devastation now, passing small children still playing ball on the sand, scavenging, seemingly impervious to the violence. She stopped briefly to chat with them, in French, in Arabic, and suddenly she revived.

A stout Belgian was dozing on a ratty blanket in his Speedo swimsuit, a cooler with a Stella Artois by his side. A Lebanese boy with dark curly hair stole up to the blanket, nipped his shoulder bag, and ran off.

"Pierre called," she suddenly told him, as though the sight of the boy reminded her of the Lebanese lawyer who had arranged Weiseman's kidnapping in Tehran. "I gave him hell for the way they treated you. This time you'll see the Sheikh."

*I'm stuck.* Her words echoed in his head, and the image of Gramont at the stained glass windows returned. And am I stuck, too? he wondered. The two of us hostage to our masters.

Alone with her on this beach, he realized he wanted her now, more than more answers. Later, there would be time to speak of where she fit into Laurent Gramont's plans, and who was betraying whom.

**SHE STEERED THE** black sports car north along Lebanon's Mediterranean coast, past the mountain forts left by the Romans, and the ruins of ancient wars. Arafat had been holed up farther along the road, she told him, just shy of the Israeli and Syrian borders, until Hafez Assad's assassins came for the itinerant Palestinian leader, and he barely escaped to Tunisia.

"Over there," she continued with the same precision he had noticed in her tutoring of him on Iran before he flew to Tehran. But now he was focused less on her incisive history lessons than on how her golden hair blew free in the breeze.

Shortly after the car entered Byblos, she turned into a palm-shaded driveway of a private cottage with an orange gabled roof.

She took him around her compact hideaway, filled with books and impressionist-style paintings she had done of the Mediterranean landscape, aquarelles she had painted of the Côte d'Azur, and sketches of Iran and Iraq and the Lebanese coast. The cottage, she told him, is where she came to recuperate after her ordeals in Paris with Laurent Gramont.

"Remarkable," he said. "Your two lives, in Europe and the Middle East."

From a balcony off the room, he could watch the vast Mediterranean, stretching out as far as the eye could see. It was strange—such an idyllic scene, scant miles from the rocket attack. She stepped out next to him, and he suddenly turned, pulled her close. They kissed, and afterward she took his hand and led him back inside.

Later, they strolled hand-in-hand through the old city, by tourist sites they barely noticed. She led him to the sandy beach, and they sat under a big beach umbrella with the colors of the French and American flags.

As the sun began to fade in the darkening azure sky, she sighed and finally broke the languorous silence. "It's done," she said. "Alain spoke to Gramont, and Laurent surprised me by going along."

"Meaning what," he asked, abruptly alert again to things he hadn't been thinking about.

"Meaning, Khomeini returns. Alain said Gramont got it approved by the Élysée. It's a fait accompli. But then, we do what's necessary to squeeze the Islamists, to contain the revolution."

"Françoise, it's a con. You know Gramont. Once Khomeini is back, the ayatollahs will take over, they'll be in control. They won't need Paris, except for Jacques's weapons . . . on credit."

"David. Alain is on our side. He told me it's too late to find a successor to the Shah, that we need a placeholder who can be removed when we find a permanent successor."

"I see," he said. So Gramont had won this battle. But not yet the war. And if this now enabled them to join forces, to tighten the grip on the ayatollahs with the help of de Rose's operatives, well, why not.

Her eyes willed him not to betray her. There was not a word of Ankara, perhaps because, as Weiseman now suspected, Trevor may have shared that with Gramont. Weiseman had suspected for a long time that the two of them had been plotting together, sharing ideas without telling him. He had seen enough powerful men to recognize that power and amorality were dubious companions.

But then it was as if there was nothing more to say; everything was on the table now. They walked slowly back to the cottage, then more quickly to the bedroom, ignoring the ringing of the phone call they knew must be from Trevor or Gramont.

## 16

# THE SHEIKH

**B**ACK IN TEHRAN, the rendezvous with Sheikh Khalaji was postponed three times. Finally, on Saturday night, Pierre Jubril picked up Weiseman in his red Ferrari. In Byblos, Françoise had described the lawyer as a champagne radical whose leftist politics reserved space for a high lifestyle.

Jubril steered carefully along the length of Tehran's Pahlavi Boulevard, past the dim café where Madame Zed performed her card tricks, past the gloomy American embassy where Lyman Palmer had directed that barriers be installed, apparently awaiting the imminent arrival of the ayatollahs.

Finally, a seedy sector of nightclubs and discos came into view.

Weiseman thought, *This* is where I'm to meet the Sheikh? Perhaps the idea was to throw off Hanif and his henchmen.

Jubril slowed and parked the car, camouflaged under a tree with wide branches at the foot of a hill a few blocks away from the clubs. "We'll walk," he mumbled, then tossed a coin to a sallow teenager who took up his post as car watcher under the shadow of Mount Damavand.

They hiked up the windy hill. Weiseman had no idea where they were. Every time he met up with the Islamists, he noted, it was in a dark, isolated place. It gave him a queasy feeling.

They arrived outside a Catholic church with a gold cross dominating a spectacular green dome and a slim spire that stretched up through the starry night toward the heavens. Jubril led Weiseman up the steps to the front door, where a huge, muscular man with a trim mustache stood under the doorway's arch, his skin tanned by the sun, illuminated by the moon.

It was Guido Montana, just as in the photo Trevor had wired him. Jubril left Weiseman and went to speak to him. A half dozen men Weiseman hadn't noticed previously, suddenly gathered at the base of the steps, conferred together briefly, then dispersed, disappearing from sight around the perimeter. Weiseman was getting bad vibes and he didn't trust Jubril. He considered leaving, but how? He was surrounded. What's more, he needed to see the Sheikh; he'd been working toward this meeting for months.

Suddenly, Jubril was back. "The meeting's in a different place," he said.

Montana led them down the stairs and across the square. Weiseman watched him, and Jubril, warily. They passed a swath of strip clubs with erotic names rendered in French. Young women dressed in short skirts and tank tops moved seductively in storefronts, inviting the bearded men watching them inside. When Montana approached, the men backed off quickly. He led Jubril and Weiseman down a narrow alley, into a club. Au Lapin Agile.

It was a boîte, a place for drinking and dancing. Fluorescent lights blinked, illuminating posters that imitated paintings by Toulouse-Lautrec. One close to the entrance depicted a naked blonde with one leg propped on the edge of a table to paint her toenails blood red. An admirer, possibly a client, looked on.

Weiseman made his way past a muscular guy in a tight yellow T-shirt bumping and grinding with a woman on the dance floor. Once they reached the far side of the dance floor, Montana said, "Wait here," and disappeared into a back room. An orange sign read: CABARET DES ASSASSINS.

"What the hell is this?" Weiseman demanded of Jubril, jutting his chin at the sign.

"Don't worry," Jubril said, puffing furiously on his cigarette. Beads of sweat ran down his face. "It's the former name of this joint."

The door opened. Weiseman could see a half dozen men in a smoky room, crowded around a table. "This way," Montana said, gesturing toward the room.

"No." Weiseman decided it was his turn to change plans. "We meet in the square," he insisted. "There are tables out there where we can talk. The Sheikh and me. Alone."

The big man got into his face, silent and imposing, towering four inches over him.

Weiseman stood his ground. He saw Montana's big hand grip the dagger in his belt.

"That will do, Hamid," an eerie, high-pitched voice suddenly said. Its owner wore a shiny, gray, double-breasted suit and a white, open-collared shirt with green enamel cuff links.

"I think Mr. Weiseman and I will take some air," said Khalaji.

He linked arms with Weiseman and they walked slowly to the outdoor terrace, where they sat at a table. Weiseman studied him—a beak-like nose, gray eyes under rimless dark glasses, fleshy lips. The Sheikh rested two arthritic hands on his lap, gnarled into fists that gripped onto green and white worry beads. "I believe you wanted to see me," he said in his reedy voice.

Set the rules of engagement at the start, Weiseman thought.

"My government has no official contacts with your . . . representatives."

"Of course, Mr. Weiseman. America stands with the Shah. But soon the Shah will be gone, and with him your good friend Hosein Hanif."

Khalaji looked up into the starry sky, as if asking, is there some reason you wanted to meet with me. His thumbs set the glass beads in motion, round and round, headed nowhere.

"Do you have a message? From your president?"

"I have no such message."

"Then why are we here?"

"To open up a channel, to explore our respective concerns."

It added up to just about nothing, but in a strange way it was all Weiseman could say. He was there to open a line of communication in case the Islamists seized power despite his best efforts. He knew that, even with this limited effort, he had exceeded his authority, and he did not expect to get anywhere with this man. Diplomacy often worked this way. You make all the preparations, take risks, political and physical, and then what? Nothing. It was an exercise in constructive ambiguity, passing smoke signals across a chasm of distrust. But it usually was better than war.

He had to wait almost a minute for an answer. "Ours are a pious people," the Sheikh finally said, his large hands gesticulating now. "Violence is an unfortunate part of life. To us, tradition matters most, and justice under the laws of Islam." A brittle cough interrupted his homily. "America has a religious tradition. Your president is said to be a religious man. The Ayatollah, bless him in heaven, does not desire violence against anyone."

"The Shah—"

"The Shah is a dead man," the Sheikh said softly, but with certainty, as if he had been briefed by the Shah's doctor. "He has cancer. He'll be gone by his sixtieth birthday. Perhaps sooner."

Weiseman said, "Perhaps Allah himself has decided to make a peaceful change in Iran."

A waiter came by. One glance from the Sheikh sent him scurrying away.

"Please, Mr. Weiseman. We are not politicians. We are men of God. We desire America's support in removing Pahlavi, Hanif, their entire corrupt entourage."

"And why would we do that, Sheikh Khalaji?"

The Sheikh sipped his tea. He grasped the paper napkin in his twisted fingers and dabbed at his lips. Under the streetlights, his eyes seemed opaque.

It was only then that Weiseman realized: The Sheikh was blind.

"Because," the Sheikh said, and pushed himself up from his chair, casting those sightless eyes upon Weiseman "because God is on our side. We will prevail and you will lose your voice in Iran, the way you lost in China and Cuba and Vietnam."

As the Sheikh stood, Montana, standing back by the pub, took the cue that the meeting was over and began striding toward them, with Jubril just behind him.

"One more thing," Weiseman said, and the Sheikh raised his right hand. The others stopped, some fifty feet away.

He needed *something* from this meeting, for Trevor, to keep the channel open.

"The United States is concerned about human rights—political freedom and religious tolerance. Would a new regime in Iran share our concerns?"

The Sheikh's face became a quizzical frown, jaundiced in the overhead lights. "That is an American question," he finally said. "We will rule according to the Koran, glory be to God."

"And the Ayatollah Khomeini?" Weiseman said.

The beads jiggled. "What is your question?"

"Our countries have worked to keep peace in your region. That could continue, or—"

The lights from the square seemed to capture the Sheikh in an eerie glow as he curtly signaled for Montana to come get him. "It is the will of Allah, all praise be to Him," he said, then slipped off with his escort, now seeming an insignificant man in a cheap Western suit.

From the distance, an accordion played what struck Weiseman as a totally incongruous "La Vie en Rose," as he watched the Sheikh disappear into the crowd in the square, his cane tap-tapping across the paving blocks. It was like the final scene of a movie.

Jubril came close to him and whispered, "What did he say?"

"That God was on his side," Weiseman muttered. "Let's get out of here."

## 17

# *RAMADAN*

**T**HE DIRTY PONTIAC WAS STIFLING. The usually voluble Shapour was silent, almost sullen. When they passed a poster of the Shah and Empress hanging on a gray building, he sliced his index finger across his throat.

Much had changed in the last weeks, even days.

The lobby of the Intercontinental, previously thronged with business-men in slick haircuts and cuff-linked shirts and silk neckties, now held clusters of bearded clerics in round black turbans. Women sat in separate clusters, wearing chadors instead of the designer fashions of just days be-fore. People spoke in whispers, a hand covering every mouth. The hotel restaurant, which once served rather good European cuisine, was now a cafeteria where all offerings were halal—properly slaughtered and prepared, permissible for the faithful to eat.

A husky young man passed by in a black suit with an open-collared black shirt and Ray-Ban sunglasses. "I'm Jafar," he whispered. "Trita's brother. Let me know when and where," and then he was gone.

It took Weiseman a moment to recall how Seyyed had asked him to help his acolyte Trita's brother, whose name was Jafar. Weiseman had agreed because of the important role in the transition he envisioned for Seyyed, but he sensed the small favor was about to become something more complicated.

He turned toward the elevator and there was Daud, with the usual manila envelope, telling him it was from the palace and urgent.

In his room, the minibar had been stripped of alcoholic beverages. On the walls, the Ayatollah Khomeini had replaced the Shah. He opened the window and heard the calls to prayer drowned out by the sirens of police cars speeding to a demonstration. In the street below, young mullahs marched in ranks, brandishing signs demanding that the Shah leave the country. SAVAK forces patrolled the streets but stopped no one.

Weiseman turned on the TV and saw the Shah addressing the nation. It was Constitution Day, which coincided with the start of Ramadan. Weiseman followed the speech, courtesy of English subtitles. Modernization. Reforms. A more open society. Words to delight a Western democrat. Expansion of the White Revolution: health and education. Iran would soon be a first world country. If only, Weiseman thought.

Outside, the Shia madrassa students were becoming strident. More sirens signaled SAVAK reinforcements. The wails intensified from the mosques. The country was tumbling into chaos.

Weiseman went to the washroom, doused his head and face with cold water. After a moment he remembered the envelope and went back to the desk. The handwritten note was from Empress Farah.

"Our friend, David. We wish to take your counsel."

Well then, he thought, it was a golden opportunity to win the Shah's confidence.

Lyman Palmer wouldn't give the Shah any advice. Come to think of it, Weiseman realized he hadn't seen a cable from Palmer in weeks. It was as if Justin Trevor had waved his wand and the American ambassador had gone up in smoke.

Better call him, though, he decided. Palmer would be enraged if Weiseman went to see the Shah without him. But Palmer wasn't in the embassy when he phoned him, nor was he in the residence. A maid told him the American ambassador was now into his third week of home leave.

Thomas Foster called Weiseman back. "I was wondering when you'd call."

That evening at the Brit's residence, Weiseman told Sims and Foster of the message from the palace, then got to the point: He had received a defection request from a SAVAK officer, a brother of one of Seyyed's acolytes. Could they help?

"Yes, of course," the two men answered nearly in unison.

"You'll need to take a trip south, to Abadan," said Foster. "Our people will be there to assist. But he's your man. You'll do the handoff."

Sure, thought Weiseman. How many years in Evin for kidnapping a SAVAK officer?

Millicent strolled in, perfectly timed to cut off debate. "I was with Farah this morning. We wrote that note together. I told her you would help Reza. She's very worried about him."

"Of course, Millicent," said Foster. "He can trust us."

Like your husband can trust you with Foster, Weiseman thought grimly, recalling his suspicions at the familiar way Millicent and Foster had interacted at the lunch in the British club shortly after he had arrived in Tehran.

Foster told him that Ambassador Palmer would be back in time to be the scapegoat. "Trevor will see to that," he said "Palmer will seek to shift the blame to me, which is what he does to deputies."

Weiseman said nothing, but quietly took in that Foster was no fool. Because it was much more likely that, actually, Palmer will point the finger at Weiseman himself if anything went wrong.

**THE NEXT MORNING,** Daud was waiting in the lobby in his snug morning coat. Weiseman gave him a nod and proceeded outside to the waiting Cadillac limousine. A stiff-necked Iranian in a tailored chauffeur's uniform touched his hand to his heart and opened the right rear door. Weiseman turned and spotted Daud watching him from the lobby, mopping his brow with an outsized yellow handkerchief.

A quarter hour later, sentries waved the limo rapidly through the palace's massive wrought iron gates as if they wanted to prevent anyone from seeing him enter. Then they let him cool his heels in the courtyard while the Shah's coterie inside decided what to do with him. Weiseman stood under the smoggy morning sky, the sun beating down, drops of perspiration sliding down his face, pools of sweat gathering under the arms of his freshly laundered white shirt. He could imagine Hanif in there, arguing to the Shah that he should not be wasting his exalted presence on this presumptuous troublemaker.

It was true, Weiseman thought. The Shah had just done what he had urged him to do; he had reached out to his people and promised them modernization and health and education. And what had it led to? Street demonstrations, opposition agitprop, and police brutality. Iranian society was shattered, with no compromises in sight. The middle ground was truly empty . . . unless the Shah got rid of Hanif, unless more moderate ayatollahs like Amin or Seyyed cut a deal with other moderate forces . . . unless an understanding was reached with the ayatollahs that would not humiliate the United States and consign the Iranian people to misery and repression.

Unless . . .

The sun in the courtyard was unbearably hot. He reached into his back pocket for a handkerchief and wiped the moisture from his eyes.

How did you deal with true believers, religious zealots with guns who saw no middle ground? You had to beat them. There was no other way.

But America wasn't going to war here. Iran was on the other side of the earth. The war in Vietnam had barely ended, and Carter had won the presidency by campaigning against it. Anti-war sentiment was alive and well in virtually every American household.

Besides, what would be the goal of a war here? To keep the Shah in power another year? Until the cancer took him? No. The fire was coming, and there were no hoses long enough to extinguish it.

Weiseman looked up and saw Hosein Hanif standing before him in full-dress uniform with the four stars of a full general—the beak of his hat gleaming, his shoes reflecting the sunlight. Hanif turned on his heel, and Weiseman followed him into the palace. Inside, under an enormous chandelier, the Empress stood in a straight, white silk dress, a single strand of pearls like a talisman around her neck. She kissed him dryly on both cheeks, like a family friend.

Hanif strode out of the room.

The Empress spoke. "My husband needs you," she said quietly, gesturing to the enormous double doors behind her. Then she, too, left.

It was the Shah's throne room, and as he stepped inside Weiseman saw the Shah across the room, a solitary figure standing erect—and seeming to strain to do so—in a white dress uniform with a gold, red, and blue ceremonial sash, as if ready to inspect his troops on the parade ground. He was gazing up at an illuminated portrait of an Iranian military officer wearing a fur trimmed hat with a black bill, stiff white plumes rising from a gold medallion at the top, a bushy mustache under a prominent nose, the fleshy face framed by outsized ears.

It was Reza Shah, Mohammad Reza's father.

The Shah studied the portrait as if seeking a sign. His face was nearly identical to his father's—the same nose and ears. But Weiseman was struck by the ineffably sad eyes.

The Shah turned his scrutiny, finally, to Weiseman, examing his face, his bearing, as he had studied the portrait of his father.

"Is it over?" he asked. His voice was soft as summer rain, but he was tightly wound. "Lyman Palmer won't answer me. He never does. When people with authority don't answer, it's ominous."

"It's not foreordained, Your Majesty. The United States is behind you."

They moved closer to the Peacock Throne, covered in gold and jewels, a masterful piece of Mughal workmanship to project power and fabulous wealth, with steps leading up to it so it would appear the Shah was floating above ground and closer to heaven.

But the Shah seemed weighted down from heaven now; they sat on an elegant, nearby sofa. Beno, the Shah's great black German shepherd nestled at his master's feet, chewing on a large bone.

The Shah stared at the unicorns dancing on the distant wall, as if in a trance. His distraction might have been due to his cancer medication, but was more likely out of thoughts of what was to come—his overthrow, humiliation, the end of his royal line . . .

"The situation is serious," Weiseman said candidly. "There's very little middle ground."

"I tried. I reached out . . . Did you hear my speech?"

"I did. It was . . . admirable."

The Shah waved his hand in dismissal of the empty compliment. He was determined to guard his dignity. "I don't have much time, you know."

Weiseman remained still.

"Of course you know. The doctor is American. Trevor sent him to me."

"You need to act, Your Majesty, to regain the initiative. They only win if you surrender."

The Shah eyed him intently and seemed to summon up his strength. "I won't live to see Iran ruled by a medieval shaman, David. There will be a new prime minister this afternoon. He's loyal; he'll do what I say." The Shah glanced at him, to gauge his reaction, but Weiseman said nothing. "It will give everyone something to chatter about."

He doesn't see, Weiseman thought. A new prime minister will avail him nothing at all.

"And General Hanif?" he asked, knowing the SAVAK chief would be listening in through a tap in some lamp or fixture in the throne room. "Is he indispensable?"

The Shah gripped his side and grimaced. A moment or two passed, but it seemed like forever as he absorbed the pain. The cancer, Weiseman realized, must be getting more aggressive.

"Yes," he finally replied. "Indispensable . . . until he tries to replace me."

The pain revived, and the Shah turned a pale blue. He gripped the arm of the sofa. Beno leapt up. Weiseman leaned over to help but was halted by a fierce stare.

"You tell your president I have served America well, for decades. Now I expect to count on America." He took a deep breath. "You'll stay in Tehran until the end of Ramadan. That will be the moment of danger."

Maximum danger, Weiseman thought, but nodded his assent. "Yes, of course I will."

The Shah's eyes glazed over again. "You won't do to me what Sir Reader Bullard did to my father . . ." His voice took on a faraway tone.

"No, sir."

The Shah seemed to recover his bearing. "Good. After all these years . . . America will do that . . ."

He lifted his hand as if to wave off his thoughts, but stopped, abruptly, seemingly unable to lift his arm high enough. Had he had a stroke? He lifted a small handbell from the side table, rang it, and Weiseman was startled to see the Empress suddenly gliding across the empty room like a matchstick ballerina to assist her husband. She helped him to his feet and, bearing the weight of him, slowly helped him out of the room.


COLONEL YILMAZ INVITED Weiseman back to the Polo Club for a ride in the woods. The Turkish general staff had met in retreat, then convened the National Security Council and advised the prime minister that time was running out on the Shah. Yilmaz now could assure Weiseman that Turkey was ready to support Ajax Two. Of course, Ankara had questions.

When would the plan be set in motion? How would it be executed? Who would be the successor? A general, they thought, would be best.

"Oh yes," Yilmaz added. "I forgot. There was an envoy from Paris, a revolting man. Jacques Schreiber, asking about our military plans to stage a coup in Iran. I told him nothing."

Mossad was more exacting. The prime minister understood the need for action, Moshe Regev said, but insisted on knowing every aspect of the plan. The Shah had, after all, protected Persian Jews living in Iran, and he had allowed them to immigrate to Israel. He had collaborated with Israel and Turkey to checkmate the Arabs. The prime minister was an Orthodox Jew who valued such things highly.

Weiseman told them it was time to give history a push. Operational plans were being finalized in Washington. Soon, he'd be ready to say more, and if they wished, to visit Ankara again, and Jerusalem.

He returned to Ronald Sims and surprised himself by taking the Brit more into his confidence. Weiseman briefed him on his meeting with the shaky Shah and sought his counsel on who among the many charlatans grasping for power could be a constructive partner after the Shah's departure. "We need a reliable successor. There can't be an empty throne."

He watched Sims reflect on that, then promise to take him to a certain honest business executive he had known for many years, a competent administrator who could serve as prime minister to a future shah or, if need be, in an Islamic regime. "No," Weiseman said. "What we need is someone to replace the Shah, a strong man to hold the country together."

Sims nodded. "There are two generals who would do nicely. They're loyal to the Shah, so far, but ambitious. I'll have a word . . . with your permission of course."


**WEISEMAN MET AGAIN** with the network, except this time the group had expanded. There was an air of excitement, of expectancy—finally, the Pahlavi tyranny would be gone and a new democratic government would take his place. Weiseman encouraged their hopes, tested their readiness for risk, smiled as they told him how the nation would rise as one to oust the Shah.

But he knew better. He could feel the rising risks, the tide threatening to wash the Shah away and deliver the ayatollahs to power.

When the larger group departed, he handed out assignments to Alana and Mahmoud, to Shapour and Yasmine de Rose, who, like her spymaster father, was far from naïve. They were the leaders with a grip on what must be done, on how to turn this loose team of students and middle-class idealists into an operational unit that could alter the Iranian reality. Teams would be formed in every district of Tehran; young professionals and junior military officers would be added to their student network. Protest marches would be stepped up. But now the operational focus would shift. Wall posters would go up questioning the intentions of the mullahs. The young would press their parents to join their efforts to block a political takeover by the ayatollahs and to draw on their own professional contacts to build support for a moderate succession,

Mahmoud was the one most at risk, as the double agent spying inside the Sheikh's mosque. Weiseman admired his courage but worried deeply about his safety.

Mahmoud told him that Montana and the mullahs were forming a militia called the Revolutionary Guards. "You'd be amazed at the middle-class recruits buying into their line, the thugs they're recruiting from South Tehran."

IT WAS MIDNIGHT when Hannah arrived at the safe house, breathless, palpably frightened. Hanif was on to her, she was sure of it. Weiseman ordered her to back off; he'd get her a visa and put her on a plane to Germany, or America. "After all your family has gone through—"

"No," Hannah said. Iran was her country now. Hanif had to be stopped. She had tapped his office phone with the device Weiseman had passed on to her through Alana.

"It's time," she repeated. "Hanif is on to us. He's waiting for the right moment, for the US to install him on the Peacock Throne. He spoke tonight to Washington, to a man called Trevor. 'You're our man, Hosein.' I heard him say that. It's on the tape."

She looked at Weiseman. "Who is this Trevor?" she asked.

## 18

# FIRE IN THE THEATER

**E**VERY BATTLE PLAN dies at the first skirmish, along with the men ordered to carry it out.

The assets Weiseman had assembled had nothing in common except a wish to send the Shah packing. There wasn't an ounce of trust among them. His Ajax Two plan was the least common denominator, and he figured it might only survive until the moment when it must be executed. That was when his allies could well fall out like Ali Baba's forty thieves.

He needed a hedge, a fallback strategy in case the mullahs won. In Beirut, Françoise had reminded him of Ayatollah Seyyed. Yes, he could use a worldly ayatollah with a taste for power, ready to deal with Hanif, harboring a grudge with Khomeini. Was Seyyed such a man? He wasn't sure.

Back in the hotel he strode through the lobby, ignoring the familiar manila envelope. "But, sir, it's important," Daud mumbled as Weiseman entered the tiny elevator.

In his room, he tore off his clothes and soaked under a cold shower, then dressed in a polo shirt and light khaki pants and white tennis shoes. There was a knock on his door, and he opened it to find the manila envelope on the threshold. He ripped it open. A half dozen photographs of himself around Tehran stared back at him. It was a clear threat—we're watching you at all times. It had to have come from Hanif, just as Hannah had warned. Unless it was the mullahs, or Sheikh Khalaji, or Guido Montana . . .

The phone rang. It was Karim Nasir. Weiseman pictured him, in his tweed jacket, in the room lined with books, before he took in what Karim said: "They've taken my son—"

Weiseman's instincts took over. "Not on the phone," he said.

Weiseman had to go to Abadan the next day for the handoff Foster had arranged.

"Tomorrow," he told Karim Nasir. "Can you get to Abadan?" An idea had come to him. "Can you get to the cinema there? The Rex Cinema. Do you know it?" Surely there were no listening devices in the theater, and it would be tough to spy on them in the dark.

Karim confirmed and Weiseman left immediately. He took the stairs, slipped across the back of the lobby, out into the relentless heat, and down the hill into Tehran. Ordinary Iranians bustled past shop windows, not tarrying to look in. All the lights were dimmed.

It was sea of the past, the turbans and chadors, with Western-style clothing having virtually disappeared seemingly overnight. A diplomatic colleague in Beijing once told him that Mao Tse-tung had created an anthill of human beings dressed in identical, floppy, blue suits that erased gender, making it impossible to distinguish between men and women, and stifling human imagination and creativity, thus enforcing submission. Orwell's *1984* had come to China, his friend had said, and it would only disappear when the Chinese people discarded their Mao suits and became human beings again.

The sounds of the *adhan* echoed all around as each muezzin began at the appointed time, but according to clocks that were never perfectly synchronized. Weiseman snapped out of his reverie to see two young women wearing head-to-toe chadors, one of them fingering an errant curl that peeked out of the hood of her chador. An older woman came by and stopped to scold the younger woman, who bowed her head and pulled her shroud tight around her forehead before slinking away.

Weiseman proceeded to take a series of taxis about the city, meeting with assets in affluent suburbs and shabby slums, going where diplomats never go, clad in khaki, his pin-striped suit locked away in his hotel closet. He met with students still daring to speak, and endured suspicious stares in mosques. He noted how everywhere he went people conversed in whispers.

Hanif's cops were out, their presence palpable, still a silent menace. There were more men in uniform, toting machine guns, and people hurrying down the street, trying to stay out of their reach. Religious thought patrols were out, too, warning young women to behave like pure Muslim girls.

That night, he called Françoise from a pay phone, let her know that Selim Nasir might be in danger, and told her what she must do. Then he telexed Trevor and told him that he planned to spend Ramadan in Iran, perhaps stay a bit longer. "Of course, my boy," Trevor said. "Whatever you say."

**ON AUGUST 19,** Weiseman took a train to the southern port city of Abadan, traveling second-class on hard wooden seats in a compartment full of country people dining out of picnic baskets. He greeted them with one of the few words of Farsi he knew—"Hello"—and they smiled back as they opened their baskets. Out came lamb and chicken, dates and figs. Weiseman found himself talking with the teenage boy sitting next to him. His name was Ibrahim. He knew only slightly more English than Weiseman knew Farsi, but through their clumsy exchanges Weiseman learned of the dreams of Ibrahim's family: a good education for young Ibrahim, a decent doctor to serve their village, an end to violence.

Weiseman told them Americans wanted the same things. He asked Ibrahim to ask his family what they thought of the Shah. The father, bent over from what must have been a lifetime of physical labor, took a metal medallion from the inside of his jacket where it had rested on his heart. He kissed first one side, then the other. The first side was engraved with an image of the Shah, the other with the image of the Shah's father.

Young Ibrahim watched this gesture as he must have countless times. He said quietly, "We will change old ways. We will—purify."

The mother, with her iron-gray hair in its tight bun, wept softly. She spoke no English but she understood. She had doubtless witnessed this generational debate between her husband and son many times, Weiseman thought.

**WHEN WEISEMAN ARRIVED** in Abadan, he went to the port and stared south at the oil tankers heading out into the Persian Gulf. Deeply tanned men with grimy faces labored in the yards, moving petrol products that fueled the world's industrial machine. Just across the Gulf was Kuwait. Only slightly to the north of Kuwait was Basra, the Shia capital of Iraq.

An Iranian came up to him, dressed in a white three-piece suit and shiny black wing tip shoes, a cigarette lodged between two fingers, a boutonniere in his lapel. The man eyed him warily for a moment, then approached him.

"You, Mister American." He spoke in Oxford-accented English.

"Yes?"

"I'm Hashemi."

"I'm David."

"Do you understand what's happening here?" the man asked.

"Tell me."

"I work as a local manager of the port, for Anglo-American Petroleum. My company takes a ninety percent profit on the oil we lift from Iranian soil and the Persian Gulf."

"I see."

"Do you see? England and America are exploiting Iranian resources. I work to fatten the bellies of the fat cats—you say that?"

Weiseman nodded. "Yes, we say that."

"The Shah permits this, as his father did before him. They get paid off and deposit their vast wealth into Zurich bank accounts. Our people get screwed."

"And you, Hashemi? Are you well paid?"

"Yes. You see, I'm Mohammad Reza Pahlavi's nephew."

"I see. So . . . are you paid enough to stay bought?"

"What did you have in mind, Mister American?"

HE FOUND THE SAVAK defector, in a bulky sky-blue sweater, nursing a beer in a sordid bar near the port. The three day growth of straggly black beard and brown peasant cap over his forehead failed to mask the terror in his eyes and the tension that gripped his lean body. When Weiseman took a seat, the man said, "I came the long way to avoid a trail. I didn't spot any watchers, but you never know."

He's right, Weiseman thought. All right, get to it.

"You're to walk over to the port, Jafar, only fifty yards from here. There's a speedboat waiting; the logo is DANCE PARTY. You'll be taken across the strait to Iraq, then up to Basra. A man named Christopher will take it from there."

Jafar's eyes darted about him, trusting no one. "Christopher?"

"He's one of ours."

"And then?"

"Then they'll work it out. You'll stay in Basra till things cool down here."

Jafar's face was lined with suspicion. Weiseman could only imagine what was going though his mind. The mullahs would take over Iran; he'd never come back. His family would be arrested for his defection; Trita, his saintly brother, would be banished to Evin Prison . . .

Yes, Weiseman thought. It could all happen. Something worse almost had happened to him in Germany.

Jafar downed his beer in a single gulp and ordered a shot of whiskey. "Fortitude," he said with a grimace. He downed that, too, then said, "Watch after Trita," and tugged his cap further down over his eyes. He pulled a duffel bag over his right shoulder, the kind navy men around the port area were carrying. He stood and seemed to measure the distance to the port, then straightened up, braced himself, and strode away without another word.

Weiseman watched him dodge his way forward, then saw a couple of men immediately materialize from either side of Jafar's path and begin to tail him at fifty feet. Weiseman pushed the signal on his walkie-talkie, and a half dozen young men and women suddenly were in the path of the two tails, holding hands, pointing, as Jafar kept going. The tails pointed stubby-nosed revolvers at the kids and rushed by them, keeping Jafar in their sight but not yet closing in. Jafar turned and saw them. He charged forward, making straight for the boat. One of the tails pointed a revolver. Weiseman said, "*Now*" into his walkie-talkie, and a silent bullet blew the revolver away, tumbling toward the sea.

British and American security agents swiftly surrounded the two tails, disarmed and cuffed them to a link fence, blindfolded them, and quickly disappeared them.

A leap from the dock and Jafar was in the boat. It sped away, due west for Iraq.

Weiseman went to the bar, trembling, and downed a shot himself. A man next to him said, "We did our best, but you never know. There are lots of patrol boats out there."

It was Hashemi, the man he met earlier at the other end of the port.

He asked, "And if he makes it through the gates of hell, and into Saddam's Iraq, what will become of him?"

"You'll let me know," Weiseman said.

"Of course, Mister American. I'll keep an eye out for you. As agreed."


**LATER THAT AFTERNOON,** exhausted from the blast of the 120-degree sun, Weiseman entered the Rex Cinema and took a seat in the balcony. There must have been hundreds of patrons, all Iranian—families opening picnic baskets in the theater, young couples making out. On the screen, newsreels showed the Shah, but instead of the feeble monarch Weiseman had just met in Tehran, here was an imposing leader wagging his index finger at his subjects, calling the shots.

The feature film was a Persian love story, and Weiseman felt himself dozing off. He snapped himself awake once . . . a second time . . . then let himself go and drifted away. A half hour later a tap on his arm woke him up. "I came as soon as I could; there are police all over the street," Karim said in a husky whisper.

Weiseman roused himself, sat up, and looked around at all the surrounding faces absorbed in the screen before reaching into his jacket and handing the envelope to Karim. It contained a forged French passport with his son's photograph in it, and a paper giving the name of a man who would come to Evin and take Selim to Paris. Alain de Rose had seen to that with a testy call to Hanif: "He's a young man, and he works for Le Figaro; it wouldn't do to cause an incident."

Karim stuffed it all back into the envelope looking stunned. "I owe you my life," he blurted out before trying to embrace Weiseman.

Weiseman shoved him back and shushed him, throwing a look around them to remind him where they were. The faces around them still seemed intent on the screen. "Go now," he hissed. "We'll speak again, back in Tehran."

Weiseman leaned back to watch the film and put sufficient time between their departures. The rhythm of the Farsi language promptly lulled him back to sleep.

He awoke to the smell of smoke. Patrons were in the aisle, muscling each other to get out. A man in a suit came on the stage and screamed at the top of his lungs. *Fire! Get out! Get out!*

Weiseman leapt up and looked all round, trying to gauge how to make his way through the mass of human beings desperate to escape. A curtain was ablaze; the crowded theater was already like a tomb.

An elderly lady collapsed in front of him. He stooped to help her, and someone ran up his back, stomping him to the ground. He grimaced in pain but took the woman's hand. There was no pulse. He put his ear to her chest and heard nothing. She was dead.

He forced himself up, pushing aside a large woman who pressed on top of him, flailing with tight fists. He was frightened now; he realized that he could die in this theater.

Squaring his shoulders, he pushed, shoved, and gouged his way toward the exit like the others seeking to survive. A metal exit door was locked. He pushed again and again on the metal bar that should have opened it, but it wouldn't budge.

The fire darted to a curtain nearby. All the walls were covered with curtains, and one by one they were igniting. The heat was intense. A chemical smell burned his nostrils while his skin prickled with the heat. Weiseman thought everyone in the theater would be asphyxiated before being burned to ashes. Old people were collapsing to the ground, children were screaming. Death was all around.

He banged on the metal door and screamed for someone outside to open it. The smoke and fire were a wall now, creeping forward, closing the space behind them, and forcing the crowd forward against the impenetrable door.

*You cannot die!* Weiseman commanded himself.

Summoning his strength, he charged the door like the Stanford halfback he had once been, slammed into it, then pulled back and slammed into it again. Pain shot from his back shoulder down his right side. The flames were very near now, and the bitter, poisonous smoke was suffocating. Some other men joined him, ramming the door with their shoulders, kicking it, until Weiseman raced forward one more time, and this time the door gave way. He fell forward and kept his wits enough to roll to one side to avoid being trampled by the hordes tumbling out after him.

A voice came over a megaphone, in frantic Farsi. *Get away! Hurry! Now! Now!*

He forced himself up, staggered across the street, and ducked behind a low brick wall. Turning toward the theater, he saw people stumble through the open doorway, and then the building collapsed in a conflagration of smoke and flames and a thunderous rumble. Everyone was screaming inside a thick dark cloud of smoke and debris.

Half-conscious, he told himself: *Get out of here.*

People were running everywhere, toward the Rex Cinema and away from it. He dragged himself away through the chaos as fast as he could, his right side—his shoulder, back, and leg—throbbing painfully.

Ten minutes down the road he saw a small hotel on a side street. He went in and paid for two nights in advance. In a tiny room, he took a hot bath and went to bed. When he awoke, stiff and sore, he made his way to the lobby where there was a TV. The smoke was still rising from the charred ruins of the Rex Cinema. Estimates were that more than four hundred people had died inside.

**THE NEXT MORNING,** the regime claimed that the fire was the work of Islamic fundamentalists who had attacked the cinema as a symbol of Western values. General Hanif reported that Khomeini's henchmen had used arson repeatedly in recent months, burning down over two dozen theaters and hundreds of private compaies. Later, opposition leaders blamed the SAVAK policy of locking theater doors from the outside for security purposes. Western telecasts noted that the fire department had been suspiciously slow in responding to the alarm.

Other reports noted that the Rex was not frequented by Westerners—except in this instance, it had been, by an American diplomat, no less, whose photo was flashed around the world.

Hanif, Weiseman thought.

The phone rang in Weiseman's nondescript hotel room in Abadan. Trevor was calling from CIA headquarters. It wasn't the first time Justin had found him when he was in trouble.

Trevor said, "Lyman Palmer is demanding that you be pulled out of Iran. He's cabled the State Department inspector general. He wants your head on a platter."

Weiseman sat crammed into a tiny bathtub, nursing his lower back in the piping hot bath water. "I'll leave the country tomorrow morning, Justin. Nothing would give me greater pleasure."

"Why would you do that, David?"

" Palmer—"

"Oh, don't worry about Palmer; it's his mission. And it's his fault."

"He went to the inspector general? Justin, I'm not going to fight our own people. I'm ready to resign."

Trevor chuckled. "Really, David, isn't that rather melodramatic? The IG is my creature. Rollie Atkins—you remember him, our administrative counselor in Prague."

Trevor owns us all, Weiseman thought. Always has, as long as I've known him.

"Justin, this country is ready to go up in flames, like the Rex."

"Of course it is. Ramadan ends soon. You're going to stay in Iran, keep doing what you're doing. Be back to Tehran by Labor Day. That's when the real fire will break out."

The phone clicked and Trevor was gone.

Weiseman fell back into his fugue state; he couldn't get the memory of the fire out of his mind—ordinary people out for a film, incinerated in a raging fire. He asked himself whether the fire had been meant for him. Was it a lethal lesson from Hanif for messing with his men at the dock—an auto-da-fé arranged by mullahs to dispose of an interfering American heretic? The fire had been set, he was certain, the exits deliberately locked.

Who wanted to turn a theater full of innocent Iranians into a funeral pyre?

Weiseman turned the hot water back on in the tub and slid back down into it. He felt the shock of unremitting heat, then closed his eyes and was pulled back to the Rex, seeing flames consume the theater and the Iranian people.

## 19

# AJAX TWO

**THE END OF** Ramadan fell on September 4, Labor Day in America. Two weeks had passed since the fire, and Weiseman was in his hotel in Tehran nursing his back. Messages arrived from the palace, funneled through Daud, but he didn't reply. And he stayed away from the embassy where he was persona non grata.

Debate still raged in the news media over who set the fire that destroyed the Rex and killed nearly five hundred Iranians. There were stories about the mysterious American. It was reliably known, one paper said, that he was pressuring the Shah to abdicate and that he had met with the Ayatollah Khomeini. Another said he had cast an evil spell over the monarch and was manipulating him like a new Rasputin. There was no agreement about what he might have been doing inside the Rex Cinema, except that he had not been there to watch the movie.

An "impeccable source" provided a photo of this foreign devil conversing with General Hosein Hanif under a black headline demanding to know "Who is this Weiseman?" An editorial in a paper sympathetic to the ayatollahs said he was CIA and suggested a resemblance to Kim Roosevelt, who had returned the Shah to his throne in 1953.

Lyman Palmer, asked about the American by reporters, said laconically that Weiseman had no connection to the American embassy. "He's some kind of shadowy operative," Palmer added, and he gave a noncommittal smile when asked if that meant CIA.

Trevor told Weiseman that the dig from Palmer had raised his standing with Carter.

With his steadily improving Farsi, picked up from Yasmine and the streets of Iran, Weiseman followed the Shah's doings on TV. He appeared to be guided by caprice—one day presenting new reforms that enraged the ayatollahs, the next announcing arrests of dissidents.

Shapour meanwhile reported to Weiseman that there had been a flurry of executions at Evin. Daud spoke to him of an "Action Plan" the ayatollahs planned to launch right after Ramadan.

Weiseman went out camouflaged in a ten-day beard and peered through dark sunglasses at a spreading sea of black chadors, black beards, and black turbans. Posters of the Shah and Farah were defaced with Nazi swastikas. The streets were chockablock with heavily armed SAVAK forces.

He thought he spotted the two men he had last seen chained to the link fence on the Abadan dock. He lost them in the crowds, but then, a chador appeared at his shoulder, whispered, *"Mahmoud est en danger"* and swept by.

He felt a chill of alarm. Mahmoud was his responsibility, and a vital part of his network.

He cabled Trevor. Iran was a balloon, pumped up almost to the limit and one tiny pinprick from bursting. He told the spymaster that he was going to revive Ajax Two.

**RONALD SIMS TOOK** him to meet the business executive, a tidy man in a well-cut suit who at least had the look of a prime minister: hair graying at the temples, a neat mustache, and a dignified manner that implied Oxford or Cambridge. London's man, for sure.

When the man began speaking it was obvious he was a sober-minded businessman who saw that the Shah's time was up. He was also a patriot. He said, "I won't be the Shah's last prime minister, Mr. Weiseman."

"What about a new government?"

"Well, that's another matter. Can you arrange that?"

Sims also brought him to the two Iranian generals he had mentioned, one after another. They, too, were wary, but interested. They knew how Reza Shah graduated from the barracks to the throne, stepping aside for his son at foreign insistence, but they also knew of Hanif's expertise with the hangman's noose. In the right circumstances, to serve the nation, perhaps, but well, not quite yet.

He returned to the Tehran Polo Club, and this time Mustafa Yilmaz selected a fine chestnut mare for him. Soon they were riding in rolling green fields. Yes, Yilmaz was sure the Shah's Turkish friends would offer him refuge and hospitality when he departed, but not forever, mind you. Turkey had its own interests to consider, and Iran was a neighbor, an inescapable fact of life that would remain so after the Shah abdicated, whoever or whatever took his place.

Mahmoud and Alana secreted him to cells of Iranians desperate to see the Shah depart. He told them that the moment was near, but hedged about specifics. It wouldn't do to commit himself and the United States when events were underway; nor did he wish to undermine confidence by admitting that he had no control over how it would happen or who would be the successor. He pressed these good folk of Tehran on what they would do to avoid a takeover by the mullahs.

Ah, he was always told, that comes later. One thing at a time. First, the Shah must go.

Over and over he explained patiently that, in politics, a vacuum is filled by the most determined force and that those who wait suffer the consequences. A fundamentalist regime would have little tolerance for those who later demanded a democratic government.

"We will adapt," they said, deaf to his advice. Once the Shah was gone, everything would work out fine.

**WEISEMAN WAS CONVINCED** now that there were only two options to avoid a fundamentalist regime headed by Khomeini. Either Washington would join with the British, the Turks, and the Israelis to replace the Shah with a secular leader—shifting to an expedient general—or the United States would have to cut a deal with a moderate mullah, if there was such a figure.

He mulled it over. History was replete with clever clerics who had governed shrewdly. In France alone there were Cardinals Mazarin and Richelieu as well as Talleyrand, the ideologically neutral turncoat who served as foreign minister to Louis XVI, then to Napoleon, and then again to Louis XVIII, before the defrocked priest expired along with the line of Bourbon kings. But here it would take a cleric ready and able to take on the ominous Ayatollah Khomeini, and one prepared to work with the Americans and sustain the alliance.

He went back down the alley near the palace to meet Moshe Regev. Sitting next to him was a slight bald man with large round glasses. Weiseman was surprised but managed to keep it to himself.

"Good evening, Prime Minister."

"I'm here to meet with some Iranian friends of Israel," the Israeli leader said. "Moshe has asked me to see you. He says you have a concept, but do you have a workable *plan*? We can't afford to look like fools, or destroy our relationship with Iran."

"I'm ready to offer the Shah safe passage to Rome, as in the first Ajax operation. We're reviewing possible successors but haven't yet—"

The Israeli interrupted. "There are many figureheads available. Each has his own price."

So Weiseman asked for the prime minister's advice on the generals and the businessmen, on Hanif, and last of all on Ayatollah Seyyed.

"The generals are too timid," the Israeli said tersely, pushing those outsized black horn-rimmed glasses back up his nose. "But this Seyyed, that's interesting. Will he do it? Can he?"

"We'll help, but—"

"David," Regev said. "Menachem needs the details."

Weiseman laid it out. Supply of arms and air cover. Logistics. Propaganda. Political action. Sabotage. Some of it real, arranged through Trevor and Sims, much of it still on the drawing board.

"I see," Begin said and rose to his full five foot four. He was a tiny man from Poland who had survived the Holocaust and looked more like a rabbi than a statesman entrusted with the fate of the State of Israel. "We'll do what we can. We know the Persians better than you. We have assets here. You'll work with Moshe."

"Thank you, sir. I will. We intend to count on your assets."

"Don't thank me." Begin removed his eyeglasses, took the pristine white handkerchief from his breast pocket, and cleaned them slowly, inspecting them in the light above his head before putting them back on and eyeing Weiseman. "We act in our national interests. So understand, Ayatollah Seyyed can not be installed as Imam of Iran on the wings of the Israeli air force. If you want him to replace the Shah, that's America's job. I hope you're up to it."

"Actually, Prime Minister, your security is involved more than ours. It's a team effort: you and us and the Turks. We'll have to do it together."

WEISEMAN SAW THE Shah the next morning to prepare him for the inevitable. This time, he offered no reassurances.

"It's a matter of time, Your Majesty. We're working on a compromise. We've arranged a trip to Rome for you and Empress Farah."

"Just as before."

"We hope."

"So this time you will be in Kim Roosevelt's shoes."

"They are big shoes to fill, sir."

"And yet."

"And yet," Weiseman repeated.

It was surreal. The elaborate French gold clock on the desk was set ten minutes ahead of time; on its base perched a pair of owls, omens of good and evil, like the djinn, the evil spirits.

But the Shah seemed almost relieved. He went through the motions, asked whether his son, Reza, might move up, the way he had. "If necessary . . . you understand."

"It's under consideration."

"You'll let me know when."

"Of course, Your Majesty."

**IT WAS 2:00** a.m. at the church near the Italian embassy. Seyyed wore a black turtleneck sweater and blue jeans. They were alone, watched over only by a one-eyed sexton.

"There will be a change," Weiseman said. "Soon."

"Indeed. And what do you want of me?"

"My president is a religious man," Weiseman said, "but he is also sensitive to American interests. I need to know what you wanted to tell me, before General Hanif interrupted us."

Seyyed plucked a cigarette from a black leather case and lit up. He appeared to think it over, then began to speak of his growing up near Qom, his wild days in Rome and Paris before settling down as a mullah. He talked about how he became an ayatollah, the clerical discipline that lay heavily on his spirit, about how Ruhollah Khomeini told him often of his holy mission. Martyrs for missions, he said, made him uneasy.

"And if Khomeini takes over?" Weiseman asked.

"His whole life is his mission: to restore the caliphate to Iran."

"With himself as caliph."

"Of course. But he would rely on his acolytes to run the country—Sheikh Khalaji, Guido Montana, and others. The revolutionary guards will insist on harsh measures to preserve the revolution."

Weiseman always assumed a reign of terror if the ayatollahs took over, but confirmation from Seyyed, from the inside, shook him.

"And you?" Weiseman asked.

Seyyed didn't hesitate. "In the madrassa, we were taught there was no wavering between right and wrong. Ruhollah Khomeini accepted that literally."

"And you?" Weiseman repeated.

"Perhaps I was corrupted in Rome and Paris."

"Some of the greatest kings once were corrupted priests."

"It's true," Seyyed said. "My best friend in school is now a general. He taught me that timing is everything, that you have to strike at exactly the right time."

"Well then," Weiseman said. "You asked me what we want of you. We want you to save this country. I'll be back to you soon with the details."

Seyyed nodded, committing himself to nothing but open to what might come next. Even ayatollahs needed to concern themselves with their security.

"*Inshallah,*" Weiseman said, thinking, *this may be our Persian prince.*

Iran's future could depend on whether there was sufficient lust for power in the priest's soul, and whether he'd get the timing right.

THAT EVENING, WEISEMAN called Hanif to keep him on the wrong track. He would tell him his moment of glory was imminent. Hanif wouldn't trust him—things had gone too far for that, but seeing the prize before him might induce enough self-deception to freeze him long enough.

He was told that the general was at Evin.

When he called the prison, a male clerk put him on hold, then came back on the line and said General Hanif was busy. There were reports of insurrection, threats to His Majesty. The general was preparing to round up the traitors.

Weiseman waited a quarter hour. Then, determined to reach Hanif, he called Hannah's direct line. A woman answered, a voice he hadn't heard before. She asked who was calling, then said, "The director is unavailable."

He asked to speak with Hanif's personal secretary.

"Ah, you must mean Hannah," said the new voice. "She isn't here anymore."

## 20

# MASSACRE

**F**OR WEISEMAN, THE TURNING POINT began when he heard rumors that mundane requests for permission to stage rallies for the Eid al-Fitr holiday, celebrating the end of Ramadan, were being turned down by wary bureaucrats under Hanif's thumb. But the demonstrations were staged anyway, and the government did not intervene.

Sensing weakness, the mullahs called for a general strike and confrontation with the government. Students and businessmen joined in; then so did working people. Street assemblies took place every night. Cries flew from every rooftop—*Allahu Akhbar!* God is great!

The Shah's new prime minister, a sad-looking, bald-headed man with a lisp, appeared on television and imposed the martial law decree that Hanif had worked on through the night.

Weiseman knew what that meant. Hard men did their work at night and presented the bitter fruits of their labor at sunrise.

At midnight, he received a message from Mahmoud, the brave young man who had infiltrated the mosques and was his contact point with dissident priests. Weiseman hadn't seen him in two weeks. You must take care, Mahmoud warned: "Montana is telling Sheikh Khalaji that you're a poison weed that needs to be plucked. It's very dangerous for you now."

Weiseman, recalling his run-in with Montana during his visit to Sheikh Khalaji, followed up by assigning a trusted embassy guard to shadow the young man whenever he went out.

By the morning of September 8, twenty thousand people were congregating in downtown Tehran for a religious rally. Weiseman stood within sight of Jaleh Square, recalling a soggy day in Prague's Old Town Square, waiting for the Red Army to crush the Prague Spring. Now, ten years later, he observed uniformed army troops and SAVAK paramilitary amassing on the edges of the square, and he felt a similar foreboding.

Through a bullhorn, a harsh voice shouted in Farsi to the crowd: *Disperse! Go home!*

No one moved.

And then a fusillade was unleashed upon the crowd, and the first line of demonstrators went down. Shouts and screams filled the air. Weiseman told himself he couldn't just stand there while the mayhem unfolded before his eyes. It was a sin, Johann had told him, to hide in the face of murder, to remain uninvolved, and thus be a silent coconspirator.

Despite the danger, he weaved his way across the bloodstained cobblestones, stepping around fallen bodies, searching for any of the young people who had joined the network. The smell of death hung like a macabre cloud over the square. Before him, a weeping woman hugged a child—*her child*—whose face was shattered beyond recognition.

A bomb exploded, seemingly only a few feet away, and Weiseman staggered off to find shelter in a café on the fringe of the square. Falling into a wicker chair, it took him a moment to overcome the ringing in his ears and notice the man who had literally crawled up to him, whispering "Mr. American" before ceasing to move. Weiseman felt as if his head might explode. He bent down and closed the eyelids of Hashemi, the man at the port who, because of him, decided to change sides to make a better Iran.

**THAT NIGHT, SHAPOUR** arrived at Weiseman's hotel, bandages covering his entire head, only the fierce coal eyes peering out of the slots the doctors left so he could see.

On television, Hanif stood tall in his general's uniform and recited government estimates that placed the casualties of the demonstrations at 122 killed and 1,000 to 1,500 wounded. Shapour cursed at the TV set. According to the doctor who had saved his eyes, there were 300 to 400 killed, and at least ten times that number wounded.

Outside, Weiseman heard a commotion and threw open his windows. *Allahu Akhbar!*

Another demonstration was proceeding unimpaired on the streets below. A line of high priests passed in front of the hotel. Weiseman spotted Ali Amin, his right fist shooting into the air, no longer the timid Texas professor. Ayatollah Seyyed strode alongside him, waving a green Islamist flag. Weiseman wondered, what was his Persian prince up to?

On the building across the street, the images of the Shah and Empress were gone, replaced by the fierce, penetrating gaze of Ayatollah Khomeini.

**"YOU'RE NEEDED." IT** was an hour later, a woman's squeaky voice. The operator must have connected her to his hotel room.

"Who is this?" he blurted out.

"Virginia."

"Who?"

"Not who, where. You understand?"

It was CIA. He told her he understood.

"All right, then. I have a message. See Zed. Then go back to Paris. Goodbye."

This was from Trevor, now concerned that Weiseman's life might be at stake. Justin only intervened in extreme circumstances.

Weiseman called Daud at once.

"Excellency?"

"I'm leaving for Paris tonight, Daud. The 11:00 p.m. Air France flight. Can you arrange—"

"Of course, Excellency, at your command. Consider it done."

STILL IN THE sport shirt and khaki pants he'd had on in Jaleh Square, Weiseman pulled on a windbreaker and dark sunglasses, took the back stairs, and slipped by the reception desk. He strolled down the hill and, amazingly, noticed no tail. Maybe Daud had passed the word: don't worry, he's on his way out.

At the foot of the hill, he hailed a taxi and told the driver to head toward the American embassy. Ten minutes later he got out in front of the safe house. He went in and saw Nouri, washing plates and beer mugs, drying them meticulously, one by one. The effect was hypnotic.

There was a shuffle of feet behind an amber drape that Weiseman hadn't seen earlier. A hand parted the drape. He walked through, into a dark corridor.

"Come." She turned on her heels and he followed her slowly, into a room lit by several blue and gold mosaic lanterns. The walls were covered with purple velvet. Madame Zed wore a widow's black dress. Her gray hair was covered by a simple black cloth scarf. The colored lights sparkled on her rimless glasses.

"My name is Marion Parsi," she said. "My late husband worked for the Agency. Mr. Trevor asked me to advise you regarding your trip to Paris."

On the table, between them, lay a card with the face of Ayatollah Khomeini. "The Iraqi Mukhabarat has taken Khomeini from his house in Najaf. Saddam will be glad to see him gone."

"Where is Khomeini now?"

"Laurent Gramont was here, in Tehran. He convinced the Shah it was better to have the Ayatollah five thousand miles away than across the border in Iraq."

Weiseman was incredulous. Did the Shah actually think Khomeini will stay in Paris? If so, Gramont had conned him with a ruse worthy of Justin Trevor. Or, was it Françoise?

Marion Parsi picked up a remote lying on the table. For a few seconds the television screen blinked snow, then he could see images of the dour ayatollah in black robes and distinctive black, round turban at Basra, where the frontiers of Iraq, Iran, and Kuwait come together. An Iraqi border patrol circled about Khomeini and guided him to a waiting van.

**THE TAXI FROM** Orly took him directly to Alain de Rose's Sûreté office in the massive Concierge that dominated the Île de la Cité. De Rose was waiting for him in his office, standing before a window with a commanding view of the Seine and the gothic spires and flying buttresses of Notre Dame. Down river, the outlines of the Mosque de Paris were half-concealed in the evening fog.

De Rose drew deeply on a Gauloise, then stubbed it out in a Cinzano ashtray. He pulled the drapes shut and took a seat at his small desk piled high with dossiers. In the dim light, Weiseman thought it resembled a policeman's office in a provincial town, although de Rose's white Van Dyck beard, sunken cheekbones, and gravely voice lent the scene a surreal air. De Rose was the French security official who impressed him the most.

"So now you'll have to decide what to do, David," de Rose said.

The door opened and Laurent Gramont walked in. Weiseman had been hoping Françoise would be with him. But she wasn't.

"When are you bringing him out?" he asked wearily.

"Soon," de Rose said, glancing toward Gramont, who simply nodded.

"And then?"

"Then we'll see," Gramont said. "It's really not up to us, you know."

"The Shah has to fix this himself," de Rose explained. "Unless you Americans do it for him again." He gave Weiseman a searching look, as if offering him a last chance to stop the plan Gramont had set in motion.

"Exactly," Gramont chimed in. "How many times do you save him?"

"So we get Khomeini," Weiseman protested, "and the fanatics instead—"

"Oh, no," Gramont interrupted. "*We* don't. The Persians do."

"And our interests?" Weiseman demanded.

Gramont sighed. "Tell him, Alain."

De Rose spoke in his gruff voice. "I told you. Either you preempt and install a successor, as you did in '53, or you bow to the inevitable and see what good can be made to come of it. That's what it comes down to."

Alain was correct; you act or you live with the consequences.

All right, Weiseman thought, it hadn't happened yet. But the moral abasement of it all enraged him. "You mean *appeasement*," Weiseman shot back. "Put your money on Khomeini and the mob he'll bring with him to Tehran. Sell out the decent Iranians. Well, you're good at that kind of thing."

Gramont shrugged dismissively. "Call it what you like. Nations do what they must."

"And the Iranian people? It's the twentieth century, not the Middle Ages."

"Well, it's up to them," Gramont said.

Weiseman walked to the window, stared silently at the Seine, then turned back to them. "And you, Alain. How long do you think it will take the Iranians to grow out of it?"

De Rose turned to the dossiers on his desk, acknowledging defeat but refusing to validate their cynicism.

"As long as it takes," Gramont said softly. "It took twenty-six years from our revolution until Napoleon was gone. It's been twenty-six years since you Americans brought Pahlavi back from Rome. Be patient." He smiled. "Give them time for their passions to cool. They'll see how much they need us. How could they possibly get along without us?"

**EXHAUSTED AFTER THE** long flight, or maybe more so by the meeting with Gramont, Weiseman stopped outside the building for a moment, then walked down along the river, toward the location where the Bastille had been, the spot where the French Revolution had begun two-hundred years before. He passed by the Mosque de Paris and his senses froze at the scene of young boys playing soccer, whooping it up, happy, fearing nothing. He stood there watching the soccer game, so different from the one he'd watched in Tehran months ago. Sweet young demoiselles floated by, turning their heads shyly at the boys who were playing out their dreams . . . while Iranians began the decisive phase of their worst nightmare.

**THAT NIGHT, HE** phoned the private line at Langley, and "Virginia" patched him through.

"I have only a moment," Trevor said. "They're rather unsettled in the White House."

"Everything is lined up, Justin. I've made commitments. I need a final go on Ajax Two."

He heard Trevor's trademark sigh. "Well, you'll do what you must, won't you, David. And you'll do it on your own, certainly no need to tell us about it."

He knew Trevor would say that, but still. Had he been dealing behind his back with Gramont?

"Tell me more, Justin."

"More? You have to create facts on the ground so our people won't resist, won't succumb to sentimentality. Shape the outcome for us. Is that too much to ask you to do for your country?"

"Justin, I'm asking a simple question. Is it a go?"

He heard a voice in the background—"The White House calling, sir"—and then there was only a dial tone.

## 21

# NAUPHLE-LE-CHÂTEAU

FRANÇOISE'S EDITOR AT *Le Figaro* told Weiseman she was on assignment somewhere in the Middle East; they hadn't heard from her in weeks.

Trevor had ordered him to Paris to be present for Khomeini's arrival; Marion Parsi had made that perfectly clear. Laurent Gramont and Alain de Rose had made no bones about their business. He couldn't imagine that Françoise wouldn't be in Paris, too.

He put on a light windbreaker and made his way carefully down the stone steps of the left-bank safe house, past the snooping eyes of the nosy house watcher. *"Bonjour, Madame Sylvie."* He crossed the street, dodging tiny Renaults and Simcas. A black Mercedes with CD diplomatic plates and drawn, white curtains cruised by. The sun was low. Paris was awakening.

After months under cover in Tehran, he could only marvel at the splendor of Paris, the rhythms of the city. And then, outside the church of Saint-Germain-de-Prés, he saw the same withered old man to whom he had given a coin in this same spot while heading to the dinner at Laurent Gramont's, the one where he'd met Françoise. He tapped on the man's shoulder and there was the beret, extended toward him. He dropped in a franc, and the deep bow he received in return brought a smile to his lips. Here is another survivor, he thought.

At the newsstand before the church, he bought a copy of *Le Figaro*, and there she was, on the first page: *"Entre Iraq et Iran, par Françoise d'Antou."* Between Iran and Iraq. His eyes swept down the front page column reporting on Khomeini's journey out of Iraq. There was nothing new. He flipped to the continuation page: *"Fin de Régime."* "Ali Amin, a Texas professor teaching in Sciences Po this semester, said that the rule of the ayatollahs would be moderate, that Ayatollah Khomeini would preside over the nation as a spiritual leader, like Gandhi, while technocrats governed."

That's what Amin had told him after the mullahs bound him up and deposited him at the farmhouse in the Tehran suburbs. How could she write such tripe?

Of course: for Gramont.


**WEISEMAN HADN'T EATEN** in thirty-six hours, so he wandered through the *sixième*, across Rue de Seine and Rue Mazarin, until he reached the quai, then crossed Saint-Michel and stopped along the river at a bistro he'd never noticed before. He looked through the window at the mélange of uniforms—students and businessmen, a policeman and his girlfriend, a priest in a cassock, perhaps from Saint-Séverin or Notre Dame just minutes way. At a table for four there was a man with a big paunch barely restrained by red suspenders, his slim wife in a print dress and round pasha glasses, and two kids trying to pry apart shells from a big black pot of mussels.

He stepped inside and spotted a red garter on the right sleeve of a very wrinkled white shirt, and signaled.

"*Par ici*," the waiter said, showing him to a table already occupied by a tall man in his midthirties. The man had blond hair parted down the middle, a neat mustache, half-glasses, and a small black leather bag at his feet.

"*Vous permettez?*" Weiseman asked, eyeing the dozen oysters the man was slurping with gusto from their shells. He realized that he was ravenous.

"*Bien sûr*," the man said. "They're Belons, from Normandy."

Weiseman nodded to the waiter. "*Aussi pour moi, et des quenelles de brochet Nantua.*"

"A good choice," the man said, "light as a feather, swimming in lobster sauce. Of course, not so good for the cholesterol." The accent sounded Dutch or German.

"I'm David," Weiseman said, extending his hand.

"Hippolyte Altmann, from Flanders, in Belgium. A doctor for my sins, at Père Lachaise Hospital—near the big cemetery."

"I know it," Weiseman said. "But please eat. I'm happy to smell the garlic and look out at the street."

"Yes," the doctor said. "Notre Dame, the Seine, nothing quite like it. But here, take some of the Sancerre. It's really an excellent white. I can't polish off the entire bottle."

Altmann poured. They clinked glasses. "*Santé*," Altmann said.

"*Salute*," Weiseman replied and watched the doctor shuck an oyster from its shell, swallow it down, and smile contentedly, then mop up the butter and garlic with a heel of farm bread, and finally wipe the sauce from his mustache.

At the next table, halfway through their pots of *moules*, the family remained on the attack. The father with the paunch and suspenders called for another Kronenbourg beer.

"I'm from Antwerpen," Altmann said. "It's a commercial city—textile and diamond trade. Rembrandt and Bruegel painted there." He swallowed another oyster, patted his mouth with his napkin. "And a center of medicine. My father and his father were doctors."

The waiter placed a dozen oysters in front of Weiseman, and freshly sliced bread, steaming hot, and he refilled their glasses. Weiseman said, "Another bottle of the Sancerre, please, this time on me."

At the next table, incredibly, the black pots of empty shells were being cleared away, the mounds of mussels reduced to empty containers, replaced by steak frites. Weiseman forked an oyster, sniffed its raw, oceanic flavor and devoured it. He washed it down with the Sancerre. Across the Seine, the bells of Notre Dame chimed three o'clock. Both men ate quietly for a few minutes. Weiseman thought of the Shah and wondered what was going on in Iran.

"Tell me, Dr. Altmann—"

"Hippolyte."

"Hippolyte. Tell me about your practice."

"I'm an oncologist. I treat cancer patients. I save lives. And yes, I lose them."

"Like me," Weiseman murmured, and thought of the dead Hashemi curled at his feet in Jaleh square.

"Sometimes there's nothing to be done," the doctor continued. "Just mitigate the pain . . . postpone the inevitable. It's very common, more than you might think. A woman comes in, she says, 'Help me, doctor.' You examine her and realize it's hopeless." He pushed away his plate. "Do you tell her the truth, that it's hopeless? Of course not."

"So," Weiseman said. "Postponement? That's all there is?"

"It's the European way, you know. Something has affected our spirit; perhaps it's Freud, the pleasure principle. After the First World War, all those ghastly sacrifices, no one wanted any more conflict. Once Hitler took Paris, the French gave up and just went along. Of course, everyone claimed to have been a Resistance fighter once the war was over."

Like Gramont, Weiseman thought: Resistance fighter, noble count, and appeaser, doing the dirty work of the nation . . . Like me?

Altmann's face froze a moment . . . a painful thought?

"We Dutch actually did resist. We paid a terrible price. The Germans broke my father's hands. His beautiful surgeon's hands."

The waiter came by with the food: Weiseman's quenelles, Altmann's grilled fish.

"I have to operate tonight," Altmann said, waving off a refill from Weiseman. "To buy a bit more time, to show I've tried."

Weiseman filled his own glass and lifted it toward the doctor. "To postponing the inevitable," he said.

WEISEMAN WATCHED THE mob scene at Orly on television and realized that the French had allowed the Iranian mullahs to stage a spectacle. They could have hustled the old ayatollah into a waiting limousine, and quietly away. Instead they allowed TV crews in. No—they invited them in.

Weiseman, sipping a chilled beer at a bar in the village of Nauphle-le-le-Château some twenty-five miles out of Paris, found it harrowing. The arrival at Orly seemed to invest the elderly ayatollah with towering stature. He came down the stairs of the plane, clutching the arm of an Air France steward, then stood on the tarmac in the hot airport lights alone, in complete repose—a prophet carrying out God's mission, ready to destroy the infidels. A reporter pushed a microphone his way, and a cop cast it off with a vicious karate chop, a French thunderbolt in service to the Prophet.

Khomeini was placid, as if the commotion he had aroused had nothing to do with him. But Weiseman was certain the old man was contemplating how long he would have to remain in France before arriving triumphantly at his ultimate destination.

The bartender, a big-bellied fellow with a soiled blue shirt, gestured toward the TV set.

*"Cet Arab est fou, monsieur. N'est ce pas?"*

"I wish it were true, monsieur," said Weiseman. "But he's not an Arab, he's Iranian, and he's crazy like a fox."

The bartender rubbed the stubble on his chin. *"Ah, oui,* the kind that bite. But our boys won't let him out of that big barn down the street. Another beer, monsieur? On the house."

At which point Weiseman saw, on the television screen, Khomeini speaking—indecipherably—into a microphone held by Françoise d'Antou.

**THERE WAS ANOTHER** mob scene outside the big house with blue shutters in Nauphle-le-Château when the long black Citroën limousine and the cavalcade of lesser black cars rolled into a second blinding array of TV lights. Except Weiseman wasn't watching this on TV—standing near the front of the crowd, he observed a shield of French police and Sûreté officers escort Ruhollah Khomeini slowly into the big house as though he were a visiting head of state. The French knew how to do that well, Weiseman had to admit.

Yes, the shrewd, old Iranian priest knew he'd be on the front pages of every newspaper in the world tomorrow, the lead story of every TV news show. Weiseman thought the images would put enormous strain on Iran's already severely rent social and political fabric. It would tear at the tightly strained mental state of a shah near nervous collapse.

And then he saw her, alighting from the fifth limousine, in a black shift with a single strand of pearls, a delicate peach silk scarf covering the golden hair. She started his way, a subtle smile on her face.

"*Viens, chérie.* I will introduce you to the Imam."

**THE BIG HOUSE** was furnished sparsely with straight wooden chairs, an atrocious green cloth sofa and an oak table pushed back against the wall to make room for the crowd of idolatrous supporters and conniving Persian politicians, positioning themselves for what they assumed was the inevitable seizure of power.

In the center of the room, with legs crossed on a small threadbare prayer carpet, sat the Ayatollah, seemingly unaware of the commotion his arrival had stirred. His head was bowed. His eyes were tightly compressed. He was a religious symbol, an idol around which the good and bad Iranian opposition would struggle for power and the remains of the

Shah's fortune, and, Weiseman was convinced, a hard-willed fanatic who would call the shots, convert Iran into a new kind of prison, and act as an unequivocal enemy of the United States and the West.

Over Khomeini's left shoulder stood Sheikh Khalaji, the glazy pupils of his sightless eyes somehow focused on Weiseman.

"Imam, you know Madame d'Antou," he heard the blind Sheikh say in Farsi. "And this is the David Weiseman we mentioned to you."

Khomeini slowly extended his hand to Françoise, the mottled skin seeming to slide out from the black sleeve. "Madame." The single word was spoken in a tired guttural voice that betrayed his age and the great odyssey that had led him from Iran to Iraq to this village outside Paris. A journey still incomplete.

Françoise took the hand and bowed her head, then passed the frail fingers into Weiseman's custody. A flashbulb froze him; he did not want to see himself on the front pages shaking hands with Khomeini. Trevor would . . . but a large hand reached out and seized the camera from its zealous owner, and Weiseman turned to see Montana removing the film.

The old priest took a labored breath. In a barely audible voice he said, "You will visit us soon in Qom when the revolution is fulfilled."

*The eyes*. It was impossible not to feel the intensity of the fiercely dark eyes that seemed to be hiding in the caves above the narrow cheekbones. Weiseman had met many world leaders, heroes and villains, but he had never felt as intimidated as he did now. The man's severe demeanor conveyed his overpowering self-righteousness, the utter conviction of his own rectitude. It didn't take a lot of thought to imagine the regime he would impose upon Iran.

Montana dangled the roll of film in midair, fixing Weiseman with a vicious glare.

Françoise whispered, "We'd better go now."

**SHE TOOK HIM** to an apartment he had never seen before—yet another elegant hideaway, in Neuilly, just beyond the Arc de Triomphe. It was her private haven in Paris, she said, away from Laurent and Jacques and the others who tried to run her life.

She stepped back, slowly, and removed her scarf.

It was time to talk. "Are you ready for this?" he asked.

"Yes, David," she said quietly, again the professional operative, her eyes clearly focused on him. "Together we have a better chance to get this job done."

"And Gramont?" he asked.

"David, Laurent and Justin are allies but also ruthless competitors. They are in league more than you may know. You and I will have different orders to follow but—"

"Yes, but on the important things—" he started.

"Exactly," she interrupted, "on what matters, we decide. You and me. And what matters most is . . ."

He watched the infraction in her eyes shift back and forth, from collaborator to lover. Yet over his shoulder he imagined Trevor warning him: *Go carefully, David.*

## 22

# WASTELAND

**T**EHRAN WAS A WAR ZONE, Françoise had told him, a wasteland. There were rolling demonstrations every day, hotels and businesses were being torched.

Upon his return to Tehran, the television sets at Mehrabad Airport were showing alternative sequences—first an interview by an American reporter in which the Shah froze for thirty seconds, unable to answer a question—thirty seconds on worldwide TV, a lifetime. Then came a second sequence in which the Shah, tall and straight in full-dress uniform, announced that he had sacked his prime minister and would appoint a military government to restore order. Iran was a civilized country, this more confident shah said firmly. The occupant of the Peacock Throne would not allow religious radicals to turn his proud country from democracy into anarchy.

Weiseman rushed through the terminal, thinking, *fin de régime*—it's almost over. He hailed a taxi. "Niavaran," he said. "The palace."

The driver scowled. "To see the Shah?"

He nodded.

"Then we'd better make it fast, mister."

The driver sped off on the barren highway toward Tehran. The streetlights were out; only the half-moon provided an ominous choreography for the starless stage. The windows in the graceless apartment buildings along the highway were utterly dark. Occasionally a big oil container truck would pass by, its horn shattering the evening silence.

Weiseman dozed off. The long flight had worn him down, and sitting in the economy seat between two young mullahs chanting incantations from their tattered prayer books had agitated him. He had asked one of the mullahs to excuse him so he could use the toilet, and the man kept chanting.

A commotion in the street woke him up. They had entered the populated part of the city, and he saw young people in jeans smoking cigarettes and hoisting placards on walls.

Death to the Shah! Death to America!

On a dark lamppost, a body swung in the night wind. The body was wrapped in an American flag soaked in blood. He felt an overwhelming feeling of dread, a revulsion ready to boil over. He swiveled the window down, thrust his head out, and vomited onto the street.

The driver said, "A weak stomach, mister? It's the revolution."


**AT THE PALACE,** Weiseman ignored the salutes from the uniformed sentries. He got out of the cab, paid the driver, and slowly climbed the marble staircase. When he reached the top of the stairs, he stopped abruptly. General Hanif was coming out of the Shah's throne room, passing him without a word. Hanif sat down on one of three gilded chairs near the landing, deep in concentration. Weiseman thought of approaching him, but the Chamberlain appeared and said, "Excellency, His Majesty will receive you now."

The golden doors through which Hanif had passed opened again and there was Mohammad Reza Pahlavi sitting on his throne, gazing listlessly into the distance. The deterioration in his physical appearance was shocking.

"Your Majesty." Weiseman took a seat to the monarch's right, in a gilded fauteuil.

"Trevor sent you," the Shah said, "to see if I'm really still here. Well, after all these years, I can deal with death. But to lose the country to a fanatic . . ."

He coughed and reached for a glass of water. "You saw Khomeini in Paris."

"I did, sir. He's frightening; he's convinced that he's God's agent on earth."

"I met him once," the Shah said, "when I was younger. I tried to reason with him. He was nothing but a filthy little cleric. And do you know . . ." The Shah's eyes glazed over, he was somewhere else.

"Sir?"

"Yes. I was just thinking."

"About?"

"A delegation of business leaders came here last week, with my minister of finance. They wanted me to modernize the economy. They suggested that I introduce reforms. They had no idea about my White Revolution. And after all I've done for education . . ."

"Your Majesty. Perhaps they mean—"

"General Hanif was here, just now. He asked me to appoint him prime minister. He asked for a free hand to govern under martial law."

The Shah crossed his legs, reached into his shirt pocket for a cigarette and lit it. "You don't think Hanif can be controlled, David, do you?"

"I'll be frank with you, Your Majesty. It would be the end of your reign."

"Yes, yes, Empress Farah said the same thing. I thought about that, but something must be done. There's a revolution brewing, so I really have no choice. I'll announce the new military government in the morning, after you inform President Carter."

"Sir—"

"No, David. Not Hanif; I've just dismissed him from all his posts. There will be a new man heading SAVAK. You see, I've taken your advice."

Weiseman wondered if he'd informed Hanif that he was following his advice as he watched Mohammad Reza Pahlavi snuff out his cigarette in a crystal dish inlaid with gold. "I won't let the military crush my people," the Shah said. "Gramont assured me he'll keep a close eye on Khomeini. I'm preparing reforms now . . . for my son to carry out."

"Your Majesty, may I speak candidly?"

"You always do."

Weiseman looked up to see Empress Farah. She wore a white silk dress, a diamond choker at her throat, but her tiny body barely filled the dress. She, too, had shrunk physically from what she had formerly been.

"And you must always do so," she added. "My husband must hear the truth. It's such a stranger in this place. In the palace, the Shah is told what his advisors think he wants to hear."

It's the same in the Oval Office, Weiseman thought, and saw the Shah look at his wife tenderly, for the first time in his presence revealing personal emotion. She evidently was his rock, the one he appeared to cling to for what strength he had left.

"Go ahead, David," the Shah said. The Empress stood behind him, the consort with her hand reassuringly on his shoulder.

"When we met before, sir, I urged you to reach out to your people."

"Yes, I've done that. The White Revolution—it's my legacy to them, my bequest."

"Reza," the Empress said, all pretense gone now. "Listen to what David has to tell you."

"That's just it, Your Majesty." Weiseman continued, "It's not your bequest. It's their right. Your people want to decide these things for themselves. They want the Majles to be a true parliament. They want to make their own mistakes, their own reforms. When you make all the decisions, they have no stake in them, no investment in the future you're mapping out for them."

"No!" The Shah was red in the face. "My subjects aren't ready. They lack the education. This is Iran, not rural Virginia. They'll be seduced by Khomeini, this *Velayat-e-Faqih*, this fake philosopher king who will give them Sharia law."

Weiseman shook his head but saw the glimmer of understanding in Farah's eyes.

"Don't you see?" the Shah said, breathing hard now. "It's either Khomeini or me. It's either throwing out everything I've done for thirty-seven years or repression by the fanatical ayatollahs and their thugs. And I—"

The Shah clutched his side and grimaced in pain. Weiseman rose to assist him, but the Empress was at his side, pouring water from a sterling silver pitcher into a crystal glass, handing him a tablet to swallow. The Shah's head rested on his wife's slight breast. He closed his eyes.

"Is he . . ."

The eyes opened. "Yes, David, I'm alive. But you see, I'm trapped; my country is about to descend into a long night."

The Shah pushed himself up, and Farah helped him from the chair, then slowly led her husband from his throne. Weiseman watched them go, reflecting that the drama was almost Shakespearean. The power of the Pahlavi dynasty was draining away, and Khomeini and the Shah were like two alienated brothers fighting over the inheritance, with the only sure loser being the ordinary people of Iran.

Weiseman took a last look at the throne room, suspecting it would be his last time there, then passed through the antechamber. General Hanif was in the same gilded chair, staring into space, his former vigor depleted, a gray shadow of what he had been when he and his master had ruled the country together. He looked at Weiseman curiously, as if in another world.

"General . . ."

"So," Hanif said, a glint in his eye. "You see, now I'm liberated from my oath."

Weiseman listened silently as Hanif told him how Trevor said he was America's man, how together they would stop the mullahs, how finally he would succeed his beloved Reza Shah.

## 23

# LAUNCHING THE OPERATION

OUTSIDE THE PALACE, the smog was so thick that Weiseman couldn't see the mountains surrounding the city, but there was a crowd of people wearing white masks over their mouths for protection from the polluted air. A half dozen students sprinkled among them held up placards of Khomeini's glaring face. When the Ayatollah came to power, he knew, demonstrations would no longer be allowed, but this crowd didn't know that or didn't want to believe it. Weiseman was struck by the fear that he had waited too long and lost critical leverage.

In the taxi, he pulled the typed sheet from his breast pocket and felt at least its reassurance: *Arrived safely. In Baghdad with Iraqi military friends. Awaiting your instructions. Jafar*

The cab driver pushed a tape into his audio system, and a forbidding voice filled the vehicle. "The Imam," the driver said, kissing the image of Khomeini that hung beneath his rear view mirror. "It's time for the mosque."

**WEISEMAN HAD ALREADY** laid the groundwork with the Turks and Israelis, handed out assignments to the network, and reached an understanding, however contingent, with Ayatollah Seyyed. Once he set the plan in motion, the Shah would have little choice but to take his second Roman holiday. It would be safer for him than being on hand when Khomeini arrived in Tehran.

He met them all again, one at a time.

Colonel Yilmaz told him that the Israeli cabinet was ready to go, and that General Irmak wanted to get on with it—operations deferred were opportunities lost. But Turkish politicians, like politicians everywhere, were dragging their feet. Meanwhile, he boiled down his choice for successor to the Shah to three Iranian generals—the two Weiseman had met before plus one other. All were eager to take the lead now that they thought Hanif was out of the game. They were patriots, intelligent men educated at West Point or Sandhurst, dedicated to the kind of secular republic Atatürk had established in Turkey. But such men often are—until they acquire ultimate power.

Still, Yilmaz admitted other matters had come to the forefront. "My generals are preoccupied with internal politics in Ankara. They want to get this done, to free their hands."

Weiseman took in again that there was likely a coup coming in Turkey, and told Yilmaz just that he had promised each of his candidates a role, but had so far promised no one the gold ring.

Moshe Regev, in their meeting, told him he was receiving a stream of questions from his superiors. Perhaps David would come to Jerusalem? A meeting with the inner cabinet would satisfy their curiosity. Weiseman told him they were out of time. Khomeini could be flying in at any moment. That was the heart of the matter: they needed to replace the Shah before Khomeini landed in Tehran. After that, it would come down to planning a coup against a new and ruthless regime bitterly hostile to America.

Regev shrugged, then repeated, "Menachem needs the details."

Of course, Weiseman thought, and then weeks of delay, picking them apart.

"Ajax Two is on," Weiseman reiterated to him. "It's time for the Shah to go to Rome."

**OVER THE NEXT** seventy-two hours, days and nights blended into one another for Weiseman. Final plans were laid for propaganda, political action, funding the operation, and fake passports. Weiseman set in motion a proactive program to smuggle out those in danger; that was a promise he had made to himself. And Ronald Sims quietly arranged logistical and air support . . . just in case.

Millicent called him every day for assurances that no harm would come to the Shah and the Empress, and that their possessions would be flown out of the country, not left for the "scavengers."

Lyman Palmer did his bit by remaining away on home leave.

Realizing that the odds of blocking an Islamist takeover were declining rapidly, Weiseman revved up plans to counter the mullahs. He met Seyyed every night, always in a different location. Seyyed was more and more open in expressing his distrust of Khomeini. It was too late to block Khomeini's return, but Seyyed would be his confidential agent within.

"I spoke to Madame Françoise," he told Weiseman. "She told me to trust you, to work with you."

One night as he arrived for a meeting at what Seyyed had told him was a safe location, Weiseman stopped short as he saw General Hanif, now the ex-SAVAK director general, exiting to a waiting car. When he asked Seyyed about it, the priest said he'd need to call on whatever assets he could. "Do you have a problem with that?"

"Of course not."

It set him thinking, though, about how he was pressing to overthrow the Iranian monarchy and replace it with people recommended by others that he barely knew. Once you started down this road, sheer gravity impelled you forward. How did you find an off-ramp? Should he find one now?

In his mind he asked Johann what gave him the moral authority to play God, to take on the role of Kim Roosevelt. Did vague guidance from Justin Trevor suffice? No, for Weiseman it was the moral certainty that rule by the ayatollahs would be a disaster for Iran and for the United States.

On Saturday night, Karim Nasir called, his voice ragged with worry. "My Selim never went to the airport. He's gone missing . . . Can you call Evin?"

"It was all arranged," Weiseman said, "just as I told you." Then he asked, "Could Selim have gone to ground?"—thinking, Had he gone over to the ayatollahs out of hatred of the Shah?

"I warned my son against the ayatollahs," Karim said. "But he hated the Shah and thought he knew better, that his generation would have the courage to show us what we should have done."

"I'll have my people ask around," Weiseman told him, thinking that Alana's network of young people might discover where Selim was. But he knew that they were all working twenty-four seven and didn't have time to hunt for Selim—whom, he hoped, most likely had gone underground.


## SUNDAY WAS D-DAY.

At a final meeting on Saturday night, Colonel Yilmaz suddenly asked if the United States would be ready to land troops at Mehrabad to block Khomeini's return. Before he could reply, Moshe Regev said, "I'm sorry, Jerusalem says no."

All the air left the room.

Weiseman had always known that the United States would have to take the lead in the operation, but America needed the political cover and the operational capabilities of Israeli and Turkish forces; it was to be the three allies of Iran stepping in to preserve the alliance that sustained their interests in the Mideast. Sure, Regev had warned that Israel would not take the lead, would at best operate in support of the United States. But the plan had always contemplated active participation by the IDF as well as Turkish forces. Weiseman had made that clear to the Israeli prime minister.

Now Regev had pulled the rug out from under him.

He turned to the Turk. "Colonel? Do you want to talk to Ankara about—"

"Not necessary, sir. I know what they'll say. Without the Israeli air force, the Iranian generals will back off. Turkey can't be in a position of bombing a Muslim neighbor. We have to live with Iran."

Weiseman glared at Regev.

Regev rose and placed a hand on Weiseman's shoulder. "David, it's not tragic. The mullahs will be snarled up in their reign of terror for years. They can be bought. It's the Middle East." The Mossad man cleared his throat. "And we have an insurance policy."

Weiseman excused himself, stepped out of the room and dialed the private number in Washington. From the comfort of his Wyoming Avenue home, Trevor said, "Ah, yes, I thought it would come to this. The Israelis would rather rely on their nukes."

That's what the Israelis consider an insurance policy, Weiseman thought, before hearing Trevor's signature cough. "Abort."


IT WAS 4:00 a.m. when Weiseman reached the hotel. Daud was there waiting for him at the front door. In the lobby, a handful of Iranians were gathered in front of a television.

"What's going on?" Weiseman asked.

"It's the tapes," Daud whispered. "They're everywhere. They bring them in every day on order of the ayatollahs, on the Air France flight."

On the screen, Ayatollah Khomeini was sitting cross-legged on the prayer mat in Nauphle-le-Château, speaking to the people of Iran.

"Who's the courier?" he asked Daud.

"Mullahs, Excellency. And there is the Frenchman, directing the deliveries. You've met him. Here."

*Jacques Schreiber?*

A head leaned out of a back office and someone called, "Mr. Daud, telephone, for you."

The little man shrugged his shoulders. "Will you forgive me, Excellency?"

Weiseman went to his room, flicked on the light, tossed his suit jacket onto the bed—then sensed the presence of someone behind him. He turned and saw her face, as white with terror as that night long ago at Laurent Gramont's black-tie dinner party in Paris. It was Yasmine de Rose.

"I've been waiting for you," she said.

"What are you doing here?" Weiseman asked, his voice harsh, astonished that she was in his room.

"I saw him driving by," she said, her voice as tight and tremulous as that night in Paris.

"Him?"

"The man who murdered Shirin near the Sorbonne."

She struggled to suppress a sob, and once again he sensed the heaving emotion that consumed her. Finally, eyes cast down, she was able to say what she'd come to say: "Papa has an intercept of a phone call from Nauphle-le-Château. It's of Guido Montana, telling the Ayatollah that Françoise is poisoning his mind, that she's an infidel. He intends to kill her . . . and you."


**WEISEMAN LEFT THE** hotel and went out to a telephone booth a block away. He reached Trevor on the private number.

"I'm coming back in the morning, Justin. I'm ready to answer your questions."

"Excellent. I expected you would be. A car will collect you at Dulles, take you straight to me."

"Justin, you're involved in all this with Gramont. The two of you together, right from the beginning—"

There was the slight, telltale cough.

"Well then, I'll see you tomorrow evening, on Wyoming Avenue; you know the house."

"Not tomorrow, Justin, there's something I need to do first, in Paris."

"David, the president is expecting you, so am I. Tomorrow—"

"Goodbye, Justin." He dropped the phone back in its cradle, cutting off Trevor's protests.

The phone rang again. Weiseman sat there, counting the rings . . . four, five, six . . . For a moment, he imagined Trevor's cold fury. But then his mind was elsewhere.

## 24

# *VILLA SCHREIBER*

**THEY MET AT** the Fauchon café on the Boulevard de Madeleine, sitting by the window at a tiny table for two. She seemed almost imperious.

"Tell me about your role in bringing Khomeini to Paris, Françoise," Weiseman said. "I need to know."

"Of course you do, David."

Out the window, he spotted a man who looked familiar, like a CIA officer who worked in Langley headquarters. One of Trevor's staffers—O'Brien? The man came into the shop and pretended to examine the pastries.

Françoise noticed, too. "A colleague of yours?" she asked.

Weiseman bore down. "It's Jacques, isn't it? He ran the operation."

"No, it's not Jacques."

She hadn't touched her food, she hadn't even taken a sip of her coffee. She lit a cigarette. He'd never seen her smoke before.

The CIA man was coming their way now, carrying an espresso and a croissant. He walked right by them without a sign of recognition.

She puffed nervously on the cigarette.

"Françoise, you need to know . . . we have intel, Montana has been warning the Ayatollah about you. We believe he intends to kill—"

"I know," she said, now strangely calm, as if that was a professional hazard she was expected to manage. "And you, too," she added. "You know that as well. Don't you?"

A waiter appeared and handed her a note. She read the note and folded it neatly, put it in her purse, then stood and handed him a name card. "Come to this address," she said. "Tonight. Jacques may be there. I never know."

**THE AGENT CAUGHT** his arm on the way out the door. They walked in lockstep into the Place de la Madeleine and stopped, facing the church's perfect Greco-Roman columns.

Weiseman said, "What do you want?"

"I'm Tim O'Brien. I work for Trevor."

"I know who you work for."

O'Brien lit up a cigarette, a Lucky Strike, and blew the smoke into the wind. "The ayatollahs are set to take over. Montana will run the security services. He's after your ass. He intends to do to your girlfriend what he did to the Sorbonne student."

This confirmed what Yasmine had told him, and what he just heard from Françoise. The the mullahs wanted him dead, and Françoise. Why hadn't Trevor told him this directly?

What was going on?

O'Brien smirked, as if reading his mind. "You're over your head, Weiseman. They're setting you up."

"They? And who is they?"

"The French have got you all twisted around. You're following your cock instead of your head. Klein warned you. We're watching to make sure you don't give away the store."

The spook turned on his heel and strode down the avenue. Weiseman watched him go, past the church, around the corner. He watched O'Brien disappear, then waited until he'd regained his composure, and walked past the flower stalls and headed toward the Place de la Concorde. It was time to talk to Laurent.

ONCE ACROSS THE bridge, Weiseman continued along the quai, past the bouqinistes, with their paperbacks wrapped in plastic to escape the mildew of the Seine pulsing along just below. At the Quai d'Orsay, he asked for Gramont. The clerk called up and told him, to his surprise, that Gramont was ready to receive him. A young man wearing a green tie led him upstairs and said, "The Count will be right with you."

Forty minutes later, Weiseman was still waiting and, checking his watch angrily one last time, he got up to leave. At which point the inner office door slid open, as if programmed. "David, they didn't tell me you were here. Come in . . . come in. Sit down. A cigarette? Oh, I forgot, you don't smoke."

"I saw Françoise this morning," Weiseman said.

"Yes, I know." Gramont lit up a Gauloise and took a careful puff. *"Tu permitte?"*

Weiseman watched him preening like an ostrich. He'd won and was relishing it.

"I have to fly to Washington in the morning, Laurent, to report."

"Of course, Justin will want to know."

"I want to know what you're willing to tell me."

Gramont crushed out his cigarette. Mixed with his air of triumph was a nervous tension, as if he were aware that the road ahead would be rocky, that the ayatollahs would not be so easy to control.

"Well, he's here now," Gramont said. "It's just a matter of time."

"If it's just a matter of time, why push him out?"

"Please, David," Gramont said. He spread his manicured hands, like an entertainer awaiting applause. "We get the credit this way. For helping, in our modest way."

Weiseman repeated the adage from memory. "Don't forget what Churchill said. 'You'll be amazed at the extent of their ingratitude.' Do you really think you can work with the mullahs?"

Gramont shrugged. "Who knows? They're almost completely egoistic; they have little room for understanding anyone else's interests."

Weiseman tried not to remark on the irony of Gramont being the one to make that observation.

Gramont rose, made the journey to an elegant Empire armoire, and drew out a bottle of whiskey. "A small glass?"

"A bit early for me."

Gramont poured himself a glass, swallowed it down, and wiped his lips with a starched, white cloth napkin. Weiseman studied him carefully; there were deeper lines in the Frenchman's sculpted face than he had noticed before. Perhaps even for him, playing a dirty game for the Élysée was taking its toll.

"It won't be so easy," Gramont said, partly to himself, then put down the glass and returned to his chair. "We'll have to work together after Khomeini arrives, to keep him in line."

Weiseman almost laughed. "So, you've decided we'll work together . . . now?"

Gramont shrugged again. "It's our métier, David. You know that. Justin knows."

Of course. *Déformation professionnel.*

Weiseman got up. "Is there anything else?"

"Just one thing. You want to know about Françoise. She'll tell you what you want to know. But you need to protect her, or it will be on your head."

"*My* head?" Typical of Gramont, deflecting his responsibility when he was the one putting her in danger.

"You still don't understand?" Gramont spoke so softly that Weiseman had to strain to hear him. "Didn't Yasmine tell you?"

**THE YELLOW BRICK** house on the corner of the Rue de Vaurigard and the Rue de Médicis wore a name tag in the form of a gold plaque on a stone pillar: VILLA SCHREIBER. The descending sun cast a patina of auburn light on the blue tile roof. In the glare, no lights could be seen from inside the house. Still, it was seven o'clock, the appointed time. Weiseman knocked twice on the door.

It opened, and a maid in a black dress and white apron said, *"Bonsoir, Monsieur Weiseman."*

She led him through a vestibule to a set of double doors twelve feet high.

*"Entré, monsieur. Ils vous attendent."* They're waiting for you.

He opened the doors. Françoise was seated on a love seat. She wore a straight black dress and a single string of pearls. Her hands were folded tightly in her lap. Jacques Schreiber, in a red velvet smoking jacket, sat beside her, for all appearances the husband and paterfamilias. Standing behind them in black tie was Laurent Gramont, like the godfather in a family portrait.

"Take a seat, Monsieur Weiseman," Jacques said. He tapped the ashes of a cigar into a swanlike ashtray on a side table. "Please, you're our guest."

There was an overstuffed sofa facing them, but Weiseman chose instead a straight-backed fauteuil, also facing them. "You have something to tell me," he said, and crossed his legs.

"It should come from Françoise," Jacques said dryly. "We've decided you need to know."

Gramont nodded and, as if on cue, she leant slightly forward. Weiseman couldn't help noticing the grace of her movements in the low lights.

"David, Empress Farah is my cousin."

Weiseman was rarely surprised anymore to learn of the connections between high societies in Europe and the Mideast. Still, this caught him off guard. He stared at her as she went on.

"For years we worked with the Shah's regime, like America, until the murders here in Paris. We couldn't allow the Iranian civil war to be fought here."

"*We?* Who is we, Françoise?"

"She's talking about France," Gramont said. "Me, and Françoise, and Jacques."

*Jacques?* He turned toward Françoise. "Then you've been playing me all along. All the stories about Jacques working with the gestapo . . ."

"The gestapo part was true," Gramont said. "So was most of the rest, except—"

"I was arrested after the war," Jacques interrupted. "There were, shall we say, intense inquiries in the Rue des Saussaies, the same cellars my German friends used during the occupation. I was offered a deal I could not refuse: collaboration with the Sûreté against Moscow, or the gallows." He shrugged. "*Sauve qui peut*, you might say. It was the Cold War. Over time, my network expanded, in China, the Middle East. Now Iran."

Gramont cleared his throat. "The arms dealer cover enabled him to turn up wherever he was needed. Arms dealers go to trouble spots. Using him was an inspiration, from Françoise."

Weiseman glared at Jacques Schreiber.

Jacques flicked the ashes of his cigar back into the swan ashtray. "We are a professional couple," he said. "For operations." And then, a sardonic smile. "Of course, I'm only human."

"You're not," Françoise said cuttingly, "and nothing ever happened."

Gramont fixed Jacques with the withering look of contempt reserved by a French aristocrat for the nouveaux riche. "The sordid compromises of our profession," he said wearily.

Jacques chuckled, then crushed his cigar in the swan as if he was burning it into the chest of a prisoner in the cellars at the Rue des Saussaies. "Please, Monsieur Weiseman. There's no need to be morose. Nor sentimental. *Un petit charade, c'est tout.* Nothing more."

He rose from the love seat, checked the back button on his wallet pocket as if by habit. "I think my part in this little drama is over. There is something pressing I must attend to."

Weiseman watched Jacques leave the room and slip on a suit jacket, then heard him tell the maid, "I'm going out, Celeste," before hearing the door close behind him.

Gramont poured himself a whiskey. "Françoise has been with us since she left the university," he said. "She's an accomplished agent, one of our best, but of course undeclared. It's imperative that her role remain secret."

Abruptly, he downed the whiskey.

"In fact, she's more than an agent to me. She is a special responsibility. Her father and I were comrades during the war. He died during the Nazi invasion."

Gramont kept talking. "When the two of you met, we saw our chance to work with America to deal with the murders on our streets and the *fin de régime* in Iran. Now we're at the most sensitive phase. When you see Justin, tell him our agent has won the trust of Khomeini, that there is a way ahead to protect our mutual interests in Iranian oil after the Shah departs."

Weiseman was still taking in the fact that he had been a "chance" to them—that he had been Françoise's *assignment*. "When the two of you met, we saw our chance . . ."

"And Françoise?" he spit out at Gramont. "What is your special responsibility to her, Laurent? That is, if she survives this—if Montana doesn't kill her." He couldn't help but add sardonically, "Which of course, will 'be on my head.'"

Gramont ignored his anger. "You and she will work to tighten the screws on the ayatollahs," he said, "Just as you asked. Just as she promised."

Gramont rose, straightened out his tuxedo jacket, adjusted his cufflinks just so. "You and Françoise will want to be alone now. If you like, we'll have a car take you to the airport in the morning."

"That won't be necessary," Weiseman snarled.

Gramont nodded, started toward the open door, then turned. "Oh yes, bon voyage, David. My best to Justin."

Weiseman watched the door close behind Gramont, doubtless off to some official function in his tux, the ultimate cynic, patrician, and patriot . . . like Trevor.

Françoise got up and went to a nearby side table to put on a radio—to defeat any listening devices, Weiseman guessed. "David, beyond my relationship with the Empress, there was nothing here tonight you didn't know before. In our profession we use people, often terrible people to achieve our aims."

"That's what we've been doing with Jacques—"

"And me."

She stared at him deliberately for a long moment before saying, "No longer," without breaking her gaze.

The radio played on in the background, some bad French rendering of a bad American pop song.

Finally, Weiseman said, "Watch out for Gramont," before turning on his heel.

"David—" She stopped him. "You do understand: Laurent is the one who is vulnerable here. He convinced the Élysée to take Khomeini out of Iraq, to bring him to Paris. When it all goes wrong it will be Laurent who will be at risk, and no one will know him."

Weiseman took it in and nodded. "But you and I are still the ones with a target on our backs," he said as he left.

## 25

# *FAST FORWARD*

**A**N AGENCY CAR took Weiseman from Dulles Airport to the front
entrance of CIA headquarters, where a guard led him to the director's limousine. The guard opened the left rear door of the armored
car, and Weiseman sat on the plush, black leather seat. Then he waited for
forty minutes, the same amount of time to the minute that Gramont had
kept him waiting at the Quai d'Orsay. On the minute, Trevor silently
entered the right rear seat—pride of place—and then they were speeding
down the George Washington Parkway under the canopy of pine trees
concealing the road as though it were a state secret. Trevor did things his
way, Weiseman knew, so he waited in silence until the limo pulled up
before the Washington Monument.

"Let's take a walk," Trevor said, and led him along the path beside the reflecting pool. Two crew-cut bodyguards trailed behind, tiny communication buds in their ears, their reflections bobbing images in the water. "We saved the Shah once before," Trevor said. "Not again."

"Justin, he's ready to go. He looks like a mummy."

Trevor kept moving forward. "Ajax may be dead," he snapped, "but we still need a replacement for the Shah. There must be someone. You have to give me options. That's why I sent you out there. You don't expect me to just go along with Gramont, do you?"

Weiseman stared off across the water at the Jefferson Memorial and thought, *Here we go*, then said, "There are two generals . . ."

Trevor waited for more.

"It's too late," he finally stuttered. "Things have to happen before Khomeini arrives."

"Yes," Trevor mused in hasty agreement, missing Weiseman's point and going on as if speaking to himself. "A fait accompli to checkmate Laurent. We need that."

Weiseman, walking a step behind his slowly pacing boss, was more convinced than ever that Trevor and Gramont were playing their own double games—each keeping all avenues open, all options available, never giving up until the last card was played and they ran out of options. He noted, too, that his normally cold-blooded mentor was personalizing things with Gramont . . . and he suddenly wondered whether Jacques was reporting behind Gramont's back to Trevor. Jacques, he knew, wouldn't hesitate to double-cross the arrogant count.

Trust was a limited commodity among intelligence operatives.

Regardless, Weiseman knew it was too late to find a replacement for the Shah—Trevor was going to need to form some kind of liaison with the ayatollahs

"I've met Khomeini," he said.

Trevor stopped at that, turned, and waited for Weiseman to catch up. "I've read your report. Tell me about him," he said, striding off as soon as Wesieman was beside him.

"Ali Amin says he'll be kept in Qom as spiritual leader of Iran. But that's ridiculous. Khomeini is absolutely fearsome. He'll be calling the shots."

"Still," Trevor said, "we should talk again to Amin. He's a professor at UT, isn't he?"

"Why not?"

"And there's an ayatollah who distrusts Khomeini?" Trevor was fully alert now, sensing an opening, but Weiseman wouldn't name Seyyed, not even to Trevor. Trevor had once warned him: *words fly, names fly*.

"Of course, Justin, we have assets—the ayatollah you mentioned, a network of students and businessmen and younger military officers. The Turks and Israelis. The Brits are being helpful." He couldn't bring himself to mention Tariq Aziz, even though he was sure Trevor was probably pondering an Iraqi option.

They arrived at a bench and Trevor slumped onto it. "Go on," he said.

"And there's Hanif. He's gone underground, calling in his chips. He has some kind of link to our ayatollah. He told me he had your backing."

A plane soared above them, banking for the final descent to National Airport. Trevor tracked the plane, his right hand shading his eyes from the sun. Finally, he turned toward Weiseman. "Well, Hanif *would* say that, wouldn't he."

Weiseman allowed a half smile to cross his lips. He'd always enjoyed Trevor's form of diplomatic ballet. He was his mentor, after all. "Justin, the French are ready to move Khomeini in at any moment. If we don't preempt now, we'll have to wait until the people feel enough pain to rise up against the mullahs. That will take a very long time."

Trevor merely nodded and looked lost in thought.

Like musical chairs, Weiseman thought, Trevor and Gramont are watching to see who will be left standing, with Serge Klein doubtless there to do the dirty work.

"You'll go back out there," Trevor finally said quietly. "We'll announce our support for the moderates."

"That would be the fastest way to get them killed."

Trevor's face seemed to age before him, the grooves and tributaries deepened as if plowed. Weiseman could sense the calculations underway in his patron's mind.

"Gramont called me," Trevor finally said.

Ah, finally, thought Weiseman.

But then Trevor said something unexpected. "Khomeini's people warned the French against the Shah receiving exile in Paris, that whoever takes him will pay a heavy price."

"That's outrageous," Weiseman snapped. "The Shah was our ally for thirty-seven years. Other leaders notice how we treat allies who get in trouble."

The stillness along the mall was deafening.

Weiseman tried again. "I've met these mullahs, Justin. They'll build a fundamentalist state. They'll oppose us all over the Middle East. They'll have their own SAVAK. They already have a contract killer, Guido Montana, and he's targeted me."

Trevor said, "I know about Hamid Fazli."

Now, Weiseman thought, this is the time to confront him.

"Sir, we have a responsibility, whatever the consequences."

Trevor rose from the bench and wiped an alien bead of perspiration from his forehead. "Whatever the consequences, David? You can't mean that. Consequences are all that matter."

"No, Justin. The Shah should be treated in New York, at Sloan Kettering, with no apologies. We're a humane people. The mullahs will need us when they take over."

Trevor stared at him a moment, then shook his head and rose from the bench. "You're disappointing me, David. My analysts tell me that that will lead to an outcry against us in Tehran. I want you to come up with a plan that gets us out of this mess. And tell me what we really should do about Pahlavi."

So, Weiseman thought, he's just Pahlavi now. To Justin Trevor, he's already a dead man. They'd had these differences over and over, going all the way back to Prague—Trevor telling him that only power counted and disdaining what he termed sentimentality, and Weiseman insisting that the human factor must be accounted for.

Perhaps it was a generational thing, Weiseman sometimes thought, but at bottom, he realized that when it really mattered, he was still Johann's son.


**EN ROUTE BACK TO PARIS,** Weiseman unlocked his attaché case and drew out a plastic cover with a single sheet of paper.

*You are to resume contact with Khomeini representatives. Go see Amin tomorrow. Tell him the Shah will leave on the 16th, directly for New York. Explain to him as eloquently as you did to me why we owe the Shah that much. You may cooperate with Madame d'Antou to learn the plans of the ayatollahs. Your reports should be sent directly to me, no other copies. JT*

So, Weiseman thought, Justin is ready to let the Shah come to New York. Or is this just a con, a cover for sanctioning official contacts with the ayatollahs? With Trevor you never know.

He slipped the paper into his case and pulled out the cable Ambassador Palmer had sent the day before about his meeting with the Shah. Palmer must have snorted in disgust before delivering the mealy mouthed message the high-level interagency Iran group had coughed up.

*Our support for you is steady, but it is essential to end the uncertainty. We would support a military government only to end bloodshed but not to apply the iron fist to retain your throne. A Regency Council could supervise the military government.*

Since a Regency Council could act only in the monarch's absence or incapacitation, the Shah had asked Palmer if Washington expected him to go abroad. And, of course, there was the problem of where to go, he added. Palmer's cable noted that there was a long silence until he finally told the Shah he was confident that he would be welcome in the United States.

Of course, Trevor instructed Palmer to say that; Palmer would never have said it on his own. So they were going to let the Shah come to New

York after all. Weiseman thought, maybe his pitch on the mall had made an impression on Trevor.

He drew out the third document from the plastic, the instruction encouraging all remaining US dependents to leave Iran, and the embassy's reply:

*There is a strike by Iranian civil air personnel that has terminated air traffic control services at Mehrabad. Israeli and US aircraft are no longer permitted to land in Tehran.*

**WHEN WEISEMAN ARRIVED** at the big house in Nauphle-le-Château the next afternoon, Ali Amin was almost unrecognizable. He had traded his natty Western clothes for the long black robes and turbans of the mullah fraternity; a white beard covered his face. He seemed in a frenzy, complaining that the Ayatollah wanted everything done at once.

So, just a spiritual leader? The pope of Iran would be consigned to Qom? No, Weiseman thought ruefully, I don't think so.

Amin whisked Weiseman into a room crowded with typewriters, tape decks, video recorders and microphones—the rudimentary weapons of a medieval revolution.

"I'm here on instructions," Weiseman said. "The Shah leaves Iran in forty-eight hours."

"We know that. Our reports are that he'll stop in Saudi, then the military will stage a coup, and he'll return, like Operation Ajax in '53. Hanif will be back to run SAVAK."

Weiseman brushed aside Amin's paranoia. "Hanif is out of the picture," he said, hoping it was true, but still edgy about Hanif's contacts with Seyyed. "The Shah will die without urgent medical attention," he added sharply.

"So he'll die, *Inshallah!*"

Amin sat down on a wooden chair next to a tape deck, arranged his robes carefully, and stroked his beard. Weiseman leaned forward, their eyes now separated by inches. The door to the room opened. A woman in a chador entered; only her eyes were visible through the slits in her black nijab. "The Imam requires your immediate presence," she said to Amin.

The voice. He was sure he'd heard it before, but with the head-to-toe covering it was hard to be sure.

He followed the folds of the woman's chador and Amin's robes through the ramshackle house and its clutter of modern technology, past journalists with cameras around their necks, past young Iranian lads chatting excitedly, convinced they had seen the hidden Imam. On either side of a closed door, two bearded bulky bodyguards slouched, Kalashnikovs lying idle on their laps.

"Wait a moment," Amin said. He entered the room and closed the door behind him.

"Alana?" Weiseman whispered, and the woman turned slowly toward him. "Why?" he whispered.

"Keep quiet, brother," a bearded bodyguard growled. "You're at the shrine."

The woman looked down. Had she been turned?

The door opened. Amin's hand slipped out from his sleeve. The index finger pointed toward Weiseman and curled, beckoning him to enter. He stepped in and saw Ayatollah Khomeini sitting on the same prayer mat as he had the night of his arrival in France. Sheikh Khalaji stood right behind him, and alongside Guido Montana glared, one hand on the dagger in his belt.

Khomeini trained his limpid dark eyes on him and mumbled in Farsi. Amin translated. "You have something to tell us?"

The old man coughed slightly and was offered a glass of tea, but shook his head, then nodded, almost imperceptibly.

Weiseman spoke in English, knowing it was vital to be precise. "The Shah will depart Tehran in forty-eight hours for New York where he will be treated for the cancer. He is going to die. Our purpose is to allow him to do so in dignity."

He waited as Amin translated. The Ayatollah leaned forward to hear Amin. Then Amin translated his response: "If you do this, it will bring a great disaster."

**WEISEMAN ARRIVED IN** New York in the middle of an ice storm to await the Shah's arrival. He went directly to the command post the State Department had established at the Sloan Kettering Cancer Center. The next morning the television showed Mohammad Reza Pahlavi gingerly stepping off the plane, the Empress Farah at his side. But instead of New York's snowy JFK tarmac, the Shah was being greeted under a brilliant sun by the slim, mustachioed figure of Egyptian President Anwar al-Sadat. The terminal sign in the background read ASWAN.

Weiseman watched as the Shah and Farah, with Sadat and his wife Jehan, climbed into Sadat's presidential Cadillac, with Iranian and Egyptian flags flapping from the front bumper stanchions. The vehicle turned in a wide circle on the tarmac and then drove off into the desert.

The phone in the command post rang. Ali Amin pronounced his name distinctly, and then came the accusations of bad faith. The trip to the United States had clearly been a ruse. If the Shah was so desperately ill, how was it he had time to visit Sadat?

Weiseman didn't know either, but he wasn't admitting it. "It's probably a stopover, Ali. Sadat wanted to show his respect."

But Amin wasn't buying it. "It's Operation Ajax again," he insisted. "Are you sure Trevor has told you the whole plan?"

Not very likely, Weiseman thought, but he told Amin it must have been Sadat's idea. Amin wasn't buying that either. "Sadat's a walking dead man," he said.

When the conversation ended, Weiseman needed fresh air. Out on the icy street he found himself surrounded by demonstrators in heavy parkas and ski masks waving signs. SHAH GO HOME! Even though the Shah hadn't arrived student demonstrators, Iranian and American, were circling the hospital entrance just in case.

A bus pulled up and suddenly the crowd doubled in size. The circle started to close around him. Now the signs were in Farsi. *MARG BAR AMRIKA!* DEATH TO AMERICA!

Weiseman dashed back inside. From the command center he called Trevor and asked, "Is this a double cross?"

"Absolutely not," Trevor replied crisply. He paused an instant, then said, "David, listen carefully. We have confirmation that Hamid Fazli, this Guido Montana, is after your neck."

Weiseman couldn't help himself. "No kidding," he said.

Trevor paused, as if startled that Weiseman knew. "Well, we'll try to get him before he gets you," he finally said.

**FOR THE FOLLOWING** week Weiseman watched fitfully as innumerable TV news programs showed the Shah and the Empress convalesce in beach chairs outside the villa Sadat had chosen for them, surrounded by a bevy of Egyptian bodyguards. He watched the Shah wave furtively to the press from behind a white lattice curtain and wondered whether Amin was right: Was Trevor arranging his return to Iran?

On January 26, motorcycles escorted the royal couple back to the airport.

Two hours later they landed at Casablanca, where the Shah was greeted planeside by Hassan II of Morocco. Another motorcade, with Iranian and Moroccan flags flapping in the Saharan sun, whisked them to another villa, this time in Marrakesh.

When Amin called, Weiseman said, "Ali, he's still heading west. It won't be much longer."

On January 31, Weiseman was summoned to Washington. In the L-shaped office, Trevor looked up and said, "The Ayatollah returns tomorrow to Tehran. God help Iran."

Weiseman waited. There must be more. Trevor could have told him that by phone.

"We're recalling Palmer. It's premature to send another ambassador. The president has appointed you special envoy for Iran. You're the only one of us who knows those mullahs, who can prevent them from getting unruly."

## 26

# *ISLAMIC REPUBLIC*

R EVOLUTIONS BREED MASS confusion and pandemonium, rousing hope in some and stirring fear in many. When Ruhollah Khomeini returned to Iran on February 1, 1979, the full range of emotions was present on the faces of the crowds at Mehrabad.

From his office on the seventh floor of the State Department, Weiseman watched the live telecast of the scene at the Tehran airport. He watched the Ayatollah parade under green banners with yellow Farsi script as if he were the messiah, there to lead Iran back to the Middle Ages. Cordons of bodyguards escorted him through adoring crowds grasping to touch his garment. All the women were shrouded in black, not a speck of skin or a strand of hair showing. Men beat their chests and tore at their hair. Children waved Korans at him as shouts filled the air: *Shah raft, Shah raft . . . The Shah is gone, the Shah is gone!*

A cutaway shot showed a female journalist in a headscarf asking a mullah with a white beard for comment and was told that, henceforth, the country would be known as the Islamic Republic of Iran.

Who was that mullah? Weiseman wondered. Was it? Yes. Ali Amin, a long way from Texas.

Weiseman had few illusions about what this meant for Iran. He had seen it before: shameful photos of Austrian arms rising in the Nazi salute as Hitler drove through Innsbruck and Vienna to claim his conquest; gestapo thugs and German shepherds chasing him and his father; hiding behind the hedges in the Berlin Grunewald just before the trains left for the camps.

Now was the dawn of a new despotism in Iran.

He turned back to the TV, but the Ayatollah was gone, leaving behind only the debris and the wild crowds. Depressed, he got up to store his classified documents in the new safe they had given him, and then he realized he had forgotten the combination. He forced himself to concentrate, and it came back. As he twirled the dials, he remembered what Trevor had once told him: *If you're in a sensitive position and you're any good, you'll have enemies. So don't neglect the little things; that is how they'll get you.*

**HE HEARD FROM** Ali Amin only three days later, on February 4. "The Imam has appointed me acting foreign minister," Amin said on a fuzzy phone call from Tehran. "But there's no staff, and no files. The Shah's men held a bonfire."

"We should talk, Ali, when you're ready."

"We heard about your appointment," Amin said. "We know you plan to relaunch Operation Ajax."

"That's not true," Weiseman told him, although he wished it was.

There was no response. Weiseman could hear clicks on the phone, counterpart to the field of static. Amin obviously knew his phone was tapped.

"And the Shah, he is . . ."

"Still in Marrakesh. We don't know his plans. He's told us nothing."

**SUNDAY, FEBRUARY 14.** Valentine's Day.

The Revolutionary Guards attacked the American embassy chancery in Tehran and the complex of employee apartments, taking many of the staff captive. Weiseman called Amin on the emergency number. Amin uttered what sounded like a curse in Farsi, then said, "The Revolutionary Guards will be the death of me."

That might just turn out to be true, Weiseman thought, but his task was to free those staffers. "Can you call the Ayatollah?" he asked. "You don't need this right after taking over."

He heard Amin suck in his breath. "The Imam is in Qom with Khalaji and Montana, contemplating our future. The RGs are closer to him than I am; they're like Mao's Red Guards."

This was no time for niceties, so Weiseman let him have it. He told Amin the way he handled this hostage taking would define the new regime. Amin promised to do his best—"But it may take time. You'll have to be patient."

"Let me give it to you straight, Ali. If any of our people are hurt, there will be a new Ajax."

Weiseman had no authority to say that, but it worked. Twenty-four hours later, the American hostages were freed. But it was warning enough to check on the dependents and nonessential employees, and the classified documents still there. The brief seizure convinced the embassy that it was time to draw down. US officials, always eager to avoid blame, quickly cleared the IMMEDIATE cable Weiseman drafted, instructing embassy offices to ship all but the most essential classified documents back to Washington within forty-eight hours.

Two days later, Weiseman boarded a flight across the Atlantic, heading back to Iran. At a stopover in Casablanca, an embassy officer handed him a cable from Trevor.

*Keep going: trouble in Tehran. Amin in hot water. The Shah's not coming stateside anytime soon.*

**A NIGHT LANDING** in Tehran. Everything was black, not just the sky, or the women's chadors and men's robes, but even the Alborz Mountains ringing Tehran on the north side veiled in heavy cloud cover. The country seemed to be drained of all color.

A diplomat had to sniff out what was hidden, the truths no one would tell him. Weiseman sensed that vividly now, as he experienced the omnipresent new police state taking charge—first in the airport, in the averted eyes, the excessive politeness and apologetic demands for his passport, then at the hotel, in the security man who awkwardly patted him down yet didn't miss an inch. Behind the reception desk of the hotel, Daud stood officiously, a sneer on his fat lips, no longer the bowing worm who couldn't do enough. On his lapel was the shiny new insignia of the Islamic Republic. Over his head, glaring out at Weiseman, was a portrait of Ruhollah Khomeini, proprietarily at ease where the portrait of Mohammad Reza Shah once hung.

It took eight calls for Weiseman to get through to a nervous sounding Ali Amin, who agreed to see him the next night at ten in a Tehran suburb.

Restless, Weiseman put on a polo shirt and dark pants, donned a warm jacket and wraparound sunglasses, and slipped down the hill to the main street where he purchased a ball cap. The perfumed smells of Persia surrounded him; he found them strangely seductive, awakening a belief in what this country could be. But the contrast with the waves of people in black was unnerving, bringing to mind Trevor's maxim about how people dressed to suit their political circumstances. Ordinary Iranians were seeking anonymity; they were hiding in plain sight.

Spotting a phone booth, Weiseman checked the card in his wallet and dialed Sammy's phone number. The phone rang a dozen times. Finally, a man picked up.

"I want to speak with Sammy," Weiseman managed in Farsi, then corrected himself. "Shapour."

"Dead," the man muttered in Farsi. "Shapour died."

Weiseman felt his chest tighten.

"Who is this? Who is calling?"

He hung up and moved swiftly down the street. Two big guys toting black batons stood just ahead, eyeing him closely. Looking away, Weiseman edged toward the side of the road and pretended to gaze at the snow-tipped mountain cliffs just barely visible through the smog.

Act like an Iranian, slouch a bit, stay calm. Tuck the cap down.

Okay. He pivoted to move forward and, suddenly, a woman was there, colliding into him. The niqab that covered her face must have obscured her view. Parcels in her hands tumbled to the ground and he bent to help her, his hand accidentally grazing hers.

She shrieked in Farsi, as if she had been violated.

"I'm sorry," he blurted out in English. "I was trying to help—"

The guys with the batons were on him, roughly dragging him to his feet. One of them pulled his arms behind his back and snapped on the cuffs. "Revolutionary Guards," the other one mumbled.

Montana's men, he thought. Stay calm. Speak in Farsi.

"I'm a guest of your government," Weiseman said, struggling not to betray his fear. "I was invited here by the Imam as a friend of Iran."

They looked at him suspiciously, then began to whisper to each other. The cuffs were cutting into his wrists; his hands were already numb.

He told himself, don't let on that you're American.

"I have an appointment with the Imam today, at 5:00 p.m."

They checked their watches, whispered together again. The guy who cuffed him came right up into his face, trying to read him through his eyes. There was spittle on his lips and food in his beard. He smelled like dirty socks; he clearly hadn't washed for days.

A streetcar clattered by and stopped near them.

His heart was pounding violently; he was sure they would drag him to a tiny, dirty cell in Evin Prison. He was claustrophobic, fearful that this time there would be no reprieve. "It's a misunderstanding," he said, aware that it wasn't what he said that mattered but the confidence and certainty that he could project to his captors. It was vital not to show fear. "The lady didn't see me. I was trying to help recover her parcels. I'm sincerely sorry."

The two RGs stared at him, contemplating their prize.

Keep talking, he warned himself. "The Imam will be deeply disturbed if I do not appear."

The mention of the Imam stirred them. The second guy said something abrupt, and the man who cuffed him swung him around. Weiseman smelled the rancid breath of the man who removed the cuffs.

"Thank you, brothers," Weiseman said, and he stepped away from them and climbed as casually as he could onto a nearby tram on the way to anywhere else.

**WEISEMAN RODE THE** streetcar for an hour, knowing he could be arrested at any time and tossed into Evin, into Montana's bloody hands, and no one would ever know.

He was in the part of South Tehran where Sammy and Alana had taken him before. The narrow streets were ominously quiet. The young hustlers he'd encountered the last time were absent; it seemed everyone thought it better to stay out of sight. He alighted from the tram and walked past brick buildings with shades drawn all the way down. It was as if the lively street scene he recalled was a figment of his imagination, as if this part of Tehran was a ghost town.

At the school, he pushed on the door and, to his amazement, it opened. He told himself he was a fool to be doing this, but he walked in led by some inner voice. A door opened and he heard a woman's voice. He headed that way, slowly, cautiously, and stepped into another dimly lit room where he saw the silhouette of a woman in a chador. Her niqab was lying on a nearby desk.

The woman unbuttoned her shroud, and he saw that it was Alana. A man walked out of the shadows. Weiseman was startled. "They said you were—"

Shapour smiled at him. "Dead. Yes, I know. Another associate named Shapour has been killed, and I've used that as a cover."

Weiseman turned back toward Alana. "You were with them in Paris."

"Yes, David. I had to find a way to get my father out. I managed to get in with the Ayatollah's people. It's a snake pit—"

"The Revolutionary Guards are patrolling the streets," Shapour interrupted. "Khalaji and Montana have created a Frankenstein. Only the Imam has the power to rein them in."

"They're seizing people's homes," Alana said. "Bullying professors, intimidating doctors and lawyers and shopkeepers. People are disappearing every day."

This is what Hitler's goons did, Weiseman thought, what all hoodlums do when they seize power. But now everything was happening faster than he had expected. He'd need to contact Sims, Colonel Yilmaz and Moshe Regev, and Seyyed. Jafar in Baghdad. And Françoise.

The best option now, Weiseman thought, would be to keep the mullahs off balance, lead them to make mistakes that would cause popular anger and thereby complicate the consolidation of their regime. That's what they wanted most. He wondered if it was possible to prevent it.

"The people," he said. "Do they understand they have to get out, before it's too late?"

"David," Alana said. "People never believe the worst, even when it's happening. Papa told me that before Hanif took him."

Like in Berlin in the thirties, he thought again. "And Khomeini. What does he say?"

"Mahmoud just called. He said the Imam is in Qom." Alana looked at him. "One day he'll speak to the world from his prayer mat, and then people will understand. It will be worse than with the Shah."

DEMORALIZED, WEISEMAN STAYED in his room at the hotel the next day, making calls, waiting until evening, when the car sent by Amin picked him up. The broad-shouldered bodyguard in the front seat had an oval shaped head with thinning gray hair and a bad case of dandruff. The hulking man gripped a large revolver while the driver, a young man in a blue blazer and open-necked pink shirt, twirled the dial of the car radio until he settled on rock music, gyrating and humming along with the songs.

They passed block after block of concrete apartment buildings on their way out of town, then skirted empty fields and dusty villages where stick-thin, shirtless children in tattered pants kicked soccer balls in vacant lots. Older people with pinched faces stood warily by the side of the road, eyeing the car suspiciously as it passed through their infinitesimal spot of the earth. After a half hour, the car stopped at another anonymous concrete block.

The bodyguard jumped out and opened Weiseman's door, pointing the gun at the building in front of them. "This way, brother," he snarled and marched off. Weiseman hustled to follow him, and they hurried up a half dozen stone steps to a small grocery shop, its doors shielded by steel bars. "This way," the bodyguard repeated, leading Weiseman into a stairwell beside the store, and they began climbing chipped stone steps to the second, then the third, and finally the fourth floor, where the man wrapped twice with the butt of his revolver on an unmarked stone door. After a moment, the door creaked open.

Amin, in a shabby tweed jacket, poked his head out the door; he was unshaven, distracted, looking around to see if anyone had followed them. He blinked, then led Weiseman across the linoleum floors to two chairs covered in gray cloth. Weiseman sat down in one, shifting around, trying to get comfortable. A loose spring dug into his hip.

Amin said, "They've sent thugs to staff the Foreign Ministry. They all curse America, though most of them can't find it on a map. Iran is the center of their universe."

Weiseman studied Amin—the white beard, the black-rimmed eyes struggling to keep open, the nervous tick in his right cheek. "Can you say where it's headed?" he asked.

"It's a mixed picture." He spoke without conviction. "The Imam inspires us all, but the RGs are out of control. They're beating up decent citizens who had nothing to do with the Shah. Executions have started . . .

by stoning . . . by firing squads. Lashing women falsely accused of prostitution. Banning Western music. We now have our own religious police, the Gasht-e Ershad, or Guidance Patrol, patrolling the universities, enforcing the veil . . . even the niqab and chador. RGs are filling the cells at Evin Prison. A wholesale purge is underway, intimidating the people. Anyone who's ever been to the palace is likely to disappear."

"And the government?"

"It's a floating circus of ayatollahs and ministers, lesser mullahs and intellectuals like me, surrounded by lots of charlatans. New characters emerge every day. Two new ones maneuvering for power now—Abolhassan Bani-Sadr and Sadegh Ghotbzadeh, petty intellectuals on the make politically, trying to enrich themselves." Amin paused and made a shrug of resignation. "We Iranians specialize in pretense, so it's hard to tell the patriots from the frauds. We all have a little bit of chicanery in our souls."

Amen to that, Weiseman thought, and then he remembered: *Taarof.*

"And the new prime minister?" he asked. "The one I met? I hear he's an honorable man."

"Yes, I suppose so, but the spies are everywhere. It's why we're meeting out here."

Amin got up and went into the dismal kitchen. He drifted back after five minutes or so with two gray ceramic cups of hot coffee. There was a circle of foam from not stirring it enough.

"Are you going to be all right?" Weiseman asked.

Amin cleared his throat. "I don't know, but after a half century of the Shah and his father, we have to try. I still see the Imam, occasionally; he's out in Qom with his palace guard."

Weiseman could see in his face that, despite the brave talk, he was resigned to failure.

Amin stared hard back at him for a moment with bloodshot eyes. "You know, I took a big risk for you, getting your people out on Valentine's Day."

"Yes. I understand that."

Amin held his gaze. "I'm going to need your help in return one day."

"Of course." He's already thinking about his escape, Weiseman thought. But getting people out the way Johann got him out was already a priority for Weiseman. "It's the least I can do."

Amin pulled a pack of cigarettes from his pocket and roughly shook one out. Lighting it quickly and dragging heavily, he coughed, then began hacking and put it down to wipe tears from his eyes.

"Didn't your people understand?" he asked gravely when he'd recovered. "The Imam was sure America would never allow the revolution to win. He told me, 'Our oil is for America like water is for human life.' They sent you Sheikh Khalaji to judge that for himself. He told us America was strong but lacked the will to stop the revolution. And, of course, Montana is relishing his job as the new chief executioner."

It was the same story Weiseman had learned from his father—that weakness in the face of aggression always invites far worse violence.

"We'll meet again," he said, wondering how long Amin would survive. He remembered the old adage that a revolution will devour its children . . .

"Oh, yes, David, the Shah . . ."

"I'm going there next," Weiseman said, standing, ready to go.

The door opened from the outside, and the big guy pointed the gun. "This way, brother."

## 27

# THE FLYING DUTCHMAN

**U**NDER THE MOROCCAN sun baking Rabat, Weiseman was ushered through a cluster of redbrick buildings in the government center and into the Royal Palace. Two guards in resplendent white uniforms stood at attention, gold shoulder tassels floating above curved swords set against the blue stripes down their legs. He entered an office marked Minister Eli Cohen.

Inside, a tan, trim man in his midfifties extended his hand. He wore a tropical gray double-breasted silk suit, a crisp white shirt with a spread collar, and a blue tie with powder blue doves. His hair was parted in the middle, perhaps reflecting his challenge in playing both sides of the road—Arab and Jew.

"We've been following your itinerary," Eli Cohen said. "Bienvenue."

The inner office was decorated with Persian carpets and autographed photographs from King Hassan, from Egypt's Sadat, from Shimon Peres of Israel, and from a younger shah of Iran. The message was clear: Eli Cohen was a man of standing in this part of the world.

"You know them all," Weiseman said, his eyes taking the tour of the testimonials.

"For a Jew, you mean. Actually, it's less unusual than you might think. The Arabs were humiliated by the 1948 war and the creation of the State of Israel, what the Palestinians call *Nakba*, the calamity. Arab states raised hell in the UN, but now most of them don't really give a damn. And they turn to us the way Europeans did for centuries, the French and English with the house of Rothschild, Bismarck with his banker Bleichröder . . . between pogroms, of course."

"Come over here," Eli Cohen said. He led Weiseman to the picture window, then pointed to an office across the way. Curtains blocked their view of the interior. "That's His Majesty's office. My brother Binyamin is his economic advisor. My role is to assure the King's security. He has never once mentioned my faith to me. He receives Shimon cordially when I bring him here. One day, please God, the king of Morocco will help mediate a peace between Palestinians and Israelis."

Cohen smiled and poured two glasses of schnapps.

*"Insha'allah,"* Weiseman said.

*"Le Chaim,"* Cohen said, and they clinked glasses. He motioned Weiseman to sit, then he got down to business.

"The former shah has been His Majesty's honored guest for a month, just an hour from here in a seaside villa near Marrakesh. Every day I receive Arab ambassadors protesting his presence. It's becoming uncomfortable, David."

"I see."

"We have a Red Crescent doctor, a specialist in what ails the Shah. She tells us that the Shah needs urgent treatment in a facility that exceeds our modest capabilities. There is a demon inside that is eating away at him."

Eli Cohen lit a cigar. He blew smoke rings toward the picture window. They hung in midair against the window a moment, drawing Weiseman's attention to two boys outside tossing a Frisbee across the Royal Palace grounds.

In the end, it always comes to this, Weiseman thought: a hard decision, innocent children. "Of course, you're right," he said. "The president is deeply grateful to His Majesty."

Another smoke ring floated from Cohen's mouth. The Frisbee arched toward the picture window, and a skinny boy wearing a red fez with a gold tassel leapt into the air and snatched it just before it struck the window.

"Of course, we're not asking him to leave at once," Cohen said. "Arabs are not like that. His Majesty is very hospitable." Another puff. "But soon."

"Actually, Eli, we think your Moroccan sun has done all it can. I'll take it up tomorrow."

**THE SHAH RESISTED,** partly out of lethargy, but more out of reluctance to cross the Atlantic, as if taking that fateful step would end his last forlorn chance to reclaim his throne.

The real problem, however, lay in Washington. Trevor told Weiseman that the White House thought the question of treatment in New York was behind them. The president had cracked privately to Trevor that he didn't want to put our embassy people at risk again while the Shah "played tennis in Forest Hills." Ali Amin sent Weiseman a message that treating the Shah in America would inflame the radical mullahs he was attempting to placate. Meanwhile, the Shah's powerful American friends warned the White House that the Shah would die due to American hard-heartedness, consigning him to circle the globe seeking refuge, like Wagner's Flying Dutchman.

In the last week of March, Eli Cohen slipped into Washington and called on Justin Trevor. Weiseman, in attendance, listened to Cohen say it was time for the king's guest to depart by the end of the month, and for the world's bastion of liberty to let him in.

Trevor stalled until Cohen gave him the report of the Red Crescent doctor, who said the cancer had progressed beyond treatment Morocco could provide. America's national security and diplomatic teams went into action, searching for a place to relocate the Shah. Appeals were made to foreign leaders to consider their humanitarian obligations. A budget was set aside and USAID grants, long in abeyance, suddenly were approved. Money changed hands.

On March 30, 1979, a Royal Air Maroc executive jet carrying the Pahlavis set down in Kingston, on the Caribbean island of Jamaica.

But nothing lasts forever. The day before Memorial Day, a hot precursor to the steamy Washington summer, the Jamaican ambassador came to call on Weiseman at his State Department office. The ambassador was a slender man with a neatly trimmed mustache who barely filled out a nicely cut two-button suit. His manners were impeccable, but his message was predictable.

"My PM was happy to be of service when Mrs. Thatcher called him from London." A coy smile signaled that his government knew the United States had put the Brits up to it. "But, you see, Mr. Ambassador, our Arab friends . . ." And then Weiseman barely paid attention; he could have composed the talking points himself from the script Eli Cohen had proclaimed to him only two months earlier.

Fortunately, the US embassy in Kingston had alerted Washington to what was coming. The Shah's villa on the Caribbean was exposed to tourists, to gun runners and drug pushers. *Narco-trafficantés* from Columbia and Venezuela, the embassy warned, liked to stop in Jamaica for R & R between jobs. Kidnapping the Shah of Iran would be an irresistible temptation. Best to move him at once, the embassy advised.

The State Department's European bureau had a notion about the Azores, just off Portugal, but Trevor quashed that idea. "Keep him on this side of the Atlantic," he insisted. "Try Mexico."

So another deal was done. Intractable trade problems between Mexico and the United States were suddenly resolved, and the United States boosted its purchase of Mexican oil. The president decided the time was ripe for a state visit south of the border, where he delivered the memorable phrase that his sick stomach was due to Montezuma's revenge. Mexican nationalists vented outrage, but no matter. The Palace pocketed the cash, and Mexico's president welcomed Mohammad Reza with open arms.

On June 10, the Shah and his wife moved into yet another villa, this time in Cuernavaca, their fourth since leaving Tehran in mid-January. Weiseman had a team of Navy Seals and CIA agents visit the site to guarantee security. The day after they arrived, the Shah's personal physician called Weiseman to let him know that the Shah's health was deteriorating. He took that report to Trevor, who confided that the White House didn't want to hear it. Members of Congress wouldn't tolerate the Shah coming to New York just now. A point Ali Amin drove home in their weekly phone call.

"Keep him moving, David, away from the US. Your presidential election is seventeen months away. Don't you have enough problems?"


THE WASHINGTON SUMMER brought more calls from the Shah's doctors saying the time was at hand for the Shah to go to Sloan Kettering. But no US officials were available to answer those pleas—the president was on holiday in the Florida Keys, not to be disturbed, while Trevor had taken Clarissa for a thirty-fifth anniversary holiday in a Palermo palazzo. Justin, Weiseman thought, would relish Mafia hospitality.

He heard from Françoise that she was coming to Washington on business and he arranged to visit her. It would be their first time together since their tense encounter at Villa Schreiber. She had been true to her word, providing valuable intelligence on the ayatollahs, working with Alain de Rose to checkmate Gramont, and coordinating with Yasmine and Alana's teams to arrange small acts of sabotage in Tehran.

He met her at Dulles and told her that an urgent request had arrived from the Shah's doctors that he visit Mexico. The trip would provide a chance to assess the Shah's health and to convince the Mexicans to extend his stay. As well, it had occurred to him that they could be alone for a few days at the Mexican resort. Would she like to come?

They flew first to Mexico City, where he was received formally by diplomats at the Foreign Ministry and with ineffable politeness by presidential aides in the palace on the Zócalo. He thanked them for their hospitality to the Shah and listened carefully to gauge how much longer the Mexicans would allow the Shah to stay.

Well, they told him, he's only been here two months. But of course, there are still some matters to be sorted out.

Translation: you want him to stay in our country; don't forget the rental payments due us.

While he waited for instructions, Weiseman and Françoise spent the weekend together. The first morning they walked from Chapultepec Park to the zoo, taking in the massive expanse of the park where the rich enjoyed their leisure hours and the poor fought their daily battles for survival. Coming out of the park, Françoise saw a young woman playing "The Devil's Trill" on the violin. When it was over, Françoise went to the woman, quietly placed a ten dollar bill in the open violin case, and began to speak with the woman in fluent Spanish. He had not known she spoke Spanish.

He asked what she had said to the young woman. "I told her that I took violin lessons as a girl but I gave it up, that I didn't want her to make that mistake. I wanted to give her hope."

They dined alfresco in a small café in the Zona Rosa, and the tensions of the past frantic months gave way to a nimbus of romantic banter. They ate a platter of red and green enchiladas, quesadillas and mole, and sipped a specialty cocktail with two straws, while they were serenaded by a handsome Mexican caballero.

They emerged from the café under a full moon to see a boy of three or four sipping foul water from a filthy puddle on the Paseo de la Reforma. Along the paseo, prostitutes with heavily rouged faces, short skirts, and platform shoes plied their trade with obese norteamericanos, while skinny pimps in tight suits and slicked-down hair, cigarette butts teetering from their lips, stood guard over their assets.

Around the corner from the hotel, they saw a man brandishing a gun at a well-dressed Mexican woman. "Wait here," Weiseman said. He strode straight ahead, slipped up behind the gunman and twisted his arm behind his back. A karate chop sent the weapon flying to the side of the road. The man ran off into the dark night.

"Señor, how can I thank you," the woman said, embracing him, and then Françoise.

"He's a good man," Françoise said to the woman. She turned to Weiseman and took his arm. "It really matters when you don't need to do it."

On Monday, they went on to Cuernavaca, a resort town southwest of Mexico City known for its silver mines, and proceeded to the Shah's complex. There was no hint of the Shah to be seen anywhere. Outside the gate to his hideaway, a guard pointed to the large walled villa. "He sleeps quite a lot these days."


**THE NEXT MORNING,** reality returned. Françoise received a call.

"It was Laurent," she said. "A reign of terror has broken out in Tehran. A political purge is underway, women are demonstrating, being beaten by RGs, universities being shut down."

Moments later, as if coordinated, Trevor phoned. "You've got to go back. Tell Amin and whoever else you can reach that we've got to take him in, for a short while. Tell them he's a dead man. Tell them that we can do business with them."

Trevor paused. Weiseman heard him try to suppress a telltale cough. "Tell your friend Amin that Laurent agrees."

At the airport the next day, she told him, "The cells at Evin Prison are worse than anybody knows."

Weiseman's memory called up the image of Montana dangling a roll of film in midair, fixing him with a menacing glare.

"Promise me," she insisted, "you will be prudent."

He handed her a three-by-five card with a code word to upgrade their communication and scramble their telephone and cable communications so they could speak securely. Then he headed down the ramp toward the plane.

## 28

# *REIGN OF TERROR*

**T**HE FLIGHT ACROSS the Atlantic and, after a four-hour wait in
Heathrow's Mideast lounge, the miserable connecting flight delivered Weiseman across eight and a half time zones. He was tense
from the moment he set foot in Mehrabad. Everywhere around him he
saw the suspicious stares of shop merchants and baggage handlers. With
his only bag on his right shoulder, he strolled as casually as he could
through the Nothing to Declare channel.

A hand grabbed his arm. A skinny bearded man said, "This way,
brother. Your bag."

"Diplomat," he said reflexively, and flashed his black passport.

The man said, "In the Islamic Republic, brother, everyone is equal," and he nudged him forward. And then they took his bag apart, removing all the contents and picking at them meticulously. They turned socks inside out, one by one. They emptied his toothpaste tube into a rubber vat. They ordered him to remove his shoes and then pried off the heels.

"Checking for microfilm," the skinny bearded man said smugly. "This way, brother."

Two stocky Revolutionary Guards pushed him roughly into a small room where a third man with yellow teeth and dirty finger nails gave him the most thorough and disgusting pat down he'd ever experienced. When it was done, he was ordered to disrobe, down to his undershorts. The dirty digits resumed their filthy, invasive journey; they pulled down his shorts and probed, while the other two RGs stared. He wanted to strangle the guy, but he knew that any move would mean a one-way trip to Evin Prison.

When they were done, the three men walked out of the room, leaving his clothes and the contents of his luggage in a shambles. He dressed quickly, managed to hammer his heels back on, and repacked his bag.

He waited a few minutes, controlling his rage, then gingerly opened the squeaky door and poked his head out. He saw the three men leading another foreigner toward a doorway down the corridor. He picked up his bag and slipped quietly back into the Nothing to Declare channel, through the automatic doors, and into the airport terminal. Anxious to get out, he strode past the fortune-tellers, by men offering taxis to town, beneath Ayatollah Khomeini's ominous glare.

Outside the terminal, he hurried toward the waiting Ford, but Sammy wasn't behind the wheel. And there was a woman in the back seat. Weiseman got in the front passenger seat, and the driver steered the car out of the airport toward the highway. The woman in the back seat pulled off her niqab. It was Alana. "Everything is okay," she said. "Everything is okay."

But everything wasn't okay. Shapour, Alana told him, was in Evin, packed into a tiny crowded cell next to his father's.

"Give me the details," he said. "Perhaps Amin can help."

"David, Ali Amin will be lucky if he doesn't end up in Evin himself."

The driver swerved to the edge of the road. On a billboard above them, Khomeini was seated on his prayer mat in Qom, with Sheikh Khalaji hovering behind him.

"They have an Islamic police force now," Alana said nervously. "The Sheikh runs it." And before he could ask, "Montana runs Evin."

An Islamist SAVAK, he thought. Evil remains the same, only its costume changes.

TREVOR'S INSTRUCTIONS WERE clear, although the means for enacting them weren't: *Tell the mullahs we've got to take him in. Tell them we can do business with them.*

On a hot summer day later that week, Weiseman was squeezed between two Revolutionary Guards in the back seat of an ancient Chevrolet convertible as it bumped down a potholed road. When he'd gotten in the car, one of them—a skinny bearded RG called Nejab, pressed against him, thigh to thigh—had pulled a green handkerchief from his pocket and tied it tightly around Weiseman's eyes. The swirling dust from open windows caused him to gag. The car bumped along.

It was a more harrowing reprise of his earlier kidnapping to Amin's farmhouse. The trip seemed endless, with the dust and the sweaty men on either side of him.

He heard the men swigging beer, and it made them seem all the more ominous to him. After all, Muslims don't drink alcohol. These men were more like mercenaries, with no moral code save violence. Still, it reminded him of his thirst, and he asked for a drink. Nejab slammed the bottle against Weiseman's knee, and a sharp pain shot down his leg. The car stopped and Nejab got out. Weiseman heard and smelled the trickle of urine against the road.

Time went by. The Chevy bounced down the riven road. Finally, the driver mumbled and pulled over. The pressure of the RG's thigh on Weiseman's evaporated. The car door opened on his side and Nejab pushed him out. A pair of hands untied the handkerchief covering his eyes. He blinked in the sharp sunlight and pushed out his chest, forcing himself to stand tall.

His sight was still blurry, but he drew in the scent of a woman in front of him. Amazed, he blinked again, distrusting his eyes. A chador and a black headscarf covered all but her face.

She must have followed him to Tehran, taken the next flight, there for him again.

"Justin Trevor called Laurent," Françoise said in a tight whisper. "I've spoken to the Imam." Her voice was tremulous, her body tense. "You must be very prudent here."

The two RGs led him around her and up the steps of the modest two-story, wooden building. He recalled what Yasmine had said about Montana's threat to kill her. He turned and saw Françoise led away, to another filthy car between two other RGs.

Someone pushed him inside the building. He walked slowly down a hallway, telling himself to focus.

A door opened. He heard Sheikh Khalaji's voice. "The American is here, Imam."

He tried to recall Trevor's instructions, which were not to be exceeded: *Probe gently. See if you can find a way to work with them.*

Justin had been quite clear. Things were always clear in Washington. But this was Qom—the Ayatollah's house. He turned around, expecting Montana to appear behind him.

"Come," the Sheikh said, and Weiseman walked in slowly. He heard the door close behind him and turned to see that the RGs remained in the corridor, and the Sheikh was gone. Weiseman was alone with the holy man sitting cross-legged on a simple prayer mat, only a sole bearded man sitting nearby to translate.

The Ayatollah sat, taking no notice of Weiseman. With his head down and his eyes tightly shut, he seemed deep in prayer, a mystic in touch with another world, not to be swayed by the kind of diplomatically turned, polished phrases Trevor had sent him to deliver. Khomeini had his own agenda. Above all, he must be thinking of the new Islamic Republic and how it could survive. In fact, for the Ayatollah there would be no distinction between this world and any spiritual world. The rules of one would be the rules of the other.

The priest stirred.

"So," he said in Farsi, "what message do you bring us from the Great Satan?"

Weiseman decided to forgo Trevor's talking points. They had no meaning in this place.

"We are not destined to be friends, Imam."

Khomeini held his gaze. "So it is," he said in a soft voice.

Follow his lead, Weiseman thought. Use his archaic language.

"So be it," he confirmed. "But there is a corridor of common interest, for your survival, for us to maintain our presence here. To conduct normal relations, as normal as possible."

"And Pahlavi?" Khomeini asked, his voice barely audible.

"Imam, he is very ill. He's tied up to medical machines, unable to travel."

"Then it's up to you, everything that will happen."

Weiseman stared into the fiery eyes, knowing Khomeini wasn't interested in any excuses, reasonable or otherwise. This was a man not accustomed or inclined to negotiate, but rather a religious fanatic issuing an edict, and expecting it to be obeyed. He wanted the Shah and his fortune, and the United States was not about to give him that. But surely he wanted to survive, too.

"Imam," Weiseman began, "in both of our countries, there are those seeking a confrontation between us. Influential voices, persistent people. It would be best to avoid—"

Khomeini's eyes opened widely at the cold threat to his survival. Startled, he began to cough. The door opened and Montana was there, but the Ayatollah waved him off. The door closed. Khomeini stared silently at Weiseman.

Weiseman told himself the vital point had been made, giving Khomeini something to think about. Piling on now would be counterproductive . . . and Montana was on the other side of that door.

But there were many lives at stake.

Try it, Weiseman thought. Two lives are more important than impossible dreams.

"Imam, there are two innocents locked up in Evin. Hosein Hanif put a man there. The Revolutionary Guards have arrested his son. I ask you to release them, as an act of mercy."

Khomeini's face was entirely immobile. "And Pahlavi?" he repeated.

"I saw the Shah in Mexico, Imam. He will die soon. If he comes to New York, it will be only for an instant."

The Ayatollah seemed to stir a moment, his eyes darted back and forth, as if in thought. Then he slowly raised his right hand to end the interview, and said mystically, "So be it," leaving Weiseman in the dark regarding his intentions.


**FRANÇOISE WASN'T THERE** when the RGs bundled him again into the back seat of the car between them. They kept the blindfold on and his wrists bound all the way back to Tehran. Two hours. His hands ached; the dust forced him to cough. He asked for water.

Nejab said, "This is not an American tavern, brother."

When the car finally stopped, both men gripped Weiseman's upper arms like steel hooks hauling a side of beef and dragged him out of the car and up a flight of metal steps. At the top, they undid his wrists and pulled off the blindfold. He shook his arms, blinked into flashing fluorescent lights, and then saw beneath him row after row of tiny cells.

Evin Prison.

They frog-marched him up four more flights of metal stairs, his legs buckling under him. At the top of the stairs, they reached a door and one of the RGs pushed it open. Seated at Hanif's old desk was Guido Montana; the sign on his desk now announcing his true name: HAMID FAZLI.

Weiseman tried to steel himself, not knowing if he was destined for the cell that Françoise had warned him about.

"Come in, Mr. Weiseman. The Imam has instructed me to tell you about the release of the two men you inquired about."

"When can I see them?" he asked warily, aware that he was in Montana's power, but knowing he had to try. He couldn't let them rot there.

"Why not now? Right away, in fact. Come with me."

"There's also a woman, a prisoner of the Shah," Weiseman said. "Hanif killed her father and raped her mother. There's no reason for her to be your prisoner. She supports the revolution. Her name is Hannah Wiecorzek."

"I'll check on this," Montana said. He went to a steel safe near his desk. A moment passed. A second drawer opened. He studied a dossier. Finally, he said, "Yes, the prisoner is in cellblock 293. She's not on our list; you can have her." He picked up the phone and barked something indecipherable in Farsi before hanging up. "Now, let's hurry along."

Montana led Weiseman back down the stairs, to the ground floor, out a steel door, and into a dusty yard. He saw Shapour across the yard, next to an older man who must be his father.

A woman was being led out, in a chador and blue jeans barely visible above her tennis shoes. It was Alana. RGs placed her between her father and brother.

"In a moment, Mr. Weiseman, we will release these counterrevolutionaries into your custody. But first we will release them into the custody of Allah."

A voice barked out an order. Seven soldiers clambered through a steel door.

"No!" Weiseman screamed. He ran at full speed toward Alana.

Two huge men intercepted him. Four soldiers aimed their rifles across the yard.

*"Long live Iran!"* shouted the father, then Shapour and Alana.

There was a sharp command, followed immediately by a deafening volley of shots. The three prisoners jerked and twisted as if in some sick puppet show, then crumpled to the ground.

Blood stained the wall and the dust beneath their bodies.

A soldier marched across the yard and fired a single bullet into each head.

Weiseman turned away and vomited in the dust.

Montana said, "Now you, Weiseman. You will be escorted back to Mehrabad. Don't come back to Iran again, or you'll have a very special place on that same wall."

## 29

# AFTER THE WALL

NEXPLICABLY, MONTANA HAD released Hannah. She was with Weiseman on the plane to Paris, vowing to return to Iran and avenge Alana's murder.

Weiseman was relieved by her release, but all the way to Paris the vision of the crumpled bodies tormented him and kept him awake despite his exhaustion. He told himself he should have been able to save Alana and Sammy and their father. He blamed himself for waiting too long to launch Ajax Two. He knew it would take a generation or more before the mullahs were gone and the reign of terror would give way, as it eventually did following the French Revolution, to a return to sanity, to an Iranian Thermidor . . .

Weiseman called Françoise from Orly Airport. There was no answer at the Villa Schreiber or at her number at *Le Figaro*. Alarmed, he took a cab directly to Gramont's residence. Laurent was out, but Margot Gramont—gasping at the sight of him—offered him a place to rest.

When he awoke four hours later, she gave him the address of an apartment in the sixteenth arrondissement.


**FRANÇOISE TOOK HIM** in and they stayed together in the apartment for days, explaining to each other how they'd gotten out of Iran, trying to exorcise demons that wouldn't be exorcised. She told him she had gone back to Qom against Laurent's orders, because he was there.

A week passed before Trevor called him.

Trevor uttered not a word about Weiseman's absence, nor about what had happened on his trip, except to say, "I'm glad you're safe."

"Thank you."

Then, quietly, "The Shah's health has deteriorated further. We have to face that. You need to handle this; no one else has the Shah's confidence."


**WEISEMAN RETURNED TO MEXICO.** A State Department doctor joined him to cross-examine the Shah's doctors, to confirm that the illness was as grave as they claimed. It was.

It was time to take the Shah to New York.

The Mexicans, clearly relieved that the Shah was leaving, assured Weiseman with practiced smiles that they would, of course, be more than willing to take the Shah back, after New York, if the president asked them to do so.

Weiseman flew back to Washington for the showdown.

He headed directly into back-to-back meetings in the State Department and Pentagon, where officials argued against allowing the Shah into the United States. They warned that the mullahs would take revenge, putting American diplomats in Tehran at risk. Bobby Beauford thundered about political risks to the president just to save a reviled former dictator.

On October 21, Justin Trevor summoned Weiseman and asked for his recommendation.

"If we don't let him in," Weiseman said, "the president will be blamed for his death."

"And the consequences of that?" Trevor asked.

"Justin, we ordered the embassy to draw down its personnel months ago, to burn most of the classified documents. We have aircraft at our Italian base in Aviano, ready to go in and bring out the rest of our people, if necessary."

Trevor studied the medical report, an index finger moving across every word of every line. *Lymphoma, a cancer of the lymph system that resembles leukemia . . . the lymph nodes had become painful and swollen . . .*

"Damn!" Trevor said, his icy anger seeping to the surface. Weiseman knew he hated the very idea of the Shah coming to America.

Then he said, "All right. Do it."

**THE NEXT DAY,** October 22, 1979, Mohammad Reza Pahlavi arrived in New York and was taken directly to Sloan Kettering. Françoise had flown in and met Weiseman there to greet the Shah and the Empress. Farah appeared first, struggling to maintain control. She embraced Françoise. *"Chère cousine."*

The Shah walked by, stiffly, wordlessly, as if desperate to guard some measure of his shredded dignity.

Weiseman watched the Shah disappear behind whitewashed doors that closed him off from the outside world, the way Sir Reader Bullard made the Shah's father vanish to distant South Africa forty years earlier. This time, it was too late to do the one thing that might provide a measure of solace for the newly ousted shah: to place *his* son on the Peacock Throne.

Weiseman stared at the now locked antiseptic white doors. He had a premonition that the Iranian people were entering a dark room, and there was no way to predict how long before they would be let out.

## 30

# RETRIBUTION

T HE STATE DEPARTMENT Operations Center called exactly two weeks after the Shah arrived in New York. It was 7:00 a.m. on a Sunday, November 4, 1979, a working day in Tehran. Françoise was back in Paris.

Weiseman knew immediately that something was amiss. The Operations Center only called on weekends when there was a crisis.

They told him to switch on his TV, and it took him a moment to understand what he was looking at: American diplomats being led across the embassy courtyard in blindfolds, hands bound behind their backs. Screaming students—an announcer's voice estimated the mob so far at three thousand—were still pouring over the outer walls of the embassy compound, shouting *Death to America!* and locking the gates from inside, forcing their way into the chancery. It was the nightmare scenario.

Weiseman dressed quickly.

An hour later he was in his office on the seventh floor of the State Department. Suddenly there was no news except the hostages. Nothing else mattered: not the Russians, not the Middle East, not the energy crisis, not the ravaged US economy and double-digit inflation.

The president would be fixated on this challenge, Weiseman knew. Both Carter's Christian concern for the hostages and his political instincts would impel him to focus on bringing his diplomats home. Whenever there was a great national crisis—World War II, the Berlin airlift, the Cuban missile crisis, the Vietnam War—presidential attention became completely gripped by the emergency.

Weiseman called Trevor, but the emergency number rang off the hook. He phoned the Iranian Foreign Ministry, and a nervous-sounding Amin picked up on the first ring. It would work out just like the Valentine Day episode, Amin assured him: the students were off on a lark; it was no more than a student sit-in at a US university. They'd be back to classes in a few days.

A White House secretary called to invite him to a noon meeting in the Situation Room. When he got there, he found himself surrounded by the entire National Security Council: the vice president; the secretary of state; the secretary of defense; the secretary of the treasury; the national security advisor; the chairman of the joint chiefs of staff; and the director of central intelligence, Justin Trevor.

Weiseman took a seat along the wall behind them. There was an eerie hush in the room.

The president strode in and everyone rose. He was dressed in a dark suit, white shirt, and sober black tie, a miniature American flag pin newly affixed to his lapel. He took his seat at the head of the table and motioned for everyone to be seated, then caught Weiseman's eye.

"Join us, David, we're going to be depending on you."

They proceeded to pick his brain clean, demanding to know everything he'd learned in dealing with the Iranians. Most urgently, they wanted his assessment of Khomeini. Was he crazy, an unguided missile? Would he do a deal? Would the army be with us if we intervene? What do we do if one of our people are killed?

These powerful men were angry, determined to do something. The agenda was formidable: military, economic, and financial sanctions; legal and political items; Congress and the UN. Assignments were made: contingency papers to be prepared, first drafts Friday.

"The carrier Midway is in the Indian Ocean en route to a port of call in Mombasa," the JCS chairman said. "I sent the captain a signal: divert to the Gulf, the Strait of Hormuz."

Bobby Beauford piped up. "We need to send an emissary to Iran."

It was Kabuki—a shadow play where all the actors dutifully played their parts.

Carter was running the national security apparatus like the engineer he was, but they were dealing with an ayatollah whose perspective might as well have been shaped on another planet. Khomeini didn't want a compromise. America was the Great Satan, and God's agent didn't compromise with Satan.

Trevor had told Weiseman never to say anything important in a room with more than two people in it: you and the person that mattered. Here, however, it was different. He needed to get across every nuance of the situation so the president could make the right choices.

"And the Shah?" Carter asked.

"He's still seriously ill, Mr. President."

"And how do you see it?" one of the gray suits asked.

"Sir, the Ayatollah is afraid the revolution will be stillborn. The hostages are his foreign devils, a tool to unite the nation behind his regime, to deter us from sending in the Marines."

"Go on," Carter said, barely audibly.

"It's not going to be fast. Khomeini won't let them out till they've served his purpose. I think we need to stay cool and, above all, do no harm." Weiseman paused.

"Or?"

"Or we go in and take our people out. We commit the necessary forces and do it right."

Silence. "And the Shah?" Carter asked again.

"That's what Khomeini kept asking when I saw him in Qom. I called New York an hour ago, sir. I spoke to his doctor and to Farah. He has tubes in his body now. His doctors think it will be four to five weeks before it's safe for him to travel."

"By that time," came the voice from the head of the table, "all our people could be dead, maybe one at a time, maybe all at once."

The president allowed the discussion to go on for almost two hours, then asked two questions. "What do we do if the hostages are harmed? What do we do if Iran disintegrates into some kind of civil war?" He didn't wait for answers. He told them to staff those questions, then rose from the table and, head down, deep in thought, strode out of the Sit-Room.

Weiseman heard the defense secretary say he wanted pinpoint military options prepared in case they killed any hostages, and then the secretary hurried after the president into the Oval Office. Weiseman was dumbstruck: "pinpoint military options" *after* they killed hostages!

ON MONDAY THE FIFTH, Weiseman snapped on his office TV, and the images plunged him into deep gloom. Nejab, the RG who had treated him so roughly on the car ride to Qom, was at the head of a line of Revolutionary Guards parading the hostages in blindfolds and manacles and pointy dunce caps in front of the cameras, letting the world know that the mighty United States was a paper tiger, helpless to free its diplomats. Students waved classified American cables before the international press and accused America of plotting a preemptive coup to stop the mullahs from seizing power.

Weiseman froze. *Classified documents.* They were supposed to have been returned to Washington months ago, he thought, with the few essential documents that remained to have been burned in a crisis. He bolted out of his seventh floor office and ran down two floors to the Iran desk officer. On the man's wall was a framed photograph of Ayatollah Khomeini, and next to it a poster of the Shah with a bright diagonal red line through it.

"Yes, sir," the official said. "We did recall the documents. So did DOD and CIA. But things were quiet after that, so we agreed to send them back. We couldn't know . . ."

Weiseman left the desk officer in midsentence, cursing his incompetence, and hurried back to his office. He decided to try the obvious, most unlikely thing. He picked up the phone and dialed the embassy in Tehran, and amazingly, after two rings, someone picked up.

"Den of spies," said a young, high-pitched voice, speaking in Farsi.

He asked for Chris Tyler, a young diplomat who had worked for him earlier before being sent to Tehran. "Tyler is unavailable," the voice said. "He will be unavailable for some time. Don't call back."

Then the voice broke into peels of laughter, and the line went dead.

The embassy was under the control of the RGs and students ready to carry out the Ayatollah's every wish. Weiseman turned back to the TV and saw RGs making provocative statements from their embassy command post, followed by dutiful reports of White House bulletins. Empty words flew back and forth across the earth.

His secretary buzzed him on the intercom and said the father of one of the hostages was on the phone. That meant the White House had given the families his name. He knew it would be the first of hundreds of calls. The press would be next.

He picked up the phone and heard Roger Tyler's choked voice. "Mr. Weiseman, you were my son's boss. When are you going to get Chris out?" In the background, he could hear a woman alternately weeping and telling her husband what else to ask. But Weiseman had no answer for them, saying only that he would do his best, and that they should feel free to call him again.

His secretary buzzed again. The French ambassador had arrived. He had forgotten the appointment and hurried out to welcome Jean Pascal.

The ambassador wasted no time coming to the point. "Laurent Gramont has asked me to speak with you."

Words direct from the spymaster, Weiseman thought, to be passed on to Trevor and Carter.

"Do something," the ambassador said, "or do nothing."

"I beg your pardon."

"Either send in the Marines, or show indifference until they get bored and let your people go. But don't agonize in public. If you convince them they have a trump card with the hostages, they'll hold on to them a long time."

"And France," Weiseman asked. "What will your government do to help?"

The ambassador rolled his eyes. "Monsieur Weiseman, the issue is not the hostages. They'll be sent back to you in due course, once Khomeini consolidates his authority. The issue is, well, you know my language, *l'absence des États-Unis dans le monde.* The absence of the United States in the world. That's dangerous. The Kremlin sees you are distracted and will exploit that. They can do a lot of damage while you dither over your precious diplomats."

*Your precious diplomats.* Weiseman forced himself to remain calm.

But wasn't he right? For Khomeini, the hostages were strictly an instrument of leverage. And yet, Nejab and the RGs were in there with the hostages, with no one restraining them

His secretary came in and handed him an urgent cable. One of the hostages had signed a confession confirming that the embassy was a "den of spies." The text was written in poor English, obviously by one of the RGs; the signature was a nearly illegible scrawl. God alone only knew what had been done to the poor bastard before he dragged his pen across the page.


IN TREVOR'S L-SHAPED office, an aide inserted a videotape into the player and then slipped out of the office. Images of students climbing over the barriers around the US embassy appeared on the large screen. A young mullah followed them over, and his turban fell off. Following images showed him speaking to the students, who pumped their fists in the air.

"It's Ahmed Khomeini," Trevor said. "The Ayatollah's son. Get it?"

Of course. The Ayatollah may not have ordered the hostage taking, but later, when he considered it useful, he had tendered his blessings to the invaders. Now everything would play out according to his script. The Shah, the diplomats, the students are pawns in his revolution.

Trevor got up and refilled his teacup. "For you, David? With sugar and lemon, I recall."

Weiseman nodded. Trevor said, "We've double-checked the embassy roster; there are fifty-four hostages in all, best we can tell." He passed Weiseman his tea, then took his seat behind the big desk. "This won't be over until we inaugurate a new president fourteen months from now."

So much for Justin's loyalty to Carter, Weiseman thought.

"Jean Pascal came by this morning," he said. "He said we should do nothing or—"

"Yes, yes, the French would say that, wouldn't they? But this is America. Jimmy Carter is a lay Baptist minister, not a Cartesian philosopher. Americans expect their leaders to act."

Of course, Weiseman thought. This was about more than just the hostages.

"Let me tell you what will happen," Trevor said. "The president will get bogged down in the weeds instead of deferring the detail work like he should. He'll become desk officer for Iran. He'll review every proposal. There'll be daily meetings. It will waste untold hours—"

"Justin, our people are in custody—"

Trevor held up his right hand, like a traffic cop. "Secret interagency committees will be formed. There will be leaks, proposals for punitive measures, rescue missions, carrots and sticks. The Navy will want to send warships to the Persian Gulf. The networks will make the hostages their lead story every night on TV. Khomeini will issue a religious fatwa against the United States."

Despite himself, Weiseman knew that Trevor's appraisal was accurate. He could be a coldhearted bastard, but the old pro usually assessed things spot-on.

"The good Iranians will disappear," Trevor continued. "They'll be herded into Evin and shot. Or hanged."

He paused to sip his tea. "The opportunists will swarm about like locusts. They'll do whatever Khomeini commands, and they'll feather their nests."

"And then?"

"Once Khomeini feels he's achieved his purpose, there will be diplomatic meetings in Europe. But the hostages won't come home until we have a different president."

"And we do nothing in the meantime? You can't mean that."

"Oh, no, David. Of course not. We'll try everything."

Trevor sipped his tea again. "It's not hot, this tea." He furrowed his brow. "My colleagues will talk big about what they'll do to Iran. Members of Congress will be worse; after all, they're just politicians. Our experts will tell us all the reasons we can do nothing. Our allies will agree; they'll give us words of solidarity, and hold our coat."

Trevor picked an imaginary spot of dust from his suit lapel. "You're going back in, David. CIA will give you an unaudited budget. You'll make sure we know what's going on in Iran. You'll be our channel to all those bandits and thieves in their mullahs' robes and European suits. Of course, you won't be working for us."

Deniability, Weiseman thought. David Weiseman, who's he? We don't know him.

"Of course, Justin, but you said nothing will happen until there's a new president."

Trevor stared intently at him, then said, "I want to know in advance if they're going to hang or shoot any of our people. I want to know if there are still Iranians we can talk to, or put to work for us. I want to know whether there are any governments or any adventurers with armies and cash who might help us."

"Help us do what?"

"You told me you wanted to frustrate them, put a spanner in the works everywhere they turn, find ways to make them crash, or at least let our people go."

"That's all?" Weiseman said.

"That's all, unless you can think of anything else. If you and I know the truth, we can prevent Bobby Beauford and the fools around the president from making a worse hash of it than they have already."

Trevor paused and stared off, as if deciding how to say what came next. It was a habit Weiseman knew meant that something important was coming.

"David, I've arranged some, shall we say, advanced training for you at CIA, at the Farm." Weiseman had never been to the Farm before. He was a diplomat, not a spook, even though, since Trevor had become DCI, he'd been operating as a virtual agent. But there was a lot about intelligence operations that he didn't know, and so now Trevor was offering him "advanced training." The risk level of his work, he realized, was about to rise sharply.

Trevor read his mind. "You've done well so far," he said, "but now things are going to get heavy. There isn't time for an extended regimen, so you'll have to focus."

Weiseman stiffened at the thought of what was to come. He knew how a new Islamist regime would deal with an American plotting its overthrow. He hadn't forgotten Montana.

And yet, he felt a quickened pulse at the prospect of the culmination of his mission.

"How do I communicate with you?" he asked.

Trevor pulled out a white index card from his top desk drawer. It contained a seven-digit 800 phone number, a special channel cable address, and a code name.

"Memorize this now, David."

Weiseman absorbed the information and handed the card back.

"Why that code name?" Weiseman asked. "Lone Wolf."

Trevor smiled tightly.

## 31

# *LONE WOLF*

**T**HE CIA FARM was just south of Warrenton, Virginia, on I-95, an hour from Washington.

Weiseman missed the unmarked turn, spotted the Mobil gas station, then doubled back and slowly drove up the dirt road to the cluster of redbrick houses. He showed his State Department pass, drove under the raised electronic wire gate, then watched it descend in his rear view mirror.

That night, he was given a volume titled *Intelligence Handbook*. "Read this and think about it," his trainer said. It had one page in particular earmarked for him: *Beware of people who believe*, he read. *They aren't reliable players.*

That night he thought about cultivating traitors, and recalled a line from Graham Greene: "Oh, traitor—that's an old-fashioned word." Was "traitor" old-fashioned? No. Not according to the values his father had drilled into him after they escaped from Nazi Germany. America is different, Johann had told him. America doesn't cross redlines. But of course we do, Weiseman knew. Every country does. We do, however, look out for our people.

The hostages would go through hell and then they'd come home, but not before Khomeini had milked them for all they were worth. The more we flagellated ourselves over their release, the longer it would take. Weiseman was convinced of that. And he was sure that Carter wouldn't send in a serious strike force.

America couldn't ignore them, of course. Weiseman was realistic, but he wasn't cynical. That was how he differentiated himself from Trevor. Chris Tyler was in there, a young diplomat who once worked for him, as were many other colleagues and friends. He'd find Iranians to tell him what was going on in the embassy. No doubt it would take a bit of baksheesh to get them to share their secrets; or an appeal to some attachment to America; or a visa or other way out for an endangered family. There would be those who'd sell to both sides, like Daud in the Intercon; those who'd be out for glory; and still others seeking a bit of excitement in a desperate life.

He went over and over the options, searching his mind for the magic bullet. He thought the Israelis could do it; they were masters of the rescue mission. And maybe, now that they'd seen the ayatollahs up close, they regretted the way they had scuttled Ajax Two.

But about the revolution itself. Bringing down the ayatollahs so soon was a nonstarter. The mullahs would have to burn their bridges first, to outrage the people as badly as or worse than the Shah. The middle classes and bazaari and students who clamored for modernization and for a democratic Iran would soon come to see that the ayatollahs' takeover had been the worst possible outcome. Khomeini's return meant that they had neither a modern nor democratic Iran. Khomeini and his cronies—Khalaji,

Montana, unknown others—were even now imposing a medieval Islamist authoritarian regime backed by thuggish Revolutionary Guards.

Eventually a counterrevolution could start, from within. Maybe Seyyed would lead it.

The Islamists would fall out, begin to cut one another's throats. It happened in all revolutions. One day these mullahs would take some step—out of indignation, or cold fear and paranoia, that would lead the Israelis to . . . well, Regev had said it all, when he'd referred to Israel's nuclear weapons as "insurance." Hadn't he?

**A FEW DAYS** after he arrived at the Farm, Weiseman saw a news item. Acting Foreign Minister Ali Amin had been placed under house arrest and replaced by Abolhassan Bani-Sadr. Poor naïve Amin, thought Weiseman, soaking up all those nonsensical nostrums about a technocratic government. Had he been confined to that shabby apartment, or worse, in Evin? It was bound to happen.

But Bani-Sadr? Weiseman called Trevor and asked, "Who's he?"

"He's nobody, an adventurer, just the kind of man you should deal with."

But by the end of the month, Bani-Sadr, too, had been dismissed. The new acting foreign minister was Sadegh Ghotbzadeh, who had managed the internal crackdown so far.

Weiseman asked Virginia to send him a dossier on the two men. CIA analysts said they were Western educated revolutionaries, slick and slimy, used by Khomeini to soothe Western concerns. That's what Amin did, until they got rid of him. Now Bani-Sadr had been cast off as well, after two weeks. And just how would they soothe us while they held our hostages?

Weiseman thought about all this while he was running five miles a day at the Farm, memorizing codes, studying the conceits of tradecraft, and reading CIA biographies of Persians he might be able to use to get the hostages out: Bani-Sadr, nursing grievances over shabby treatment by the revolution; or Ghotbzadeh, who seemed as if he might sell his mother for personal gain.

On December 10, the director of the Farm came to see him. "Mr. Trevor called; he wants you to stop by his residence tonight, at seven."


**CLARISSA TREVOR GREETED** Weiseman at the door of their house on Wyoming Avenue in a slim fuchsia dress, her brunette hair done up in an elegant chignon. She was a more mature version of her daughter, the lovely Regina, Weiseamn thought. She led him into the salon, sat with him on a silk sofa, a photo of Justin and herself in Sicily on the end table.

Trevor walked in pipe in hand, shook Weiseman's hand and got right to business. "We're trying to get the president out on the campaign trail. While he's running for reelection, he'll be out of our hair. The hostage crisis will become a fact of life. Americans will go about their normal lives. We can move beyond this distraction and attend to the important issues."

Once Weiseman would have been shocked—treating the president like a puppet to be dangled at will, while Trevor presumed to run the country. But it had to be done.

"All options are on the table?" Weiseman asked.

"Yes, of course," Trevor replied.

"Negotiation, bribes, military action?"

"They always are."

"As is indifference," Weiseman added.

"That's right." Trevor suddenly sneezed. He took a snow-white linen handkerchief from his back pocket and dabbed at his nose. "Though the American media isn't making it any easier. Every evening on prime time they toll the number of days the hostages have been held. We might as well send up a white flag and announce to the world America's surrender to mindless mullahs and their thuggish sidekicks."

Trevor refilled the glasses Clarissa had arranged upon Weiseman's arrival. "It's time," he said. "Your training is over. You need to get back to Iran."

**BACK IN LANGLEY** the next day, Weiseman was shown to the operation center where Trevor introduced him to Kurt Waldheim, the UN secretary-general who was off to Tehran to appeal for the release of the hostages. Weiseman proceeded to brief him and found him dismissive, a former Austrian foreign minister and now top UN diplomat who thought he knew it all.

Yet, when Waldheim arrived in Tehran a few days later, he found himself surrounded by screaming students every time he stepped in and out of his car. There was a grotesque session with mutilated and deformed victims of SAVAK who waved stumps of missing limbs in his face, demanding to know why he had permitted these war crimes. His visit to the cemetery of the martyrs of the revolution turned into a riot, forcing him to flee under heavy guard. To top it all off, the students rejected his requests to visit the hostages.

Weiseman was waiting to debrief the shaken diplomat on his return two days later to New York. Waldman told him he was glad simply to be back alive. He said, "This Ghotbzadeh, the foreign minister, he's a sneaky one. He talked tough in front of the Revolutionary Guards, but there was something slippery about him. Perhaps he could be bought."

Weiseman pondered the thought in the secretary-general's private elevator as he descended the thirty-eight floors of the UN secretariat building on the East River, with its breathtaking view of the Manhattan skyline. He needed to meet this Ghotbzadeh, he decided, this "sneaky one."

But first, there was the little problem of how he was to get to Iran and back alive, with Montana lying in wait for him?


**EVENTS WERE IN** motion, laying new obstacles in the path to a deal with the mullahs. The entire Mideast, Persian Gulf, and South Asian region had become an entangled arc of crisis.

The Great Mosque of Mecca was invaded by terrorists, a sacrilege that summoned up outrage across the Arab world.

Islamist fanatics invaded the American embassy in Pakistan, forcing diplomatic staffers to leap to their death when the embassy became a burning pyre. Two of Weiseman's friends were among the dead.

Soviet armed forces invaded Afghanistan and began systematically to shell the primitive country with modern missiles carrying high explosive payloads.

In the White House, the president announced a major increase in defense spending.

The next day, Bani-Sadr was elected president of the Islamic Republic of Iran, trouncing Ghotbzadeh 75 percent to 25 percent. Ghotbzadeh was humiliated, and, Weiseman speculated, must be fearful that he might be cast to the wolves.

Yasmine de Rose phoned for her father, telling Weiseman that two shady French lawyers had visited Bobby Beauford in the White House, lobbying on behalf of the new Iranian government that the Shah be extradited back to Iran.

A coded cable arrived from Françoise. In Tehran, the students in the embassy were speaking openly about show trials. There were Iranian proposals for a UN commission to come to Tehran and take testimony about the Shah's crimes. There was also an idea coming from President Bani-Sadr that perhaps the UN commission visit could somehow lead to release of the hostages and return of the Shah's assets.

No doubt Bani-Sadr would take a generous cut of those assets.

Well, why not? Weiseman thought, if it would get the hostages home. But Ghotbzadeh, still plotting against Bani-Sadr from the Foreign Ministry, killed the idea.

Weiseman called Trevor on a secure line and told him that Ghotbzadeh might be tempted to undermine his new president.

"Yes, that's more like it," Trevor said. "Play them along. It's the oldest game in the world: tempt them with what you might do for them, draw them close."

Weiseman called the travel agency in Morristown, New Jersey, that Trevor told him would take care of his arrangements. Next, he called Françoise in Paris. "Meet me at De Gaulle. I'm headed back to Iran."

"I know," she said.

The next morning, he boarded a plane for Paris.

**PIERRE JUBRIL, THE LEFTY LAWYER** from Lebanon, met him at a Corsican bistro in Paris, where they ate omelets and flat peasant bread and drank rough red wine. Weiseman asked about the French lawyers who had visited the White House.

Pierre told him to leave them alone. "They're adventurers; they'll talk and talk, lead your government on a fine chase but nothing will come of it." He rubbed his thumb and index finger together. "Except they'll fatten their pockets."

"What about Bani-Sadr? Ghotbzadeh?"

Pierre stared hard at him for a moment, then sipped his wine. He rubbed the two digits again. "Perhaps. But one by one, not together. They loathe each other."

"Do you know them?"

"Oh, yes," Pierre said. "Bani-Sadr, you might say, is too clever by half. He speaks Farsi in a way that no one in Iran understands where he's going."

"Doesn't he speak French?"

Pierre coughed, a long dirty snort. "Even worse. I rarely understood him."

"And now he's president."

"Yes, constructive ambiguity; it's a qualification for high office in my country, and in Iran. Also here in Paris."

*Constructive ambiguity*—that nice phrase that Weiseman had learned from Trevor.

"Ghotbzadeh?"

Pierre sliced into his omelet, chewing as cheese dribbled down the right side of his mouth. "Ah, that one is the dictator type, and quite the opportunist. I'm told he loves being foreign minister—the perquisites of office, the limousine, the women, photographers and fawning journalists, ordering people around. He'll make you think you're talking into the wind."

Pierre broke off a piece of the bread and chewed thoughtfully. "It depends what's in it for him—a way to gain the upper hand with Bani-Sadr or to show Khomeini he's the one to trust. But if you mean to use him, you'd best do it soon, before Bani-Sadr does him in."

"And you can arrange for me to see him, Pierre."

The lawyer smiled and again rubbed the two digits together, then wrote a number on the back of a Kronenbourg 1664 beer coaster: *10,000 US.*

Weiseman passed an envelope across the table. "Half down, with the balance once I see him." He lifted his wineglass and clincked it against Pierre's. He drained the glass, shuddering at the harsh taste. "It's good. I must get to Corsica one day."

**RUE CITÉ DE** Varenne, Gramont's home, where Weiseman had first met Alain de Rose, Jacques, and Françoise.

Gramont was now all business.

"Every day it's something different. They want the Shah back, they want his money back, his properties, Farah's jewels. They'll free the hostages after the election of the Majlis, the Iranian parliament, but they insist on an apology by your president."

"Out of the question."

Undeterred, Gramont went on. "The Iranian people have been affronted. One day Bani-Sadr is ready to welcome the UN commission and transfer the hostages from the embassy to government control, then release them. The next day, there are conditions. One day, Bani-Sadr says he's speaking for the Imam; the next day he fears for his life."

"And the two French lawyers?"

"You won't believe it. They proposed to Washington that the CIA kill the Shah—'pull the plug' was their phrase. Then they said," he coughed lightly, "you should substitute a dead body for the Shah's, dispose of it with due public fanfare, and continue his treatment in an undisclosed location."

They must have been dealing with Beauford, Weiseman thought.

"The pièce de résistance," Gramont chuckled, deep in his throat, "was that they forged Carter's signature on a letter on White House stationary apologizing to Khomeini, begging him to help him out of this political jam. They appear to have regular access to the White House, David. Your people must be desperate."

If he only knew, thought Weiseman.

"And what about Bani-Sadr?"

"We know him well, David. He's a rogue. He and Ghotbzadeh are your best chance. You'll have to play them off against each other. See them separately, in Europe. Out of Iran." Gramont shook his head, as if seeking to expunge a bad taste. "I can arrange the meeting with Bani-Sadr. He'll be traveling this way soon, a state visit to Paris, then down to Morocco."

"I'll do it there, Laurent. In Casablanca, after he meets the king, just before he flies home."

Gramont jotted it down in a leather notepad with his gold-plated Dupont fountain pen.

"Ghotbzadeh?" Weiseman asked.

"*Alors, mon vieux*, Pierre is taking care of that for you."

Finally, "Françoise. I called her at the apartment. Where is she?"

"David, she's in Baghdad," the puppet master said. "Helping you again. She's interviewing Saddam Hussain."

Gramont paused. Weiseman could hear the alcohol coursing down the count's throat.

"I told her not to. She said she had an idea."


**THE NEXT MORNING** Pierre came to see him. "Ghotbzadeh is willing to see you."

That was fast, he thought. Money talks.

"You'll be seeing him in Iran," Pierre suddenly added. "And don't worry about your security. Ghotbazadeh said he'd take care of Montana."

Easy for him to say, thought Weiseman.

The two digits rubbed together again. "By the way, you owe me 5,000 US."

## 32

# DESERT ONE

ELI COHEN GREETED WEISEMAN with elevated eyebrows as he entered the terminal of the King Hassan II International Airport in Casablanca. Cohen wore a lime Lacoste polo shirt and khaki pants; a gold Patek Philippe watch was on his wrist. He led the way to his red Jaguar convertible.

Soon they were riding along the coastal highway, en route to the tourist city of Mohammedia. Cohen drove with the top down to invite in the warm sun. Palm trees lined the road; the smell of the ocean and the honeyed scent of bougainvillea filled the air.

"Do you know what you're doing?" the Moroccan asked, flipping on the radio.

"Of course," Weiseman replied . . . "and I hope it works."

Arabic music filled the car. Carts ambled along, drawn by donkeys. Small children in ragged pants squatted at the side of the road, grinning, throwing dice. Aged women covered in black from head to toe watched them like mother hens.

Cohen began telling him about Bani-Sadr's talks with the Moroccan king. Weiseman listened with one ear as they skirted sand beaches where nubile young women in string bikinis frolicked in the surf, while their mothers or aunts sipped tea or lemonade through straws, their bodies and faces as fully covered as if they were on a Tehran street.

"He's changed quite a lot since I knew him years ago as a student, in Paris."

"What was he like, Eli?"

"He was a pretty boy with curly hair, our Abolhassan, adept at covering his trail. The girls liked him all right, and perhaps the boys. I would meet him for lunch from time to time. Always my treat, of course."

"What did you talk about?"

Cohen turned up the radio, and the music blew into the zephyrs dancing around the Jag. He laughed. "Our pretty boy was selling and we were buying. He'd tell us about the Shah and his enemies, who was coming up in the regime, but especially about the street folks who he said one day would upend the Shah. Some of it panned out, much was made up. It wasn't as though he cared whether the Shah stayed or went. It was a way to make money, to afford the girls."

Perfect, Weiseman thought. If one should "beware people who believe," then a cynic like Bani-Sadr could be useful.

"When did he decide to throw in with the mullahs?"

Cohen revved the Jag and scooted around a truck, then told him how the young Bani-Sadr participated in anti-Shah student demos in the early sixties. "He was imprisoned twice in Tehran and wounded in '63. The French gave him a monthly stipend in the hope that he would report to them from Iran about the Shah. Instead, he ran away to Paris and studied economics. Later, he joined the revolution and returned to Iran with the Imam. They made him finance minister because there was no one else to handle it. When Amin was jailed, he became acting foreign minister, until Ghotbzadeh ousted him from that job. President now, Bani-Sadr is still on the make, opportunistic, and still watching his back."

"Then he'll be looking for an opportunity."

"Oh, yes." Cohen steered the Jag along a curvy stretch, then suddenly slammed on the brakes. A donkey was in the middle of the road. A man with a weathered face was prodding the beast with a stick, but it stood impassively, the patience of centuries on its face. Cohen blew his horn. The donkey raised its head and shook it from side to side as if to say, *Get lost.*

They sat there while a queue of traffic piled up behind them. "Where's the Sahara desert?" Weiseman asked, for want of conversation. "How far from here?"

"Due south, after Agadir and Marrakesh. It's another world. I go there sometimes to escape, but it has nothing to do with this country. It's where Africa begins."

A siren sounded and a police car drove up from the opposite side, a trailer suitable for bearing beasts behind it. The donkey looked up again, shook its head up and down, then moved forward to the side of the road.

"Will Bani-Sadr be as clever as that donkey?" Weiseman asked.

Eli Cohen floored the accelerator and the car zoomed along the edge of the cliff, above the surfing foam of the Mediterranean. Up ahead, a redbrick arch loomed, and the Jag slipped through it, beyond the city walls. The ground was covered by white pebbles, and Weiseman asked what they were.

"There's a rock salt factory here, and yes, he'll be as clever as the donkey. You should discount at least fifty percent of what he tells you."

They drove through the deserted town: public squares dotted with palm trees, the outdoor patio of a restaurant, a sagging green tarpaulin draped over it as if to protect nonexistent patrons from the sun. Nine police cars were gathered on the far end of the square. A lean, brown policeman stood in front of each car, keeping an eye out.

A wizened old man in a sky-blue robe and white knit cap bicycled down a narrow lane toward the medina, past two overturned wicker baskets. It hardly looked like a resort town.

"Where is everyone?" Weiseman asked.

"We've cleared them out, for you and Bani-Sadr."

"And the hotel?"

"Change of plans," Cohen said. "Our Persian friends are like that, they don't trust us. You'll be meeting him in that big brick building over there, the one with the chimney spouting filthy fumes into the air. The oil refinery. Our pretty boy is here to do business with the king."

**BANI-SADR HAD CHANGED** from his photos. The curly-haired pretty-boy Eli remembered had been replaced by a sour-looking thug. Black horn-rimmed glasses circled the black pupils of wary eyes and a dense black mustache, matching a black pompadour, dominated the face. He wore a well-cut silk tweed Italian sport jacket and black knit shirt opened to show off a hairless chest that looked as though it had just been polished to a fine sheen.

They met in the office of the refinery's chief executive and sat on faux leather chairs.

"Mr. President, how good of you to receive me."

"You requested this meeting, Mr. Weiseman. What do you want?"

"We want the hostages returned unharmed. You know that, sir."

"Yes, but on what terms. You need to give me something to work with."

He was already angling for cash, Weiseman thought, perhaps a Swiss account to pay off ayatollahs. Or an annuity, for life after the revolution. One day he'd find himself wanting a visa and a new identity in California.

"I've been in touch with the White House," Bani-Sadr said sarcastically, "through the French lawyers. I saw them yesterday in Paris. Do you know about that? Are you au courant?"

"You know who I work for."

The Iranian president reached into his jacket and pulled out a pack of Gauloises. "The Shah," he said. "We want him back."

"Mr. President, you know that's not possible. I'm not here to waste your time."

Bani-Sadr suddenly bounced to his feet and went to the window. He stared out at the dirty smokestacks, shifting back and forth on the balls of his feet. "The king of Morocco has agreed to refine our oil," he finally said. "Your best Arab ally is in our pocket."

Let him rant, Weiseman told himself. Just don't let him leave.

Bani-Sadr began prowling around the office, stopping to make a point, then thinking better of it, stealing a drag on the cigarette. A man appeared in a flowing white jellaba and a red fez slightly tilted on his head, like a candle on a cake. He placed tiny red lacquered porcelain cups at their places, poured tea, and left the matching porcelain kettle.

"The Imam doesn't know I'm meeting you," Bani-Sadr said nervously. "He can be quite unforgiving. I'm taking a risk."

Weiseman said nothing. Let him work himself up to the matter at hand.

Bani-Sadr slid back into his seat and dashed the half-smoked cigarette into a metal ashtray. He sipped the tea, as did Weiseman, who found it much too sweet.

"If we can't get the Shah, we have to expose his crimes. My people need a catharsis."

"You mean the UN commission," Weiseman said. "Taking testimony from victims."

"That, but Pahlavi's assets, too. They must be returned."

"That can be discussed, but it would be linked to the release of the hostages. I understand there's an idea to have the students transfer the hostages to Minister Ghotbzadeh."

Bani-Sadr was up again, lighting another cigarette, then cackling harshly, and suddenly the black horn-rimmed glasses and mustache were inches from Weiseman's face. "*Students?* They were cleared out after a week," he said, before drawing back and glowering at Weiseman. "The only ones in the embassy now are Revolutionary Guards, who report to Khalaji and Montana."

A bottle of scotch appeared from a desk drawer, as did a single tumbler. Bani-Sadr poured himself an inch and downed it. "Don't trust

Ghotbzadeh. He'll make you pay for everything twice, and then he won't deliver."

Good, thought Weiseman. Play them off against each other.

"Mr. President, if we are able to reach a deal, will the Imam go along?"

Bani-Sadr shrugged, showing that he didn't know, or perhaps didn't care to know.

"Thank you for your time." Weiseman rose. "But I can't engage my president this way."

The Iranian was taken aback. He grasped Weiseman's elbow. "It's all right. You'll have to visit Tehran again. Nothing can happen without the Imam. He remembers you."

"And Montana?" Weiseman asked. "I believe he remembers me, too. I seem to be on his list for the firing squad."

The Iranian president again got in Weiseman's face. He pulled off his horn-rimmed glasses and, for an instant, Weiseman was looking at the pretty student in Paris.

*"Moi aussi, Monsieur Weiseman."* He gripped Weiseman's elbow. "I am, too."

Weiseman drew a sealed white envelope out of his breast pocket. "Then you may be able to put this information to good use, Mr. President."

Bani-Sadr cast his eye over the contents, and then grinned. "So, our friend Montana is wanted on murder and arson charges in France and the United States." He slipped the envelope into his pocket and raised a glass. *"A bientôt a Tehran."*

"Mr. President, we've settled nothing here today. You do know that."

"Yes," Bani-Sadr said, "but we may have begun everything."


THINGS WENT FROM bad to worse as reports emerged of an Evin Prison bursting with new guests, and of embassy hostages subjected to new and indecent outrages. Red Cross inspectors allowed to visit the embassy observed American diplomats in solitary confinement, and staffers laying cheek by jowl along paper thin cots on a hard floor, men and women alike. When one of the men sought to defend a female colleague from the groping hand of a captor, he was punched in the head and hauled off to solitary.

Something had to be done. In college, Weiseman had read Reinhold Niebuhr, the Catholic foreign policy realist who shared Johann's view of life and human propensities: never give up, do what is doable, even if imperfect. Iran, with its array of bad choices, was the case model for this philosophy, he thought ruefully. Weiseman knew nothing short of a military operation would free the hostages until the Ayatollah had no further use of them. But there was always something one could do. Johann had taught him long ago: If you can't do everything, at least do what you can. The worst enemy was resignation and indifference.

He spent the next month circling around Iran's borders, taking the temperature, arranging refugee receiving centers in the Gulf emirates, and working out contingency security plans with the directors of Jordan's and Turkey's intelligence services. Then he flew to Jerusalem.

Regev met him at Ben Gurion Airport. This time his Israeli hosts were ready to engage. They had agents in Iran who spoke Farsi and knew their way around, seasoned men and women, Regev said. Of course, they had to be sure that Washington was serious, that the White House would act, and do so effectively.

Regev took him to a nondescript building on the outskirts of Tel Aviv to meet Mossad's "technicians," the experts at rescue missions, the specialists at sabotage and disinformation, and the ones who conducted black operations and destabilization. Listening intently to a briefing, Weiseman spotted faces he had seen in Amman and Ankara—including Jafar, whose escape Weiseman had arranged. Weiseman greeted him and promised to pass a message to his family that he was okay.

And then Weiseman realized who the person sitting in front of him was. He turned his head toward Regev and his expression said it all. *Tariq Aziz in Tel Aviv?*

Regev told him simply, "When things get sticky, we do what's necessary."

Weiseman took it in and turned to look at Aziz, sitting there in this Israeli bunker with his silk Italian suit, the trademark oversized glasses and white mustache; he could have been a rich Israeli businessman, or an émigré in Brooklyn. When the spokesman for the butcher of Iraq finally noticed him, Weiseman stifled his disdain and asked, "Is there anything you want to tell me?"

Tariq Aziz's facial muscles crinkled into a sly smile. "Just one thing," he said. "You have a beautiful and brave friend who is very convincing."

But bringing Françoise into it only intensified Weiseman's disgust for the man.

**A SHORT HOP** on an air force helicopter from Jerusalem to Beirut and he was reunited with Françoise. Dropping politics for a weekend on a beach near Byblos, Weiseman said nothing about his excursion to Tel Aviv.

She told him, unprompted, about her visit to Baghdad. "Saddam was in a vile mood. He knows Khomeini better than anyone. All those years he got nightly reports from his Mukhabarat. He knows now that he should have handed Khomeini to his security service, to dispose of, without asking the Shah. He's convinced it was a big mistake to let Khomeini go. He said Gramont tricked him—that Gramont told him Khomeini would be kept under house arrest in Paris. Saddam said one day, there will be a war."

Weiseman wondered, Did she tell this without hedging to Gramont?

And then, after an early dinner, Jimmy Carter's solemn face was on the flickering television set, telling the nation and the world about an attempted rescue mission he'd authorized. "Late yesterday, I cancelled a carefully planned operation in Iran to position our rescue team for later withdrawal of American hostages who have been held captive there since November 4. Equipment failure in the rescue helicopters made it necessary to end the mission."

Weiseman heard only the details of failure. Eight helicopters had taken off from the U.S.S. *Nimitz* in the Arabian Sea to rescue the hostages, to meet at a rendezvous point in the Iranian desert, code-named

Desert One. Rotor blade failure . . . a cloud of suspended dust . . . helicopters separated . . . malfunctions, hydraulic problems. He remembered the heartbreaking phone calls from Roger Tyler and so many other spouses and parents.

"To my deep regret, eight of the crewmen of the two aircraft which collided were killed, and several other Americans were hurt . . . The responsibility is fully my own," Carter said solemnly.

Damn right, Weiseman muttered to himself, imagining the image of Bobby Beauford whispering to Carter on how the mission could save the faltering election campaign.

# 33

# *DASH TO THE FINISH*

**B**ACK IN WASHINGTON, in the aftermath of the aborted rescue mission, Weiseman observed the condition of the hostages grow worse. Students and RGs took retribution for the aborted rescue mission by depriving the hostages of food and sleep and medical supplies, by masking their eyes and restricting their movement with chains and confinement. A religious group allowed to visit the hostages returned from Tehran to say that the captors took sadistic pleasure in meting out harsh treatment. One hostage, who told off the RGs in Farsi when they said he was a spy, was placed in solitary for months.

Spring turned to summer and, on July 27, 1980, the official Tehran radio laconically announced, "The bloodsucker of the century has died."

The Shah of Iran was laid to rest on the banks of the Nile where his father had been interred after three years of exile in South Africa. Weiseman recalled seeing the Shah stare in awe at the portrait of his father, seeing his shy demeanor . . . yet he'd also seen his support for Hanif's brutal methods. Mohammad Reza had brought his father back for burial in Iranian soil. Who would do that for him?

In Iran, dissent reached new levels. The sagging economy and repressive regime led to daily disturbances. An Islamic court, obeying orders from Qom, condemned a doctor to death. Montana's firing squad carried out the execution, and doctors went on a sympathy strike. Women directed to wear the chador in government offices staged demonstrations in Western clothing and were dismissed from their jobs. Scholarships were cancelled for those studying abroad. The "students" at the embassy demanded the removal of Bani-Sadr and Ghotbzadeh, blaming them for dallying with the Americans—like David Weiseman.

Saddam Hussein, watching Iran disintegrate, began to stage raids along the border.

The Iraqi ambassador came by to warn David that it could come to war. Weiseman called Trevor, who reminded him of priorities. "You know the old saying, the enemy of my enemy is my friend. Saddam is a mad dog, but now he's our mad dog. Let them go at it."

"And if they go to war, Justin, what do your experts say?"

"It will go on for years, hundreds of thousands will be killed or wounded, on both sides."

"Hundreds of thousands? And you can justify all that slaughter?"

"Yes, David, I can. One day there'll be a truce between Saddam and Khomeini. In the meantime, they'll leave us alone. Tell the Iraqi ambassador we understand his concerns."

Weiseman mulled that over and called Françoise on her private phone. He told her about the visit from Saddam's ambassador.

"You'd better take it seriously," she said. "I interviewed Saddam forty-eight hours ago. He means to preempt, to strike Iran before it's too late. He said—"

Then the line was broken, and suddenly Weiseman heard Bobby Beauford's voice talking to him. Beauford had broken into the call as if his White House ID card gave him carte blanche to do so.

"Dave," he said, "we need an October surprise."

Of course you do, thought Weiseman. Plot an assassination. Kidnap the Ayatollah. Anything to win the election.

"What do you have in mind?" Weiseman asked.

"That's your job," Beauford replied and rang off.

Weiseman asked the Iraqi ambassador to return to the State Department and then told him he had reported his démarche to higher-ups. He didn't convey Trevor's encouragement of Baghdad, but he didn't discourage the Iraqi either. He knew the ambassador would sniff out the meaning.

He recalled Trevor's tutelage on his first posting, in Prague: *To achieve your ideals, you may need to be ruthless. There is nothing like well-placed leverage to secure noble ends.*

**FRANÇOISE CALLED. HER** voice was so clear, he thought she was in Georgetown.

"I'm in my embassy in Baghdad," she said, and they went secure. He entered the codes and waited till the static cleared. The call resumed in classified format, the static gone, blocking out intruding ears.

"The intermediary made the arrangements," she told him. "Khomeini has given me assurances for your security. He'll receive you, if your talks go well."

The Imam was the only one who could free the hostages and ensure his safety. Or could he? Did the Ayatollah control Montana and the RGs?

"David," Françoise interrupted his thoughts. "Watch out for Serge Klein. He's been seen with Hosein Hanif."

My God, Weiseman thought, Hanif again, first with Seyyed, now Klein. What was that about?

He took the elevator down from his office and strolled outside, moved slowly to the Mall, and stood at the reflecting pool. It was Labor Day. Carter and his Republican opponent, Ronald Reagan, were in Detroit, launching the final stretch of their campaigns.

He was about to put himself at great risk, and he wasn't doing so for Jimmy Carter and damn sure not for Bobby Beauford and his blasted October surprise. He was doing so for the hostages.

He stared at Lincoln on his stone throne and thought, *we're all hostages*. The men and women trussed up in the embassy. The Shah, who tried to live up to his image of his father. Hanif, who had ruthlessly served two now-dead shahs. Khomeini, who had emerged from exile to carry out macabre dreams. Carter, whose political fortunes were dependent on how the crisis played out. Françoise, who remained at least somewhat beholden to Gramont. And me, he thought ruefully . . . restitution for his escape from Berlin long ago.

He caught Lincoln's stony stare. There comes a time, Weiseman told himself, when you have to act, to do something, if you're going to justify the life your father saved.

He strode back to his office and phoned Françoise back. He told her he would be away, pulling loose threads together. He didn't want her going back to Iran, and he kept secret the Israeli talks. There were still outer bounds.

He called Trevor and told him he was ready to go.

"Good," Trevor said. "Time is running short. Anything that works. Do it!"

SURPRISINGLY, HIS ARRIVAL at Mehrabad went smoothly and was hassle-free—thanks to Bani-Sadr, Weiseman surmised, surely not Klein. When he left the terminal, he walked over to a bus stop and climbed aboard an ancient vehicle with peeling paint and blemishes of rust. It was packed with Iranians from the provinces, arms filled with wailing children and suitcases tied with heavy ropes. The odor of charcoal and cooked meats filled the air. A man in the row ahead of him clung tightly to a squirming, flapping chicken. A four-year-old girl with dark eyes reached over and touched his arm. "Nice man," she said in Farsi.

It took two hours for the bus to make its way through local villages, past local mosques, and to finally enter the center of Tehran, affording him one more view of this elusive country. At the last stop before Tehran, the little girl who'd called him a "nice man" hopped off her mother's lap and climbed onto Weiseman's, kissing his cheek. "Nice man," she repeated, then scampered down, taking her mother's hand and stepping gingerly from the bus. From outside, he saw her blow him a kiss, and he sent one back, wondering whether this nightmare would be over when she was old enough to be a student, and kidnap more Americans.

By the time the bus finally stopped at the Intercon, a newsreel of failures was racing through his mind: the Carter visit on New Year's Eve 1977 when he told the world how he admired the Shah's Iran; the collapsing monarchy in 1978; the flight of the Shah and Khomeini's return, with the proclamation of the Islamic Republic, in January 1979; the seizure of the American embassy hostages in November 1979; and the Desert One rescue fiasco in April 1980.

How, he wondered, could we have gotten it so wrong . . . so often?

THE NEXT MORNING, a car arranged personally by Trevor, with tinted windows for extra security, picked Weiseman up for his appointment to see Sadegh Ghotbzadeh. On the way, he stared out the window at the swirl of traffic passing by as smog enveloped the city and hid the surrounding mountains. There was tightness in the way people walked, glancing over their shoulders as if aware of perpetual danger.

Within ten minutes the driver turned into a narrow alley and stopped before a nondescript one-story brick building on which a black plaque whispered, PRIVATE OFFICE. The front door opened. A man in a shaggy gray sweater led him down a drab hallway, knocked on a door, and then opened it. "He's here," the man said and drifted away.

Weiseman recognized Ghotbzadeh from the photos the CIA had

provided. The foreign minister, wearing a black turtleneck sweater, sat on a blue fabric Scandinavian sofa, manipulating green and white worry beads. "Come in," he said, rising to shake hands, revealing a massive body grown soft. The face was almost handsome—black wavy hair, soft eyes, and a nose that flared above a strong mouth, but with a growth of graying beard. There was something wary about the way his dark eyes measured his visitor.

"Is this about the hostages?" Ghotbzadeh said. "Look, I don't give a damn about the hostages. The Ayatollah is ill. He's in hospital."

"My condolences," Weiseman said, wondering how that might affect the hostages.

"The Revolutionary Guards are filling the vacuum," Ghotbzadeh said. "They're hoodlums, squeezing me. Can your government do anything about *them*?"

"Perhaps we could help you with Bani-Sadr," Weiseman said.

"Fuck Bani-Sadr. Gramont briefed you before you came here, didn't he? Don't you see what's going on here?"

Ok, thought Weiseman. Let him have it.

"Sure. It's about power, and here's my message. You're dealing with a superpower. My president will do whatever is necessary to free the hostages. If you want to stay in power, you'll lend a hand. Do *you* get it?"

The Iranian became agitated, but he visibly willed himself to settle down. He let a moment go by, then said softly, "You know, I went to college in America."

"Right, and so did I, as did Amin, your predecessor. You saw what happened to him."

Ghotbzadeh stared hard at him before drinking from a tall glass of Perrier. "I studied economics," he said. "I learned it always comes down to money."

So, it was to be another shakedown.

Ghotbzadeh got up and led Weiseman to a round table at the center of the room. "Sit," he said, then disappeared through a door. Two minutes later, he came back, flipping the pages of a thick leather binder. "The mullahs are saying Bani-Sadr and I are selling out to America. Bani-Sadr will get it in the neck." Ghotbzadeh emitted a shrill laugh. "I've learned to speak like a mullah," he said. "To show respect to the Imam."

He flipped further to the black binder and passed it over to Weiseman. There were ledgers, filled with dollar figures, and lists with headings for the Shah's assets, military equipment, and other entries Weiseman couldn't translate. He had Ghotbzadeh explain it to him, knowing he wouldn't get a copy. He was fairly sure that this was Ghotbzadeh's own wish list and that Khomeini had never seen it, much less Bani-Sadr. It came to over $10 billion.

"After you kidnapped our diplomats? You're dreaming."

Ghotbzadeh waved his hand dismissively. He pointed to an item at the bottom of the chart for over $5 million. There was no descriptive heading.

"It's for you, isn't it? Your commission."

"This is Persia, Mr. Weiseman. Nothing's free."

Weiseman stifled the temptation to tell him to stuff it. Instead he played along. After all, he was here to corrupt this greedy fat man, not to reform him.

"Well," he said. "Now that we know your price, tell me what we get for our money."


BACK AT THE Intercon, Weiseman strode by Daud and rode the elevator to the fourth floor, then hurried toward the presidential suite. Inserting the key, he opened the door, turned on the light, and stopped in his tracks at the sight of the intermediary with whom Françoise had arranged his visit to Tehran, sitting on the edge of the bed.

"*You?*"

"Better hurry," Jacques Schreiber said. "There's a helicopter on the roof."

"A helicopter?" Weiseman asked. "The presidential palace is right across town."

"*Monsieur Weiseman, Bani-Sadr est—comment dit-on?* Incapacitated."

"They handed their own president over to Montana?"

"Bani-Sadr is in hiding," Jacques said, and pointed toward the door. "Hurry. We're going to Qom. To the Imam."

He started up the shaky wooden ladder to the roof, and Weiseman followed behind.

Sometimes one had to sup with the devil.

**THEY TRAVELED IN SILENCE.** Strong winds buffeted the helicopter in the smoggy darkness; the only light inside emanated from Jacques's cigar.

The layers of intrigue were deep, fed by fear and greed, resting on power and money. Seyyed conspiring with Hanif. Jacques Schreiber now helping him, on orders no doubt from Gramont, who had played him from the beginning. Trevor, at least, had given him fair warning: trust no one.

When they finally landed near the Ayatollah's house, Weiseman jumped out and hurried up the steps without a word to Jacques, his gaze rapidly scanning around for Montana.

A door opened. Sheikh Khalaji said, "The Imam is ready."

Khomeini sat in a straight wooden chair beside the prayer mat, the translator at his left elbow. A nurse hovered to his right. Behind her was a tangle of wires and tubes—blood transfusion equipment.

The old man spoke so softly that Weiseman had to move very close to hear him. "It is time to settle our affairs," the Ayatollah said, as if he were dictating his will. "The Islamic Republic will go on—" Khomeini coughed and his face turned red. The nurse edged closer to him, but he shook his head and she receded.

The Ayatollah leaned closer to his ear. "The hostages have served their purpose."

Finally!

"We will establish ordinary relations with America, just as with other countries."

Khomeini began to cough again, and now his face turned white, as if the blood had seeped out of his skin. This time the nurse ignored his headshakes of protest. She pushed aside her niqab, found the spot with her rubber glove, and injected a hypodermic needle into his arm.

The Sheikh stepped forward. "That's enough, you have weakened the Imam."

Weiseman hesitated, afraid Khomeini would die in his presence. He and the hostages would be killed in retaliation. He rose to go, but the Ayatollah's fingers grasped his sleeve.

A guttural whisper. "You will see. I will make this happen. Soon."

Despite himself, he bowed slightly to the ailing leader. He hated everything Khomeini stood for, and he deeply doubted what he had just heard, but something impelled him to acknowledge the man's power— his unique position in history.

When he emerged, he saw Montana with a dagger in his belt, lurking on the side of the house. Jacques called out from the helicopter—"*Vite, trés vite—*"

Weiseman raced down the stairs toward the helicopter, its motor revving, and hopped quickly in. Out the window, he saw Montana rush toward him. From a second helicopter hovering above them, a shadow leveled a high-powered rifle toward their copter.

"*Allons-y!*" Jacques shouted, as the pilot revved the motor.

Weiseman saw the rifle rise, then abruptly shift. The burst of fire was deafening.

Montana's huge body went down, spurting blood, as their helicopter rose into the sky. Weiseman cranked his head to look up at the other copter, floating high above, tracking them. Was it there to safeguard their return to Tehran . . . or to terminate it?

"*A toute vitesse!*" Jacques shouted. Faster . . . faster.

The other helicopter dived toward them, skimmed across the grass fifty yards away, then began to climb again into the sooty sky . . . But not before Weiseman saw the assassin's face.

Hosein Hanif.

They drifted through the misty Persian sky in silence. Weiseman thought Shirin Majid had finally been avenged, as had Alana, Shapour, and their father.

He tried to piece together how Hanif fit in to the counterrevolution he had been promoting, how he had survived. Sitting next to him, apparently composed after the terror of the departure, Jacques said, "We're safe now, you can relax. Hanif was here to provide security, and to take down Montana."

Of course, Weiseman thought, Hanif would have had the backing of his hard men of SAVAK, along with access to the safe houses, the networks of informers, and all the weapons he had bought from Jacques Schreiber and from the United States. For Hanif, the choice was either to leave the country or to fight the mullahs who had brought down his Shah. For such a man, exile would be a curse. So, now he was allied, however temporarily, to Seyyed, to Jacques, and only he knew to whom else.

And then Weiseman remembered what Trevor had said to Hanif: "You're our man, Hosein." And he recalled another Trevor adage: *Never break entirely with any adversary, you never know when you'll need them one day.*

Jacques lit a cigarette, finally breaking the silence. "Don't worry about Françoise. Our people took her to a safe place right after you arrived."

Weiseman felt a wave of relief wash over him. "Thank you, Jacques," he said.

"What happened with the Ayatollah?" Schreiber asked.

"I don't know," Weiseman said, thinking, *tell him nothing.* "It could be everything or nothing. Maybe it was a deathbed wish."

Jacques Schreiber didn't say another word; he just stared into the night.

The helicopter followed them all the way to Tehran, before veering away into the sky.

**ON SEPTEMBER 10,** the Majlis issued a statement spelling out the conditions for the release of the hostages: the United States would have to unfreeze all Iranian assets and transfer them back to Iran; commit to no US military or political intervention in Iranian affairs; and return all the Shah's assets to Iran, or at least commit to assisting the Iranian government in pursuing those assets in American courts.

Two days later, on September 12, the Ayatollah issued a statement with more or less the same terms. Washington was ecstatic, for it seemed the Iranians might really be serious.

Then came a call from an Iranian diplomat named Sadeq Tabatabai. He wanted to meet in four days, in Bonn with an American authorized to discuss details of the hostage release. Now it appeared that Iran was in a hurry.

Weiseman phoned Ghotbzadeh, who told him that the Tabatabai family was of distinguished lineage in Iran. "He's a relative of the Imam by marriage. He's part of the inner circle."

Weiseman passed this on to Trevor, who told him that the deputy secretary of state and a technical team would be in Bonn on Sunday, empowered to negotiate. "You're not going," Trevor said. "It will go on and on. They'll fight for every dime."

Mystified at being left out, angry after all he'd done, Weiseman started to push back, but Trevor cut him off. "It's decided."

Giving in, Weiseman called Tabatabai. The Iranian of noble lineage said, "Tell the deputy secretary we expect the US to supply the Islamic Republic with military spare parts."

Still angry, Weiseman relayed the message to Trevor.

"Understood," Trevor replied. "Oh, by the way, there's just been a coup in Turkey. The military has taken over again. You can come home now, David."

"Actually," Weiseman said, "I'll be staying on awhile in Tehran. Things to do . . ."

"Well, David, that's different. But remember, no prints."

## 34

# NO PRINTS

**K**ARIM NASIR GAVE WEISEMAN a private base of operations in the back room of his house in the woods near Tehran University. Weiseman knew the White House had only one interest—to get the hostages out and secure an October surprise—and that there was little chance of upending the ayatollahs any time soon. They were consolidating their power through the time-honored practice of revolutionary terror. It would take time before Iranians, ecstatic at the departure of the Shah, would feel the lash of the new tyrants sufficiently to rise up against the economic hardship, the corruption, the repression. But the unbending certainty of the mullahs and their thuggish enforcers would alienate the people. Eventually.

Atatürk's insight when faced with opponents of reform gnawed at him: "One should not wait before crushing a reactionary movement. One should act at once." Or else, Weiseman realized, be prepared to pay the price over many years. The question was how effectively the film of Iranian history could be fast-forwarded. US hands must not be seen sabotaging the regime; that was clear. To do so would end the talks to bring the hostages home and would put them in danger, even though Khomeini had promised to let them go. No, for Weiseman the task was to cramp and complicate consolidation of the ayatollahs' regime in ways that could not be traced back to American hands. That's why the United States needed allies, and needed Iranians upfront.

With his agents in place, Weiseman could begin organizing demonstrations, funding opposition newspapers, developing channels for spreading propaganda, smuggling in weapons, arranging acts of subversion, setting off the occasional bomb near sites important to the mullahs, and corrupting the likes of Bani-Sadr and Ghotbazadeh.

This wouldn't bring down the ayatollahs, not at once. But it could shake them, make them ever more repressive, and stir the anger of the population. With Montana dead, he thought he might have more latitude, but whispers soon disabused him of that notion. The mullahs had spread the word that he and Hanif were working together. And every day, power was accruing to the Revolutionary Guards, the Iranian gestapo.

There was something else. He would need to find escape routes for those in the opposition, especially his agents who faced retaliation by the regime—including himself.


**IN A SMALL** university office with windows taped over with sheets of brown paper, in the philosophy department of Tehran University, Weiseman met with Ronald Sims and Thomas Foster. Karim Nasir sat in the corridor just outside the office, at a chipped yellow desk, conducting a tutorial with a female student, keeping watch, ready to sound the alarm if any RGs came snooping around.

Sims and Foster were good. They knew Iranians who would help, some with family members in Evin, others with financial resources. Sims said the border with Iraq was porous; his people knew it well. The Brits had been dealing with the Iraqis for a long time.

"You remember Jafar," Foster said. "Trita's brother. The military officer we slipped out to Iraq. He's in touch with Iraqi colonels and is sending us reports."

A soft knock on the door brought a tense Weiseman out of his chair. Karim Nasir leaned into the room. "Strangers are roaming about the campus," he said. "You should finish up."

The door closed.

"The Ayatollah will need another foreign devil," Sims said softly, "after he lets your embassy people go. Saddam will be the perfect choice." His eyebrows rose. "Khomeini wants a chance to get back against his jailer."

"Yes. I can see that."

Sims had more. "Millicent drove to the border a few days ago and talked with a general who was once close to the Shah. He said the Ayatollah had ordered them to make every preparation for war. The general told Millicent the ayatollahs were amazed that America gave up after that bungled rescue mission."

Weiseman thought this general was someone he should meet.

There was another knock on the door. "Hurry!"

Sims peeled aside the edge of the frayed drape covering the window. "RGs," he said.

"Who can we count on?" Weiseman asked hurriedly. "Inside the regime."

"Well, you've met the president and foreign minister," Sims said, "but they're compromised—useless. Find someone the old man needs, to lend a touch of respectability."

Weiseman wasn't surprised it had come back around to Ayatollah Seyyed. He nodded to Sims, and then they hustled out the rear door held open by a nervous Karim Nasir.

**THE WORD FROM BONN** was that the hostage talks were stuck. Sadeq Tabatabai was bargaining like a fishmonger, while in Tehran the RGs hauled the hostages out for daily humiliation before the waiting cameras of the world press. Every night, American television networks announced the number of days the hostages had been held. Jimmy Carter, his reelection prospects fading like a wilted flower, sat chained to his desk the way Trevor predicted he would be, devoted to his duties, in fear that he would be greeted with disdain on the campaign trail.

The plans Weiseman concocted with Sims began to unfold. Middle-class families, bazaari who once led demos against the Shah, now took to the streets. A small private plane crossed Tehran's evening sky dragging a fluorescent banner proclaiming, ALLAHU AKHBAR, God is great. The same words that routed the Shah were now being turned against the mullahs.

Over the next week, while the RGs unsuccessfully sought to trace the plane and pilot that Weiseman had obtained with the help of Moshe Regev, citizens crowded onto Tehran rooftops and chanted, *Allahu Akhbar.*

Enraged, the RGs lashed out, further cramming the cells at Evin.

Printing presses cranked up. A new broadsheet appeared, *Allahu Akhbar*, tarring the ayatollahs for shredding Iranian traditions and undermining the hopes of the people.

At the Tehran Polo Club, Weiseman helped Millicent out of a dilapidated VW bug. A tall man climbed out of a waiting military sedan, dressed for a walk in the woods. The general, who prudently withheld his name, told Weiseman he had been a young lieutenant during Operation Ajax, when Mossadeq was removed as prime minister. Now he said there would have to be another campaign of civil uprisings, each night in another part of the city. Peaceful demonstrations and acts of sabotage throughout the country would be necessary until Khomeini's regime was chasing its tail. "It's astonishing what people power can do," he told Weiseman.

The next day, a hooded youth rode his motorcycle along the Qom highway to within a hundred yards of the Ayatollah's house. He pulled a chord on his backpack and became the first martyr resisting the revolution.

Outside the American embassy compound, peering through high-powered binoculars, Weiseman watched the daily parade of hostages, searching for Chris so he could report to Roger Tyler that his son was still alive and well. He saw RG Nejab again, this time in a filthy golf jacket, leading on the American chargé d'affaires. Next came the bent bodies of those hostages who had refused to knuckle under and so had landed in solitary. Two women hostages, hair stringy, faces blotched from sleep deprivation and a rotten diet, were prodded to move faster by a notorious female captor called Bloody Dora, who was said to be the worst of the lot.

Finally, he spotted Chris Tyler. The RG goading him forward was Selim Nasir, Karim Nasir's son. The young man had found his calling.

**THE FIRST PERSON** Weiseman helped to get out was, indeed, Karim Nasir, who had been under house arrest after a female student he tutored had broken down under torture by the Revolutionary Guards and accused him of being a Shah supporter. Colonel Yilmaz arranged to slip Karim across the Turkish border. "We're in charge in Ankara now," Yilmaz said. "No protesters to worry about."

Many others followed across neighboring borders. Some were soldiers, many middle-class businessmen, police, teachers, and students, the fabric of civil society repressed first by the Shah and Hanif, then by Sheikh Khalaji and Montana, now by self-righteous Islamists and RGs who claimed to have captured their future. No country was more eager to welcome Persians than Israel, which knew well the value of acquiring human talent. "Such a waste for Iran," Moshe Regev told Weiseman, as Israel doubled its immigration quota for Iranians.

Weiseman paid special attention to the young people who were Iran's future. After the loss of Alana and Shapour, he was determined to save as many of those in their network as wanted to leave Iran. It was the least he could do to honor their memory.

Camouflaged in worker's clothes and a film of black earth covering his face, he personally drove a large fruit and vegetable truck toward the Turkish border at midnight, with a dozen students or more—he wasn't quite sure how many—including Mahmoud, secluded among the packing crates. The truck was stopped and searched repeatedly at police blockades. Miraculously, no one was discovered.

At the last blockade, only a mile to the Turkish side of the border, a squad of five RGs forced him from the truck, at gunpoint, holding a photo—his photo—and shining flashlights in his face. Two men twisted his arms behind his back and cuffed him. The squad leader reached for a radio phone. Weiseman heard him utter the word he most feared.

*Evin.*

There was nowhere to run. Flashlights were fixed on his eyes and the cuffs singed his wrists. A dozen young Iranians—his responsibility—faced death under the tarpaulins.

RGs with machine guns strode toward the rear of the truck and began to remove the tarpaulins. Weiseman heard screams and gunfire. It was over. He felt sick with despair.

To die on this dusty border.

And then, Mahmoud came around the truck with two timid teenage boys, who suddenly turned and emptied their pistols into the squad leader and the two RGs who were detaining Weiseman.

Moments later, his cuffs removed, the tarpaulins back in place, the dead RGs dragged to a ditch at the side of the road, Weiseman drove the truck across the Turkish border where Colonel Yilmaz's men escorted them to safety. They immediately drove him back to Tehran in a Turkish military sedan, wearing the uniform and broad rimmed cap of a Turkish general.

The two teenagers insisted on returning with him. When he left them off in a mountain village outside Tehran, he asked them why. "It's our country," they said.

A few days later, Mahmoud led a young woman into Karim Nasir's house, where Weiseman was hiding out. She removed her chador. "I'm back," Hannah Wiecorzek said breathlessly. "I heard you were getting people out."

**TIME WAS RUNNING** short. On September 21, Weiseman, in the brown robes and hood of a Muslim priest, visited a small mosque. He told Ayatollah Seyyed that Khomeini was gravely ill and that financing would be available to work against the regime, to counter the likes of Khalaji and the RGs and to turn Iran back to its people.

The reticent priest surprised Weiseman. He said he had recruited a coterie of counterrevolutionaries who shared his concern about what Khomeini was doing to the country and the good name of Islam. Behind Seyyed, in the half-light, he saw Trita and his brother Jafar, back in Iran to support Seyyed's campaign.

"Don't expect Ruhollah Khomeini to die anytime soon," Seyyed said. "He's been frail as long as I've known him. He may yet outlive you and me."

Seyyed said Khomeini had invited him to join the Supreme Council of Ayatollahs. He was going to accept. It would place him in a position to know Khomeini's inner secrets, and to subvert them. He would have to indulge in unorthodox measures. It would be dangerous.

Weiseman did not ask for details of his plan. He handed Seyyed a picnic basket stuffed with francs, marks, and pounds sterling. To get his people out, he gave Seyyed a point of contact, Mahmoud, who so far had mastered the art of survival, and Hannah.

And he provided Seyyed with a code name: Persian Prince.

On his way out of the mosque, he exchanged salutes with a bearded Hosein Hanif—whatever his ultimate motives, now a collaborator in the campaign to undermine the ayatollahs and RGs.


**THE NEXT DAY,** September 22, the armed forces of Saddam Hussein crossed the border near Basra and Abadan and invaded southern Iran. Khomeini summoned the rage of the gods and declared jihad on Saddam's Sunni infidels.

Tariq Aziz, Saddam's foreign minister, passed a message to Weiseman through Moshe Regev. "You see, you can depend on Iraqis as partners."

Justin Trevor, no doubt drawing deeply on his cigar and savoring his vintage port, sent Weiseman his own message: *God has smiled on us; now they may let our people go.*

## 35

# *MORNING IN AMERICA*

**B**ACK IN THE State Department, Weiseman read the cables on the numbing negotiations ongoing in Algiers with Tabatabai, but his mind was on the spreading war along the Iran-Iraq border; on the Iranian patriots and foreign agents he had set in motion in Iran; on Seyyed, his Persian Prince; and on the hostages themselves, still held by the Revolutionary Guards in the American embassy. He stayed in touch every day on a secure line with Françoise, who said she was working closely with Alain de Rose, and kept him current on Gramont's maneuvers.

The White House was pressing for a deal before the November 4 presidential election, but the Iranians were not backing down on even one of their extreme demands. Some in Washington called for a halt to the talks, but Trevor brought Weiseman to the Oval Office to explain to the president that Iran would only concede when time ran out. Weiseman cited examples of the Iranian bargaining tactics he had encountered in Tehran. The president instructed his delegation to stay in Algiers.

Weiseman thought back to the moment four years ago in the fiberglass-enclosed, bulletproof, inaugural parade reviewing stand in front of the White House, the marching bands, the strutting majorettes, the fantastic floats. Jimmy Carter in his moment of triumph, bringing Democrats back into power for the first time since Lyndon Johnson went down in the ashes of the Vietnam War.

Nothing ever turned out as expected.


**TWO WEEKS BEFORE** Election Day, Trevor called Weiseman to say he was flying to Sacramento to brief Governor Reagan on foreign policy developments. "The DCI does this with the opposition candidate before every election," he said. "Iran's the big issue; you should come with me."

They flew across the country in Trevor's specially equipped air force plane, one of the backups to Air Force One, landing at McClellan Air Force Base, just outside the city. From there, they were driven to the California State Capitol with its huge gold dome. Climbing the marble stairs, Trevor said, "Reagan will be the next president."

Weiseman smiled, thinking, if Trevor thought so, it might well be true. After all, unmanageable crises are rarely conducive to presidential reelections.

Ronald Reagan greeted them in his big plush office, under the California flag with the golden bear. They all sat down in green leather chairs at a highly polished round table. Reagan thanked Trevor for taking the time to fly out to California. Then he flashed Weiseman a broad smile. "I've heard a good deal about your exploits, Dave."

Reagan was getting older, but he still had movie star good looks and a natural charm that put people at ease. He had a fat knot in his necktie and a slick pompadour, and he began to regale them with political jokes that soon had both Trevor and Weiseman laughing out loud. Weiseman had never seen Trevor so amused.

"Well, Director, I suppose we should get to the business at hand," Reagan said.

Trevor nodded and passed a black leather briefing book across to the governor, but Reagan left it unopened. "Why don't you just tell me what I need to know," he said.

As Trevor took Reagan on a *tour d'horizon* of international hot spots, Weiseman reflected on the stark differences between this sunny, casual Californian and the driven, meticulous Jimmy Carter who read every memo, checked every last detail. As Trevor continued talking, Reagan nodded at times. Weiseman had no idea how much he was absorbing.

"Governor." Trevor's tone became more sober. "David is our point man in Iran."

Reagan snapped to attention, the smile gone, his eyes focused. "That *is* important," he said, and then Weiseman was briefing Reagan on the negotiations, on Khomeini, on his trail of agents in Iran, though without naming any names.

Reagan glanced at his gold watch. "Oh, my, time flies. Well, I have just one question." He grinned. "Are you folks going to get the hostages home before January 20?"

Trevor turned his head toward Weiseman. "David? You're the expert."

"Well, Governor, our people are working twenty-four seven on it. I'd guess Khomeini will sign off on it a few hours before you take the oath."

"That'll be good enough for government work," Reagan said, and stood up. He escorted Trevor and Weiseman into the marble corridor outside the governor's suite, spinning tales, elevating his eyebrows, laughing at his own jokes. "I'm going to miss this place," he said, as if he really meant it, then turned and strode like John Wayne back into his office suite.

It was only then that Weiseman realized he had told Reagan he expected him to take the oath as president.

As he and Trevor walked down the marble staircase, he finally asked

Trevor the question that had bedeviled him since his most recent escape from Qom, when Hanif had gunned down Montana. "How did you orchestrate that one?" he asked.

"Oh, that," Trevor said nonchalantly, and put on his sunglasses to shelter his eyes from the California sun and Weiseman's view. "Klein had a word with Hanif. I told you we'd take care of that."

Amazing, Weiseman thought, and the true Trevor—cold-eyed, cynical, pragmatic—but when needed, watching out for him, while hiding his bottom-line views behind an opaque mask.

"Justin, whose side are you on actually?"

Trevor chuckled in his trademark dry laugh. "David, on the American side, as always. But you see, the other sides keep changing."


THE NEXT EVENING, back in Washington, Weiseman watched Ronald Reagan turn his head again, smile as he did in the governor's office, and ask Jimmy Carter in the presidential debate whether America was better off than it was four years earlier, when Carter first took office.

The American side, Weiseman thought, was about to change as well.

Brains aren't everything, Weiseman's father had told him long ago. Life is about character, Johann said.


IN THE END, Carter, the engineer, missed his November 4 deadline for freeing the hostages, and Ronald Reagan, the actor, won the election, just as Trevor predicted he would. Sitting in his patron's Wyoming Avenue home on election night, Weiseman watched one state after another break for Reagan, forty-nine out of fifty, leaving Carter shattered.

Justin Trevor, the ultimate Washington survivor, sipped his brandy and lit a Havana cigar. "Life goes on," he said.

While Carter recuperated down in Plains, Trevor moved quickly to fill the vacuum. At his instruction, Weiseman called Sadeq Tabatabai to say that President Carter was ready to continue negotiations for the release of the hostages.

"Carter?" the Iranian repeated. "Isn't Reagan president now?"

Weiseman sighed and calmly explained that there would be a transition period until January 20, which would enable the president-elect to prepare his agenda and appoint his cabinet and principal advisors. Until then, Iran would still be dealing with President Carter.

"I see." Tabatabai paused a moment. "All right."

The Iranians had always wanted the deal to be done before November 4, because they had wanted to avoid dealing with Reagan. Now the prospect of beating Reagan to the White House gave them a second chance. "But there's a deadline," Weiseman told the Iranian. "It's January 16. That will give us just enough time to implement the complex financial transfers. Otherwise you'll have to deal with Reagan."

"Yes, I can understand that," Tabatabai said soberly. "Of course, it's not up to me. Your people will have to be generous. The Imam must approve whatever is agreed upon."

And so the hard slog resumed. The Algiers talks squirreled down into the minutiae of what the Iranians wanted and what the Americans could legally do. Carter had no political stake in the talks—it wouldn't win him back the presidency—but Weiseman marveled at the way he threw himself back into the mission of freeing the hostages. Throughout December, the deputy secretary of state and his experts flew back and forth between Washington and Algiers as if it were the DC-New York shuttle run, pressing ahead with the grueling negotiations.

On New Year's Day, 1981, Weiseman told Trevor it wouldn't work unless the Iranians saw actual legal documents on the transfer of assets. Until that happened, they'd suspect a trick.

Trevor convened a group of Justice Department lawyers and Treasury financial experts to draft those documents. Weiseman was the group's political advisor, there to ensure the documents were watertight enough to preclude a last minute Iranian double cross, but not so provocative as to arouse suspicions and prevent the release of the hostages.

The last week of Carter's presidency was mired in the arcane paperwork for the transfer of assets by fourteen banks in five nations. There were also the practical details of having aircraft on standby to take the hostages out—assuming it all worked. On January 19, with twenty-four hours left in Carter's term, Trevor told Weiseman the president hadn't slept all week.

As the morning of Inauguration Day dawned, Weiseman already was in his office. At 8:00 a.m. he read a FLASH cable from Algiers, and his heart stopped for an instant: *The transfer of assets is complete, the hostages will be released today.*

He dialed Wyoming Avenue and Trevor pressed a button on his phone that connected them directly into the Oval Office. "Mr. President, David has some good news."

He read the cable to Carter and heard him pause a moment; apparently he was too exhausted to celebrate. Finally, Carter said, "Thank you, I'll tell the president when he comes over to see me at eleven."

The president? Weiseman was thrown for a moment. Ah, yes. Ronald Reagan.

"Oh, one more thing," Carter said. "Will the hostages be airborne before the oath? On my watch?"

"Mr. President," Trevor said, "we just don't know that."

There was silence for a moment, then Carter's wistful voice. "Yes, of course. Well, stay on it, will you? Someone needs to be at the helm. Let me know as soon as the hostages are airborne. Call me in the Oval Office, the limo, the Capitol, or wherever I am."

His voice trailed off, and Weiseman felt himself choke up. Whatever else he felt about Carter, the man had given it all he had. It was more than you could say about most people.


**INAUGURATION DAY, AND WEISEMAN** sat in the State Department Operation Center, waiting for word that the hostages were airborne. On his right was the dedicated telex machine on which the cable would arrive, on his left, the television set showing the president-elect's limo pulling up to the entrance to the West Portico of the White House. Behind those double doors, where presidents often stared out of their gilded prison, Jimmy Carter was bracing himself to yield power, no doubt praying that the hostages would be freed before twelve noon, when Reagan would take the oath.

Weiseman stared at the three telephone numbers Trevor had given him. "One of these will reach the president," Trevor had told him.

Time dragged on. He had telexed Tabatabai twice that morning, first at 8:00 a.m., when the financial transfers were completed, then again at 10:00. There had been no reply. TV talking heads chattered on, speculating about what the two men in the Oval Office were discussing, and about when the hostages might be freed. They hadn't a clue about either. Then again, thought Weiseman, neither did he.

At 11:30, the two men walked out of the White House, toward the presidential limousine, Carter grim faced, Reagan smiling, gesticulating with his hands. The TV showed Reagan smiling, exuberant and presidential in his blue suit, pearl-gray double-breasted waistcoat and tie, a square white handkerchief tucked into his pocket, waving to well-wishers. Carter wore the same attire but, as he climbed into the back of the waiting limo, seemed lost in thought, his presidency already a memory.

The car began the slow drive up Pennsylvania Avenue to the Capitol, past cheering crowds who were seemingly happy to brave the frosty weather.

At 11:40, the phone rang, startling Weiseman. They're airborne, he thought.

But it was Jimmy Carter. "Any news?" he asked.

"Mr. President, not yet."

Five minutes later the limo pulled up at the Capitol, and the two men were escorted into the ground floor entrance by a team of Secret Service agents. Moments later, they appeared on the grandstand to await the transfer of power. The phone rang again in the Op-Center and Weiseman snapped it up. "Monsieur Weiseman?" a man said.

"*Oui.*"

"It is Jacques Schreiber, from Paris. It seems there's been a falling out in Tehran. Sheikh Khalaji has issued an order for the arrest of Bani-Sadr *and* Ghotbzadeh."

Weiseman squeezed his eyes tightly shut.

"Are you there, Monsieur Weiseman?"

"Schreiber, the money has been transferred. Are they going to come through?"

"*Je ne sais pas.* The revolution is eating its own. I don't know—"

The line went dead in midsentence. Up on the TV monitor, the chief justice stepped to the center of the stage. Reagan came forward to face him, a heavy black overcoat and white wool scarf shielding the Californian from frigid Washington weather. He recited the oath, repeating the Chief Justice's words without error. He was an actor, after all, accustomed to memorizing his lines.

There was a great roar from the crowd that extended across the plaza, all the way from the houses of Congress to the Supreme Court across the way. The trees swayed under the ice and snow that burdened their branches. Weiseman heard a TV announcer say that America was entering a new epoch, virtually the same words that had been said exactly four years before. Weiseman wondered, How would it turn out this time?

Now president, Ronald Reagan began his inaugural address. Even over the TV, Weiseman could pick up the vibes, the hopes invested in what the democratic process had wrought. Up on the stage, constructed in the shadow of the Capitol dome, hard men who served the past administration and would serve this one squinted into the icy sun, harboring their memories and dreams and doubts. To Reagan's left, at the front of the platform, Jimmy Carter fidgeted, no longer president.

Weiseman picked up some phrases—"orderly transfer of authority . . . the business of our nation goes forward . . . government is not the solution to our problem; government is the problem . . . special interests"—but the telex machine was stirring. He leaned over it, tapping its side, urging it on.

A piece of paper began to slide out of the machine, then stopped. There were only two words on it: *Test Run.*

*Damn.*

He swiveled back to listen to Reagan's speech. "We have every right to dream heroic dreams . . . to perform great deeds . . . we are Americans."

A great roar came forth from the crowd. A banner rose from the masses shivering before the Capitol, saying, Morning in America.

The president finished his address and waved to the crowd. The Marine Band played a Sousa march. A soprano stood before the crowd and sang the "Star Spangled Banner."

The telex machine remained quiet.

They were all up now. As Jimmy and Rosalyn Carter headed toward the rear of the Capitol, the former president looked over his shoulder as if he'd forgotten something. Then he and Rosalyn made their way slowly down the great marble steps.

They boarded the waiting helicopter and the camera panned back to the top of the stairs, where Justin Trevor waved to them, then turned, and strode back into the Capitol. Weiseman watched with the rest of the nation as the helicopter lifted up and headed toward Andrews Air Force Base in nearby Maryland. A half hour later, Air Force One took off for Plains, Georgia.

Then it came to him—the realization of what his mentor had done. Justin had separated him from Carter's team in Algeria and taken him on the trip to Sacramento. The old survivor had dressed him all up nice and pretty so the new president would take him on.

Suddenly, the telex machine came to life, exactly five minutes after Carter had climbed dejectedly aboard Air Force One: *The first plane with the hostages has taken off from Mehrabad. The second is taxiing up the runway and will be airborne in moments.*

After 444 days.

He picked up the phone and called the number at the Capitol that Trevor had given him.

"Yes?"

"Mr. President, the hostages are on the way home."

He heard the infectious laugh. Ronald Reagan said, "Thank you, David. It seems we're off to a good start."

**A MONTH LATER,** Assistant Secretary of State for Europe David Weiseman, at home on a Sunday morning, browsed through the newspapers. He saw the clipping in the *Post*. Iranian President Bani-Sadr had been dismissed and had fled to Paris. Ex-Foreign Minister Ghotbzadeh had been arrested and promptly executed by firing squad.

Françoise stepped into the room, and he remembered something he wanted to ask her.

"I saw Justin. He said they've replaced Gramont."

She nodded. "That's right. The Élysée decided that Gramont's strategy had failed, that it was time to get tough on the mullahs. Alain de Rose has replaced him He's asked me to work with him."

"First, tell me about Gramont," he said. "Why now?"

"Sometimes they even cut the strings of the puppet master," she said. "The Islamists demanded that France extradite exiles who fled Iran after the revolution. They sent suicide bombers and assassins to Paris. It was just like they'd done before, as if nothing had changed. So, Laurent had gotten us nowhere."

Weiseman nodded. "Your new job sounds important," he said.

"I'll be his station chief at the French embassy in Washington," she said.

Weiseman gave her a surprised look, then a broad smile, as he rose and said, "Let's go for a walk."

She took his arm and they made their way down the tree-lined sidewalk, the breeze flirting with her miniskirt. He spoke about the news from Iran. "They were crooks," he said, "both Bani-Sadr and Ghotbzadeh. They took big chances. But to destroy them like that . . . to exile one, to hand the other over to the RGs . . . it's indecent."

"Oh yes," she said, "there is one other thing that may interest you. You remember your Mossad friend."

"Of course, but don't tell me—"

"It seems that Regev met alone with Alain and presented him with a detailed dossier on Jacques's wartime work for the Nazis in France and Poland. Jacques is now in solitary in Israel's maximum security prison, near the Dead Sea. We won't be seeing him again for a very long time."

"Sometimes we get lucky," he said. "By the way, one of Reagan's aides asked me to stop by the White House. It was about Lyman Palmer. He was America's last ambassador to Iran. We didn't get along very well."

"What did he want, this 'aide'?" Françoise asked.

"Palmer was being considered for another ambassadorial appointment, in Italy," Weiseman said. "You won't believe it. This guys looks at me, says Palmer's name, then puts his thumb up, then down, then asks me, 'Which is it?'"

Her eyes opened wide, relishing the moral quandary in a way Weiseman found particularly French.

"So, David, you had this man's career in the palm of your hand. What did you say?"

"He's worthless; he caused me a lot of trouble."

She gave him a flinty look.

"What did you say?"

"Well, I was offended by the way the White House guy presumed to play God so I decided to support him." Weiseman gave her tight smile. "For an opening I knew about in Paraguay."

She laughed despite the chilly breeze.

"Let's go home," Weiseman said. "Promises to keep."

## ACKNOWLEDGMENTS

**IT WAS MY 27-YEAR CAREER IN THE UNITED STATES FOREIGN** Service, with the professional diplomats of the State Department and of the countries to which I was privileged to be accredited, that prompted me to tell this tale of a young American detailed to work for a CIA director and cast into the demanding dilemmas of an Iran catapulting into crisis—the slipstreams of authoritarian monarchial rule, revolution by fundamentalist authoritarians, and the personal turmoil of long-suffering Iranians. His task: extricate the country from its choice of one or the other kind of harsh rule, assist the decent moderates of civil society to survive, and safeguard American interests in the tumultuous Mideast region. It is a story familiar to many of my former and present diplomatic colleagues, and one similar to my own experiences, and choices, in the Philippines some years later.

The list of professional and personal relationships that opened my eyes to challenges and opportunities are too numerous to list here, but some have been of particular relevance to this work. From my Foreign Service career, Robert Schaetzel, my first ambassador, at the US mission to the European Union in Brussels; Jonathan Dean, who led our team in Bonn that coordinated negotiations with the Soviet Union, the United Kingdom, France, and the two Germanys which transformed the security scene in Europe; the twenty-three delegations of NATO and Warsaw Pact nations who I was fortunate to join in Vienna in negotiating the historic treaty on conventional forces in Europe; to my friend Steve Bosworth, whom I served as deputy in the State Department Policy Planning Staff and as American Minister in Manila; to the brilliant Peter Rodman, a dedicated patriot known to be Henry Kissinger's stellar student, and who served with distinction in the State and Defense Departments and the National Security Council; to Admiral Jim Stavridis, a polymath sailor, academic dean, writer, businessman and public servant; to colleagues in and partners in two law firms, first Patton Boggs and now Berliner, Corcoran Rowe; to the many Europeans, Filipinos, and other Asians, and those I came to know and respect in Africa, the Mideast, and Latin America.

I salute my indefatigable agent Ron Goldfarb and his colleague Gerrie Sturman, who drew on years of seasoned expertise and sustained commitment to bring this debut novel to publication.

This book also grew with the counsel of collaborators. The late Sol Stein, the novelist Alan Furst, whose mastery of the historic spy novel set standards I have sought to emulate, and to editorial tutors. Special thanks are due to the professionals at Melville House, above all publisher Dennis Johnson whose support and lethal pencil made the book better in many ways; Valerie Merians, his co-founder and publisher; managing editor Mike Lindgren and the impressive group of marketing, publicity, and sales experts who make the Melville House train run smoothly, to publication.

And to my family, my son Douglas, whose support and dedication has been constant and dependable. Above all to my wife Barbara, the love of my life and my bride since our graduation together from the University of Connecticut, who has read every draft, enriched the book with her love, her comments and her humanity, who remains my bride every day.

### A NOTE ABOUT THE AUTHOR

Philip Kaplan spent twenty-seven years as a diplomat in the US Foreign Service. Now retired from the State Department, he is currently practices law in Washington, D.C. This is his first novel.